# The Third Wife

He thinks she's his wife. He's wrong.

A.M Jones

Jones Thrillers

**The Third Wife**

© 2025 A. M. Jones

This is a work of fiction. Names, characters, places, and incidents are either the product of the author's imagination or are used fictitiously. Any resemblance to actual persons, living or dead, events, or locales is entirely coincidental.

**Content Warning:**
This novel contains references to pregnancy, miscarriage, psychological manipulation, coercive control, and grief. Reader discretion is advised.

ISBN (Paperback): 978-1-9192578-0-8
ISBN (eBook): 978-1-9192578-1-5

Published by Jones Thrillers

# Contents

# Dedication Page

*For those who see the cracks in the perfect marriage.*

# Epigraph

"We are never so easily deceived as when we imagine we are deceiving others." – La Rochefoucauld

# ACT I - The Pact

# Chapter One
## The House of Three

The house breathed his name.

Kevin paused on the steps, cardboard box sagging in his arms, and glanced up at the second-story window. The iron vent above the door exhaled again, dragging a thin hiss through the ductwork that, if he held his breath and tilted his ear just so, sounded like *Kevin*. The syllable was stretched until it frayed into air, but still it raised the hairs at the back of his neck.

"Just wind," he muttered.

The porch boards were swollen and soft underfoot. The three gables hunched toward each other like conspirators, shadows slanting under the streetlamp's cold glow. By daylight, the place had looked like a fairy-tale Victorian; at night it was a crooked mouth daring him to walk in.

Behind him, the moving van's engine ticked as it cooled. Samantha balanced her own box against her hip, hair pulled tight in a knot, her smile precise as a blade. She always looked so composed—even now, with paint flecks on her jacket sleeve and dust smudging her knuckles.

"My strongman." She nudged him with her elbow. "Going to stand there and spook yourself, or open the door?"

Kevin shifted the weight of the box, grinned despite himself, and mounted the last step. "House said hello."

Her laugh rang out too quickly. "You're hearing things. She's old, she creaks. That's all." She leaned in and kissed his cheek. "Come on, Kev. Home."

The lock turned with more resistance than it should have, as if the house were weighing their worth. Inside, the air was thick with lemon polish over dust. A vase of white lilies already sat on the entry table. Kevin frowned—he hadn't seen Samantha carry them in.

The wallpaper was a faded pattern of climbing roses. In the half-dark, they resembled thorns.

He set his box down, flexed his arms, and tried to shake the unease. *Old house. Old lungs. Of course it sighs.*

Then the vent above the stairwell sighed again. The same dragged-out consonant, almost a whisper of his name.

Kevin forced a chuckle. "You really don't hear that?"

Samantha tilted her head as if humouring him, her expression too smooth. "Hear what?"

"Never mind," he said. He wasn't about to start their first night with talk of ghosts.

They ferried boxes until the van was empty, footsteps echoing in the hollow rooms. Somewhere between trips, another bouquet appeared on the kitchen counter—daffodils this time, bright as coins. Again, Kevin hadn't seen her bring them in.

He told himself she must have slipped them from her car earlier, a surprise. He told himself she was always thinking two steps ahead, arranging details to perfection.

Still, the breath of the house followed him. Each time he passed the stairwell, the vent seemed to pull at him, exhaling secrets in syllables just beyond hearing.

When he carried the final box upstairs, he caught a thread of laughter tangled in the hiss. Two notes, overlapping. He froze.

"Kev?" Samantha's voice floated from the bedroom. "Come on, I need your muscles for the mattress."

He swallowed, adjusted the box, and forced his legs to move. *Wind. Just wind in the ducts.*

But the sound followed him up the stairs, curling after him like a whisper that knew his name too well.

The bedroom was half-assembled by the time Kevin dragged the mattress into place. Samantha directed him with a practiced efficiency, tapping one corner of the bed frame, then the other, as if she were conducting a symphony only, she could hear.

"Left, Kev. No, your other left." She laughed, quick and light, and he felt the tension of the house ease a fraction.

By the time the sheets were smoothed and the blanket stretched taut, it almost looked like they belonged here. Almost. The crooked windowpanes distorted the streetlamp glow into bent ribbons across the floorboards, and in the glass, Kevin's reflection warped into someone older, heavier. He looked away.

"See?" Samantha said, brushing her hands together. "Baseline civilization."

They retreated downstairs for food—cold pizza out of a tilted box, eaten standing in the kitchen. Samantha perched against the counter, chewing thoughtfully, as if even pizza were a task to be optimised.

"You're awfully quiet," she said, wiping grease from her fingers.

"Long day." Kevin took a pull from his beer, but his mind was back on the stairwell vent, the hiss that had sounded suspiciously like laughter. He forced a smile. "House is... different at night."

"Old houses always are." She shrugged, dismissing it as if she'd already made peace with the quirks. "You'll get used to it."

Her certainty was contagious. That had always been her gift: to bend reality into whatever shape she preferred. Kevin had followed her lead through job changes, apartment hunts, even marriage vows. If Samantha said this was home, then damn it, he would believe it.

Still, he couldn't help noticing things. The daffodils on the counter glowed too brightly in the dim kitchen, their yellow almost aggressive. Samantha had sworn she hadn't bought them, yet there they were, arranged just so.

After they ate, he dug through boxes for a toothbrush while she padded around in socks, humming under her breath. The tune was unfamiliar. Normally, she hummed Motown or old pop songs, things he could half-sing along to. Tonight, it was something softer, almost tuneless, like a lullaby without words.

"You've got a new one stuck in your head," he said, brushing his teeth.

She blinked as if surprised he'd noticed. "Do I?" Then she smiled and swished water from the sink. "Guess it's nothing."

Later, in bed, Samantha curled against him, her knee slotting between his like it always had, her arm draped across his waist. The familiarity was a comfort—the weight of her hand, the warmth of her breath against his shoulder. He let his body sink into hers, the new house fading into the background.

But when he tilted his head and kissed her, he caught a trace of scent that made him pause. Lighter than usual. Lemon soap, maybe, instead of the amber perfume she favoured. He wondered if she'd switched brands, or if it was simply the flowers permeating the room.

"You, okay?" she murmured against his jaw.

"Yeah," he said, forcing the hesitation out of his voice. "Just... tired."

Her lips curved against his skin. "Then sleep. Tomorrow we'll make this place ours."

She turned, curling into her pillow, hair spilling across the sheets like ink. Kevin watched her for a moment. She looked exactly like the woman he'd married, every line and angle of her face familiar. Yet there was something faintly rehearsed about the way she breathed, too even, too measured.

He lay awake longer than he meant to, listening to the house sigh. The vent exhaled again, a softer sound this time, less like a name and more like a fragment of conversation. He tried to piece words out of it, but they dissolved into the creak of wood and the shuffle of settling pipes.

When he finally drifted toward sleep, his last thought was that Samantha felt just a degree too warm beside him, as if the house itself were lending her its breath.

Morning came with thin light through the warped windows, the wallpaper's roses brightening into something almost innocent. Kevin sat up slowly, stiff from the mattress still half-wrapped in plastic, and rubbed his eyes. Beside him, Samantha was already awake, pinning her hair with quick, sure motions.

On the dresser lay a folded slip of paper. She smoothed it with her hand as though it were important, then caught him watching.

"Housewarming," she said lightly.

He reached for it. Blue ink looped across the page in careful strokes: *Welcome home, Sam.* A small heart curled beneath the final letter.

"From who?" he asked.

"From me," she said, amused. "My past self is thoughtful."

Kevin forced a smile. They'd played this game before—she left notes for herself in books, on mirrors, inside jacket pockets. But something snagged his attention. He'd seen her handwriting plenty of times: lists pinned to the fridge, checks written out, sticky notes on his lunch. Samantha's letters were usually upright, neat, teacher-perfect. This note's curves leaned extravagantly, the "S" curling like smoke, the cross of the "t" slanting upward.

He held it a beat too long before passing it back. "Pretty," he said.

Samantha tucked the paper into the drawer with a flick that seemed too casual, too dismissive.

They ate breakfast out of moving boxes—toast from the temperamental toaster, coffee brewed thick and bitter. Samantha slid a yellow legal pad across the counter. Her printing was blocky, businesslike: milk, flour, sugar, eggs. The letters stood upright, severe. He blinked. On this page, her "S" was straight-backed, not looping at all.

She caught him staring. "What?"

"Nothing," he said, folding the pad shut.

He tried to push it away, but the thought clung. The handwriting from the note and the handwriting on this list didn't belong to the same hand.

By mid-morning, contractors drifted through—the plumber muttering at ancient pipes, the electrician complaining about cloth wiring. Kevin kept out of the way, carrying tools or holding ladders when asked, but his mind circled back to the note. When he fetched his wallet to pay for takeout, he slid the folded scrap inside, tucked behind his health card, as though it were evidence.

Later, while unpacking the kitchen, he opened a drawer in search of a spatula and froze. Three identical black combs lay nested side by side, their teeth worn differently, plastic gloss dulled by years of use.

"Bulk buy?" he called.

From the hallway, Samantha's voice came too brightly. "Oh, those. Old. I'll toss them."

She appeared in the doorway, smiling with quick precision, and moved to take them. Kevin shut the drawer first. "Keep one. For the guest bathroom."

"Sure." Her smile softened, too smooth. "You're sweet when you try to domesticate me."

The drawer sighed as it closed, the combs clicking faintly like teeth.

That night, the vents exhaled again. Kevin lay awake listening, the note in his wallet a weight against his hip, the handwriting already burned into his mind. The house whispered something he couldn't quite make out—maybe laughter, maybe names. He pressed his hand to the mattress beside him, felt Samantha's warmth, and wondered which version of her had written *Welcome home, Sam.*

***

Kevin padded into the kitchen after midnight, throat dry from dust and nerves. The house was silent, save for the low hum of the refrigerator and the occasional sigh through the pipes. He poured water into a glass, drank, and leaned against the counter.

The daffodils had begun to droop, their cheerful yellow faces bowing as if in exhaustion. He reached out, touched one petal—it crumbled at the edge, though they'd been fresh just that morning.

He set the glass in the sink. A second clink answered the sound, sharper, like another glass settling. He frowned, opened the cupboard. Only one glass missing.

The hair on his arms lifted.

He shook his head, muttering, "House noises."

When he turned back toward the hall, something tugged at him—an itch to check the utensil drawer. He slid it open.

Empty.

The three black combs were gone.

He stood there longer than he should have, staring at the bare drawer, as if the combs might slide back into place if he waited. The silence pressed in. He could almost imagine the sound of teeth clicking together, just beneath the floorboards.

From the stairwell, the vent sighed. Not a word this time, but something close—a shiver of sound that made his name without letters.

Kevin shut the drawer softly, as though not to disturb whoever had taken the combs, and climbed back upstairs.

Samantha was already asleep, hair spilled across the pillow, her breath steady and even. He slid in beside her, careful not to wake her, and stared at the ceiling until the ceiling blurred.

The last thing he heard before sleep claimed him was the house exhaling again, this time with the faintest edge of laughter.

# Chapter Two
## Rules of Samantha

The next morning, Samantha shepherded Kevin into the kitchen like a teacher guiding a student into class. The daffodils had already been replaced, fresher, taller stems lined up in a glass vase as though someone had swapped them while he slept. He wanted to ask when she'd gone out, but her energy brooked no interruption.

On the refrigerator door hung a brand-new whiteboard, laminated, with colour-coded markers clipped neatly to the edge. A printed heading, bold and cheerful, announced: HOUSE RULES.

Kevin blinked at it. "We have rules now?"

Samantha beamed, holding the board steady with one hand as if unveiling a masterpiece. "Every household needs structure. Old house, new routines—it's the only way to keep chaos out."

There were five rules written in tidy, upright script:

No doors locked against family.

Rotate chores weekly, sign off when done.

Shared spaces stay tidy.

Meals eaten together whenever possible.

One face to the world—always united.

Kevin leaned closer. The first one snagged him like a hook. "No doors locked?"

"Safety," Samantha said smoothly, as though anticipating his concern. "Old wiring, finicky plumbing—I don't want anyone trapped if something sparks. Besides, we shouldn't need locks, should we? No secrets in this house."

She capped the red marker with a decisive snap.

Kevin forced a nod, though the word *family* lingered oddly in his mind. He and Samantha were family, yes, but she had no siblings—at least, none she spoke of often. The rule felt like it was aimed at more than the two of them.

Samantha clapped her hands, snapping him back. "Let's assign chores. You take trash and recycling; I'll do shopping and meals." She scribbled their initials in alternating colours like a teacher assigning classroom duties.

He wanted to laugh—grown adults, married less than a year, suddenly living by a laminated chart—but the brightness in her eyes made it difficult. She radiated certainty, the kind that swept objections aside before they were voiced.

"You're serious about this."

"Of course." She tapped the final rule with her fingertip. "Structure is love, Kev. Without it, things fall apart."

He studied the board again, uneasy, but said nothing.

***

Later that afternoon, the laminated board already gleamed with neat initials and tick marks as if it had always been part of the kitchen. Samantha had washed the markers, lined them in a row, red to black to blue to green. Kevin leaned against the counter, coffee in hand, watching her.

"You ever have rules like this growing up?" he asked.

Her back stiffened almost imperceptibly as she smoothed a dish towel over the sink handle. "Every family does."

"I mean... exactly like this." He gestured toward the refrigerator, toward the cheerful proclamation that no door could ever be locked. "Feels like you've done this before."

Samantha turned, smiling with practiced warmth. "My mother believed in order. She said routine keeps people safe."

"Sounds strict."

"It worked." She tucked a strand of hair behind her ear, eyes sliding just past his. "We were... close."

Kevin studied her carefully. "We?"

She picked up her coffee mug, sipped, and set it down. "Neighbours. Cousins. You know how families blend."

The answer slipped too easily, like a coin sliding into the wrong slot. Kevin remembered the wedding reception, how she'd avoided talk about siblings, how her photo albums stopped at middle school and then resumed abruptly in college.

He pressed, gently. "You never mentioned brothers or sisters."

"Didn't I?"

"No."

Her smile tightened, eyes holding his with a steady brightness. "Then I must not have had any worth mentioning."

The silence after landed heavy. Kevin swallowed the rest of his coffee, the bitterness clinging to his tongue. He told himself not to push, not to make their second morning in the house a fight over something that might not matter.

Samantha slid the dish towel into place, all tidy corners. "What matters now is us," she said softly. "This house, this marriage. We'll keep it together because we're together. Isn't that what you wanted?"

"Of course." He kissed her temple, the gesture automatic, but her skin felt a degree colder than it should have.

The refrigerator hummed louder, as if it too disliked the silence that followed.

Kevin glanced again at the laminated board. The rules stared back, numbered and final, like commandments. He wanted to joke about it, to break the tension, but the words stuck.

Samantha was already moving on, talking about paint colours for the parlour, her voice brisk and bright. But Kevin felt the hole she'd left with her evasions, and he couldn't shake the thought that her rules had been written long before this house ever belonged to them.

By evening, the laminated board was already part of the rhythm. Samantha had cooked a simple pasta, set the table just so, and reminded him to rinse his plate before stacking it. The rules—only a few hours old—were spoken like old habits.

Kevin played along, nodding, doing the chores as assigned. He rinsed, wiped, stacked, all while stealing glances at the bright white surface gleaming on the refrigerator.

The handwriting stared back at him. Upright, schoolteacher neat. A blocky "N" in No doors locked, a careful "M" in Meals eaten together. Not the same hand as the curling *Welcome home, Sam.*

After dinner, Samantha disappeared upstairs to run a bath. Kevin lingered in the kitchen. He could hear the water rushing through the old pipes, the sound echoing faintly in the walls. The house always seemed eager to carry voices where they didn't belong.

He picked up the red marker, tracing the edge of the first rule with his fingertip. The plastic surface squeaked faintly under the pad of his thumb. He pressed the cap against paper towel, twisting, and left a faint impression of the ink.

Not much—just a smudge. But enough. He folded the towel neatly, slipped it into his pocket, and told himself he wasn't crazy. Evidence was evidence, even if it was only marker strokes and scraps of paper.

Samantha padded back into the kitchen in a robe, hair wrapped in a towel. "You're still up?"

"Couldn't sleep." He smiled, holding a mug of water. "Figured I'd make peace with the rules."

Her eyes softened, pleased. "You'll see. It keeps things clean, simple. No secrets."

Kevin raised the mug. "To no secrets."

She clinked her glass against his, lips curving in that familiar smile. For a moment, he felt ashamed for pocketing the towel, for doubting her. For imagining things.

But when she kissed him goodnight, he smelled that faint lemon again—sharp, citrus-bright, not the warm amber perfume she'd worn their whole first year together. He kissed her back, but the question lingered.

Was it Samantha changing? Or was it something else—someone else?

Later, lying awake in the dark, Kevin slipped his hand into his pocket, feeling the folded paper towel with its faint red trace. A fragment of handwriting, a piece of a puzzle he wasn't sure he wanted to solve.

The house sighed through the vent above the bed, soft and steady, as if it too was keeping score.

***

He lay there another minute, the red-smudged paper towel a warm square in his palm, then slid out of bed. The house held its breath as his feet found the hallway runner. He didn't turn on a light. In old places, light felt like a challenge; darkness was a courtesy.

Downstairs, the kitchen clock ticked with the stubbornness of something wound too tight. The whiteboard gleamed in the refrigerator's halo. Kevin crossed to it and stared until his eyes watered. Upright printing. The blocky N again. He touched the edge of the board and felt the faintest texture beneath the laminate, as if older ink—older rules—had sunk into the surface and were trying to rise.

He lifted the board carefully off its magnetic hooks. On the steel door beneath, a fine dust of eraser crumbs clung in a rectangle. He set the board on the counter and turned it over. A piece of masking tape, yellowed at the edges, was stuck to the back. A single word ran along it in faded marker: together.

He pressed his thumb against the tape and felt a whisper of grit, as if the word had been traced a hundred times by a worried finger. He put the board back exactly as he'd found it.

The junk drawer slid open with a squeal that seemed too loud for the hour. Elastics. Menus. A tangle of keys that didn't match anything he knew. He fished them up. One was brass, ornate, old as the house. Another was modern with a blue plastic cap. On a whim he tried the basement door. The brass key didn't fit. The blue one turned easily—too easily. The door swung inward a finger's width, then stopped. A wedge. He reached down and found a flat rubber doorstop pressing the door open.

No doors locked against family.

He left the wedge where it was and eased the door shut without fully closing it. On the way back through the kitchen he opened the cupboard to pour water and paused. Two identical glasses sat side by side on the shelf. The one he reached for had a faint ring of water drying along the base. The one next to it was dry. He told himself he was imagining it. He took the dry one.

At the sink, steam clouded the window. He wiped a circle with his wrist and looked out at the yard, a rectangle of black punctured by the shine of the alley lamppost. Near the garden gnome at the back fence, a shape shifted, small and furtive—cat, raccoon, imagination. When he blinked, it was gone.

He washed the glass, set it upside down to dry, and turned to go. The whiteboard caught his eye again. He stepped closer, not for the rules now, but for the handwriting. He raised his phone, took a quick photo, then another. Insurance against himself. Proof for the man he would be in the morning when doubt came calling with its reasonable voice.

Upstairs, the bathroom door was ajar, a stripe of light across the hall carpet. The mirror was fogged from Samantha's bath. He wiped a clean band with his forearm so he could see to brush his teeth. Two toothbrushes lived in a tumbler by the sink—same brand, same colour. One bristle head had flared just slightly, the way a brush does when someone presses too hard. The other's bristles still stood straight, stiff as soldiers. He lifted one, then the other, feeling the different drag of wear against his thumb. He set them back precisely how they'd been.

In the fogged mirror, someplace above his head, a small shape cleared itself, an oval lip of not-quite steam, as if a fingertip had drawn there earlier. A curve. Another. A vertical stroke. He leaned in until the glass chilled his breath. Letters refused to appear, but the arrangement had the stubborn geometry of writing.

"House tricks," he whispered. "Condensation."

Behind him, a floorboard spoke near the bedroom: a soft complaint and then a settling. Kevin glanced over his shoulder and saw nothing but the dark rectangle of the hall. The air carried the faintest trace of lemon.

He went back to bed and found the mattress warm. Samantha lay curled toward his side, her hand fisted near her mouth like a child's. He told himself the different scent came from the bath, new soap, new house. He willed sleep to take him and finally, grudgingly, it did.

***

In the morning, Samantha moved through the kitchen with cheerful efficiency, already dressed, hair scraped into a symmetrical knot. The red marker squeaked as she drew two neat checkmarks beside DISHES and COUNTERS on a to-do grid she must have added while he slept.

"You're up early," he said.

"Couldn't wait to get us squared away." She kissed his cheek—quick, perfunctory—and pushed coffee into his hand. "Electrician's due at nine. I'll meet him. You can handle the grocery run?"

He nodded, still surfacing. "Sure."

She held his gaze an extra beat, as if confirming compliance, then smiled brilliantly. "We're going to make this beautiful, Kev."

He looked past her at the board. The blocky printing stood immaculate. The masking tape word—together—scratched at him from behind the laminate like a splinter under skin. "Did you... rewrite these?" he asked, casual.

"Rewrite what?"

"The rules. They look—fresh."

"I touched them up." She lifted a shoulder. "Markers dry out."

He sipped coffee he didn't want and watched her place a stack of folded dish towels in the drawer. They fit so perfectly it was as if the drawer had been built for them.

"What was your kitchen like growing up?" he asked. "You said your mother liked routine."

Her hands paused a fraction, then continued. "Small. Yellow curtains. We took turns—" She stopped, smiled, corrected. "*I* took turns making dinner when I was old enough."

"With...?"

"Whoever needed feeding." The answer was glib but landed wrong, like a step on an uneven stair. She changed the subject before he could climb back up. "List's on the counter. Don't forget allspice."

"Allspice?" He tried to make the word a joke. "That specific?"

Samantha's eyes warmed, and for a second he felt the old ease. "Pie fixes everything," she said. "You'll see."

He pocketed the grocery list and his wallet, felt the folded paper towel with its red smear, and told himself to let it go. Let the house be old. Let the rules be rules. Let the handwriting be a quirk of sleep and light.

On his way out, he hesitated at the refrigerator and moved one magnet—not far, a half inch. The whiteboard hung slightly askew. He wanted to see if, when he came back, it would be straight again.

The morning air bit his face with the pleasant cruelty of early spring. He walked down the porch steps and glanced back. The upstairs bedroom curtain stirred, then stilled. No silhouette at the window. He told himself he hadn't been hoping for one.

\*\*\*

The grocery store felt like a different planet—fluorescent lights, tinny pop music, aisles so straight and bright no secret could hide there. He bought flour and sugar, eggs and milk, cinnamon and allspice, tossed in extra coffee as a talisman against last night. At the bakery kiosk, a tray of lemon tarts shone under glass. He nearly ordered one, then thought of the other bouquet that had appeared without explanation and chose a baguette instead.

Back home, the kitchen smelled like lemon again. The vase of daffodils had been replaced with lilies, white throats open, sweet as surrender. The whiteboard on the fridge sat perfectly level.

He set the bags down. "Electrician come?"

"Mm-hmm," Samantha said without turning. She stood at the counter labelling glass jars with tidy block letters: FLOUR, SUGAR, RICE. The labels matched the rules: upright, careful, as uniform as a row of teeth.

He pulled the baguette from its paper and tore off a heel. "You always label like that?"

"Like what?"

"So... exact."

Her pen paused. "It helps," she said, and resumed writing.

He reached past to set the spices down and brushed the edge of the label sheet. The pen lifted and, for a microscopic beat, hovered between two ways of forming the letter S. When it touched the sticker, it chose upright. Clean. Schoolteacher neat.

"Looks good," he said softly.

She glanced up, searching his face for something he hoped he wasn't showing. Whatever she saw satisfied her; she smiled, bright as a switch being thrown. "Teamwork."

He looked at the door to the basement—still propped open with the rubber wedge—and at the neat, uncompromising line of rules on the fridge. He wanted badly to be the kind of man who could surrender to the comfort of being told what to do.

"Teamwork," he echoed.

Somewhere in the house, a vent exhaled, so soft it might have been a memory. It sent a draft through the kitchen that made the lilies trem-ble. One petal fell and landed face-down on the counter, leaving a wet crescent like a thumbprint.

Kevin pressed the petal under his fingertip and felt it give, thin and slick and real. He lifted his finger, and the petal stuck to the skin a second before letting go.

No secrets, he thought, staring at the rule. But the house already knew better.

# Chapter Three
## Sugar & Flour

T he Claremont Lane Bakery had been in business longer than the house had been standing. Kevin knew because Samantha had told him—three times, in fact, weaving the fact into conversation like it was essential background. "Established 1901," she'd said, pointing at the fading sign above the door, her voice warm with local pride as though she were the town's historian.

This morning, he parked across the street, baguette crumbs still on the seat from yesterday, and stared at the painted windows until the cold nipped him into moving. The bell over the door chimed, heavy with a century of footsteps.

Inside, the air was thick with sugar and yeast, butter melting into everything. Glass cases gleamed with rows of croissants and tarts, loaves stacked like bricks of gold. Kevin stood in line behind a woman with a stroller, trying to remember the exact list Samantha had drilled into him. Flour. Sugar. Allspice. Cinnamon. He checked the note in his pocket, her printing upright, uncompromising.

When it was his turn, the clerk looked up from the register with a sunny familiarity. "Back again so soon? You must really like the cherry turnovers."

Kevin blinked. "Sorry?"

The young man's smile didn't falter. "Your wife picked up a half-dozen last week. Said they were her guilty pleasure. I told her they'd ruin her figure, and she said, 'What figure?' and winked. I mean—" He stopped, suddenly aware he was rambling. "Anyway. Nice to see you both becoming regulars."

Kevin's throat went dry. "Last week," he repeated.

The clerk nodded, bagging his flour. "Yup. Same day, Tuesday morning. Pretty sure she was headed to the farmer's market after. She had that—uh—scar?" He drew a finger above his right eyebrow. "I noticed because my brother has one just like it, soccer injury. She said hers was from falling off a bike."

Kevin felt the bottom drop out of his stomach. "Scar?" he asked, too sharply.

The clerk faltered, then smiled uncertainly, as if replaying the memory to check his own accuracy. "Yeah, just a little white line, nothing major. Gave her kind of a cool look. Sorry—was that not your wife? I mean, she looked exactly like her. Same voice. Same laugh. I'd have sworn—"

Kevin forced a chuckle, paper-thin. "Probably wasn't her. She's never had a scar."

"Really? Huh. Dead ringer, Mario had said, then. Sorry about that."

The register dinged, spilling coins into the tray. Kevin paid in silence, the sound of change-like nails tapping on glass.

When the clerk slid the receipt across the counter, Kevin tucked it into his wallet without glancing at it. But he felt the dread bloom low in his gut, already knowing what he would see later: handwriting that didn't belong to Samantha.

***

He didn't make it to the door. Three steps from the threshold, something yanked in his chest like a poorly tied knot catching. He pivoted and drifted to the end of the counter where a bulletin board displayed curling flyers: piano lessons, a dog-walker, a sketch of a missing grey cat with one black ear. He pretended to read, then slid the receipt from his wallet with the care of someone handling a live wire.

CLAREMONT LANE BAKERY in faded thermal print. Date: last Tuesday, 10:18 a.m. Cashier: MARIO. Items: 6 CH TURNOVER, 1 CAPPUCINO. At the bottom, a flourish—*Thanks, Sam!*—in blue pen, a looping S that unfurled like ribbon. The 7 in the phone number for feedback wore a confident bar.

Kevin's thumb held the paper still while the bell over the door chimed behind him for other customers, strangers with simpler mornings. His heart thudded hard against his ribs. Samantha's lists were always straight-backed, no loops, no bars on numbers unless she was being cute. She'd never been cute on a receipt.

"Everything all right?" The clerk—Mario—had drifted a few paces down the counter to restock napkins, concern edging his sunny voice.

Kevin folded the receipt once, twice. "Yeah, sure. I just—reminded me I forgot something. Do you carry allspice?"

"Two shelves over by the cinnamon." Mario's grin returned, relieved to be useful. "We expanded our spice section last fall. Your wife—uh, sorry, *the woman* I thought was your wife—she knew exactly where everything was. She said, 'I can navigate by smell.' That was funny." He paused. "I thought it was funny."

"It's funny," Kevin said, and found that his mouth could still approximate a smile.

He moved to the spices and stared at the neat little tins like they might rearrange into sense if he stared long enough. Allspice, cinnamon, clove, nutmeg—his hand landed on a tin, but his mind stayed with the receipt, the loop of the S, Mario's finger to his eyebrow describing a thin white line that did not belong to the woman Kevin kissed every night.

*Dead ringer,* Mario had said. *Same voice. Same laugh.*

Kevin unscrewed the tin and inhaled: warm, round—*a kindness of a spice..* Warm, round scent. A kindness of a spice. It didn't make him feel any kinder.

At the register again, Mario slid over a pen for the signature. "Sorry if I made it weird," he said, earnest, the way people apologise when they don't know the shape of the thing they've bumped into.

"It's fine," Kevin said. "People look like other people." He scrawled his name and almost laughed—his K dipped differently depending on how much coffee he'd had. Handwriting wasn't a fingerprint; it was a mood. A performance. A mask.

"Exactly," Mario said, encouraged. "I see doubles all the time in here. Yesterday there were two guys who could've been brothers and they swore up and down they weren't even related. Wild."

Kevin pocketed the receipt and his change, nodding like a man in agreement with the world. He took two steps toward the door, then paused again, the knot pulling tight.

"Quick question," he said, turning back. "When you say she... laughed. What kind of laugh?"

Mario blinked. "What kind?"

"Loud? Soft?" Kevin gestured vaguely, aware he was entering a kind of madness from which there wasn't an elegant exit. "Sharp, like—like a bark? Or warmer?"

Mario considered, leaning on the counter with both palms. "Bubbly? But quick. Like she's saving part of it. Not a snort or anything." He flushed. "Sorry, that's not helpful."

"It is," Kevin said, and it was. Samantha's laugh ran the length of a room and lit it up. He loved that about her. This other laugh—bubbly, quick—felt like a laugh edited for space.

"What earrings was she wearing?" The question slipped out before he could stop it.

Mario's face brightened. "Little hoops. One caught the light and I said something dumb about how they looked like pastry rings. She laughed at that, too."

Hoops. Samantha wore studs almost every day. Hoops for parties. Or for pretending to be someone who wore hoops to a bakery on a Tuesday morning.

"And the cappuccino?" Kevin asked. "Cinnamon on top?"

"Cocoa." Mario nodded, pleased to have a concrete answer. "She said cinnamon made it taste like Christmas, and she didn't want to rush the year."

Cocoa. Samantha always asked for the cinnamon shaker, calling it her "pie dust." He knew because he'd teased her about being eighty inside.

"Thanks," Kevin said. His voice sounded normal—he marvelled at it, the body's commitment to keeping the mask on even when the mind gaped. He pushed the door and the bell chimed and the cold outside hit him like a clear instruction.

He stood on the sidewalk with his purchases cutting into his fingers and watched his breath turn white. The receipt burned in his pocket. He took it out again and studied the loops like a jeweller hunting flaws in a precious stone. The capital S swept high and then sank in a graceful tail; the lowercase m leaned into itself; the heart punctuating *Sam* was tended—no hurried dash, but a tidy, almost symmetrical shape.

He thought of the note in his wallet at home—*Welcome home, Sam*—and the tender heart beneath the m. He thought of the rule board's upright letters, the blocky M, the careful N. He thought of the two identical toothbrushes and the one with flared bristles, the three combs nested in the drawer and then gone.

A bus hissed to a stop up the street. An older man stepped off, glanced at Kevin, and kept going, the small mercy of a stranger's disinterest. Kevin flexed his hands to keep blood moving. The knot in his chest loosened into a different sort of ache.

This was absurd. There were a dozen explanations, most of them boring. Samantha could have bought turnovers and a cappuccino with cocoa on top because why not. Maybe she'd tried hoops for a day and decided against them. Maybe a scar appeared in bright bakery light where none existed at home—shadows make liars of faces, he knew that. Maybe the S looped when you wrote standing up and stayed straight-backed when you wrote sitting down. Maybe his own need to fix the house in his head as either haunted or harmless had turned everything into a clue.

***

He started toward the car, head bowed against the wind. A woman coming the other way called out, "Morning, Sam!" and he looked up in reflex, ready to laugh and correct, but she sailed past him to a second woman behind, the two of them identical in bulky coats except that one's scarf was red and one's was grey. They hugged and chattered, splitting the morning between them.

Twins were everywhere once you looked for them, he told himself. Doppelgängers. Patterns. Confirmation bias. You saw what you looked for; you heard your name in pipes because you were listening for it.

He reached the car, dropped the bag on the passenger seat, and sat with his hands on the steering wheel. The residual warmth from the drive over had left the cabin smelling faintly of baguette and something citrus. Lemon, maybe, though he hadn't bought anything lemon.

On impulse, he pulled out his phone and snapped a photo of the receipt. He took another, closer, until the loops of the S filled the frame. He texted the image to himself, then deleted it, keeping only the photo in his camera roll. and kept the photo in his camera roll because it seemed less insane to keep a picture than a theory.

The engine coughed to life. He drove the long way home, circling two extra blocks so he could roll past the farmer's market Mario had mentioned. Tents billowed, bright as a row of teeth; a chalkboard offered honey and pears. He imagined Samantha—hoops catching the sun, cocoa dusting her lip, a thin white scar arching like a whisper above her eye—and felt the unreality of it slant the street.

At a red light, he lifted his hand to his own eyebrow, touched the place where a scar might live. Nothing. Smooth skin. He laughed—one short, saved piece of a larger laugh—and startled himself with the sound.

The light changed. He drove. The house on their street hunched into view, its three gables leaning toward each other like conspirators in mid-sentence. On the porch, a package leaned against the rail—brown paper, no return address, tied with string like something from an old movie.

He parked, climbed the steps, and read the label: SAMANTHA in upright, careful print. No loops. No heart. The 7 in the tracking code was plain.

He brought it inside and set it on the table. The lilies flooded the foyer with sweetness so thick it turned metallic at the back of his tongue.

Wind pressed at the door as if something outside had changed its mind and wanted back in.

He stood over the package with a paring knife and watched his hand shake just enough to make the blade a bad idea. He set it down.

"Samantha?" he called.

Her voice came from upstairs, bright, immediate. "In here!"

He laid his palm flat on the package and felt the solidity of whatever was inside. The whiteboard on the fridge shone in his periphery, unwavering, its rules unbothered by the day's discoveries.

He reached for the string. He didn't pull. Not yet.

He wanted one more boring explanation before he crossed into the kind of knowledge you don't climb back out of.

He wanted to be a man who could walk into the kitchen, present flour and sugar and a tin of allspice, and listen to his wife talk about pie.

He wanted to open the package and find nothing but measuring spoons. He wanted to believe in measuring.

He lifted the tin of allspice from the bag and set it by the stove. The metal clinked like a small bell announcing mass.

"Pie," he said to the room, to the rules, to himself. "Pie fixes everything."

The house breathed out through the vent above the door, a soft, even hush, as if agreeing. Or warning. He couldn't tell which.

# Chapter Four
## Sonia's Quiet Hands

S onia knew the house by the sounds it made when no one was trying to listen. A good house told on itself. This one confessed in the nails.

She knelt on the upstairs landing with a folded towel under her knees, the stair runner peeled back like a tongue, a pry bar cradled against the third tread from the top. That tread had flex, the bad kind, the whisper of a split around one of the old cut nails. She could hear the complaint when anyone heavier than she was came up the stairs—tik, tik, keening little protest—and it made her jaw clench because small things turned into big things when you said "later" to them. Later was how houses got mean.

Samantha's voice floated from the bedroom, low and clear, not speaking to anyone, not at a volume meant to carry. Most people would call it humming. Sonia knew it for what it was: rehearsal. Samantha liked to lay the route in her mouth before she walked it. Words went down smoother that way.

"Pie fixes everything," Samantha said, and then again, a shade brighter, like she'd painted a smile onto it. "Pie fixes everything, Kev."

Sonia levered the pry bar beneath the tread and eased it up. The old wood gave with a small sigh. From the other end of the hall, water ran; someone had turned on the bathroom tap to fog the mirror for a scene. The house took it all and moved it around so the timing worked.

"If you don't mind running back for the cream," Samantha's voice tried next, warm with gratitude. "You know the one—heavy, not light." Sonia exhaled through her nose. "You know the one," she whispered, soft, affectionate. She could hear the points Samantha would hit, where she'd stand, where she'd tilt her head to look up at him through lashes. That tilt worked, always had, even on Sonia when they were girls and Samantha wanted the last peach slice or the better pillow or the permission Sonia couldn't say no to. The tilt said don't ruin this.

The tread lifted, exposing the dark pocket beneath. To anyone else: dust. To Sonia: history. She slid two fingers into the gap and found what she knew would be there, because she put it there herself when the move began—a cloth roll of tools, the good ones, oiled and wrapped, and a small tin where she kept spare finish nails sorted from the salvaged boxes. She worked quietly, fast, the way people do when they've learnt to make their contribution in the time no one's paying attention.

A laugh travelled the length of the house and gathered itself around her spine. Not Samantha's—lighter. The bounce to it made you think of birds. Sarah, then, unless Sonia had forgotten the sound of her own voice, which frightened her more than she would admit.

"You're early," Sonia said under her breath, though Sarah wasn't close enough to hear. She set the pry bar down, slid a shim beneath the cracked stringer, and seated a new nail with the smallest, precise taps that wouldn't be heard over water and practice talk.

The pact had never needed writing down, though Samantha put it into words later to make it real. Before it had sentences, it was just the way you learnt to live when one wrong knock could bring a certain kind of attention. One face to the world, or none of them got to keep one. They'd been good, better than good, perfect in the way that wore out your bones. Sonia had always been the one who could smooth an edge with her finger and make it disappear.

She seated the tread, leaned on it, heard only the bland, sweet hush of a stair doing its job. Satisfaction flickered and went. There was no joy in work finished when work never finished; there was only the absence of failure.

\*\*\*

"—and then we can take a walk," Samantha was saying, that bright ribbon of a voice she wrapped around him. "Just you and me, no projects, no contractors." A pause, as if she'd glanced at the whiteboard and smiled. "We'll be so good, you'll see. Structure is love."

Sonia closed her eyes. The words had been their mother's first, but Samantha wore them like skin.

Downstairs, the front door opened. Male feet—Kevin—slower on the last two steps as he shifted the bag to his other hand. Sonia sat very still, the towel under her knees absorbing the thud of her own heart. It was one thing to move through the house when he wasn't home, to lay out the props and switch them again so he never saw doubles. It was another to be here with him between rooms, a single misstep from the wrong face around the wrong corner.

She folded the towel, slid the tool roll back into the hollow with the ease of habit, and eased the runner flat. The brass stair rods would hide a multitude of sins; the pattern in the runner—three vines that braided and unbraided—hid the rest. She set a palm against the wood and felt the house's breath come up through it, warm as a dog's breath. It made her shiver.

"Samantha?" Kevin called.

"In here!" Samantha answered, and the room changed shape to suit her.

The urge to be seen came at Sonia quick and ugly. It always did right after she fixed something. She wanted a thank you lodged in her throat so badly it ached. Look, I made it not hurt you, she wanted to say, as if that might buy her the right to stop pretending for an hour. As if the work could earn her the permission to be a person.

Instead, she took the urge and folded it the way she'd folded the towel, neat, small, hidden under the tread where the house could keep it for her until she fell through and needed it to break the first impact.

She stood, dusted her palms, and padded down the hall, keeping to the rug so the boards wouldn't say her name. In the bathroom mirror, a fog-streaked version of herself blinked back like a twin who'd had a different life. She loved and hated that mirror for what it knew.

At the top of the stairs she paused, listening to Samantha and Kevin in the kitchen below. Samantha's voice ran ahead of her like a ribbon unfurling while Kevin tried to hold the end of it. He said something about a package and she said something about "oh! measuring spoons," and the relief in his laugh made Sonia grip the newel post until the bones across her knuckles stood sharp under the skin.

She sank to a sit on the top step and opened her hands in her lap. They weren't pretty hands. She'd stopped wanting that when she was fourteen and discovered they could do other things better: turn a stripped screw, set a hidden hinge straight, coax a dead lamp to light by sanding a corroded contact with patience and love. Her hands were what she had to offer. Samantha had faces, Sarah had fire; Sonia had the quiet that made other things work.

Down the stairs, she went—silent, the way a person walks when she knows all the boards that tattle. Halfway to the landing she stopped and reached under the runner where the tread met the riser, to the slot where she kept not the tools but the fears. Her fingers found the small cloth pouch by touch alone. Inside it: the brass key with the ornamental bow and a notch cut wrong for any modern lock; the key that belonged to the house's before. She'd found it trapped in a seam of old paint beneath the third coat of white, the way forgotten things sometimes crawled back into the light just to be helpful.

She palmed the key and slid the pouch closed with her thumb. It was heavy in that satisfying way dense small things were, like a coin worth saving.

Samantha laughed; it ran up the stairwell wrong—a note too sharp in the chord. Sonia tucked the key into the sole of her slipper and kept walking.

In the kitchen, Kevin stood by the island with a bag of groceries open like a lung. The whiteboard on the fridge stared patient and righteous, and the lilies in the entry had hit the hour where their sweetness tipped toward rot. Samantha had a paring knife and a string and the open package; the twine curled on the counter like something that had died and decided to be decorative.

"What is it?" Kevin asked, and the question sounded too careful, as if he wanted to be pleased and was begging the world to let him be.

"Measuring spoons," Samantha said, and lifted a nested set by the ring. They chimed: a clean ladder of notes. "See? Specificity. Tablespoon is not teaspoon. Precision is kindness."

"Who sent them?"

"Aunt Clara," she said without a heartbeat's pause. "She saw our registry too late and panicked." She kept her eyes on the spoons, kept her mouth turned in that smile that let you love her without looking too close. "She's always been charmingly frantic."

Sonia leaned in the doorway where, if Kevin glanced over, he would see only a shadow shaped like a woman. Samantha's lie sat light on the air, but the house knew the physics of it; it had to put that weight somewhere. Sonia felt it in the rods that held the runner in place. One day those rods would spit the lie back. For now, they held.

Kevin unwrapped the tin of allspice and set it near the stove. "Pie," he said. "Fixes everything."

"Exactly," Samantha said, and in the small space between them, a loop of ribbon tightened. If he walked forward into it, it would tie around his throat and he would call it a necklace.

Sonia had to look away. She could feel herself dissolving into the paint, like a moth that might be mistaken for a pattern if she kept still. "Basement," Samantha said brightly, already moving the scene towards its safe close. "Kev, would you bring up the stand mixer? There's a box at the bottom of the stairs."

He smiled, happy to be useful, and turned towards the basement door. Sonia's body moved before her mind agreed to it. "Careful with the third step," she said, and both of them flinched at the sound of her voice in their room. She kept it light. "A little soft. I wedged it, but—" She shrugged one shoulder. "Old houses like to flirt with ankles."

Kevin's face restored itself around relief; he wanted the explanation that made things practical. "Thanks," he said, and smiled at her in the simple way men smiled when you made their lives easier. "I appreciate you taking care of it."

She felt the thank you in her bones like a clean shot of something warm. She ducked her head and let it pass through without showing on her face.

When he disappeared through the basement door, the charm in the room snapped back to its angle. Samantha set the spoons down with deliberate care and looked at Sonia across the island, the way one acrobat looks at another when they know the net is tired.

"You can tell him later," Samantha said, ignoring their rules by speaking the thing. "The steps. When it's your turn."

"My turn." Sonia wanted to laugh and felt instead the urge to bite. "We said we wouldn't—"

"We said we'd be careful." Samantha wiped the knife clean and set it in the sink, as if order could absolve. "He doesn't want the truth. He wants a good marriage." She tipped her head, performed the warmth for Sonia that she planned to perform for Kevin and then—later, when schedules demanded—for Sarah. "Don't make a scene."

"I fix things," Sonia said. "That's my contribution. Not scenes."

"You fix things," Samantha agreed. "So let me do mine." She lifted the spoons again, watched the light in them as if they were proof of something. "Precision is kindness."

The basement door banged open before Sonia had to answer. Kevin reappeared with the mixer box balanced against one hip. He was careful with the third step; she loved and hated that, because it meant she mattered and could be replaced.

"Got it," he said, breathless, manful. "This thing weighs a ton."

"It'll earn its keep," Samantha said. She moved to take the box and let her fingers brush his wrist, a small spark timed to a heartbeat. He blushed with the pleasure of being touched in the exact right place and looked at Sonia because he was kind.

"You'll stay for dinner?" he asked, hoping he was asking the right question. "Pie, apparently."

Sonia smiled in the soft, sweet way that made people feel better. "I'll stir," she said. "I'm good at that."

The kitchen relaxed around the decision as if a tight muscle had finally let go. Samantha began to move like a recipe, reading aloud the steps they all already knew. Kevin stood between them and handed her what she asked for, glad for a world where tasks had endings. Sonia washed the apples and pared them like a prayer—thin, even spirals, peel to peel to peel. She lined the slices in the pie plate in concentric circles and watched the geometry of obedience make something that could feed all of them without asking questions back.

***

While the pie baked, she slipped out "to check the upstairs window where the sash sticks," though what she wanted was the hall closet with the false back. The brass key was a coin in her slipper that had pressed a hot crescent into her skin. In the closet, behind the linen shelf where the towels sat in precise thirds, there was a panel she'd eased once and set back. It came forward for her now with a sigh. The cavity took the key like a throat takes a pill. Inside: the scrapbooks their mother had kept until Samantha told her to burn them. Their mother had burned the ones that had faces in them. Sonia had salvaged these.

She didn't pull them out. Not today. She only touched the spine of the top one, felt the drag of cheap vinyl under her finger. She had a vision so clear it stole the air from her: coming up here with Kevin and lifting the panel and saying, We, and watching his face change.

The house creaked, a warning. Downstairs, Samantha laughed and it ran up the stairwell wrong, a note too sharp in the chord. Sonia flinched and set the panel back, slid the linen neatly into place, smoothed the towel edges. She came down composed.

Kevin was at the counter with his phone, looking at a close-up of something—loops of ink, maybe, or light on a metal ring. He clicked the screen off when he saw her and smiled the way people smile when they want to prove there's nothing in their hands.

"Smells amazing," he said as Samantha opened the oven and the kitchen filled with sugar and spice and the high, unsteady note of caramel hitting its edge

"See?" Samantha said without looking at either of them. "Pie fixes everything."

They ate slices standing up because plates felt like a ceremony none of them deserved. Kevin burned his tongue and laughed and swore softly, and Sonia handed him a glass of cold water without thinking. He took it and looked grateful enough to hurt.

***

When it was done—the pie, the laughter, the momentary peace—Kevin rinsed the plates and slid them into the dishwasher as if rule-following could be an exorcism. Samantha wiped the counter to a shine. Sonia took the trash bag out and knotted it, the plastic cinch biting the skin of her fingers so that the mark of it lingered when she'd tossed the bag in the bin out back and come in again.

"Stay," Kevin said when she moved towards the hall. "We could watch something. Or—hey, I didn't show you—the downstairs has this creepy little sewing room? You'd love it. You love creepy."

"Tomorrow," Samantha said lightly, not looking up from the whiteboard where she was drawing a new grid for the week. "Let her go. She's tired."

"I'm fine," Sonia said, and was lying. Fatigue had a way of filling her from the ankles up like water in a well. Soon it would reach her mouth and she'd drown if she tried to speak.

"We have an early start," Samantha said, and the ruleboard gleamed behind her like a cooperative god.

Kevin nodded because he was built to nod. "Tomorrow, then."
Sonia hesitated at the doorway, the house pressing against her back like breath. She turned.

"Kevin," she said, and he looked up quickly, hopeful, as if her voice might unwrap a gift. "If the stair talks again—if it complains—I can—" She faltered, realised she was saying I'll be here, realised she couldn't promise that and keep the rest of her promises. "Leave me a note," she finished, hating herself for the cowardice of it. "On the board. I'll fix it."

"Thank you," he said, simple and good.

She nodded, then looked at Samantha. For a heartbeat they were girls again in a mirror—one face, two faces, one—and then Samantha smiled the small, razor smile that meant be useful, be quiet, be kind. Sonia slipped into the hall and stood with her back against the wall until her heart remembered how to beat without making sideways decisions. She took the brass key from her slipper and closed her fingers around it until the points bit, a star pressed into her palm.

On her way up, the third stair held, solid as a promise kept that no one would notice. The vent breathed a word that could have been her name if you were a house and had never had to say a name aloud. In the bathroom, the mirror had cleared. Her face was only hers, until she tilted it and found Samantha's there too, and if she moved it another degree, Sarah's mouth looked back, bruised by laughter.

She touched the scar she did not have and imagined one anyway, a thin white line to make it easier for a man to tell them apart. Then she wiped the thought away as you erase a dry-erase board: quickly, carelessly, leaving a ghost of what had been written for anyone who cared to look close.

In the dark of the bedroom that wasn't hers, she sat on the edge of a bed where no one slept and listened to the pipes hum. The key warmed in her hand. She thought about walking back down into the bright kitchen and saying we to a man who wanted anything but we and thought about the house and its old, loyal nails. She pictured the stair that didn't wobble anymore because she'd loved it into holding, and she let that be her victory, small, exact, the size of a brass key.

Downstairs, Samantha laughed again, the laugh she wore for him, and then cut it short, saving the rest for later. Sonia leaned back against the headboard, closed her eyes, and pressed the little star in her palm deeper until it hurt enough to feel like truth.

When she rose to go—quiet, almost a rumour—she tucked the key not into the slipper but into the hem of the curtain in the spare room, a place where fabric folded on itself and made a pocket. She smoothed the line; the hiding vanished.

On the landing, she paused over the stair she'd repaired and bent, pressing her ear to the runner as if she could hear future footsteps choosing to trust her. I am here, she thought, which no one would ever put on a board, which was the only rule that had ever mattered to her.

She went down on cat feet. In the kitchen, the rules gleamed, and Kevin's laughter came soft from the other side of the wall, and Samantha's voice braided through it with a promise nobody could afford. Sonia reached into the trash can and retrieved the length of string from the package, wound it into a neat coil, and slipped it into her pocket. It might hold something together later.

Before she left, she set a finger against the bottom corner of the whiteboard and nudged the magnet not a half inch, but a whisper—less than a lie, just enough to see. If it hung straight tomorrow, she would know how tightly the day had been rewritten.

She closed the door softly behind her and felt the house breathe out, then in, as if relieved she'd chosen silence again. On the porch, the air was colder; the night threw a different set of sounds into her arms. Sonia stood a long moment, willing the outside to fix the inside. When it didn't, she went down the steps, counting them out of habit, her fingers closing around the little coil of string like a rosary.

Behind her, the house kept their secrets the way a body keeps breath: reflex first, then choice.

# Chapter Five
## Sarah's Smoke

Sarah liked her cigarettes best when they tasted of defiance.

She sat on the back steps, toes bare against the cold wood, hoodie zipped to her throat, and flicked ash into the flowerbed where the lilies leaned heavy-headed. The house exhaled through the kitchen vent above her, a low, steady breath. Sometimes she thought it was mocking her. Tonight, she let it.

The lighter clicked shut in her hand, warm from flame. She leaned her head back and blew smoke into the dark. The gnome by the fence kept her secret, squat ceramic belly hollowed by her careful work with a screwdriver last week. She'd prised the cork stopper loose, shoved the bottle of prenatal vitamins inside, and wedged the plug back. No one had noticed. No one ever noticed the right things in this house.

The sickness had started early that morning, same as the last week—sharp, sour waves that bent her double over the bathroom sink before the coffee brewed. Samantha had noticed, of course. Samantha noticed everything, but she'd said nothing, only handed Sarah a glass of water with that faint, razor-smile that meant I know and I'll use it when I want to.

Sarah ground out the cigarette against the step and lit another immediately, daring the nausea to come faster. She was stubborn that way—daring the body, daring the house, daring her sisters. That's how it had always been. Samantha wanted order, Sonia wanted peace, and

Sarah wanted the fire that came when you pressed against both.

Her stomach turned at the thought. Fire and smoke. Inside and out.

You're reckless, Samantha's voice said in her head, crisp and certain.

Sarah snorted smoke and muttered back, "And you're suffocating."

The porch door creaked open behind her. Sonia, of course. Sonia who couldn't let a silence stay. Sonia who patched and smoothed like wallpaper over cracks.

"You'll ruin your lungs," Sonia said softly, stepping into the spill of moonlight. "And the garden."

Sarah blew smoke sideways, away from her sister, though she hated herself for the courtesy. "Garden was dead before we got here."

"You could at least—" Sonia stopped, sighed. She folded herself onto the step beside Sarah, knees drawn up, arms around them like she was holding herself together. "She knows, doesn't she?"

Sarah tapped ash into the dirt, watching the glow at the end fade to nothing. "Of course she knows. She knows everything. That's her trick."

Sonia pressed her lips tight, eyes shiny in the dark. "Then what are you going to do?"

"What do you think?" Sarah snapped, then softened at Sonia's flinch. She reached over, squeezed her hand once. "I'm going to live. As me. Not as her, not as us. Just me."

The word me hung dangerous between them. They weren't supposed to use it. Me meant separation. Me meant the pact was cracking.

"You'll destroy it," Sonia whispered.

"Good." Sarah lit another cigarette, let the flame flare too long before she snapped it shut. "Let it burn."

***

The sickness hit again in the middle of the night. Sarah stumbled into the upstairs bathroom, gripping the sink as her body turned inside out. She caught her reflection in the mirror between waves—eyes bloodshot, hair stuck damp against her cheek. For a moment she saw her mother in that face, the same tilt of jaw, the same tired fury.

She spat, rinsed her mouth, and whispered, "I'm not her. I'm not you either." She didn't know which sister she was addressing.

When she turned, Samantha stood in the doorway, robe cinched, face calm as a pond.

"Rough night?" Samantha asked, voice soft but angled.

Sarah's grip tightened on the sink. "Stomach bug."

"Mm." Samantha's gaze slid to the bin. Sarah followed it, saw the crumpled paper sleeve from the prenatal vitamins she'd accidentally dropped, pale plastic glinting at the edge. Her pulse spiked.

Samantha's smile didn't change. "You'll want to be careful with your health." She reached out, smoothed Sarah's hair like she was a child again. "We can't afford sloppiness."

Sarah jerked away, bile and fury tangling in her throat. "You don't get to tell me what I can afford."

Samantha's smile widened, serene and sharp. "I always have. That's why you're still here."

The bathroom light flickered, once, then steadied. Sarah wondered if the house agreed.

The next morning, Kevin sat at the kitchen table flipping through the newspaper he pretended to read. Sarah breezed in, pouring coffee she wouldn't drink, her sleeve riding up enough to show the faint bruises on her wrist from gripping the sink too hard. Kevin looked up, eyes catching, concern starting to form on his lips.

Samantha swept in before he could speak, bright as sunshine, pressing a kiss to his cheek, handing him his mug exactly the way he liked it. Sonia followed with a plate of sliced fruit, soft smile smoothing edges. Sarah stood in the corner, cigarette still ghosting her fingers, and thought, We're a play. We're a script. And I don't want my lines anymore.

***

She took a bite of fruit, sour in her mouth, and said, clear enough for the house to hear, "I might take a trip into town today. Alone."

The silence that followed was quick, sharp. Samantha's head turned, eyes flicking to Sonia, who froze mid-slice. Kevin looked between them, confusion sparking. Sarah chewed, swallowed, and smiled with all her teeth.

"Why?" Samantha asked sweetly.

Sarah shrugged. "Because I want to."

The word I landed like a stone in still water. Ripples spread through the room. Samantha's smile thinned but held. Sonia lowered her gaze. Kevin blinked, clearly missing the depth of the exchange, but uneasy all the same.

Sarah licked juice from her thumb, daring them all. Inside, beneath the taste of citrus, the nausea coiled again, fierce and certain. She pressed her palm to her stomach, a silent vow.

Mine, she thought. Not ours. Mine.

Kevin cleared his throat, the paper rattling as he turned a page he wasn't reading. "If you go into town," he said, careful, "take my card. Treat yourself. Pie from Claremont? You like the lemon."

Samantha didn't look at him, only at Sarah. "She's been nauseated," she said, light as a weather report. "Lemon won't help."

Sarah's smile widened. "How attentive."

"We live together," Samantha said. "I notice things."

"You notice control," Sarah said, and the room tipped a degree, as if the house had leaned in.

Sonia slid the fruit plate between them like a peace offering. "I can come with you," she murmured to Sarah. "If you want company."

"I don't," Sarah said, soft but flint-edged.

Sonia flinched and hid it by reaching for a tea towel. Kevin set his mug down too hard; coffee lipped over the rim and streaked his knuckles. He didn't seem to feel it.

"Be back by dinner," Samantha said. A request that wasn't.

Sarah licked her thumb clean of citrus and left the kitchen without answering.

Upstairs, she shut the bathroom door and leaned against the cool wood until the nausea crested and receded. She rinsed her mouth, patted her face with a damp towel, and looked at herself the way you look at a stranger you've seen before. Her eyes were their mother's; her mouth was no one's but her own. If she dragged her thumb along her brow, she could almost carve a pale line there, a pretend scar to make Kevin look twice.

She whispered to the woman in the mirror, "I'm not sorry."

Her phone was hidden in the fake-bottom of a makeup bag—a habit so worn it felt like a prayer. She took it, sat on the edge of the tub, and thumbed through contacts until she reached Riveredge Road Women's Clinic. The line rang four times before a voice answered, bright with practised gentleness.

"Riveredge Road, how can I help you?"

"I need to be seen," Sarah said. "Soon."

"Name?"

"Riveredge road, how can I help you?"

Sarah swallowed and heard the lie arrive before she chose it. "Sam

Ward."

"Okay, Sam," the receptionist said, typing the invented letters into a system that wouldn't know how many faces wore them. "How far along do you think you are?"

Sarah shut her eyes and let the memories stack like cards: the missed period, the nausea that wove through her days like thread, the night the world tilted and the pact made everything cheap and expensive at once. "Eight weeks. Maybe nine."

"We can see you this afternoon at 3:20. Does that work?"

"Perfect." She forced a smile the woman couldn't see. "Thank you."

"Bring a photo ID."

Sarah glanced at her wallet, at the card that would match the name and not the name. "Left it at home," she lied briskly. "But I have insurance."

"That's fine. See you at 3:20, Sam."

Sarah hung up and stared at the tile. The appointment confirmation sat in her call log like a lit coal. She opened a notes app, typed 3:20—Riveredge Road, and then deleted it. The house had a way of finding anything that stayed. She slid the phone back into the false bottom, wiped a smear of condensation from the mirror with her wrist, and put her face on—the one that fit whatever room she entered.

Outside, in the yard, the gnome kept his belly pressed to the fence like a drunk in a confessional. She went to him, crouched, and lifted him without grunting, because grunts travelled through vents like gossip. The cork popped with a dry kiss. The pill bottle glinted in the darkness, white and certain. She held it a moment—what a simple shape, for something so complicated—then tucked it back. The cork seated with a satisfying push. She replaced the gnome, adjusting him by a degree until his painted eyes stared past the kitchen window, not at it.

"Where are you going?"

Sonia's voice, close enough to make Sarah jump. She turned. Sonia stood by the back door, a tea towel in her hands, like she'd forgotten to put it down when she followed.

"Town," Sarah said.

Sonia nodded, twisting the towel. "Do you want me to—"

"No."

Sonia swallowed. "Will you at least text when you get there? So I know... so I can say..."

"So you can manage it," Sarah said, not unkindly. "You don't have to manage me."

"I don't know how not to," Sonia said, and the admission made her look twelve.

Sarah leaned in and pressed her forehead to Sonia's for a heartbeat, a trick from childhood when the world got loud. "I know." She pulled back. "I'll be back by dinner... if I want to."

"Be careful," Sonia whispered.

"Of what?"

Sonia didn't answer. They both knew.

The house's front door fought her with a sticky latch; she jiggled, lifted, got it. The porch steps counted her out—one, two, three, a repaired hush on the fourth where Sonia's nail sang true. The sky wore thin cloud. She walked fast because walking slow invited decisions.

***

On Claremont, the bus heaved up to the kerb and wheezed its doors open. Sarah took a seat in the back, where she could see everyone and no one could watch her too closely. The bus smelled like old coats and last night's rain. A teenage girl in a varsity jacket slept with her forehead against the window. A man mouthed words to a song only he could hear. Sarah let the city move around her like cover.

She got off two blocks early to make the extra distance feel like privacy. On Riveredge Road, the clinic windows were frosted halfway up, the lower halves painted with flowers so cheerful they made her teeth hurt. Inside, the receptionist looked exactly like the voice: organised cheerfulness in a cardigan.

"Sam?" she called, and when Sarah stood, the woman's relief was genuine. Names were promises, and this one had been kept.

Forms. Insurance. A finger-stick for iron because she looked a little pale. Sarah watched the red bead bloom and thought, Hello, you. Hello, you.

In the exam room, she stared at the poster of a foetus floating like a moon jelly. Your Baby This Week, it said, as if there were no alternate grammar available to lives like hers. Nine weeks, the poster promised, was a raspberry. A cluster of cells building towards a face.

The nurse was brisk and kind. "Any cramping? Bleeding?"

"Just nausea."

"Worse in the morning?"

"And when people talk too much."

The nurse laughed. "I'll keep it short."

"Please don't," Sarah said. "If it's short, I'm left with my thoughts."

"Noted." The nurse took her blood pressure, made approving noises, and left her with a paper gown that rustled like shame until Sarah tamed it under her palms.

The doctor knocked and entered—a woman with tired eyes and calm hands. "Sam," she said, sitting as if they were equals on a train, facing forward. "How are we doing?"

"We," Sarah repeated. "We're here."

"That's a start."

They talked. Family history, everything and nothing. Sarah lied where she had to, and told the truth where it mattered. The doctor asked a question gently and let it land with time around it.

"Do you feel safe at home?"

Sarah considered the word home and chose the path that would get her to 3:20 without alarms. "I'm not in danger."

"Good. If that changes, you tell me." A business card slid across the counter. "If you need anything in between visits, call. And—Sam?"

"Mm?"

"Whatever decision you make, it's yours."

Sarah nodded. The word yours knocked gently on her ribs, asking to be let in. She didn't open the door, not yet.

After, the clinic gave her a small white card with 3:20 and the doctor's name and a smiley face that felt like a plaster. She tucked it into her pocket, and when she got back to the alley behind the house, she slipped it into the gnome's belly with the vitamins, the cork sealing a future she hadn't said aloud.

Inside, the house had changed its weather. The kitchen was hotter, oven on, sugar browned to the edge of bitter. Samantha moved like choreography between counter and stove, spoon and bowl, voice a metronome. Kevin hovered with offerings—apples, a lemon zester, his attention. Sonia took up as little space as possible and still managed to make the place hold together.

"Good trip?" Samantha asked, all lightness. Her eyes flicked to Sarah's pockets like magnets.

"Uneventful," Sarah said. "You know you shouldn't leave the oven open when you're not standing at it?"

"I was," Samantha said, as if the debate had already been won.

Kevin held up the zester like a contribution to peace. "We're experimenting. Allspice and lemon. Is that... a thing?"

"It is now," Samantha said.

The house listened. It always did. Sarah felt the vents pull at the edges of words, as though storing them as future ammunition.

She washed her hands at the sink and stared out at the garden. The gnome sat like a little drunk sentinel. The fence beyond him needed paint. Beyond that, sky.

"Walk after dinner?" Kevin asked, hopeful. "All of us? See the neighbourhood?"

"Rain later," Samantha said, consulting a weather app that could have been a scrying bowl. "Maybe tomorrow."

"Maybe never," Sarah said, smiling without warmth.

Kevin winced like she'd tapped his knuckles. "I didn't mean—"

"I know what you meant," Sarah said, and softened, because Kevin didn't deserve the whole of her anger, only the part that formed his shape.

They ate pie. Sarah swallowed two bites and pushed her plate away as the nausea rose. Samantha said "stomach bug" with the right amount of sympathy for Kevin's benefit, and Sonia stood to fetch tea, grateful to be given a job. The ordinary choreography soothed nobody and impressed the house.

After the dishes, Samantha announced a chore shuffle with the prim joy of a headmistress. "We're a week ahead," she said. "We should behave like it."

"Like what?" Sarah said.

"Like a family," Samantha said, and the word clanged.

"Tomorrow morning," Sarah said, "I'm going to the market."

"Lovely," Samantha said. "We need flour."

"Alone."

Samantha's jaw clicked the smallest degree. "Of course," she said, and meant no.

Sarah smiled, a baring of teeth that read as charm if you didn't look at the eyes. "Good talk."

She excused herself before they could build a fence out of sentences. In the hallway, the lilies were dying into sweetness; she pinched a brown edge from a petal with two fingers and let it fall. The stair runner held true under her feet. Halfway up, she stopped. The vent at the landing breathed out—warm, human air. For a second she smelled smoke, not from her cigarettes but from an old house fire she didn't remember living through, only being told about until it felt like memory.

In the spare room, the curtains stood still. Sarah shut the door and locked it on reflex, and then, guiltily, unlocked it—Rule #1 pulsing behind her eyes. She rounded the bed, dropped to her knees, and reached under the frame. The shoebox was where she'd left it, half-lidded, ready to be grabbed. She opened it. Inside: a driving licence with her hair a shade darker and a different last name; cash folded into a long, tight ribbon; a key she'd never seen a door for. She added the clinic printout—appointment card number two the nurse had made "in case"—and closed the lid.

Her stomach swooped. She pressed her hand there, palm flat. "Stay," she said to herself, to the cells making their private mirror of her body, to the part of her that wanted to rip through the house like a storm. "Stay if you're mine."

The floorboard under her knees answered with a small complaint, like someone else had put a knee there once and promised the same thing and failed.

She stood, shook her hands out, and went to the window. Below, the yard wavered. Sonia crossed with the bin bag, hair pulled into a low knot, shoulders hunched against a wind that hadn't started. She looked up suddenly, right at Sarah, as if she'd felt eyes. Sarah didn't move. Sonia raised a hand, a small, foolish salute, like sisters inventing a language from scratch. Sarah lifted two fingers off the sill—a word that meant nothing and everything—and let the curtain fall.

Back on the landing, she heard Kevin laugh at something on television, his laugh in pieces, edited for space. Samantha matched it with her own, perfectly timed, and then cut hers short, saving part of it for later, like always. The house swallowed both sounds and kept them.

In the bathroom, Sarah splashed water on her face and wiped it with a towel that had been folded in precise thirds. She unfolded it and left it crooked on the rack, petty vandalism that felt like a declaration. She opened the medicine cabinet and stared at the clean rows: aspirin, bandages, cotton swabs, nothing out of place. She set her travel-size bottle of mouthwash on the second shelf, off-centre by an inch, and shut the mirror. When she opened it again a minute later, the bottle had been centred. She hadn't heard footsteps.

"Of course," she said aloud. The house preferred its own symmetry. Or Samantha had passed, quiet as an apology, and fixed it without leaving a reflection.

She turned off the light and went to bed in the spare room because she could. No one stopped her. No one had to. The ruleboard didn't read Beds, but it might as well. She lay on her side, cupped her stomach, and listened to the pipes hum. Somewhere in the walls, a whisper found her, thin, like a secret folded until it almost broke.

She whispered back, "I hear you."

The whisper—hers, the house's—didn't answer. It didn't need to. She knew what it said.

You have started. Don't stop.

She slept like someone about to run. In the middle of the night she woke with her heart kicking and the certain knowledge she'd been standing at the foot of Samantha's bed in a dream, saying her own name over and over until it sounded like a stranger's.

Morning would bring coffee and lists and chore grids, and she would smile or not. She would go where she wanted. She would be what she wanted. She would say me and mean it, even if the word came out of a mouth the world thought belonged to someone else.

She rolled onto her back and laughed once, short, saved, edited for space.

Downstairs, the vent answered with a hush that might have been a warning and might have been applause.

# Chapter Six
## The Handwriting Test

K evin had never thought of himself as the suspicious type. He trusted people too easily—that was what his father always said, half as a complaint, half as a compliment.

But now he found himself at the kitchen table with three scraps of paper in front of him, scrutinising curves and tails of letters like a crime-scene analyst.

The first was a shopping list Samantha had handed him two nights ago: milk, flour, sugar, allspice, cinnamon. Upright print, no flourishes.

The second was the bakery receipt he'd folded into his wallet: Thanks, Sam! with the looping capital S that climbed and dipped like a rollercoaster.

The third was the note he'd found on the dresser their first night—Welcome home, Sam—same loop, same tidy heart under the m.

He set them side by side and stared until the lines blurred. Same woman, three hands. Unless… unless what?

He pulled out a pad of yellow sticky notes from the drawer, wrote the word Sam himself. Once fast, once slow, once with a deliberate flourish. They all looked like variations of him. Maybe that was all handwriting was—moods and speeds, not secrets.

But when he compared his experiments to hers, the differences were too sharp. One style was a ruler-straight schoolteacher. Another was

whimsical, playful. A third was careful, like someone forging themselves.

Kevin rubbed the back of his neck. He wasn't crazy. He wasn't.

The folder began as an accident. He'd left the folded towel with the
red marker smudge on the counter overnight, meaning to throw it
away, but in the morning he found Samantha had refolded it neatly and
put it in the laundry pile. That decided him. Evidence couldn't live in
open air.

He bought a cheap manila folder at the chemist's under the pretence
of needing office supplies. Into it went the towel, the bakery receipt, the
dresser note. He added photos on his phone: the whiteboard rules, the
spice jar labels, even the twin toothbrushes he'd held in his hand one
night. He printed those out, trimmed the edges, and slipped them into
plastic sleeves. Organised paranoia felt less like paranoia.

At dinner, Samantha chattered about the electrician again, about
how the breaker box would need replacing, about how the contractor
"thought he'd seen worse." Kevin nodded in the right places but tested
her.

"What was the name of that Italian place we went to last summer?"
he asked suddenly, between bites of pie.

Samantha's fork paused. A beat too long. "Gianni's on the Hill," she
said at last, bright, certain. "The one with the mural of Venice."

Kevin smiled. "Right."

But it hadn't been Gianni's on the Hill. It had been Trattoria Sorella,
and the mural had been of Florence. He remembered because she'd
teased him about mixing them up.

Later, when he checked his phone log, he saw she'd texted Sonia at
exactly that moment—an innocuous emoji. He wondered if it was a
signal, a lifeline across the table.

The next morning, he tried again. "What's our anniversary?"

She laughed, kissed his cheek, said, "As if you'd forget. 12 June."

12 June was right. But the way she'd hesitated—half a second too long, just long enough for someone to check the whiteboard, maybe.

He told himself he was being cruel. But he kept testing anyway.

That night, he sat in bed with a notebook open, jotting dates, descriptions, and words like a detective with no crime but his own marriage.

The house sighed around him, carrying voices through vents. This time he caught phrases—Did you— and Not yet— overlapping, braided like rope.

He wrote them down. Time: 11:47 p.m. Location: upstairs vent, bedroom. Heard: two voices, female, similar timbre, overlapping laughter.

Samantha stirred beside him, murmured his name in her sleep. The scent on her hair was lemon again, sharp and clean, but when he kissed her temple he swore he smelled smoke too, faint and bitter, clinging from nowhere.

The notebook closed with a snap. He slipped it under the mattress, above the bed base. The house creaked like it disapproved, like it had wanted him to keep the words out in the open where it could use them.

Kevin lay back, staring at the ceiling until the ceiling blurred into a shifting grey.

I'm not crazy, he thought, gripping the edge of the mattress. I'm not.

But the house breathed out through the vent, warm as a whisper, and he thought he heard his name spoken twice—two voices, the same, and not.

***

The next morning, Kevin decided to test his theory the simplest way he knew.

"Can you jot down the shopping list?" he asked casually over coffee. "I'll swing by the shop on the way back."

Samantha was halfway through buttering toast. She smiled, set the knife down, and reached for the pad. "Of course."

He watched as she wrote: coffee, onions, chicken, thyme. Her letters were precise, upright, the pen pressing firmly enough to leave faint grooves in the page beneath.

"Anything else?" she asked, tearing the sheet and handing it to him.

He shook his head, folded it into his wallet with steady fingers, and kissed her cheek.

In the car, he unfolded the slip beside the bakery receipt. One Sam looped like ribbon; the other marched upright like soldiers. He held them side by side until sweat prickled under his arms. Same woman. Same name. Two hands.

At the shop he bought everything on the list, added gum he didn't need, and asked for a pen at the till. On the back of the receipt he wrote the same words: coffee, onions, chicken, thyme. His script wobbled compared to hers. The clerk handed him change without comment.

Back home, Samantha looked up from the sink, smiled, kissed his cheek again. The slip of paper went into the folder as soon as she turned her back.

That night, after she'd gone to bed, Kevin prowled the downstairs rooms like a thief. The house's old study still smelled faintly of dust and lemon polish. He opened the roll-top desk and found a stack of envelopes bound with twine.

Most were bills. A few were notes from neighbours—So glad to have you in town, Sam—but the handwriting varied. One envelope, post-marked only weeks earlier, bore a graceful looping S in the return address. Another, tucked deeper, bore the straight-backed letters he now associated with Samantha at home.

He spread them on the desk under the dim light, his heart drumming. Three different hands, all answering to one name.

The vent above the desk exhaled. Kevin froze, eyes lifting to the grate. The whisper came thin at first, then doubled, then tripled—three overlapping streams, not words but syllables, like voices practising to sound the same.

He fumbled for his phone, hit record, and held it towards the vent. The whisper braided itself into laughter, soft and sharp all at once, and then dissolved into silence.

Kevin played it back, heart hammering. The recording caught only static, a hiss of air. No voices. No laughter.

He shut the desk, shoved the envelopes back, and crept upstairs with the phone sweating in his hand.

Samantha lay curled in bed, hair spilling like ink across the pillow, her breathing steady. Kevin slid under the sheets, listening hard. The vent whispered again, this time with nothing but air.

He pressed his palm against the mattress, felt her warmth, and told himself over and over: I'm not crazy. I'm not.

But the folder under the mattress thickened, and the house above him breathed like it knew better.

The vent answered with three soft breaths. Not words. Not yet.

# Chapter Seven
## The Pact

S amantha knew exactly when a house decided whether you belonged. It wasn't the day you carried the boxes in. It wasn't the night you christened the bedroom and called it home. It was the moment you learnt how to speak the house's language and the house learnt yours—and one of you refused to budge.

This house understood her immediately. It creaked in the places she expected, sighed at predictable hours, kept the sort of secrets that rot under paint unless you scrape them clean. It had vents that carried laughter and closed doors that didn't care to stay closed; it had a temperament like an aunt who loved you best when you were useful. It liked to be told what to do. That was why she'd love it. That was why it would love her back.

She stood in the upstairs hall with a towel over her shoulder and watched Sonia on her knees with a pry bar, quiet as prayer. Good. Sonia had remembered: solve small problems before they perform as large ones. Sonia didn't know she'd learnt that from Samantha, who had learnt it from their mother.

Sarah was outside smoking on the back steps, a coil of defiance that could unspool to noose or lifeline depending on who held the end. The smoke climbed through the kitchen vent and reached Samantha where she stood as a taste of tin on her tongue. She didn't flinch. She adjusted the towel and stored the information.

"Pie fixes everything," she said into the empty air, then again, lighter, a shade of warmth to give the phrase body. Pie fixes everything, Kev. There. There was the angle. She could hear the beat where he'd offer to help, because he always offered when given something easy to offer. She would give him an apple to peel, a tool to hold, and he would not notice that he had become a tool himself. He loved being useful. Useful men were loyal.

The pact had not been a ceremony, not the way people imagined when they said the word. It had been a slow sediment of choices that turned into bedrock while no one was looking. When they were thirteen, their mother had said, "One face keeps you safe." She'd said it because a man at the corner shop knew the difference between a freckle and a birthmark and made it his business. She'd said it because the landlord liked Sarah's laugh better and took rent in compliment currency until he tried to collect more. She'd said it because their mother had grown up knowing that life is not a thing you get to keep unless you keep it organised.

So Samantha had organised it. She learnt which of them could be spotted by the way she wrote a 7 with a bar and coached a change. She taught Sonia how to tuck her anxiety behind her teeth until it tasted like sugar. She taught Sarah how to round off her laugh so it wouldn't cut men open and make them bleed wants all over the floor. "One face," she said, pressing faces together in mirrors like thumbs moulding clay. "One voice." She taped rules inside their skulls with late-night repetition. She burned the scrapbooks their mother cried over, the ones with three faces looking back instead of one. She let Sonia rescue a few spines under the sink; she let that mercy stand because mercy was expensive and therefore valuable. She kept the most important pages in her own head, where fire and men couldn't reach them.

Order had been survival, and it had worked. A landlord left them alone. A corner-shop man stopped asking for Sarah because he couldn't be sure which girl he wanted. Their mother slept once in a while. Samantha catalogued the victories and learnt to enjoy the quiet in between.

When Kevin appeared, he had a handsome kindness and a habit of handing his heart to the person in the room who sounded most certain. Samantha could be certain on command. The first time he said he loved her, she tasted relief like cold water. The second time, she tasted power. He believed in efficiency, in lists, in supper at six; he had grown up on rules that hadn't tried to kill him and so did not fear the ones she hung on refrigerators. A blueprint man. She could build a life on him the way you build onto a sturdy wall. And he was good. God help them, he was good. Goodness was the one quality you could not counterfeit long-term without bleeding to death. She chose him for that and married him for everything else.

Now the house. Now the rules again. Now the old language, learnt and spoken with grace. No doors locked against family. The rule had always been about more than fire. Locks were lies you could hear. Doors, in their nature, wanted to be opened; she honoured that nature. She would enforce it gently until she needed to enforce it hard.

*\*\**

She took the towel off her shoulder and went to the bathroom to fog the mirror. Mirrors tell on you if you let them sit cold. Warm them first; then the face slips easier into the face. She exhaled, watched the glass cloud, and wrote a single word with her fingertip where condensation would remember it later: together. The letters faded as the room cooled. Good. A ghost belongs better than a sign.

The door creaked softly. Sonia's reflection arrived over her shoulder, a careful oval in the fog.

"He's home," Sonia said. "Package."

"Measuring spoons," Samantha answered, already choosing the weight of her smile. "Aunt Clara sent them late." The lie laid itself down and the room took it.

"You're pushing," Sonia said gently.

"If I didn't, we'd be driftwood," Samantha said. "Is the stair quiet?"

"It will be," Sonia said, and it sounded like a promise to God. "For a while."

Samantha turned and pressed a kiss to Sonia's temple, a small payment. "You're a treasure."

"I'm a patch," Sonia muttered.

"Same thing," Samantha said. "Without patches, everything spills."

She moved through the upstairs hall the way a captain moves a ship in a storm—hands on the right rails, weight in the right foot at the right moment, eyes on horizon and compass both. She didn't hurry. Hurrying made people look. She let the house bend the sounds of Kevin in through the vent: the paper bag, the cautious question, Is that for us? She felt a smile lift to meet him before she saw him.

In the kitchen she made domestic sorcery—string and spoon, box and laugh—turn into a scene where he could rest his heart. Look, we are an ordinary marriage. She gave him a taste of belonging to calm the itch she felt under the skin of the day, the itch named Sarah.

Sarah had always been too bright in the corners. When they were children, Sarah's teachers had described her as "spirited" with a smile that worried the word like a rosary bead until it meant "unmanageable." In crowds, Sarah found the person who needed a match, struck it, and warmed herself on the reaction. It was beautiful and exhausting. Samantha spent a decade sanding Sarah's edges down to an acceptable glow. Some girls dolled up; Samantha edited. She cut syllables off Sarah's sentences until the words didn't slice new mouths in men's faces. She taught her how to love like an actress—felt, precisely lit, self-exiting.

Now the nausea had come. Sarah hid it badly, guarding her stomach with a palm, moving like a woman who had decided to be a body all of a sudden. Samantha noticed. Of course she noticed; she noticed the heat of a day before the forecast did, the shift of air when a man remembered a lie, the way a woman's perfume told on her mood long before her mouth did. If Sarah wanted to set the house on fire, Samantha would build the exits and stand at them.

She tied the spoon ring and let it chime against her knuckles. Kevin smiled at the sound like a boy in a shop where his allowance might buy everything. "Precision is kindness," she said, giving him a philosophy he could repeat like grace. He liked philosophies you could stitch on a pillow, even if he'd never have a pillow that loud. He said he'd get the mixer; she said careful with the third step and waited for Sonia to be seen, to be thanked. Sonia drank the thank you like water and breathed easier. Good. Reward compliance. Reward competence. This was training as much as tenderness; she saw no real difference between the two.

When Kevin thumped down to the basement she set the spoons on the counter and looked at Sonia. The moment unrolled.

"You can tell him later," she said.

"Tell him what, exactly?" Sonia said, tired already.

"Whatever helps," Samantha said. "A house story, a childhood anecdote. He needs narrative or he starts building his own."

Sonia's mouth twisted. "He's already building. He collects paper like it can save him."

"I'll save him," Samantha said, and meant us. "As long as he believes. As long as Sarah doesn't—"

Sonia said nothing. The quiet made a shape in the room, a Sarah-shaped hole like the negative of a photograph.

***

They all heard the front door. They all knew the step. When Sarah moved, air moved around her as if it had been waiting. She brought the outside in on her clothes like a challenge.

"Good trip?" Samantha asked. She let her voice be brightness and curiosity; she hid the ledger she kept in the next breath, where the maths lived: 3:20 p.m., Ridge Street, a call answered with a wrong name, a future making teeth.

"Uneventful," Sarah said, touching the sink like she could bless it. "You shouldn't leave the oven open."

"I was right here," Samantha said, and then they were orchestra again, the piece she had written and conducted: Kevin with offerings, Sonia with the string of silence, Sarah with defiance curdled into charm.

They ate pie. They pretended chewing could be communion. Samantha performed encouragement with economy, an efficient kindness like a good coat: keeps you warm, doesn't show stains. When it was done, she drew a neat grid on the whiteboard and talked about chores because she knew what to do with chores. Chores were proof to frightened people that they could still arrange the world into small, solvable squares.

Later, when the house was fat with dinner and the television murmured from the front room, she stood alone at the sink and washed a single spoon very clean. The spoon didn't need that much attention. She gave it anyway, because attention is how you bless small things into meaning. She hung it with its brothers. She dried her hands on a towel that was folded in precise thirds. She noticed when the mouthwash bottle in the cabinet stood half an inch left of centre and she slid it to middle again. These were the tiny orders she could enforce without blood.

From upstairs the vent breathed and the house coughed up a sound like laughter edited for time. Samantha closed her eyes. For a second the kitchen tilted as memory slid under present and made a slick. She was fourteen again, standing in a rented kitchen that smelt like fried hands, watching her mother tape a sentence to the inside of the cupboard: One face keeps us safe. Her mother's hands shook as she smoothed the tape. Later, their mother would peel it off and burn it over the sink because you couldn't keep a rule like that on paper. Later still, when their mother died, Samantha would hold the sentence between her molars and feel its edges until she bled a little from chewing it.

She opened her eyes and the room went back to level. She checked the whiteboard. The magnet was a whisper off centre; she nudged it right. Either Sonia had tested her or the house had. She felt a smile lift and settle. Good. Be tested. Pass.

Kevin came to the doorway and leaned his shoulder against the frame like a man at peace. She opened her face to him; he poured his calm into it without looking to see if it leaked. "Walk later?" he asked.

"Rain's coming," she said, glancing at the window as if she'd divined it, though she'd checked the weather an hour ago. "Tomorrow, though. I'll show you the route by the river."

"Tomorrow," he said, relieved to have something to hold onto. He crossed to kiss her, a good man's kiss, square on the mouth, polite enough to pass in any room. She kissed back with enough of herself to remind him of all the ways he belonged.

When he'd gone, she leaned her hands on the counter and counted her breaths, an old technique to scrape the nerves off feeling. It worked. The jitter settled. The hunger didn't. It never did. Control is expensive to maintain; you have to feed it or it begins to eat you.

"Sarah," she called lightly, and Sarah appeared as if the house had said her name aloud in the vents. "A word?"

Sarah crossed her arms in the doorway and cocked her hip, a posture that made men confess sins they'd never committed. Samantha had spent a long time sanding that from her; the edge was back, newly sharpened by nausea and something like hope. Oh, that was interesting. Hope made people meaner, in Samantha's experience. Mean people destroyed systems. She could make use of that before it burned them all.

***

"You're going to say 'stop,'" Sarah said. "I'm going to say 'no.' Let's skip to the end."

"I'm going to say 'careful,'" Samantha said, as if the distinction mattered. "You move like a match. A breeze will do the rest."

"You engineered the breeze," Sarah said. "You live for weather."

Samantha considered whether truth would work better than theatre. Truth could be so efficient, when it didn't cost too much.

"I don't intend to lose what we built," she said at last. "Not to a... miscalculation."

"The word is baby," Sarah said. "Say it. Not pregnancy, not situation. Baby."

Samantha arranged her mouth around the syllables. She could, in fact, say it. "Baby," she said evenly. "Babies require names. Names require faces. Faces get us killed."

"You're afraid," Sarah said softly, almost with pity. "You've always been afraid, Sammy. You just call it being prepared."

"I've kept us alive," Samantha said. "Through men with hands like doors and landlords with friend prices and a mother who loved us so hard she scraped us raw. If you want to call that fear, fine. Fear is a tool. I use it well."

Sarah's jaw worked. "You won't use it on me."

"You're the only person it has ever worked on," Samantha said, and let the cruelty sit between them like an open drain. "Because you care about Sonia more than you care about being right."

Sarah flinched and recovered in the same movement. "Sonia's not a lever."

"She is a person," Samantha said. "She makes a very good lever."

"God, you're ugly," Sarah said, and the word landed with relief because it fit so well over the shape of the moment.

"Ugly keeps," Samantha said. "Pretty breaks."

Sarah's eyes shone. She was beautiful when she was furious—too bright to look at, too simple to live. "The baby is mine."

"The story is mine," Samantha said. "Pick your battle."

They stood looking at each other until the house coughed again and a thread of Sonia's careful humming drifted in, an old lullaby with no words. It steadied them both. They hated that. They were sisters after all.

"Dinner was nice," Sarah said, lying like a kiss. She pivoted, walked away, and left a smell in the doorway that wasn't her usual. Lemon.

Clever girl. Or coincidence. Coincidences, in Samantha's experience, were just undiscovered plans.

She went to the hall closet with the false back, the one she'd instructed Sonia not to open yet, and pressed the panel with her fingers until it scooted back and revealed the little black spine of a book their mother hadn't burned. She didn't take it out. She only touched its back. Some afternoons she needed to feel the thing she chose not to do.

Her phone buzzed. A text from Kevin, two rooms away: *Need anything?* A photo of the TV programme accompanied it—two identical actresses in a sitcom buying the same dress and arguing about it. Cute. Too on the nose. She let the image sit without a response and turned the buzz to silent. He would ask again in ten minutes. It was a mercy to let him.

The whiteboard gleamed at the edge of her vision. She crossed to it and corrected a letter she'd purposely miswritten earlier to see if anyone would notice. No one had. The N in No doors locked now wore its right angles perfectly. Precision is kindness. Precision is control. The Venn diagram was a circle; she lived in the overlap.

She set out three perfumes in the bathroom, each with a different note—amber for warmth, lemon for newness, nothing at all for days when silence was safer. She moved them as a musician moves chords, not to deceive but to harmonise the whole. Under the sink she stored two identical compacts; in the dresser, two pairs of hoops. She knew exactly which version of *Samantha* each room required at which hour. Mirrors told her, like windows in churches tell you where light wants to fall.

When the house settled around nine, she sat on the edge of her bed and let exhaustion pour through her bones. Control is weight-bearing; it turns muscle into steel if you do it long enough, and steel rusts in the blood. She breathed through the ache until it made a manageable shape. She lay down, then sat up again because lying down felt too much like surrender, and crossed to the vent at the far wall. She pressed her palm to the metal and felt the old lungs of the house push against her hand. She whispered: "We are one."

The vent whispered back something like agreement. Or maybe it whistled because the screws needed tightening. She would tighten them in the morning. That, too, was love.

She pictured Kevin at the kitchen table with his neat little folder, late-night detective in his own home. She forgave him the folder because she had taught the world to be afraid of losing what it could list. He was doing his best to say *I believe you* while collecting proof that belief had a shape. He would choose her, because she would make that choice easy, because she would bury him in kindness until kindness felt like oxygen. If he pushed too far, she would show him a truth he could live with and hide the others in plain sight. She had practice.

The doorframe darkened. Sonia stood there, small as she could be without vanishing.

"Sleep?" Sonia asked.

"Soon," Samantha said. "You?"

Sonia shook her head. "I can hear the stairs."

"They're quiet," Samantha said. "You made them quiet. Thank you."

Sonia stepped into the room and pressed the coil of string into Samantha's palm. "In case," she said. "Later. Things come loose."

Samantha closed her fingers around the string. It bit, a soft geometry. "They do," she said. "But we tie them again."

Sonia nodded. "I love you," she said, so baldly it was embarrassing, so bravely it was enviable.

"I know," Samantha said gently. "That's why it works."

After Sonia left, the dark grew kind again. Samantha coiled the string and put it in the drawer with the spare keys. She glanced at the clock and thought of Riveredge Road and a gnome with a belly that made hollow sounds when you tapped it. She could go into the yard right now with a flashlight and the correct kind of patience; she could take the belly off and take the bottle out and take control back into her hands. She did not move. She measured her power not only by what she could do but by what she could afford not to. Tomorrow would be soon enough. Tomorrow, the walk by the river, the market, the whiteboard edits Sarah would hate. Tomorrow, the next small correction.

She slid into bed then, finally, and let herself lie flat. The house exhaled once, twice, as if syncing to her lungs. That pleased her. She closed her eyes and apportioning the next day's labour in her head: market with Kevin (hold his hand at the first corner, say *We* three times before the bakery to shut the hounds in his brain), move the mouth-wash to see if Sarah notices, check the basement for carbon monoxide tags because old furnaces get ideas. Put the brass key back where Sonia would find it when she needed to feel chosen. Leave the spare hoop earrings on the dresser where Sarah could mistake them for a gift and remember she was loved.

Then the final thought, a clean line laid like a ruler across a cluttered desk: *Whatever it costs, we stay one.* If Sarah wanted to be a fire, fine. Samantha had been weather for years. She would be rain until fire hissed, wind until fire roared sideways, a sealed window when fire wanted oxygen. She would be the woman who kept the rules and rewrote them when the rules no longer kept them.

Outside, a faint scatter of rain began, as if the sky had listened politely and agreed to try it her way for the night. In the next room, Kevin turned over and sighed in his edited sleep. Down the hall, Sonia's careful footsteps went from two to one, her weight easing as she finally let the day climb off her back. Farther, somewhere behind the walls, Sarah laughed once in her own dark—sharp, saved, a blade tucked under a pillow.

Samantha smiled into the pillow. She would know where the blade was when she needed it. She always did.

***

And because she was who she was, she got up one last time and walked barefoot to the whiteboard. In the moon-washed kitchen she took the blue marker and, under the last rule, wrote a sixth line in small neat letters only she would notice in the morning: If one breaks, the others restore. If one falls, the two become one.

She capped the pen, avoided her reflection in the oven door, and let the house settle around her order like a quilt. Precision is kindness. Precision is survival. She slept with both sentences in her mouth like sugar and a blade.

# Chapter Eight
## Cracks in the Script

Sonia baked when words failed. Flour made a clean weather inside a room; you could watch it fall and know exactly where it landed. She whisked like a penitent, wrist flicking until the eggs went glossy and the sugar dissolved, until something unruly turned obedient under her hand. The kitchen breathed around her—oven ticking as it warmed, vent sighing, a faint sweetness from yesterday's lilies surrendering to brown at the edges.

"Can I help?" Kevin asked from the doorway, trying to sound like a man who belonged in an ordinary morning.

Sonia's first answer was always yes. "Slice the apples?" she said, even though the bowl on the counter already held thin moons arranged in careful arcs. "Thinner is better. They fit together when they're thin."

He smiled in relief. "Got it."

His presence was a heat source that had nothing to do with the oven. He worked carefully, too carefully; every slice looked like it was auditioning for a part. His knife knocked now and then against the board, the sound small and apologetic. Sonia tried not to wince at each mis-hit. She was the sort of person who heard mistakes like other people heard thunder.

"Rough night?" he asked. He kept his eyes on the apples, polite, the way a kind man learns to be—seeing without making someone feel seen.

"Old house," she said lightly. "They talk."

"They?" He glanced up, half-smile. "Plural?"

"Everyone's a chorus," she said, and the joke landed flat in her mouth.

He studied her a beat too long. She returned to the bowl, poured in sugar, salt, a pinch more cinnamon than Samantha would have sanctioned—Samantha rationed spice like truth. Sonia's hands trembled as she pinched; brown dust fell like weather on the fruit. She shook her fingers to hide the shake and managed only to make it worse.

Kevin set down the knife. "You're shaking."

"Caffeine," she lied.

"You drink tea."

"Then nerves." She made herself meet his eyes. "Sorry."

"Don't apologise to me." He tried a small grin. "Apologise to the apples. I slaughtered them."

"You did fine." She took a slice, chewed it, forced a smile that didn't quite unstick. "See? Survived."

He leaned on the counter, casual, as if leaning didn't brace a question. "Everything okay with Samantha? With Sarah?"

Sonia's throat went tight around the word okay. Kevin's careful weight on the question made it heavier. She turned to the drawer, took out the pie dish, and line-danced with tasks because tasks had steps if you knew them by heart. The crust went in like a sheet tucked neat, the apples in concentric rings that felt like prayer when you did them right.

"People are tired," she said. "Moves are loud."

"That they are." He paused. "You patched the stair. Thank you."

Sonia felt the thank you strike clean, a bell note in her chest. "Of course."

"You always fix things." He said it gently, not as praise exactly, more as a diagnosis.

"It's what I'm good at." She smoothed a palm across the crust's edge, press-and-turn, a small choreography. Her hands steadied under the repetition. "Samantha cooks order. Sarah—" She stopped, let the rest sit, and tried not to picture smoke curling from the back steps. "I mend."

He picked up the paring knife again, turned it once in his hand, set it down. "Does anyone mend you?"

She laughed before she could help it. It came out wrong, a thin thread cut short. "That's a very Kevin question."

"I hate that you made that a type." He smiled to show it wasn't a wound. "You don't owe me an answer."

"No." She pressed the tines of a fork along the pie's rim, tiny equal marks. "But I owe someone one."

"To who?"

She looked up before she could swallow it. To the house almost came out. To the whiteboard. To the idea of us. She shook her head. "To time," she said, and Kevin looked like he wanted to be the sort of man who understood and settled for being the sort of man who didn't ask again. He wiped his hands on a towel and reached for the sugar tin without being told. The gesture made Sonia's eyes sting—useful men were rare. Even rarer were men who didn't need to be told where the sugar lived. She turned aside to hide the slick of tears and the house, delighted, carried Sabrina Carpenter from the radio in the living room like a breeze that had learnt a chorus. Samantha had left the volume low, practising the day's temperature.

The oven pinged ready. Sonia slid the pie in, closed the door with two hands because the hinge caught if you didn't love it a little. On the glass she saw their reflections side by side: Kevin a solid blur; Sonia a smear of movement. She wiped a circle in the fog so a face could sit there properly.

"Coffee?" he asked.

"I'll jitter through the roof."

"Tea, then."

"Please." She listened to him run water, open the tin, take the bag he always took because he'd watched once and remembered. He didn't push her. The relief of that made her legs feel unreliable. She leaned against the counter and let the laminate be a back.

"You're doing too much," he said softly without turning.

"It keeps me from other things."

"Like what?"

"Like stopping." She lifted the kettle before it boiled; the whistle felt like something that announced a spill. "Stopping means hearing. Hearing means—" She cut herself off and set the kettle back.

He slid the mug towards her. Steam rose. He blew on his own like a man with a reason. "If you need anything, ask me," he said. "You never ask."

"That's because you already do it." The truth arrived and embarrassed them both. "You lift when something is heavy. You carry bags. You listen like it's your job."

"It is," he said, as if he'd chosen the position and was pleased to be hired.

Sonia took a sip. Her hands had stopped shaking. "You missed a slice," she said, nodding towards the cutting board. "The end piece. They always get left."

He smiled and ate it, obedient. He chewed like a man trying to deserve his life.

An hour could have passed that way—quiet, pie, the low industry of two people pretending to be alone in a room. Sonia wanted it long enough to believe she could have it. Then the whiteboard magnet clicked—a small, precise sound, like a sentence correcting itself. Samantha, or the house with Samantha in it. Kev's shoulders tightened a fraction. Sonia set her mug down and smoothed the towel by reflex.

Samantha came in with rain on her hair and sunlight in her tone. "Smells perfect," she said, kissing Kevin's jaw like a reward. She touched the oven door with fingertips as if testing doneness through temperature and will. Her smile to Sonia was warm, exact. "You're a marvel."

"Patch," Sonia said.

"Quilt," Samantha countered, and opened the refrigerator as if the word had the power to make yoghurt appear.

Kevin took his cue and became helpful sunlight. "I mangled the apples," he confessed. "Sonia rescued them."

"You're both heroes," Samantha said, and let the word make a little shelter for everyone to stand under. "We'll eat in an hour. Walk after, if the rain holds."

"That'd be nice," Kevin said, and he meant it so purely that Sonia wanted to put her palm against his cheek and tell him to keep that part of himself someplace safe.

The vent above the stove breathed. Three breaths? Two? Sonia couldn't tell; she had become the sort of person who counted inhales to predict storms. She wiped a non-existent smear off the counter, felt the tremor try to return, and pinned it under her hand until it was still.

"Kevin," Samantha said with bright innocence, "what's our anniversary?"

"June twelfth," he said, pleased, like someone who'd studied and been given the exact question. "I'm learning."

"Of course you are," Samantha said, and in the tiny silence after, Sonia heard the script rustle. The room adjusted around it the way a train adjusts at a junction—barely felt but undeniable to someone who listened to rails.

Sonia's tea had cooled. She drank it anyway. She told herself she was fine. She told herself that fixing a stair and lining apples counted as a life. She told herself she could keep being the quiet between their voices.

Then she looked at Kevin's hands and saw a hangnail torn to blood, and she went too fast for a plaster so she could have something small to save. He laughed and let her fuss. When she pressed the white tab down she realised she was breathing too quickly. She made herself slow it.

"You're good," he said, flexing his thumb. "You always are."

Sonia turned away so he wouldn't see what his kindness did to her face. The oven light glowed in the door, a small golden weather that promised an ending if you waited the correct amount of time and did not open early to check. She wanted her life to be a pie, measurable and precise. She knew better. She still wanted.

From the hall came Sarah's laugh—short, saved, sharpened by something that wasn't joy. The sound hit the room like a utensil dropped behind the stove: you couldn't reach it without moving the world.

Sonia set both palms on the counter. "I'll... check the linen closet," she said, the sentence that meant I can't stand here another second under all this good intention without breaking. Samantha nodded like a conductor releasing a second violin to retune. Kevin looked like he wanted to offer help and knew not to. The oven ticked on, indifferent. The house held its breath as she slipped down the hall, and for once she let it hold some of hers too.

***

The linen closet was Sonia's excuse, but she lingered longer than the excuse required. She touched folded sheets, ran her palm along towels, counted pillowcases the way a priest counts rosary beads. Softness steadied her. Thread count meant something that rules couldn't.

But softness didn't last. Kevin found her, of course. He had that kind of quiet step, polite enough to announce itself with a cough at the end so no one felt ambushed.

"You okay?" he asked.

Sonia turned with a practised smile. "Fine. Just checking stock. Samantha hates surprises."

He leaned against the doorframe, arms crossed loosely. Not interrogating, not cornering. Just there. "You looked pale back in the kitchen."

"I'm always pale."

"This was different."

She smoothed a towel and placed it on the top shelf. "You notice too much."

"I don't notice enough," he said. "Not until lately."

The honesty in his voice broke something soft in her chest. She sat on the low stool inside the closet and folded her hands like a schoolgirl caught out. "What do you think you've noticed?"

Kevin hesitated, and the pause was heavy. "Little things. Words, handwriting, the way Samantha..." He trailed off, searching for the right shape. "The way she shifts."

Her throat closed. If she told the truth, the pact shattered. If she lied, the guilt pressed harder against her ribs. She compromised with a half-truth. "She has moods."

"Don't we all?" he said. "But this is—different." He crouched, bringing himself level with her. His eyes were steady, kind. Too kind. "You're scared."

The word landed with precision. Sonia flinched, then shook her head too quickly. "No. Just tired."

"Tired of what?"

Her voice cracked. "Holding things together."

Silence filled the closet. The towels smelt faintly of lavender; her hands pressed into their folds until her nails left crescents.

Kevin reached out, gently touched her wrist. "Sonia…"

Her name on his lips was too much. She pulled her hand back and whispered, "Don't."

"Why not?"

"Because if you keep asking, you'll find answers you can't live with." Her voice shook. "And I'll be the one who told you. I can't carry that too."

His breath hitched, but he didn't push further. He sat back on his heels, studying her like a man at the edge of a map. "I don't want to hurt you."

"You won't. But Samantha will." The words slipped before she could catch them. Her eyes went wide.

And that was the moment the air shifted. The click of heels. The faint sweet tang of lemon, sharp enough to erase lavender. Samantha stood in the doorway, smile bright as glass.

"What's all this?" she asked, cheerful, effortless.

Kevin straightened quickly, guilt flashing across his face though he hadn't done anything wrong. "Just checking on the linens."

Samantha's eyes lingered on Sonia a fraction too long before flicking to Kevin. "You're good at that. Always thorough."

Sonia stood, forcing her legs not to tremble. "I was—restocking."

"And patching," Samantha said warmly. "Always mending what frays. My sweet sister." She reached out, smoothed Sonia's hair back like she was fixing a page in a book. "We're lucky, aren't we, Kevin?"

Kevin swallowed. "Yes. Very lucky."

The script slid neatly back into place. Sonia felt it like a collar, snug around her throat. She nodded, obedient, but her stomach rolled with the lie.

Samantha's hand rested a moment longer than necessary before falling away. "Dinner in ten. Pie will be perfect, thanks to you both."

Then she was gone, gliding back down the hall, humming softly. The house carried the hum through the vents like applause.

Kevin lingered a beat, searching Sonia's eyes. She dropped her gaze to the towels. "Go," she whispered. "Before she comes back."

He hesitated, then left.

Alone, Sonia sank back onto the stool. The towels blurred as tears filled her eyes. She pressed her palms together as if in prayer. She hadn't meant to say Samantha's name like that. She hadn't meant to betray the pact. But the word had escaped, and words once spoken couldn't be gathered back.

From the vent above, the house exhaled. Sonia swore she heard it whisper her name, stretched and doubled, as if testing which version fit best.

***

The house had gone quiet, but Sonia didn't trust quiet. Quiet was Samantha's favourite disguise.

She retreated to her room and shut the door—careful not to lock it, Rule #1 pulsing at the edge of her mind like an open wound. Locking was forbidden. Locking meant secrets. Locking meant rebellion.

But secrets could live other ways.

She crossed to the wardrobe, pulled open the bottom drawer, and slid her hand under the liner she'd folded there weeks ago. Her fingers found the slim notebook she'd hidden, its cover plain black, smaller than her palm. Sonia had bought it years ago with cash at a corner shop while Samantha distracted the clerk. She hadn't written in it then. She'd only carried it, a talisman.

Now she opened it, spine creaking faintly, and stared at the blank page. Her pen hovered.

Samantha's rules marched through her mind, whiteboard-clear: No doors locked against family. No lies that break the face. No secrets that shatter the pact.

Sonia wrote her own in tiny, cramped script.

Rule 1: Everyone needs mending. Even me.

She underlined me. The word looked dangerous, glowing like coal on the page.

Rule 2: A patch is not a prison.

Her hand shook, but she pressed the letters hard, leaving grooves.

Rule 3: If one burns, don't smother the flame. Let it burn the rot.

Her breath came fast now, like the words had stolen air from her lungs. She shut the notebook quickly, slid it back under the liner, and pressed her hand flat to the drawer as if holding the words in place.

The vent above the wardrobe sighed. For a moment she thought she heard laughter—three voices, overlapping, one trying to be the other.

She whispered into the stillness, "Not this time."

Her whisper sounded small, but it was hers.

Sonia stepped back, smoothed the bedspread until the fabric lay flat. She pinched the lamp chain and pulled; light winked out. In the dark, she pressed her palm over her heart and mouthed her rules again, silently, like prayer.

For the first time in weeks, her body felt steady. The house could breathe, Samantha could direct, Sarah could rebel—but Sonia had written something no one else controlled.

And paper, even hidden paper, was proof.

# Chapter Nine
## The Lie at the Table

The table gleamed like it had been waiting for guests. Samantha had polished the wood until Kevin could see the reflection of the chandelier in its surface, a perfect halo over the meal she'd orchestrated. Roast chicken, potatoes crisped at the edges, green beans lined like soldiers. Pie cooled on the counter. It was the sort of dinner you put in a magazine spread, though no photographer would capture the tension in the air.

Kevin sat at the head of the table. He'd once teased that it made him feel like a patriarch; Samantha had smiled and said it was only practical. Tonight, the position felt like a witness stand.

Sonia sat to his right, quiet, hands folded so tightly her knuckles whitened. Sarah sprawled to his left, fork tapping against the rim of her plate in a rhythm Kevin couldn't quite place. Samantha sat opposite him, smiling with that precise brightness that meant she was already calculating the outcome of conversations that hadn't started.

Kevin tried to focus on the food. The chicken smelled wonderful; the potatoes were golden. He carved carefully, passing portions with deliberate hospitality. His father had taught him that civility was a shield, and tonight he needed one.

"Looks perfect," he said.

"Perfection is practice," Samantha answered smoothly, placing beans on her plate in careful thirds.

"Or luck," Sarah muttered. She stabbed a potato wedge and bit it savagely.

"Luck doesn't last," Samantha said, still smiling.

Sonia's fork hovered halfway to her mouth, then lowered again. "We should be grateful," she murmured. "Some families don't sit together at all."

Kevin nodded, grateful for her attempt at peace. "That's true."

But as they began to eat, the small details pressed in. Samantha's cadence had a hairline crack — she said *oregano* with the stress in the wrong place, a slip he never would've noticed a year ago. Sarah chewed like she was biting a grudge. Sonia's hands trembled so badly she spilled beans onto her napkin.

Kevin reached for his wine and almost knocked it over. Samantha caught the stem before it tipped, her hand fast, steady. "Careful," she said softly.

"Sorry," he muttered.

"Nothing to apologise for," she said, setting the glass back in front of him. "We look out for each other."

The words landed heavy. Kevin smiled, but it didn't reach his eyes. The vent above the table sighed once, as though the house agreed or mocked — he couldn't tell which.

***

Sarah speared another potato and leaned back in her chair, chewing slowly, deliberately, like she had all the time in the world. Her eyes flicked to Samantha across the table. "You know," she said, voice casual but sharp at the edges, "not everything has to be perfect."

Samantha smiled without looking up. "I wouldn't call this perfect. Just... cared for." She sliced her chicken with elegant precision, each bite the same size.

"Same thing," Sarah said, tossing her fork onto her plate with a clang. "Care. Control. You call it one word, it's really the other."

The air shifted. Kevin felt it in his chest, a subtle pressure, like before a storm. He looked from one sister to the other. Samantha's smile didn't falter, but her eyes had gone hard. Sarah leaned forward now, elbows on the table, daring her.

Sonia broke first, of course. "Sarah," she said gently, "don't. It's dinner. Please."

"I'm just talking," Sarah said, shrugging. "Or is that a rule now, too?"

Kevin cleared his throat. "I think what she means is—"

"What she means," Samantha interrupted, her tone warm but cutting, "is that peace is precious, and some of us still value it."

Sarah barked a laugh, short and sharp. "Peace? You mean silence. You mean obedience. You mean *don't rock the boat or Samantha will drown you yourself.*"

Kevin froze. The words were jagged, thrown like stones. His instinct was to smooth them, to laugh them off, but the weight in Sarah's eyes told him they weren't stones at all. They were truth, sharp and dangerous.

"Sarah," Sonia whispered, shaking her head. Her hands trembled in her lap. "Please. Don't."

"Don't what? Tell the truth?" Sarah snapped. She turned to Kevin, eyes blazing. "She doesn't want a marriage. She wants a script. And you—" she jabbed her fork at him— "you're too busy memorizing your lines to realize it."

Kevin opened his mouth, but no words came. His heart thundered. He looked at Samantha. She was still smiling, still calm, though her grip on her knife was tight enough to whiten her knuckles.

"That's a cruel thing to say," Samantha said, her voice perfectly measured. "Kevin loves us. I love him. You—" she fixed Sarah with that serene stare— "don't know what love is."

Sarah slammed her hand on the table. The plates rattled. Sonia flinched so hard her glass tipped, water spreading across the wood.

"Don't you dare," Sarah hissed. "Don't you dare say I don't know love. I know it more than you ever will. Because love isn't control, Sam. It's freedom. It's choice."

Sonia scrambled with a towel, blotting frantically at the water. "Please," she begged, voice cracking. "Both of you. Stop. You'll ruin everything."

"No," Sarah said, rising halfway from her chair. "I'm done pretending everything isn't already ruined."

Kevin pushed back his chair, unsure if he should stand, unsure if that would help or make things worse. His hands shook. He wanted to tell Sarah to sit down, to tell Samantha to let go, to tell Sonia to stop crying. But he couldn't find the words.

Samantha's calm deepened into something colder. "You're reckless," she said softly, each syllable like glass. "You're going to burn us all down, and for what? A tantrum? A whim?"

Sarah leaned forward, fists on the table. "Not a whim. A life."

The silence that followed was suffocating. Sonia's shoulders shook as she pressed the towel against the spreading water, eyes squeezed shut. Kevin's chest ached with the weight of everything unsaid.

The vent above them sighed again, louder this time, almost a moan. Kevin glanced up, startled, but the others didn't react. Or maybe they were too practiced at ignoring the house's voice.

Sarah sat back down, breathing hard, eyes locked on Samantha. "I won't be quiet anymore."

Samantha's smile flickered, just for an instant. Then it returned, polished and precise. "Then we'll find a way to make your noise useful," she said.

The threat was velvet, but Kevin felt it land like a knife.

***

Kevin tried to breathe, but the air in the dining room felt thick, like the walls had crept closer. Sarah and Samantha glared across the table, Sonia trembling between them like fabric pulled too tight.

To break the tension, he forced a laugh. "It's just dinner," he said weakly. "We don't need to—"

"Tell him," Sarah cut in, her voice low, shaking.

"Tell him what?" Samantha asked, all soft innocence.

Sarah's fork clattered onto her plate. "That it's not just him. That we—" She stopped herself, lips pressed white.

Sonia's hand shot out, gripping Sarah's wrist. "Don't," she whispered, desperate.

Kevin's chest tightened. His heart beat against his ribs like a fist. "Not just me?" he echoed. His voice cracked. "What does that mean?"

Samantha's smile didn't falter, but her eyes sharpened. "It means Sarah likes to provoke. She always has. You know that."

"She's lying," Sarah spat.

"Or you are," Samantha countered, light as silk.

The room tilted. Kevin stared at Sarah, her face flushed, eyes wild. Then at Samantha, serene, composed, too composed. His gaze drifted to Sonia, who sat frozen, mouth trembling, eyes fixed on the spreading water stain in the tablecloth as if it were safer than either sister.

Kevin swallowed hard. "Someone tell me the truth."

"The truth?" Sarah demanded, half-rising again. "The truth is that I'm pregnant, Kevin. And you should be asking yourself *whose baby it is.*"

The words detonated.

Sonia gasped, a small animal sound. Kevin's knife fell to the plate with a clatter. Samantha's smile finally cracked, just a hair, just enough to show the steel beneath.

"You're out of control," Samantha said. Her tone was ice. "Sit down."

Kevin's ears roared. Pregnant. Whose baby. The sentence looped in his head, jagged, impossible. His chest heaved. He looked at Sarah. She stared back, defiant and terrified all at once.

"Kevin," Sonia whispered, pleading, "don't—"

But he pushed back from the table, chair legs screeching on the floor. He needed air, needed space, needed out. The chandelier swayed slightly, though no one had touched it. The vent exhaled a long, low groan, like the house itself was repeating Sarah's words: *pregnant... whose baby...*

Kevin stumbled into the hall, folder-thoughts screaming in his head. Handwriting samples, rules, combs, laughter edited short. None of it added up. Or all of it did, and he just couldn't face the equation.

Behind him, the sisters' voices tangled, high and low, sharp and soothing. He couldn't tell them apart anymore. He pressed his palms to his ears, but the house carried the echoes through the vents, feeding him their noise.

He staggered into the kitchen, grabbed the counter with both hands, and bent double. His reflection stared back from the oven door: pale, sweating, eyes wide. A man who no longer knew who sat across the table from him.

From the dining room came a single, chilling silence. No clatter. No raised voices. Just stillness.

The house sighed again, a sound almost like laughter, and Kevin understood—he wasn't the one asking the questions anymore. He was the one being tested.

# Chapter Ten
## The Whiteboard

The house wore morning like a disguise. Sunlight rinsed the kitchen clean; the lilies pretended not to be dying. The Whiteboard gleamed on the refrigerator with the serenity of a shrine. House rules said the cheerful printed header, as if cheer could hold nails in wood.

Kevin stood in front of it with a mug gone cold in his hand and felt like a man about to address a court. He had slept badly—if he had slept at all. Sarah's words kept flaring in the dark: *I'm pregnant… you should be asking yourself whose baby it is.* The sentence didn't settle. It ricocheted.

He told himself he would not start a fight. He told himself he would ask questions. He told himself that questions were kinder than accusations. Then he read rule 1 again—No doors locked against family—and remembered the way Samantha had smiled as she said, *We shouldn't need locks, should we? No secrets in this house.* And something heavy in him shifted.

Samantha came in trailing a tempered brightness that had fooled him for months. Lemon lifted off her skin—new bar of soap, same intention. She took in his posture the way she took in a room for fire hazards.

"You're up early," she said, opening the cupboard like this was any other morning where milk could be trusted to be only milk and not metaphor.

"So are you," Kevin said.

"We're in a season of early," Samantha said lightly, and poured herself coffee. She moved to stand beside him, shoulder almost touching his. A partner, a co-pilot. "Checking the sacred text?" Her smile was all air.

"I was thinking we should add something," he said. He sounded almost calm. Good. Calm makes people honest.

"Oh?" Samantha tipped her head, hair sleeking over one shoulder with the obedience of a well-trained animal. "What does our constitution lack?"

"A rule about truth," Kevin said. "Something simple. *No lies in this house.*"

"Strong," Samantha said approvingly. "But unworkable. People lie, Kev. Sometimes it's kindness."

"Is it?" His voice tightened. "Is that what last night was?"

"Last night," Samantha said, and her tone laid a sheet over the corpse. "Was emotion. Sarah enjoys... spectacle."

"Spectacle," Kevin repeated. "The word you use when you want to make a person feel like a show."

Samantha sipped, then set the mug down with precise care, the way a person places something fragile in a museum. "If you want me to answer something, ask the thing. You're better when you say it."

He turned to face her fully. The whiteboard stared at him from the corner of his eye. "Are there things you haven't told me?"

"Of course." Samantha's smile didn't falter. "Everyone keeps something back. It's how we survive ourselves."

"Like... sisters," Kevin said, and the word made a shape between them.

Samantha regarded him, and he saw the tiny calculation tick behind her eyes, a jeweler appraising a flaw. "Sisters," she said neutrally.

"You don't talk about your childhood," he pressed. "You never have. Your pictures start at nineteen like you didn't exist before."

"Some people prefer beginnings," she said. "It's a style."

"And handwriting," he said, swallowing, surprising himself by leaping there. "Styles change too?"

"Of course," she said. "Cursive, print. Speed, pen, mood."

He pulled the folded slip from his pocket. The shopping list she'd written yesterday—coffee, onions, chicken, thyme—stood upright, clean as teeth. He set it on the counter. He pulled the old bakery receipt from his wallet and placed it beside it: *Thanks, Sam!* with its friendly loop and bar on the 7. He added the first-night note, the one he'd kept like a talisman—*Welcome home, Sam*—with the tiny heart she never drew on anything else.

He watched her face the way you watch weather from a window.

Samantha considered the three scraps as if they were art prints she was trying to hang level. "And?" she said, a smile still soft at the corners of her mouth.

"They don't match," Kevin said. "One person. Three hands."

"Three moods," she countered.

He pointed at the heart, absurdly tender on its thin paper. "You never draw those."

"I did that day," she said kindly, as if reminding him of his own memory.

He felt heat crawl up his neck. "And the 7? The bar?"

"Some Europeans bar their sevens," she said, almost playful. "Maybe I felt continental."

He stared at her. The kitchen light made a halo on the whiteboard. "Who picked up turnovers at Claremont last Tuesday?"

Samantha's smile thinned. "I did," she said, not missing a beat. "I wanted to surprise you. They were out by the time you went."

"They weren't," he said. "And the clerk—Mario—remembered you. The cappuccino with cocoa. The hoops. The scar." He lifted a finger to his own brow—high, right side. "He described a little white line."

Silence slid into the room like cold under a door. Samantha's eyes didn't flick to his brow. They didn't flick anywhere. They held his, steady, perfect.

"Light plays tricks," she said gently. "You know that."

"You don't have a scar," he said. "I would've seen it."

"Would you?" Softly. Not accusation. Invitation to doubt himself. It almost worked; it always almost worked. He felt the floor tilt and forced his weight back onto his heels.

He tapped the rule board with his knuckle. "Rule 5," he read aloud. "*One face to the world—always united.* What does that mean, Sam?"

"It means we don't embarrass each other," she said immediately. "It means we show up for one another. It means we're a team."

"It sounds like something you wrote a long time ago," he said. "Before me."

She smiled. "You're flattering yourself."

He took the marker from the clip—red—and uncapped it with a click that felt like a small weapon cocking. "Then you won't mind if I add mine."

Samantha said nothing. She only watched. He could feel the vents lean in.

He wrote under the last rule, block letters shaky with the weight of what they meant. 6) Tell the truth.

It looked childish on the glossy white, like a scrawl on a refrigerator door in a house where the parents didn't think their child would reach the marker.

He recapped the pen and turned. "Can you live with that?"

Samantha took a breath that filled the room with lemon. She reached past him, uncapped the blue, and drew a neat box around his line. She wrote in her own upright hand beside it: (Kindly.)

He stared at the addition. A parenthetical. A leash.

"Truth with rules," he said.

"Truth without kindness is cruelty," she said. "And cruelty kills."

"What about unkind truths that keep people alive?" he asked, and the moment the words left his mouth he realized he'd made a mistake: he had shifted to her ground. Survival. Strategy. Philosophy.

Samantha smiled, relieved, as if he'd walked into the shape she'd left for him. "Then we practice kindness so hard it becomes muscle memory," she said, tapping the parenthesis. "We use it even when we don't want to.

***

The back door creaked. Sonia entered in soft slippers, eyes tired and tender. She saw the whiteboard and stilled, reading as if the letters might bite. Her gaze jumped to the sixth line and widened.

"Kevin added a rule," Samantha said, meeting Sonia's eyes in the way weathermen read wind. "Truth—kindly."

Sonia nodded once, too fast, then again, slower, as if trying to convince her body to agree. "Good," she said. "Good."

Kevin lifted the grocery list, the note, the receipt, and held them toward her. "Do you see differences?"

Sonia didn't take them. Her hands stayed folded around the mug she had reached for without noticing. "Handwriting changes," she murmured.

"Does it?" Kevin asked, hearing a thread he couldn't stop pulling. "Yours?"

"Yes." She swallowed. "When I'm tired."

"When you're someone else," he said before he could stop himself.

Sonia's eyes shuttered. Samantha's smile cooled. The house let the refrigerator motor kick on; the sound filled the freeze.

"You're not well," Samantha said softly to Kevin, as if she were offering him a place to set his pain. "Last night rattled you. We should slow down."

"Slowing down won't change facts," he said. "Sarah is—" He broke off, felt the word wedge in his throat. "She needs a doctor."

"She has one," Samantha said before Sonia could speak.

Kevin's head snapped up. "How do you know?"

"Because I know my sister," Samantha said evenly, and it landed in his ear like the wrong key pressed against a lock. *My sister.* She had never said those words to him. Not like that. Not with ownership shaped into them.

He looked at Sonia. Sonia looked at the sink. "Riveredge Road," she whispered, as if answering a question she hadn't wanted to hear asked aloud.

Kevin stared. "You took her?"

"No." Sonia's eyes flicked to Samantha and back to the sink. "She went."

"When?" His voice rose without permission. "When, Sonia?"

"Yesterday," she said, so quietly he almost missed it. "Three-twenty."

The time struck the memory he'd stored by feel—him in the car, circling the market, the house leaning toward him from its three gables like a conspiracy whispering.

"Did she... say anything?" he asked, throat raw. "About... me?"

Sonia's chest moved like someone had placed a stone on it and she was trying to breathe around the weight. "She said *mine,*" she whispered. "She didn't say a name."

The word rolled through him, heavy as midnight. *Mine.* Not *ours.* Not *yours.*

He turned back to the whiteboard because it was easier to look at plastic certainty than flesh uncertainty. His sixth rule glowed like a red wound with its blue bandage. *Truth (kindly).* He wanted to laugh, but laughter felt like a thing for rooms without vents.

Samantha touched his wrist. He flinched. She let her hand fall, unoffended. "Walk with me," she said. "Now. Before it rains."

He looked out the window. Sun stamped the yard like a guarantee. "It's not going to rain."

"It is," she said softly. "Soon."

He almost told her he was done being moved by her little prophecies. Then the sky dimmed a fraction—as if a thin cloud had remembered its cue and stepped in front of the sun. He hated how that made him believe her again in all the wrong ways.

*** 

Sarah came in then, eyes bright in the too-bright way that meant she'd slept hard or not at all. She went straight to the sink, rinsed a glass, filled it, drank. Her gaze flicked to the board. She saw the new line. She smiled without warmth.

"Truth," she said. "What a concept."

"Kindly," Samantha said, just as pleasantly.

Sarah met Kevin's eyes. For a moment he saw the girl she must have been under all the angles—tired, scared, stubborn. Then the moment closed. She set the glass down with a clink.

"I'm going out," she said.

"Where?" Samantha asked, the softness in her tone the softness of fresh ice.

"Out," Sarah said.

"With who?" Samantha's smile didn't quiver.

"With me." Sarah wiped her hands on a towel, leaving two dark wet prints like small maps. "Rule 6, right? Truth? There you go."

"You're not well," Samantha said again, and now the gentleness had teeth.

Sarah laughed, short. "I'm not compliant. That's different."

"Are you taking the bus?" Sonia blurted. "Do you want—"

"I want to breathe," Sarah said, almost kind. "Stop trying to be air."

Sonia's hands tightened around her mug. It took a second for Kevin to unclench his jaw enough to speak. "At least text when you get there," he said. It came out too parental. He hated himself for the shape.

Sarah's eyes softened a millimeter. "I'll think about it," she said, which was as much as she would give. She reached for her jacket, then paused, looking at the board again. "Add another," she said to Kevin. "Rule Seven. *No writing on other people's lives.*"

"That's not how rules work," Samantha said calmly.

"It's exactly how they work," Sarah said, and the two sentences hung side by side like a test only one person could pass.

When the door closed behind her, the house breathed out, relieved or bereaved. No one could tell.

Samantha set her mug in the sink with a little too much control. The porcelain clicked like a bone. "She is not going alone," she said.

"She just did," Kevin said, exhausted.

Samantha turned, full weather. "Sonia. Shoes."

Sonia looked between them, panic opening her mouth and then closing it. "She asked for space."

"She asked to run," Samantha said. "We don't let her run into traffic."

Kevin braced his hands on the island. "You can't follow her forever."

"I can," Samantha said, and smiled a small, terrible smile. "It's what I'm built for."

Something in him snapped. "No," he said, startling himself with the certainty in his voice. "No more surveillance. No more edits. No more—" He gestured at the whiteboard, at the marker still in Samantha's hand. "Governance. She's a person, not a rule."

Samantha looked at him like he'd finally said the magic word and it was the wrong one. "You think letting her set the house on fire is care," she said. "That's adorable."

He swallowed the heat rising in him and tried again, smaller. "I think you're afraid."

"Of course I'm afraid," she said, and it was almost tender. "Fear is intelligent. Fear keeps us hymned together so we don't fly apart."

"Hymned," he repeated, and for once the word showed its seam. You could pull a hymn apart if you found the right thread.

He stepped to the whiteboard and, before he could think better, wrote below Truth (kindly): 7) No writing on other people's lives. His letters slanted; his hand shook. It still felt good. He underlined *No* without asking who he was defying.

Samantha watched, measuring. When he capped the marker, she took a step closer and he smelled lemon, yes, but also the smallest blade of metal, like the tang of nicked skin.

"Then don't write on mine," she said. "Stay out of my childhood. Stay out of my systems. If you want truth, you earn it by not weaponizing it."

"How would I even weaponize what I don't know?" he asked, hoarse. The anger slid away and left the emptiness visible. "I'm drowning in not knowing."

Sonia made a sound then, tiny but decisive, like something falling into place. She set her mug down carefully and stepped to the board. "Add one," she whispered, not looking at either of them. She took the black marker, and in handwriting smaller than both of theirs, she wrote under Kevin's rule: 8) A patch is not a prison.

Samantha stared. Kevin did too. The line sat there, quiet as a breath, more dangerous than any of his.

Sonia backed away as if she'd spoken in church. "I have to—" She gestured vaguely toward the hall and fled. The house swallowed her footsteps and offered no forward address.

Samantha laughed once, incredulous, then bit the sound in half. "Congratulations," she said to Kevin. "In one morning you've turned the board into graffiti."

"Maybe it always was," he said.

She blinked slowly, like a large cat considering whether to pounce. Then she picked up the eraser.

A chill ran through him. "Don't."

"Truth, kindly," she said, and erased 7) with two efficient strokes. "House rules must maintain coherence."

"Leave it," he said, hearing his voice break and hating the break for revealing so much. "Leave mine."

"I left your heart on the dresser," she said. "It's pretty. It doesn't belong here."

He put his hand on the board, palm flat, blocking. For a second, their arms touched. He felt the heat of her and something underneath the heat—weariness, hard as metal. The lemon on her skin soured into something like panic and vanished as soon as he noticed, the way heat dissipates when you step out of sunlight.

"Move your hand," she said.

He didn't. He looked at the smudges on the glossy white where old letters had ghosted. Under No doors locked, a palimpsest of words; under Meals together, a shadow of a G where there should have been a V. How many times had this board been rewritten to make a life that wouldn't budge?

He took the red marker again, drew a circle around 6) and 8)—his and Sonia's—and wrote in clumsy print above the circle: TEMPORARY. He didn't know why he did it until he heard himself say, "Nothing is permanent. Not even your rules."

Samantha looked at him for a very long time. When she smiled, it wasn't her practiced, polite smile. It was something older. "You think I don't know that?"

Rain tapped the window—honest-to-God rain, small and early, a polite agreement from a sky that liked her better than he did. She opened her palm as if to show him the weather landing there, then closed her fingers and made it vanish.

"Walk?" she said again, voice gone gentle like the world had remembered how to be kind. "We'll talk where the boards can't listen."

"The boards listen everywhere," he said.

"Then we'll make them a song worth repeating," she answered.

He almost said yes. Then he thought of Sarah's wet handprints on the towel and his own name spoken twice by a vent. He looked at Truth (kindly) and at the parenthesis that made it safe and false all at once.

"I'm not going anywhere until she comes back," he said. "I'm staying here."

Samantha nodded once, as if she'd expected that, as if every exit he thought he was choosing was a room she'd built last year. "Fine," she said. "Then we'll tidy until she returns."

She wiped the counter until it reflected the underside of the cabinets. She aligned the spice jars so the labels faced dead centre. She closed the cupboard doors with equal pressure on both sides to keep the hinges from aging wrong. Kevin watched, horrified by the comfort those rituals offered him. It was easier to fear the big things when the small ones obeyed.

The front door opened and closed. All three of them turned—the house with them, it seemed. Sarah stepped in, damp hair curling at her temples, eyes storm-bright. She saw the board. She read the new lines. She laughed once, glad and mean.

"Nice circle," she said to Kevin. "You draw like a hostage."

He flinched without wanting to. "Did you... see the doctor?" he asked, the question small in his mouth.

"Did I see a doctor," she repeated, amused, like he'd asked whether she'd seen a comet. "Yes. I saw a woman who told me choices have names and consequences do too."

"And?" Samantha said, nearly kind.

"And none of you get to name mine," Sarah said. "Not anymore."

The room didn't explode. It inhaled. Kevin felt his lungs fill with air that didn't know which storm it belonged to. Samantha stood very still, as if movement might crack something she needed to hold. Sonia appeared behind Sarah like an echo, breathless with choosing to be there.

"What do you want?" Kevin asked, because sometimes the only way to be kind to truth was to ask it to identify itself.

Sarah's mouth trembled, like the hard line she'd drawn for herself ran over soft ground. "To stop living as a rule," she said. "To stop being a face. To be *me*."

"We can't afford—" Samantha began, reflex.

"We can't afford not to," Sonia said, shockingly firm, and Kevin watched Samantha absorb that like a blow.

"Tidy away the knives," Samantha said to no one, to everyone, and went to the drawer to do it herself, because if knives behaved there was a chance people would too.

The rain ticked harder, polite upgraded to sure. The board shone, plastic and stubborn, circled rules like a child's idea of a treaty. Kevin stood very still and listened to the house breathe.

In the reflection on the oven door, three women moved as one shape and then three, then one again, like a flipbook going forward and backward too fast to tell a story.

He set his cold mug in the sink. "We'll eat later," he said, ridiculous and necessary.

"We will," Samantha said, equally ridiculous, equally necessary.

Sarah smirked. "We'll see."

Sonia closed her eyes, as if praying for stairs to hold that no one would notice.

The vent exhaled a word that might have been together if anyone in the room still believed the house had learnt their language. Kevin didn't. Or he did and wished he hadn't.

He pressed his palm to the circle he'd drawn, smudging the red into a soft halo around Truth (kindly) and A patch is not a prison. His skin came away pink. He wiped it on his jeans. Rain kept time against the window.

He stayed. They stayed. The rules stayed, altered and alive. The house waited, patient as a court that knows the verdict is coming and enjoys the performance more than the sentence.

# Chapter Eleven
## The Break

The house woke to rain that meant it. Not a polite tapping but a steady hand, drumming the porch roof, filling the gutters until they gurgled like a throat clearing for a speech. The lilies bowed so low their petals brushed the sill. The kitchen was a chapel of small sounds—fridge hum, kettle ticking, the whisper of Sonia's bare feet skimming tile.

Samantha laid out breakfast like evidence—bowls, spoons, the box of oats she approved of for its fibre and its predictability. She placed them on the island at exact distances, three inches apart, the kind of precision that felt like kindness if you didn't count too hard. Kevin stood near the window, watching the rain ladder the glass and trying to breathe in a way that didn't make the room pay attention.

The whiteboard gleamed behind them, new rules circled, old ones soldiering on: No doors locked against family. One face to the world—always united. Truth (kindly). A patch is not a prison. The circle Kevin had drawn looked like a bruise, his thumb-smudge drying to a pink halo.

Sarah came in with water still thinking about her hair. She wore Kevin's old sweatshirt like a dare and bare ankles like a season she wanted the house to remember. She passed the board without looking at it and went to the cupboard for a mug, not the one Samantha had set out, but the chipped yellow one with a cracked smiley face—the one Samantha kept on the top shelf for painting days and bad moods, because even chaos had assigned cups.

"Good morning," Samantha said, honeyed. Not a peace offering; a leash.

"Morning," Sarah said, pulling the mug down. She set it under the kettle's mouth and let steam climb her throat. She was paler than yesterday; or maybe the rain made everyone look like a version of themselves that had already made hard choices.

"We'll eat together," Samantha said, voice pleasant and absolute. "Then we'll do the market. You and I."

"I'm not going to the market," Sarah said. No flourish. No flinch.

Sonia froze halfway to the drawer. Kevin glanced between them, the way a driver glances between mirrors when a siren rises.

Samantha's smile didn't move. "We need flour."

"Use the flour we have," Sarah said. She reached for the tea tin, took the bag she liked—peppermint, unruly—and dropped it into the mug like a coin into a slot that would not return change. "I have an appointment."

The word hung. It was not coy. It was not a test. It was a door.

"With who?" Samantha asked. Lightly, like names were weather.

"With myself," Sarah said. "Rule Seven." She nodded at Kevin's circle. "No writing on other people's lives."

"That was erased," Samantha said, not looking, which was how you looked at things you intended to vanish.

"I rewrote it," Sarah said. "In here." She tapped her temple. "Permanent marker."

The kettle clicked off. The rain pressed its case against the window. Sonia set a spoon down as if setting a bird she'd found back in its nest.

"We'll eat," Samantha repeated, as if repetition could reknit the morning. "We'll—"

"No," Sarah said, and the word was so simple that it made the boards consider their allegiance. "I'm not hungry."

"You need food," Samantha said. "You're unwell."

"Pregnant," Sarah said, too calmly to be anything but angry. "The word is pregnant."

"Sarah..." Sonia's voice trembled. "Please."

Sarah looked at her and softened. "I know," she said, and the gentleness broke something in Sonia's face. "I know, bird. But I'm not letting a bowl of oats stand between me and a door anymore."

She turned to the whiteboard then, not quickly, not dramatically. She picked up the black marker with two fingers like it might bite and wrote beneath Truth (kindly), in a script looser than Samantha's and angrier than Kevin's: 9) No rules about my body. She underlined *my* twice, the lines a little ragged where her hand shook.

Samantha's smile thinned so slightly only a house could have measured it. "We don't legislate bodies," she said. "We legislate safety."

"You legislate control," Sarah said. "I'm repealing."

Kevin's mouth opened and closed. He could feel the conversation narrowing to a corridor where he didn't fit, where every word he wanted to offer would be taken as a weapon by someone he loved. He moved toward the island like approaching a rail on a high floor. "We can... talk," he tried. "About options."

"Options," Sarah echoed, a tired laugh escaping. "I've had options my whole life. *Be the face or be the problem.* Today I'm the problem."

Sonia gripped the counter. "Just—text me, okay? When you get there?"

"Probably," Sarah said, which in their language meant *I love you but I'm choosing me.*

Samantha moved then—three slow steps to the board. She uncapped the blue marker, the one that made parentheticals, and wrote next to Sarah's Rule Nine: (Safely.) The word sat there like a seatbelt you could strangle in.

Sarah watched the parenthesis appear as if it were a hand closing around her wrist. "Erase it," she said.

"We don't erase safety," Samantha said.

"Erase it." No raise in volume. Just the weight of a woman who had found a wire in herself and pulled.

Samantha didn't move. She capped the marker with a clean click that sounded like a small door shutting. "Breakfast," she said instead, turning a bowl toward Sarah the way a priest turns a chalice toward a mouth.

Sarah stepped to the fridge. She took the whiteboard with both hands and lifted it off its magnets.

No one breathed.

She held it for a second, heavy but manageable, a glossy tablet of certainty that had set the tempo of their days. Then she set it down face-first on the counter with a flat slap, reached for the dish towel, and wiped hard. The top line—HOUSE RULES—squealed under the cloth, ink smearing, the cheerful font turning into weather. She scrubbed through No doors locked, through One face, through Kevin's red Truth and the blue parentheses, through A patch is not a prison that Sonia had written with hands that shook and a heart that wanted to hold. She wiped until the board was a storm cloud.

"Stop," Sonia whispered, and it wasn't obedience she wanted. It was mercy. "Please."

Sarah lifted the towel. The board was grey with ghosts.

Samantha's eyes had gone very calm. "Put it back," she said.

Sarah turned the board over. The masking tape on the back—the old strip with together written in faded marker—stared up like a relic dug out of sand. Sarah touched it once with her thumb, as a person touches a scar not to confirm pain but to name it. Then she hung the board back on its magnets and left it blank as a sky that refused a forecast.

"We'll eat," Samantha said again, softer now, as if the volume switch changed the truth.

Sarah picked up the chipped yellow mug. She walked to the doorway and paused, one palm flat against the frame, a woman bracing herself to pass through a bright threshold into weather she knew would cut. "No," she said, without bite, without theatre. "I'm done obeying rules I didn't write."

She stepped into the hall. The floor accepted her weight like it had been built to do nothing else. The house exhaled through the vent at the landing, and if it spoke, it kept the word to itself.

Kevin stared at the blank board and felt a sound in his chest he'd never made before. Relief braided with terror. The kind of sound a man makes when the map he's been following turns out to be a mirror.

Samantha lifted the dish towel, folded it into a perfect square, and set it precisely beside the sink. "We'll fix this," she said. She could have meant the mess, the morning, the life.

Sonia reached for Kevin's sleeve and didn't find it. Her hand closed on air. "Text me," she whispered to no one, to the stairwell, to a sister shaped like smoke.

Rain narrated all of it, patient and thorough, as if the sky had declared itself neutral and then decided neutrality was a kind of siding. The board shone blank and wet-looking, a promise waiting to be named.

From somewhere near the front door came the soft complaint of a chain sliding across wood. Not a lock, exactly. Not yet. But something learning the shape of one.

***

The silence left behind by Sarah's departure was not silence at all. It was a pressure system. The kind that makes the air feel heavy before a thunderclap. Kevin leaned against the counter, mug forgotten in his hand, staring at the board's blank face like it had betrayed him.

Samantha moved first. She always did. She picked up the dish towel Sarah had left twisted, smoothed it flat, and folded it into a clean square. She placed it precisely by the sink, hands steady. "Drama," she said softly, almost affectionately. "She's always been dramatic."

Kevin's head snapped up. "She just said she's done obeying. That isn't drama. That's—" He stopped, the word *revolution* catching in his throat.

Samantha's smile was thin, weary. "She's tired. Tired people say cruel things."

"She meant it," Kevin insisted. "You saw her. You heard her."

"I heard a girl lashing out," Samantha said. She poured herself fresh coffee, stirred with unhurried precision, clink of spoon against porcelain a lullaby of control. "She'll come back. She always does."

Sonia hovered by the stove, wringing her hands around the hem of her sweater. "Maybe she's right," she whispered.

Samantha's head turned, slow, graceful, and fixed on Sonia. "Right about what?"

"That... rules don't fit everyone. That maybe—" Sonia faltered under Samantha's gaze, words shrivelling in her mouth. She dropped her eyes. "Nothing."

Kevin stepped in, desperate. "No. She's not wrong. The rules—" he gestured at the whiteboard, its wiped face gleaming like a wound—"they're not laws of nature. They're yours. And Sarah just said she won't follow them anymore. That matters."

Samantha stirred her coffee again, once, twice, as if each swirl unwound his words into harmless liquid. She set the spoon down neatly, the handle aligned with the cup's rim. "Rules are scaffolding," she said. "They hold up what would otherwise collapse."

"They're chains," Kevin snapped. The words surprised him with their own sharpness. "She's choking."

Samantha's expression softened. She crossed to him, laid a hand on his arm. "You're frightened. I understand." Her voice was a balm, slow and low, the tone she used when coaxing him out of his darker moods. "But you mustn't confuse rebellion with truth. Sarah loves spectacle more than survival."

Kevin pulled his arm away. The rejection startled them both. "Survival isn't life," he said.

For the first time, Samantha's smile faltered. Her eyes darkened, something flinty rising beneath the calm. "Life without survival is nothing."

The vent above the fridge sighed, loud enough that Sonia jumped. Kevin flinched too—it sounded eerily like a laugh cut short.

Samantha tilted her head, listening as though the house itself agreed. Then she turned back to him, face serene again, mask reseated. "We'll fix this," she said. "We always do. Sarah will come back. She'll eat, she'll sleep, she'll remember who she is. Who we are."

Kevin shook his head. "She doesn't want to be *we*. She wants to be *she*."

Sonia made a small sound, like a bird striking glass. "Don't say it so loud," she begged.

"Why not?" Kevin asked, rounding on her. "Why are you so afraid of words?"

"Because words stick," Sonia whispered, eyes darting to the vents. "Because once they're in the air, the house keeps them."

Samantha placed her coffee cup down, gently but with a finality that made Kevin's stomach turn. "Enough," she said. "Sarah will come back when she's ready. Until then, we keep order. We keep us safe."

Kevin stared at her, really stared, and for the first time the calm he had once loved looked dangerous. Not serenity, but strategy. Not composure, but a mask too well-worn to peel away.

"You're not keeping us safe," he said slowly. "You're keeping us yours."

The air thinned. Sonia's breath caught. Samantha didn't move, but her eyes—her eyes told him she'd heard it not as an accusation, but as a declaration of war.

She smiled, but it was no longer soft. "Kevin," she said, as if tasting the syllables. "Careful."

The rain hammered harder against the windows, drowning the silence her words left behind.

***

The slam of the front door cut through the house like a gavel. Footsteps, quick and sure, crossed the foyer. Sonia startled, hand flying to her mouth. Samantha didn't move—her stillness a net, waiting for the next fish to swim into it.

Sarah appeared in the kitchen doorway, wet hair plastered to her temples, rain dripping from the cuffs of Kevin's sweatshirt. She looked alive in a way Kevin had never seen—fierce, trembling, beautiful with fury.

"I'm not leaving," she said, before anyone could speak. "Not until you hear me. Not until you *see* me."

Samantha's voice was a blade wrapped in velvet. "We've always seen you."

"No," Sarah said, shaking her head. Drops of water spattered the tile. "You've seen the part of me you could use. The part that fit the story. The part that didn't make trouble. But the rest of me—the me that laughs too loud, the me that wants to breathe, the me that makes mistakes and lives with them—you buried her."

Her voice broke, then sharpened. "You buried me, Sam. But I'm still here."

Sonia stepped forward, eyes shining, hands half-lifted as though she could patch the moment with touch alone. "Sarah, please—"

"Don't beg for me," Sarah said gently. "Beg for yourself."

Kevin's throat ached. He wanted to go to her, to put his arms around her, to say he believed her, but his legs felt rooted. The board behind him seemed to hum, blank and waiting.

Samantha finally moved. She crossed to the fridge, took the eraser, and set it deliberately on the counter. Her smile was serene again, but her eyes were cold steel. "If you insist on destroying what keeps us alive," she said softly, "don't expect the house to save you."

At that, the vent above the stove exhaled. Not a sigh this time, but a long groan, layered—three voices, braided and broken. Kevin flinched. Sonia whimpered. Sarah only straightened, chin lifted.

"Then let it choose," she said, looking up into the metal grate like she was staring into the mouth of God. "Because I won't obey anymore."

The words crashed through the kitchen, echoed in the pipes, rattled the chandelier until its crystals sang. Kevin swore the house repeated them back, distorted but clear enough: *I won't obey.*

Rain thundered harder. The light flickered once, twice. For a breathless instant, the house seemed to lean, as though it might crack itself open to make room for her defiance.

Samantha's hand tightened on the counter. Sonia clutched her own arms. Kevin stared at Sarah and realized, with a shudder that cut to his bones, that he didn't know if her rebellion meant salvation—or ruin.

The house whispered again, softer now, like a verdict sealed but unreadable.

# Act II – Cracks in the Mask

# Chapter Twelve
## The River Walk

The morning after the whiteboard was wiped clean, Samantha prescribed a walk beside the river the way a doctor prescribes water and rest. She said it lightly—*Let's take some air, Kevin. A bit of movement will clear our heads*—and tied her hair with the careful efficiency of someone lacing a wound shut.

The air smelt of damp brick and diesel. Last night's rain still wept from guttering in thin silver threads. Kevin pulled up his collar and watched her button her coat. Lemon lifted off her skin—new bar of soap, same intention. He used to find that scent reassuring: bright, fresh, a domestic sunrise. Now it announced performance. He wondered if she knew he'd learnt the meaning.

They took the towpath. Cyclists ghosted by with quick bell pings; dogs hauled their owners like tugs; joggers clattered out small weather with their shoes. Samantha slipped her hand through his arm and steered him minutely round puddles, low kerbs, a fisherman's bucket. She didn't look down to guide; she just knew where things would be. She had always been good at anticipating hazards.

"You see?" she said. "Movement helps."

"It does," he said, because sometimes the truest thing he could do was not start the argument he needed to have. The river ran brown and swollen, carrying bottle-tops and a drowned crisp packet towards the lock. A moored barge rocked against its ropes; its paint flaked, bright blue revealing red, revealing primer, revealing metal. Layers of self kept showing through.

Samantha pointed. "That one. Blue hull, red trim. We ought to hire it in summer. Float away a week. No phones."

"You couldn't bear it," he said, half-teasing, half-hoping the tease would draw something real. "You'd last an hour before you tried to tape a list to the porthole."

She laughed. It was the right length, the right warmth, and rang wrong anyway. "We'd set the day in order. Breakfast, read, walk, a nap. Heaven."

He said nothing. *Heaven* sounded like a well-behaved timeline.

They passed a warehouse whose windows had long ago been bricked in. Samantha's grip tightened for a moment on his forearm. "You've been very tense," she said. "It doesn't suit you."

"You prefer me tractable," he said, and let it hang as if he didn't mind the taste of the word.

"I prefer you well." She tipped her face up, the softness precise, cut to measure. "You're my anchor."

*Or ballast,* he thought. Something heavy a ship carries so it doesn't tip when the wind arrives.

He told himself to do what had worked before: small tests. He didn't want to test the woman he loved. He didn't want to need a case file to understand breakfast.

"So—Riveredge Road," he said, as if a random topographical thought had arrived. "Do you know it?"

"Of course," she said without looking at him. "By the chemist with the blue shutters. Opposite the café with terrible scones."

"The shutters are blue?"

"You never notice shutters." She smiled and steered him round a child on a scooter. "I do."

He filed the answer, the way he'd starting filing everything: a calm sentence stacked like paper. *Blue shutters.* He had walked Riveredge Road yesterday in circles, heart stuttering, eyes so wide the shopfronts had blurred. He hadn't seen the shutters. That didn't mean they weren't there. It meant she was right—or that she'd stood under them at three twenty and he hadn't.

A bench waited beneath a plane tree.

***

Ducks scissored the brown water for crusts; a cormorant lifted black wings to dry like a priest deciding whether to bless or scold. Samantha brushed a non-existent fleck from the bench before she sat. Kevin stayed standing a moment, hands in his pockets where his fingers could find the cool rectangle of his phone. He kept his voice gentle.

"The boy at the bakery remembered you."

"He should," she said. "I've bought bread there twice this week. We keep forgetting breakfast."

"He mentioned earrings." He kept his gaze on the river. "Hoops."

"Hoops are fashionable." She turned her face to the weak sun. "Even I know that."

"And a scar," he said, tapping his own brow where Mario had sketched the memory with quick, certain words. "Here."

She looked up at him with honest amusement. "Kevin, if I had a scar there, you'd have kissed it. Often."

"Would I?" He crouched slightly so her face filled his view. No line. No pale seam. Skin as smooth and composed as the rest of her.

"Paranoia makes the world cruel," she said, reaching up to cup his cheek in a hand that smelt of lemon and heat. "Don't let it make you cruel to us."

He took her wrist, not unkindly, feeling the live thrum under the fine bones. "I don't want to be cruel. I want to stop feeling like I'm failing a test I didn't know I was taking."

Her eyes narrowed the faintest degree—calculation ticked once, clean as a metronome—and then she smiled her brighter smile. "Then stop treating our life like an exam and start treating it like a picnic."

"That's a lovely sentence," he said. "It isn't an answer."

"Then ask the thing you want to ask," she said, no irritation in it at all. "You're better when you're plain."

"Whose baby is it," he said, the question docking clumsily because he couldn't make it pretty. He saw how it hurt her anyway, like he'd shoved a splinter further in.

She inhaled. A barge downriver knocked its fender with a rubbery thunk. "We will be kind about this," she said. "Whatever we do next, we will do it kindly."

"That isn't an answer either."

"It's the only kind that keeps people alive." She rose, brushed no dust from her coat, and threaded her arm through his again. "Walk."

They came to the iron bridge just as a commuter train hammered across.

\*\*\*

The girders sang their stressed song, which any sensible person knows is merely metal complaining about weight and weather. But Kevin had stopped crowding sensible explanations to the front of every queue.

Three tones braided in the hum: a high thread, a lower echo, and something between that refused to settle. He touched the cold steel and flinched. It felt—only for a second—warm. Not warm the way sun warms metal, but warm the way a living throat is warm.

"Do you hear that?" he asked.

"Hear what?" Samantha lifted her face into the grit-scented wind as if offering it time to change.

"The... sound." He knew how mad it would sound. He said it anyway. "It's like voices trying to match pitch."

"Metal sings when it's stressed," she said, soothing a child. "Nothing more. You see patterns because you're afraid."

"I see patterns because they're there." He took his hand from the iron and rubbed it on his coat like you rub off a dream when you don't want to carry it into the kitchen.

"Then stop collecting ghosts," she said lightly, and there it was again: the policy of kindness, delivered like a leaflet through a letterbox at dinner-time.

They walked on to the lock where the water frothed white and impatient. A gull screamed and dropped; a dog shook water onto a passer-by who laughed because some people still believed in good humour without effort. Kevin took out his phone, pretended to check the time, and thumbed the camera.

He lifted it as if he might want a picture of the river and snagged Samantha's profile instead, pale against the iron sky. Later—when he could be alone with the folder—he would enlarge the image until each pixel was a question. A scar is either there or it isn't. Unless it's sometimes there.

"No photographs," she said, gentle as a hand on a hot pan to prevent a burn. "Let's keep this ours."

He slid the phone back. The choice of pronoun made him cold.

They took a turn beneath a stand of chestnuts where their boots scuffed conkers loose. She told him about a neighbour's stray cat she'd coaxed from the hedge with tuna; she told him about a butcher who cut too thick and was kind anyway; she told him the exact order they should do the market in the afternoon to avoid queues and arguments—bakery last so the bread would still be warm, greengrocer first for the best apples. Her voice did what it had always done: made the path ahead sound like a plan you could survive. He nearly let himself step into the comfort she offered and decided not to. Comfy chairs can swallow you.

"Do you remember the mural?" he asked, his tone faux-casual, as if they were mid-game and he had picked a card. "At that Italian last summer."

"Florence," she said promptly. "Not Venice. You always say Venice when you mean Florence."

It had been the other Samantha who had corrected him at the table last month with that exact little tilt of triumph. He felt the click as information slotted into his private filing cabinet. He didn't want a filing cabinet inside his head. He had one now.

He stopped at the top of the slipway where rowboats slid in summer. The wooden planks were slick with algae, green as old coins. "What would it cost you to tell me the truth?" he asked.

"To tell you one would be to break all of them," she said gently. "Truths travel in packs. Ask the wrong one and you make a mess of the rest."

He almost laughed. "That's philosophy. It isn't an answer."

"It's what keeps people from bleeding to death when they don't have to." Her eyes were soft and tired. For a flicker he saw something under the polish—weight, not performative but earned the hard way. He did not forgive her anything with that flicker; he only saw it.

They looped back, the path now crowded with late risers. A sandy-coloured dog trotted past with a stick in its mouth so wide it had to tilt its head to keep from knocking ankles. Samantha smiled at it with real pleasure.

She always had time for animals; they didn't ask the sort of questions men asked. Up ahead the towpath narrowed by a café hatch cut into a wall. Steam made temporary clouds against brick; coffee, hot milk and burnt sugar braided the air.

"Tea?" she offered.

He nodded. She stepped to the hatch and ordered two. She didn't ask how he took it. She already knew. The barista slid over a loyalty card and a short blunt pencil to initial the square. Samantha wrote a neat S with a straight tail, no loop. She smiled at the girl, set the card down, and moved aside for a mother with a pushchair.

Kevin took the pencil like it was evidence and, when she turned to pass him the tea, flicked the card and saw she'd initialled twice: the visible S, upright and sensible—and beneath, faint against the card's slick, another initial in a different hand. Looping, pretty. It had either been written and wiped or written with a poor pencil that didn't take. Ghost-writing.

He slipped the card into his pocket as if it were change. She didn't notice. Or she noticed and let him have it, which was worse.

They stood with their cups, facing the river.

***

He had to hold his with both hands to keep from spilling. His palms sweated in the steam. Behind them, the hatch clinked and hissed, a friendly machine's heart. In the corner of his eye the bridge girders held their breath.

The sound of water was a grammar you could live inside without nouns.

He thought about Sarah lifting the whiteboard off its magnets and scrubbing through the old sentences until everything smeared to weather.

*No rules about my body*, in a looser script under the blank. He thought of Sonia's hands moving without permission towards whatever was most broken in the room. He thought of the coin of lemon on Samantha's wrist, bright as a flag.

"Whatever comes next," he said, and heard how formal it sounded, like a declaration at a table with minutes and witnesses, "I need you with me in it, not directing it from above."

"I am with you," she said, not defensive. "I live with you in the day we make." Then, because she knew he would keep pushing if she didn't hand him something, she added, "I didn't erase what you wrote."

"You erased Rule Seven," he said. "No writing on other people's lives."

"Because it was rhetorical, not practical." She sipped her tea. "We don't have the luxury for rhetoric."

He looked down at the loyalty card edge peeping from his pocket and pressed it further in with his thumb. "And practicality has never been used to hurt anyone."

"It's been used to keep people alive," she said, and he realised they were speaking not to each other but to a long line of ghosts who had put sentences in their mouths and told them to practise.

A barge engine coughed and started. Pigeons clattered under the bridge, startled into small grey commas. He took a breath that filled his chest to the corners and let it out slowly, like a diver returning from depth with one hand on the ladder because he didn't trust the sea to give him back if he rushed.

"Do you love me?" he asked, not because he doubted it but because the shape of the question sometimes made the answer honest.

"Yes," she said, immediate and unperformed. "The boring way and the bright way."

He nodded. "Then help me stop feeling mad in my own kitchen."

"Come home," she said, and her voice went so soft it scared him more than shouting would have. "We'll make lunch. We'll lay the day out like cutlery. You'll see what is real by touch."

They walked back on the far side of the path, swapping the river for a low wall where wild fennel sprouted. The city made its ordinary music: a van reversing somewhere with a patient beep, someone swearing at a dog in affectionate exasperation, a bell from a bicycle, the flat chatter of teenagers being braver than their bones.

It would have been possible, if you wanted, to believe that your marriage was a place you went to hide from the world. It had been that for him, once. Now the world kept arriving through vents and mirrors and the soft tick of a string measuring a stair tread.

They crossed by the small footbridge with padlocks. Lovers had fastened their names to the railing in cheap brass and painted hearts on them in nail varnish that the weather was already lifting. Samantha paused, glanced at the locks, and he watched it pass—the thought, the micro-recoil, the near-smile. She was a woman who would never padlock a love to a bridge because the rule was no locked doors.

He almost said it aloud—*You wouldn't*—and decided not to hand her the pleasure of being seen that precisely.

***

On the street near home, he saw Mrs. Hart from number twelve coming towards them with two carrier bags. She squinted, then brightened. "There you are! I thought I saw you yesterday, love," she said to Samantha. "But then there you were again five minutes later in a different coat and I thought I was losing my marbles."

Samantha's smile was swift, warm, perfect. "I'm everywhere," she said cheerfully. "Like a rumour."

Mrs. Hart laughed, pleased with the joke and herself for understanding it. "You tell your sister I've got her tin—she left it at ours last week. Lovely sponge."

Samantha didn't flinch. "I will." She touched the bags. "Do you need a hand?"

"No, no." Mrs. Hart waved her away and stumped past. Kevin stood very still until the woman's back had turned the corner and swallowed the evidence of her mouth.

Inside the garden gate, he said, "Your sister."

"She means Sonia," Samantha said at once, easy and true in the tone, the way a person might say *she means the cat*. "She returned it, I expect. People never see the errand, only the cake."

"I expect," he said. He could not tell whether the quickness of her answer was grace or guile. He could not tell whether not being able to tell was a sickness or a sign of waking.

The house met them with the ordinary sound of the letterbox clack.

***

The hall held a damp cool and the faint smell of lilies curdling sweet. He had a moment of double-seeing—their reflection in the black glass of the oven door beside the kitchen and the reality that reflection pretended to translate.

In the glass they were neat and symmetrical, two people who could be introduced. In the room the table waited, a blank whiteboard on the fridge glimmered as if primed for a primer, and a dish towel lay folded into severe thirds. The lemon rose to greet its home.

Kevin put his keys in the bowl. They sounded loud. "I'll make sandwiches," he said, because sandwiches were facts with knives.

"I'll slice," Samantha said. "Thin, or it feels spendthrift."

He took the bread out of the bag and set it on the board. She reached for the knife and he could not help himself: "Where were you at three twenty yesterday?"

She placed the knife flat, not down, not up. "Here," she said. "Where else would I be."

He nodded as if she had said what he already knew. He opened the drawer and found the loyalty card tucked it where receipts lived and the elastic bands that always multiply in darkness. He would add it tonight to the folder. He would enlarge the photograph of her profile until it pixelated and then he would try anyway to read truth in squares. He would write in the notebook the question he could not stop writing: How many hands can one life wear.

Samantha reached into the fruit bowl, chose an apple, and cut it into moons thin enough to see light through. "You're shaking," she said, absolutely gentle.

"I'm cold," he said.

"It isn't cold," she said.

"It is where I'm standing."

She set the blade down and put both hands round his, warming them as if the river had required it. For a moment he let the warmth enter him without checking it for poison. For a moment he let the history of her be true and kind in his body and didn't ask for papers. It was easy and terrible. Then he drew back and the moment left the room obediently.

"Whatever we write there," he said, nodding at the blank whiteboard, "it has to be true."

"Kindly," she said.

"True," he said again, because sometimes you had to choose a word and say it twice to keep it from being edited as it left your mouth.

She smiled, and for an instant he saw the girl she might have been if no one had taped sentences inside her head. Then the smile set and became useful.

From somewhere in the bones of the place came a low, resonant sound, not a sigh, not quite a groan—more like a lock gate swinging shut on a river. Three heavy clanks, measured as if by a metronome he could not quite locate. He felt it in the soles of his feet.

"Old pipes," Samantha said promptly, before he could ask.

"Metal sings when it's stressed," he said.

She did not answer. She cut the apple into a final thin crescent and laid it on the plate like a moon you could eat if you were careful.

He decided that tonight the folder would grow a spine. He would not stop. Not even if the truth arrived with a body count and the house clapped in the vents. He would make a line in a hand no one else could forge and he would keep it somewhere that didn't need a lock to stay honest.

When he looked up, the whiteboard shone as if waiting for weather. He could almost see the ghost of the circle he had drawn round Rule 6 and what Sonia had written after, but that was memory, not ink. He picked up the marker, uncapped it, and wrote the smallest word he trusted.

We.

He capped the pen and stepped back. Samantha read it, then met his eyes and nodded once. Not approval, not surrender. Recognition. It would do for now.

The house held its breath, or he imagined that it did. He took a bite of apple—sharp, clean, real—and let it cut his mouth a little. Pain, when it stayed small, proved you were awake. He chewed, swallowed, and turned the page inside his head to whatever came next.

# Chapter Thirteen
## The Nursery Question

Sarah told herself she wasn't going to buy anything. She said it out loud before she pushed open the charity shop door, as if the bell above it might accept declarations in place of money.

*I'm looking, that's all.* The bell gave its little tin laugh anyway.

Warm dust and lavender polish drifted off the rails. It was raining again, light and steady, varnishing the pavement a deeper grey. Inside, the shop held its own weather: the soft rustle of hangers, a radio murmuring yesterday's love songs, the hush people bring to places where things have already had a life.

A pram waited near the window with a crocheted blanket draped over the handle.

The wool was the particular white of something that had been washed and sun-dried until its brightness gentled. Sarah stopped, pinched the edge of the blanket, and rubbed the bobbled softness between finger and thumb. Her throat tightened without warning.

"Lovely, isn't it?" the woman behind the till said. She had red lipstick and a cardigan with a knitted poppy stitched above the heart. "Came in this morning.

Never used, if you can credit that. The lady said her daughter changed her mind."

Sarah lifted a corner of the blanket, then let it fall. "Happens," she said. "People change their minds."

"They do," the woman agreed, as if they were discussing chalk and not lives. "Everything all right, love? You look peaky."

"I'm fine," Sarah lied. "Just wet." She pushed damp hair behind her ear and moved deeper into the shop.

The baby rail sat halfway down, labelled with a cardboard tag in loopy handwriting: 0–3 months. A tangle of sleepsuits, tiny hats, socks like thimbles. Her fingers found a muslin, soft from many washings, printed with faint grey stars.

She pressed it to her cheek without thinking; it smelt of clean cotton and someone else's laundry powder. For a moment she could see a future the shape of that cloth: three in the morning, the muted weight of a shoulder, milk turning the air sweet and animal, the quiet kind of love you do with your hands.

The picture scared her as much as it pulled.

Her phone buzzed in her pocket. The screen showed a number saved as Ridge. She didn't answer at once. She stood among other people's small shirts and small hopes and let the vibration run its message through her palm.

At the end of the rail hung a cardigan knitted in a neat, serious pattern—one of those garments that understands the weather better than you do. She thumbed the price tag. £2.50. Ridiculous. She could afford it easily and she could not afford anything at all.

"Want me to put anything aside?" the woman called cheerfully. "We can hold till Saturday if you like."

Sarah folded the muslin once and then again, as if those careful quarters might make a decision. She pictured the whiteboard at home hanging blank as a sky that refused to be told. *No rules about my body.* A bullet point where numbers used to be. Her own handwriting, too big for the space. She put the muslin back.

"Not today," she said, and heard how adult the refusal sounded.

"You're wise," the woman said, either meaning it or knowing how to make a customer feel sound. "There's always more."

*There isn't,* Sarah thought, and left before she could change her mind.

***

On the pavement she stood under the awning and finally called back. "Hi. It's me."

"Hello, *Maisie*," the clinic voice answered, bright and trained. The alias sat on Sarah's ear like a borrowed hat; it fitted well enough to wear for a while. "You answered from a different number last time."

"Payphone," Sarah lied. "Signal's poor in my building."

"No problem." Keys clicked at the other end. "We can fit you in for a scan on Thursday. Three fifteen. The sonographer's very good. You'll be under the name you gave."

"Thank you," Sarah said. The thank you felt like smuggling.

"If you change your mind—"

"I won't," Sarah said, too quickly. "I mean—no. Thursday."

"We'll text to confirm." A warm pause. "Are you safe?"

The question caught at her chest. Such a small thing, that word. It opened into rooms. "Yes," Sarah said. "I'm... careful."

"That's good," the voice said. "We'll see you Thursday."

She rang off. The rain had settled into a proper, patient fall. She breathed it in until the sensation of someone's knitted cardigan, someone's muslin—someone else's—left her hands and she could step back into the day she had chosen.

***

By the time she reached the house, the lilies on the hall table had collapsed into themselves. The water in the vase smelt faintly of rot. She would have tipped it, scrubbed the green scum off the glass, rinsed the stems and given them another chance, like a person who can't bear for anything to be over until it states its intention clearly. She didn't touch them. Let the lilies tell their own truth.

No one was in the kitchen. The whiteboard glimmered like weathered enamel; yesterday's smear had dried into a matt sheen, as if the words had been rubbed into the skin of the board rather than off it. Beneath the clipped magnet, in her looser hand, her bullet point remained: • No rules about my body. Samantha had added nothing. Mercy or strategy. Sarah couldn't tell.

She made tea, because hot water in a cup is one of the few things the human race does right. The kettle ticked, the radiator clicked back into itself, the pipes muttered like someone politely clearing their throat.

***

She carried the mug downstairs to the basement sewing room, where the light was always a little bad and the air always a little older than upstairs.

They had called it the sewing room because Sonia mended there, feeding old clothes through the Singer's steady motor until they behaved. It was really a hoarder's nest the previous owner had abandoned when his heart packed up during the cricket. They'd cleared it just enough to make space for the table, the machine and their boxes. The rest watched from shelves and from the shadowed corners like an audience waiting for a punchline.

Sarah set the mug down and stopped moving.

The wooden animals on the narrow window ledge—three battered toys she'd noticed on the first day—were no longer facing the garden. Yesterday the giraffe had cheered the dandelions with its split grin; the elephant had presented its stump tail to the glass; the lion had glared outside like a bouncer. Now all three faced inward, looking at the room. Looking at her.

"Very funny," she said aloud, though no one had that sense of humour. Samantha wouldn't waste a joke on a window ledge and Sonia wouldn't move a thing without apologising to it first. "Ha."

She crossed the floorboards—warped, when they felt like it—and turned the animals back one by one, placing them carefully as if not to startle them. When she'd finished, she looked over her shoulder and felt the particular stupid prickling that comes when you know you are alone in a room and you cannot make your body believe you. The house made a small noise, like a breath held too long and let out through the nose.

"Don't," she said, to the house or to herself. "Not today."

She set to tidying the table because she couldn't bear the way threads collect around places where decisions will be made. Pins rattled into a tin. A tape measure draped itself over her fingers and tried to be a pet; she rolled it into a neat snail and flicked it back into the drawer.

Under a stack of calico scraps she found a jam jar with old buttons inside—two-hole black, mother-of-pearl disks, a couple of novelty stars with chipped enamel. She held the jar up. Something dull and heavy thudded against the glass.

It wasn't a button. It was a metal screw the length of her index finger, blunt-ended, with a flattened slot where a screwdriver would bite. The metal was warm to the touch in the way forgotten things sometimes are, as if they have stored a hand against the possibility of being found.

She tipped it into her palm. There were faint numbers stamped on its side, one worn almost to nothing.

She rubbed her thumb across them until the pattern arranged itself. M 6. Useful only if you were assembling something specific, something stubborn, something that came with an instruction sheet explaining where each screw belonged and what class of failure would occur if you used the wrong one.

A crib uses screws. She saw the word in her head and hated it there. She saw the frame, the rails, the neat little bolts, the firmness with which you are advised to fasten everything because if you do not the world can turn on what you didn't tighten.

She saw a room in this basement, or one like it, where someone had once planned that fastening.

"No," she said, not to forbid the thought but to keep it from running ahead of her.

She turned the jar upside down over the table and shook. Buttons knuckled out in a small rush; at the bottom, as if it had been waiting, a tiny plastic castor rolled and clacked against the wood. A wheel off a toy. There was dust in the jar that wasn't dust from sewing. There was a sweetness to the smell under the must—something like talc and something like a memory you would put your knee through if you weren't careful.

Sonia's voice came light on the stairs. "Down here?"

"In the lair," Sarah said, still looking at the screw. She closed her hand and put it into her pocket before Sonia reached the door.

Sonia took in the turned animals at a glance and tried not to show she'd seen. "Tea?" she asked, as if the mug on the table might be a decoy and the real one could be conjured by kindness.

"Already brewed," Sarah said. "I won't share, though. I've become selfish."

Sonia smiled, because her face knows that shape even when her heart doesn't feel it. "I could make more."

"Later," Sarah said. "Did you move these?"

"What?" Sonia followed her gaze. "No. Heaven forbid. They like to look out."

"They're turned," Sarah said. "Someone wants them to watch the room."

"Not me," Sonia said. She lifted the elephant, turned it towards the window, and placed it back very gently, as if the toy might complain. "I promise."

Sarah wanted to show her the screw and couldn't. The impulse to tell and the need to keep this one thing inside her went to war and her mouth stayed shut. Sonia leant her hip against the table and tilted her head like a question mark.

"I've got a scan Thursday," Sarah said, because not telling anyone meant the silence had started to feel like a lie you could bump into. "Three fifteen. Don't tell Samantha."

Sonia's eyes did that soft widening that makes you want to promise to be better. "You shouldn't go alone."

"I'm not alone," Sarah said. "I'll be with me."

"I could wait outside."

"No," Sarah said, too fast, and then corrected it into kindness. "No, bird. This one's mine."

Sonia was silent for a beat. She turned the giraffe a fraction, as if a better angle might cure a day. "Are you... all right? With it."

"I'm..." Sarah searched for a word that wouldn't feel like treason once it left her mouth. "I'm not asking permission any more."

"That's not what I asked," Sonia said.

"Isn't it?" Sarah let herself smile, small and tired. "I'm frightened. And I'm furious. And sometimes I'm happy in a way that terrifies me because if I admit it out loud somebody will write it down and make it a rule."

"I won't," Sonia said, with sudden, strange ferocity. "I won't write anything down again."

They both looked, reflex, at the ceiling where the kitchen sat with its blank whiteboard. The house took the chance to make a noise in the pipes. Sonia flinched; Sarah didn't. People learn different things from the same lessons.

"I'm going to bring the crib down from the attic," Sonia said suddenly, and then put her hand over her mouth as if to catch the sentence back. "Oh, listen to me. There isn't a crib in the attic."

"Is there?" Sarah asked, almost laughing. "Has Samantha been storing one for the day a decision could be made by committee?"

"There isn't," Sonia repeated, and shook her head. "I'm tired."

"You're always tired," Sarah said, gentler than it looked. "You carry the weight of other people's sleep."

"I mended the hem of your coat," Sonia blurted, because some kindnesses are thrown like ropes when the water gets fast. "It was catching on the stair and I didn't want you to fall."

"Thank you," Sarah said, and meant it in her bones. "Stay for five minutes."

Sonia stayed for ten, turning the lion fractionally to face the glass again and then, when it held, allowing herself to breathe. When she left she kissed Sarah's hair in the doorway the way people do when they have paid for something with coins they can't afford to count.

The house listened to the kiss through its joists, then decided not to comment.

***

Alone, Sarah took the screw from her pocket and rolled it in her palm. The weight of it was out of scale to its size. She tried to picture where in the house it had once belonged.

Not the bed they slept in; Samantha would never allow a screw to go missing from a bed. Not the Singer; that had its own tidy bag of attachments, each slotted into its place. She thought of the gnome outside with its hollow belly and secret bottle. She thought of the false-back cupboard upstairs that Samantha had told them not to touch before pretending she had never said it. She thought of the way a plan looks when you draw it; how it looks when you live inside it.

She slipped the screw back into her pocket and lifted the jar to return the buttons. One of the mother-of-pearl discs caught the light in a brief, beautiful flash—one of those domestic glories that makes you want to forgive the world its violence.

She held it between finger and thumb and saw, very suddenly, a small hand reaching for it, curious, impatient, alive. The image hit so hard she had to sit.

"No," she said again, but it sounded different this time. Not refusal. Not prayer. A promise to herself whose terms she would need to write later.

The radiator ticked as it cooled. A draught fussed at the back of her neck; the door wasn't fully shut. She rose and nudged it with her foot. The wooden animals barely moved in the corner of her eye, which is to say they did not move and she refused to give the feeling any sentence to stand on.

***

Back upstairs, the kitchen had gathered the afternoon around it. She stood by the whiteboard and read her line: *No rules about my body.* Underneath, in a different pen—blue she didn't remember being left—someone had written (safely) in small parentheses. Samantha's hand, tidy and certain.

Sarah uncapped the marker and underlined *my* again, harder. The pen squeaked on the plastic. The sound pleased her. She capped it and set it flat, not upright, so it could not perform its usefulness at once. Then she made another cup of tea because it was, still, one of the few things that worked.

By the time she went back down with a clean cloth to wipe the Singer, a memory had packed up its bags and announced itself. When they first moved in, she'd found a ball of crumpled paper behind the table leg and smoothed it flat.

*House Rules* written across the top in the same cheerful font as their own board, but older, yellowed. The list beneath had not been theirs. No stairs after nine. No windows open at night. No music in bedrooms. No strangers. And, at the bottom, in a different, more urgent hand: She hears. She knows. She had shown it to Sonia; Sonia had said they shouldn't tell Samantha because Samantha would only make something useful from a ghost.

Sarah had thrown the paper away and missed it afterwards, like a missed bus that turns out to have been the right one.

***

She wiped the Singer. The cloth came up grey. She folded it, found a better square within, wiped again. When she put the cloth down, something on the floor caught her eye: a neat, rectangular absence in the dust, as if a small piece of furniture had been dragged away in the last year and nothing had been set there since. The absence was just wide enough for a crib.

The realisation stood up inside her like a person in a cinema who finally acknowledges they're in the wrong row. She felt dizzy with it.

She crouched, pressed her palm flat to the floor where the weight had been. The boards were cold. There were little half-moons pressed into the wood where castors had once parked. Not imagination. Marks. The house had long memories and no sense of shame.

She sat back on her heels and laughed once, quietly, because what else do you do when the room you've been using for patching and lies shows you its true name without asking permission.

Then she stood, put the jar back on the shelf with the buttons inside and the one secret she would keep in her pocket for now, and told herself she would get through Thursday. She would go under an alias, in a building that had never heard the house's voice, and let a screen tell her what she already knew.

*** 

On the way out, she turned the animals to face the window again.

The lion wobbled and settled. The giraffe leaned into the light.

The elephant regarded the rain with small, sensible approval. She placed her palm against the wall and felt, or imagined she felt, a faint answering warmth, like someone on the other side, unwilling to knock.

"Watch outwards," she said to the animals, and to herself, and to whatever in the house had arranged the screw precisely where her hand would find it. "We're not living inwards any more."

# Chapter Fourteen
## Sewing Room Secrets

The sash had been catching for weeks.

Every time Sonia tried to open the basement window, the lower frame juddered halfway and stuck with a stubborn clunk, as if the house had clenched a jaw and refused to show its teeth. She had tried the easy things first: candle wax along the runners, a dab of oil, a cloth folded between her fingers to polish grit off the paint. She had whispered a quiet "sorry" to the wood the way she might to an old dog coaxed to stand. None of it took.

Today she had patience, a flat-head screwdriver, and the need to make at least one thing behave.

The sewing room kept its own weather—cooler than upstairs, light always thinned by the narrow panes, the air faintly metallic from the Singer's motor even when it wasn't running.

Sonia had claimed the space without ever quite owning it. The previous owner's shelves still watched from the corners: tins whose labels had peeled into curls, a crate of yellowing magazines about first aid and fencing, a jam jar of nails marched by size.

She set her tea on the worktable, tucked the cloth under the mug so it wouldn't ring the wood, and glanced at the window ledge. The three little wooden animals Sarah fussed over—giraffe with its split grin, lion proud as a doorman, elephant stolid and kind—were facing the garden again. Good.

She liked them that way; rooms should look outwards.

She slid the screwdriver blade under the lower sash and levered carefully. Paint cracked with a soft sound like sugar breaking under a spoon. The frame lifted a hesitant finger's breadth, then stopped. She eased again, feeling for give rather than forcing it. You learnt that—if you pushed, old things splintered; if you asked, sometimes they surprised you by helping.

A sliver widened. Dust sifted out and drifted on the draught.

She peered into the gap, expecting spider silk and timber dark with age.

Something else glimmered instead: a darker patch behind the paint and wood, a shadow not quite shadow.

She tilted her head, fished with the screwdriver tip, and coaxed a curled scrap forward. It broke against the metal and fell onto her palm.

The paper was brittle and singed round the edges, black crispness flaking onto her skin. Smoke lived in it still, years after the burning.

Her heart ticked oddly. She set the first scrap on the table and tried again, patient, lifting the sash just enough to reach behind the panelling. More fragments came: corners with half-letters, a strip with a tear through the middle, a triangle whose scorch had eaten two sides to lace.

She nudged the sash higher and discovered a small cache tucked neatly in the cavity as if someone had slid a sheaf in and pushed it to hide.

She pressed the screwdriver handle under the frame for a wedge, then pinched a larger piece by its safe edge and brought it out to the light.

Rule

The word staggered across the paper in permanent marker, black enough to resist the fire longer than the fibres had. The rest of the sentence had charred to nothing. Sonia touched the letters as if they might bite. She turned the fragment gently; on the back, ghost print from a magazine advertisement showed a smiling woman whose eyes had gone to ash.

She swallowed. Whoever had fed this stash into the gap had wanted the rules undone and, failing that, had wanted them hidden. It was the kind of housekeeping that looked like violence if you squinted.

She worked slower, minding the edges.

The cavity yielded one more object, heavier than paper. Her fingers brushed metal. She pinched, pulled. A small brass tag slid forward and dropped with the soft clink of something worn more by being carried than used. She rubbed it on her sleeve. Tarnish gave way enough to show two stamped letters: S.W.

The full stop dots were deep, deliberate.

Not a flourish.

Not someone idly scratching initials on a school desk. A marking.

"Hello," she whispered to the tag, because talking to things made the world less likely to loosen under your feet. "Who were you."

The house did not answer. The radiator clicked in the corner, slow cooling sounds. On the garden side of the window a fat fly bumped dumbly against the glass, tried the same square of air three times, then discovered space and went.

Sonia stood very still, feeling the weight of the tag in her palm and the word *Rule* looking up at her from the table like a pupil summoned by name.

She gathered the fragments with both hands cupped, careful not to crush what the burning had left her. She lifted the sash another inch and peered all the way along the cavity, hunting for more.

A few brittle cinders clung to the timber, nothing with writing left in it.

Whoever had done this had been thorough and hurried; the scorch marks were uneven, a heat applied in a rush and a panic.

She closed the sash slowly so it settled evenly onto the sill, wiped her sooty fingers on the cloth round her mug, and sat on the stool.

S.W.

She tried the initials on every face she knew and none of them fitted. She thought of the taped "House Rules" she had found when they moved in—a photocopied sheet in a box of cleaning products left by the door, the cheerful font, the cheerful bossiness, the bottom corner where some previous tenant had written in biro, She hears. She knows. How many layers of rule had this house held? How many had cracked?

Her hands began to shake in the small, exhausted way that meant she needed a purpose or a chair and she already had the chair. She chose purpose.

She picked up the brass tag; she picked up the paper with its one surviving word; she climbed the basement steps, counted them while the fear had a tantrum and then pretended to be ordinary again by the time she reached the hall.

*** 

Upstairs, her bedroom knew her in the particular way a room knows the person who apologises to it when they move furniture. She closed the door, not locked—never locked, Rule 1 had insisted, and even in rebellion the muscles still remembered obedience—and crossed to the wardrobe.

The false bottom she had glued in months ago lifted with the practiced ease of a careful secret. The small, black notebook lay beneath, its elastic loop crisp. She had bought it years ago with cash, "for lists," she had said lightly to Samantha at the till; Samantha had smiled like a person pleased by the idea of lists before the idea of the person.

Sonia sat on the edge of the bed and opened to a fresh page. Her handwriting was small, a little pinched. She wrote:

Brass tag—found behind sewing room sash. Letters: S.W. Burnt paper flakes. One fragment with "Rule" legible. Hidden deliberately.

She paused, then drew a careful box beneath and wrote, in a hand that tried to be neat and failed on the last word because her heart had a stutter in it:

Private Rule: *Tell the truth when silence harms.*

She underlined *harms*. The pen dug a tiny groove in the page. Above her, the ceiling light blinked once, twice, three times—sharp, measured, like a code. She looked up. The bulb glowed steady again. The hair on her forearms lifted in a small rash.

"I heard it," she murmured. "I heard you." It wasn't prayer, and it wasn't a joke. It was the form of respect you give to a thing you don't understand and have to live with.

She slipped the brass tag into the notebook's back flap and slid the whole book under the false bottom again, hands moving faster as if a late idea might catch her at it. She settled the base in place, pressed the corners, smoothed the skirt over her knees once, twice. People tidy when they don't have a better weapon.

***

Back downstairs, she put the blackened scraps into an envelope and wrote window on the front. She didn't know why. She didn't like things lying around without names on them. She placed the envelope on the highest shelf behind the unlabelled tins.

She told herself she would show Kevin later. She told herself she would not show Samantha. She told herself a lot of things when telling one thing would have done.

The afternoon slid into its domestic tasks—the small salvation of them. She made a stew and then made it obedient to taste. She wiped ring marks her own mug had made and apologised to the table for the circles. She mended the hem of Sarah's coat; the stitch line looked like a neat pulse on the dark cloth, regular, calming.

When she fed the thread through the Singer, the motor sang its clean, practical note. If the house wanted to hum, it could hum in time.

Kevin came down once to root in the toolbox for a tape measure. He said, "You're a marvel" without looking up properly and she smiled because she had been given a name for the day.

Samantha drifted through later and frowned lovingly at the window, then kissed her fingers and touched the wall as if a blessing might help the plaster set.

Sarah paused on the step and reached for the giraffe's head and then didn't, like a person who has promised herself something and intends to keep it.

All evening, the brass tag tugged in Sonia's mind the way a thread tugs in a seam when you've missed a stitch. S.W. She said the initials under her breath while she wiped the worktop with the folded cloth and turned it to a clean square and then again to another clean square because order heals in small steps. S for Samantha; W for—what? Wives? Ward? White? The word *Wren* came unbidden and made no sense. She pictured other female names with W—Wendy, Willow, Winifred—none of them sat in the mouth with the right weight.

After dinner—egg on toast because everyone had run out of appetite for anything more elaborate—Sonia loaded the plates into the dishwasher and listened to the house counting down to night. Upstairs, doors made their little courtesy noises as they closed. The radio in the front room clicked off after the news. Rain started again, light enough to make a sound on the kitchen window like someone tapping with a fingernail. She dried her hands and went up to her room.

***

She didn't look at the wardrobe; she didn't look at the false bottom.

She looked at her phone.

The doorbell camera app icon glowed its polite blue.

She tapped it with the guilty hunger of someone checking an ex's social feed without the courage to admit the word *ex*. The timeline came up in squares: a cat at three in the morning, fogging the lens with its curiosity; a courier on Tuesday who ignored the "leave with neighbour" note and took the parcel away like a moral victory; Samantha on Wednesday, neatly zipped into her grey coat, scarf methodically tucked, bag on her right shoulder.

Sonia pressed play. Samantha stepped out, turned left, and went with a purposeful walk that cheered you if you believed purpose guaranteed safety.

Sonia scrolled further. Monday. The same coat. The same bag. The same step. She tapped play. This Samantha turned right. The scarf was looped differently. The timestamp said 14:12. The Wednesday video had been 14:08. Four minutes apart. Two exits, two directions, two women who were the same woman and also not, because one of them had corrected him to Florence and one had not.

Kevin's voice arrived in her head uninvited: *The handwriting changes.* She watched both videos again, back to back, and this time her stomach went cold because she saw it: the tiny hitch where one shoulder sat higher than the other; the micro-pause before the second one reached to close the gate; the half-second of facing the camera head-on before she stepped away. Details Samantha could practise, copy, rehearse. Details that slip anyway when you wear a face for long enough and forget where yours lives.

She scrolled to the bottom where older recordings fell away into Load more. She pressed. A week back: the grey coat again, the bag again. Sunday morning. She tapped play. Samantha stepped out, glanced up at the sky like a farmer reading cloud, then looked directly—*directly*—into the bell camera and smiled. Not the house smile. Not the social smile.

A quick, private smile with a slant to it Sonia had seen precisely two times in her life: once when Sarah had won a raffle with a ticket she'd bought for Sonia because Sonia never bought the lucky ones; once when they had found a perfect frying pan in a charity shop for £1 and Samantha had said, with awe, "People give away treasure." The smile was real, which meant it belonged to one of them and could therefore not belong to all of them.

The coat hood shadowed the brow; if there was a scar, the camera's low angle and the grey day hid it.

Sonia's thumb hovered. Her throat closed. Her heart did an unhelpful, frightened quickstep. She locked the screen and held the phone to her chest until the beating under it slowed enough not to show through. She unlocked it again and stared at the grid as if numbers might become words and tell her which day the world had tilted and nobody had told her.

The ceiling light flickered once—blink—paused—blink—paused—blink. Three clear, separate stutters. She lifted her head and breathed, in and out, until her hands accepted the suggestion to stop trembling. "I know," she whispered, and didn't know to whom. "I know."

She almost went to Samantha's door.

She almost knocked and said *I found burnt rules and a brass tag with S.W. on it and your coat has been leaving in two directions four minutes apart and you've been everywhere like a rumour.*

She pictured the conversation: Samantha smiling into wrath, smoothing the facts into something kind enough to swallow, and the part of her that still wanted to be saved saying yes to the spoon. She stood in her bare feet on the landing and did not go.

Instead she went to the bathroom and ran the tap and wondered, pointlessly, whether you could drown a secret in five minutes if you held it under with both hands. She held her wrists under the cold and felt the skin teach her its own unreasonable lessons.

She turned the tap off, dried her hands, lined the towel's edge with the grout line because patterns help when nothing else does.

When she lay down, she left the lamp off.

The dark made a kind of sense the light had not.

She put the phone face down on the bedside table and then, because this house was teaching her to treat devices like mirrors that could betray you, slid it under the pillow.

She closed her eyes.

Beneath her, the house creaked itself into whatever it believed night should be. Somewhere a pipe knocked decisively. From the street, a laughing shout rose and went.

Sonia let her mouth form the words she had written and not said: *Tell the truth when silence harms.*

She repeated them until the rhythm of the sentence settled under the rhythm of her breath and they could share the work.

Sleep came in patches. In one patch she was back in the sewing room with her hand braced against the sash while the window breathed warm air up her sleeve. In another she was a child in a car at night, counting lit windows in blocks of flats and telling herself stories about the people behind them because loneliness does not survive being given names. In the patch just before morning, Sarah sat on the stool and turned the wooden animals to face the room again and said, "They want to watch us, not the weather," and Sonia said, "We'll turn them back after," and Sarah said, "There isn't an after."

She woke to her lamp buzzing as if a moth had trapped itself in the bulb. It flickered once, twice, three times, and steadied. She looked at the ceiling. "All right," she said, half-cross and half-grateful. "All right."

She reached for the phone and opened the bell camera again. The squares presented themselves like a game she did not wish to play. She scrolled past yesterday, past Wednesday, to the earlier part of the month. There—Tuesday. Samantha in grey, scarf tucked. Three minutes later—Samantha again, scarf looped. In one, a whisper of shadow under the right brow. In the other, smooth. In both, the same bag, the same shoulder, the same precision. She watched each twice and then a third time and then she noticed the tiny, ridiculous thing that undid her: in one, the zip of the bag's outer pocket was pulled to the left; in the other, to the right.

No one would spot it except a woman whose life had trained her to see the way the world moves two millimetres when it wants to lie.

Her hand went cold. She scrabbled under the pillow for the notebook, then remembered she had put it away, and that perhaps was best, because writing anything down now would make it real and she was not ready for real. She whispered to the air: "I'll tell him. I will." The words were a promise turned into a dare.

***

Morning lifted itself like a slow curtain. In the kitchen, Samantha was already moving through the day the way a conductor steps through a score before the orchestra looks up. "Good, you're awake," she said, a smile in place. "I've written a list for the market. Apples first, baker last." She held out the paper.

Sonia took it and did not touch Samantha's fingers.

"Thank you," Sonia said. "I'll go after I mend the sash."

"What sash?" Samantha asked, all innocence.

"In the sewing room," Sonia said.

"Oh," said Samantha, as if only now remembering the existence of the room they all lived in. "Be careful of splinters."

"Always," Sonia said.

***

She went downstairs and stood in the doorway and looked at the wooden animals and the jar of buttons and the Singer waiting quietly for someone to ask it to help.

She pulled the screwdriver from the pocket of her cardigan and set it on the sill. She lifted the sash gently and it moved, almost compliant. She breathed out, the small victory as precious as a large one.

She could have kept the brass tag in her pocket. She could have kept the burnt fragments of someone else's rules in an envelope at the back of a shelf and told herself she was collecting curiosities, not confessions. Instead, she fetched the envelope down and opened it and spread the scraps like a hand of cards. She turned them and tried the edges against each other, as if they might make a corner that proved a sentence. The fibres snowed a little black onto the table. She reached for the rubbish bin and then stopped, because the impulse to throw away always belonged to the part of her that wanted to pretend and she was done with pretend.

She wrote on the envelope again: Keep. She put the envelope back on the high shelf where even Samantha would not casually see. She slipped the brass tag out of the notebook where she had tucked it and held it up to the window.

The tarnish gave it a greenish bruise; the letters S.W. caught what little morning there was. She pressed the metal to the glass for a heart-beat, then to her wrist, then into the pocket of her cardigan so it could learn her heat and she could learn its weight.

Her phone buzzed in her back pocket; she flinched and nearly dropped the tag.

She put it on the table and pulled out the phone. Kevin: Can you check the bell cam for Tuesday 2pm? Sonia stared at the screen until the letters swam. She typed: Already looking. Her finger hovered. She erased Already and wrote Yes and sent it.

She opened the app again, scrolled to Tuesday, and pressed play on both squares. She didn't watch them through. She watched just long enough to feel the shape of the lie and the shape of the fear and then she closed the app and put the phone face down on the table. She stood in the centre of the room with her hands at her sides until her body accepted that no one was coming to write a script over this moment.

Upstairs, the front door latch clicked. A voice—Samantha's, cheerful, fixed—said, "Back soon," to no one. Sonia did not climb the stairs. She didn't need to. The bell camera had taught her enough; hearing the line spoken aloud did not add truth to it.

She walked to the Singer and put her foot on the pedal. The motor whirred the way a reliable friend hums a familiar tune. She fed a scrap of calico into the needle and stitched a straight line, then another, and then a third, because the day had pointed its light in sets of three and she refused to ignore a pattern when it offered to become a comfort instead of a threat. The light above the table flickered once, twice, three times, and steadied. She smiled at it properly for the first time all week.

When the stitching was done, she cut the thread on the small blade at the side of the machine and wrote, on the back of her left hand with a biro that lived by the pincushion: Tell him. She didn't specify who; there was more than one him in a house like this, and perhaps the sentence would force her to choose. She capped the pen and placed it neatly with the other tools. She turned the wooden animals a fraction, not to face in or out but to sit at a human angle, looking across the room at the Singer as if watching someone work were the only way to prove there was still work to be done.

Her phone buzzed again. She looked. A new square had appeared at the top of the bell camera feed—today's exit, time-stamped 10:02. Grey coat, scarf tucked, bag on the right shoulder. Sonia tapped play and watched Samantha step onto the pavement and turn left. The camera blinked; the recording ended. Beneath it, already saved, another square loaded itself into place—10:06. Grey coat, scarf looped, bag on the right shoulder. Sonia didn't hit play. She didn't need to. She saw the second Samantha in her mind turn right and she felt, physically, the world tip as if she were standing on a boat that had been tied securely and then someone had cut one of the ropes.

Sonia pressed the phone to the worktable to stop her hands shaking. "All right," she said to the brass tag, to the burnt scraps, to the little animals, to the Singer, to the house that had knocked and flickered and told her in three blinks what people refused to say. "All right."

Her throat tightened. Panic climbed, quick as a spider. She held onto the table edge and made herself count backwards from fifteen, then from twelve, then from nine. By the time she reached three the panic had softened enough to let her swallow.

She picked up the tag, slipped it into her pocket, and went upstairs to make tea because some rituals deserve to be preserved even when the rest are being rewritten. She filled the kettle and did not look at the whiteboard. She knew what would be there: the blank sheen, the bullet point Sarah had written—*No rules about my body*—underlined twice. She knew the house would be listening to the kettle climb to boil and she refused to provide commentary.

When the water sang, she poured, dipped, pressed the spoon against the bag, and carried the mug back to the sewing room. She sat, set the tea down, and opened the doorbell app one final time. She played the 10:02 and the 10:06 exits through once more, back to back. Then she took a breath that filled her ribs to their hinges and sent Kevin a message that made her stomach flip even as her fingers typed it.

There are two recordings today, four minutes apart. Same coat. Two directions. I'll meet you at the river at five. I'll tell you what I found.

She hit send before she could be brave or not brave about it. The message went. The little delivered tick appeared and then the second tick filled in blue. Upstairs, a footstep crossed the landing. Sonia did not look up. The lamp above the table flickered once in approval, twice in warning, and a third time in something like applause.

The sewing room held its breath. The house listened. Outside, the rain began again, as if to say: keep going.

# Chapter Fifteen
## The Folder Grows Teeth

Kevin used to think evidence was something only other people dealt with—detectives, lawyers, men in suits spreading photographs across polished tables. He had always been the type to throw receipts into a drawer, to bin loyalty cards once the free coffee was earned, to trust memory and affection to carry him through. But now, late at night, under the yellow light of the dining room lamp, he sat before a manila folder that had grown so swollen he could no longer close it.

The folder had started small. A chemist's receipt that didn't match what Samantha had told him. A loyalty card with initials that looked wrong. One scrap of handwriting on the back of a bill. Little things, easy to dismiss. But each time he tried to dismiss them, another appeared. Another slip. Another inconsistency. He began saving them all. Now they sprawled across the table in uneven stacks, as if mocking the neatness he had once prided himself on.

He reached for the chemist's receipts first. Two slips of paper, nearly identical, timestamped four minutes apart. Same items. Same price. Same card. He smoothed them flat with his thumb, lined them up edge to edge, stared until the numbers blurred.

One transaction, then another, too close together for sense. He tried to picture Samantha inside the shop, smiling at the pharmacist, paying for paracetamol or plasters. Did she queue, pay, leave—and then re-enter as if the first time hadn't happened? Or was it someone else, with her face, carrying her card, moving through the same motions with tiny variations?

Kevin's stomach tightened. He shifted his gaze to the loyalty card. The chemist had initialled one square in neat, upright strokes. The next square bore the same initial, but looped and slanted. Both claimed to be Samantha. Both sat side by side, proof and contradiction bound in cardboard. He held the card under the lamp, angling it so the impressions caught the light. The neat S had pressed firm, biting into the card. The looped S barely dented the surface, as though the hand had been lighter, hesitant.

The house muttered around him. A pipe ticked. The fridge compressor rattled, then fell silent. Upstairs, a board groaned like a sleeper turning over. Kevin swallowed, pushing the folder shut for a moment as if afraid it might breathe.

He whispered, "Stay small."

But the folder did not stay small. It bulged, restless. Each paper scrap had become a rib, each receipt a tooth. He imagined it sliding open on its own, corners sharp, ready to bite.

*** 

The next morning, Kevin decided to test her.

He waited until Samantha was in the kitchen, buttering toast, hair pinned neat, her perfume a lemon brightness in the stale air. He laid a fresh sheet of paper on the table and set a pen beside it.

"Could you jot me a shopping list?" he asked, casual. "Block capitals, so I don't misread it."

She looked at him once, her expression unreadable—suspicion? amusement?—then nodded. "Of course."

She wrote carefully:

APPLES. MILK. EGGS. FLOUR. SOAP.

The letters were tall, square, evenly spaced. She slid the paper towards him, kissed the top of his head, and went on humming. Kevin folded the sheet with deliberate precision and placed it in the folder. Another tooth for the jaw.

***

That evening, when he came home, the whiteboard above the counter bore a list. Same five items, again in block capitals. But the hand was not the same.

The O in SOAP was oval, not round. The F in FLOUR had a tiny serif flick. The spacing was looser, more generous, as if the writer had taken their time. Kevin stared until his breath fogged the board. He reached for the folder, retrieved the morning's paper list, and laid it beside the whiteboard. Two hands. Same list. Same message. Same house.

His pulse hammered. He pulled out his phone and photographed them both—angles, close-ups, the way a detective might capture fingerprints. When he lifted his head, his reflection glimmered faintly in the whiteboard's gloss. For an instant, he thought he saw not one man but three, standing behind his own eyes.

A voice behind him broke the thought.

"Making dinner?"

He flinched. Samantha stood in the doorway, coat still on, scarf looped. She smiled, cheeks flushed from cold.

"Just checking what we need," he said.

"Then we'll be fed," she replied, opening the fridge.

Kevin closed the folder swiftly, heart thundering.

That night, sleep came only in patches. When he did doze, he dreamed of the folder moving across the table by itself, its corners snapping like jaws.

***

He woke with sweat cooling on his chest, the room dark, the house humming in its bones.

He crept downstairs barefoot, drawn to the kitchen.

The whiteboard gleamed in moonlight. One of the lists was gone.

Kevin stopped, pulse loud in his ears. Only faint ghost letters remained, ridges in the gloss where pen pressure had bitten. Tilted against the light, the traces revealed themselves: the arc of the R in FLOUR, the oval of the O in SOAP. Someone had wiped the board, quietly, carefully, but not perfectly.

He pressed his thumb to the ghost R. The board was cold beneath his skin. "Who?" he whispered.

The vent above the fridge sighed. Long and low. Then again. Then again. Three exhalations, measured, deliberate.

Kevin jerked his hand back. The house was answering.

He went to the table, spread the folder wide. Receipts, loyalty card, lists, photographs—evidence that felt like curses. The papers stared back, an impossible deck. He felt the folder rising, breathing, corners sharp as teeth.

"Teeth," he muttered. The word sounded foreign in his own mouth.

The radiator cracked loud as a snapped bone.

***

By morning, he resolved to carry on as though nothing had changed. He went to work, nodded at colleagues, answered emails. But inside him, the folder whispered.

That evening, in the garden, Samantha clipped dead heads from the lilies, scissors glinting in the fading light. The soil smelt damp, the air thick with decay. She hummed the same tune as yesterday.

Kevin stood beside her. "Do you remember when we walked by the river? Near the barge? I pointed out the mural on that Italian place."

She didn't hesitate. "Florence. You always say Venice when you mean Florence."

His blood ran cold. The Samantha by the river had said that. But this one hadn't been there. The correction was too swift, too polished.

He studied her profile. Smooth brow. No scar. His stomach flipped.

"That wasn't you," he said softly.

Her scissors stilled. She turned, smiling still, but her eyes glittered like steel. "What do you mean?"

"You weren't with me," he whispered. "Not that day."

Her smile widened, generous and terrifying. "Oh, Kevin. You're tired. Seeing patterns in shadows."

"Florence," he said again. "You shouldn't know that."

The house groaned above them, beams aching. Samantha laid the scissors gently on the table, stepped closer, and placed a hand on his arm.

"Come inside," she said, syrup-sweet. "You're cold."

He pulled away. "You weren't there."

They stood in silence, the lilies bowing brown heads like mourners. The house breathed around them, patient and knowing.

Kevin thought of the folder upstairs, swollen with truths no one else would admit. He thought of its teeth closing round the next scrap of evidence. He thought of the day it would bite and not let go.

And he knew, as clearly as if the word had been spoken aloud, that the woman smiling before him was not the one who had walked with him by the river.

***

# Chapter Sixteen
## Pact Maintenance

S amantha woke at 6:01 because 6:00 was theatrical. Six-oh-one felt earned—proof she ruled the minute, not the other way round. She lay still a breath and listened. The house made its small confessions: a cooling tick in the radiator, a throat-clear in the pipes, a single board in the landing giving the soft complaint it saved for dawn. Nothing urgent. Just the building reminding her that everything wanted tending.

She set the quilt square, smoothed the pillows, corrected the lampshade that had drifted a shy degree to the left. People noticed perfection more than they realised; it made them trust the day. She opened the wardrobe and inhaled lemon—three bottles aligned, each two fingers from the shelf edge, all facing forward. The grey coat hung centre, flanked by its twin. Shoes paired heel to heel, laces tucked. Shirts graded by colour and calm. Her pulse slowed to the rhythm of inventory.

Downstairs, the kitchen presented last night's stew as a smell that had decided to linger. She opened a window to the width of two fingers, no more, and let in air that smelt of wet pavements and the neighbour's overachieving jasmine. Lights on. Kettle on. Whiteboard wiped to a low gleam. She capped and uncapped the marker to warm the nib, then wrote in confident capitals:

8:30 KEVIN CALL

10:00 CHEMIST

12:00 SONIA — BLUE DRESS HEM

17:30 MARKET (APPLES FIRST, BREAD LAST)

Underneath, in smaller hand, Dinner with neighbours? with a polite question mark. The answer was already yes; she'd said so last week. But people absorbed orders better if they had been offered the pantomime of a choice.

She placed the pen parallel to the board's frame, exactly two inches from the corner. The order pleased her like a clean laugh.

Mugs next. Sonia's chipped one—tiny flaw at the rim she refused to let anyone replace because it "tasted like home." Sarah's thick pottery cup, heavy enough not to slosh when her hands trembled. Kevin's old university mug, hairline crack in the handle she checked every week and never mentioned. She added ginger slices to Sarah's, set aside a saucer of plain biscuits for the hour when queasiness would arrive and pretend it hadn't.

The kettle began its chamber music—small notes gathering to a boil.

On the table, Kevin's folder sat where he'd left it, mouth slightly ajar. It had grown since yesterday; she could feel it without touching. Let it swell, she thought. Let it eat what you feed it. You can own a hunger if you keep it on a schedule.

She didn't open it. She moved it half an inch so the edge aligned with the grain of the table and went on with breakfast.

Sonia padded in first, hair in a sleepy knot, cardigan misbuttoned—third hole to second button, as usual. She rubbed her forearms like someone warding off a draught only she could feel.

"Tea," Samantha said, bright enough to lend the room a little backbone. She passed the chipped mug and a slice of toast with the crusts removed. "Sit."

Sonia smiled on reflex and obeyed. There was jam on her lip within the minute. Samantha swept it away with a thumb and wiped her thumb on a folded napkin. Sonia's eyes flicked to the whiteboard, then back to her plate with a quick, guilty swallow. She was always reading the day for signs. It wasn't her fault; some people had been born to patch other people's fears and left none of their own to mend with.

"Busy," Sonia said softly.

"Manageable," Samantha corrected. "We like manageable."

Sarah drifted in after, pale and beautiful in the way a tired person can be, cheekbones doing more work than they should. Samantha put the heavy mug into her hands before she could ask for coffee and watched the rebellion start and die in her face.

"Ginger," Samantha said. "Small sips."

"I can pour my own," Sarah muttered, but didn't set the cup down. Her gaze snagged on the whiteboard. The faint bullet under the appointments—*No rules about my body*—still ghosted there in blue. Samantha had left it, a concession and a leash. It was important to display mercy. Mercy made the next instruction less visible when it arrived.

Kevin came in last, old habit—feed everyone else, then himself. He kissed Samantha's cheek automatically and missed the exact place by a centimetre. She slid the milk towards him before he reached, placed his spoon, rotated his bowl so the pattern faced him the way he liked from a lifetime he had never named as a preference. He set the folder on the table with a softness that suggested it contained a child, or dynamite.

"Morning," he said to the cereal.

"Morning," Samantha said to the part of him that still trusted her.

He ate in that distracted way that made you want to protect someone from the objects in their own kitchen. She poured her tea and pretended not to notice that he kept glancing at the board and then at the folder, as though words might leap across the gap and rearrange themselves before his eyes.

"Meeting at eight-thirty," she reminded, tapping the schedule. "I'll see to the chemist."

Kevin nodded.

She looked at Sarah. "You have Sonia at noon for the hem. After, rest."

Sarah's mouth twitched. "Yes, mum," she said, sweet enough to sting.

Samantha smiled with all her teeth and none of her anger. "If you rested when you should, I wouldn't need to mother you."

Sonia coughed small peace into the air. "I can move it to one if—"

"No," Samantha said mildly. "Twelve. Then the market. Apples first, bread last."

"Why apples first?" Kevin asked, the sort of question he'd never asked when the house was young.

"Because they bruise," Samantha said. "And because the queue at the greengrocer is shorter at five-thirty than six." She didn't add: and because moving through a market with a plan keeps people from having thoughts that wander towards the edges of things. Not every reason belonged in the open.

She slid a plate of sliced fruit into the middle of the table. Sarah took none. Sonia took two pieces and looked grateful to the apple as though it had consented to be eaten. Kevin took one, chewed as if it were paperwork.

When they had finished, Samantha stood and cleared plates with cheerful efficiency. Rinse, stack, wipe. She handed Sonia a folded list for mending—blue dress hem, Kevin's shirt button, the tea towel that liked to fray itself on principle.

"I'll do them all," Sonia said quickly, relieved to be useful.

"Of course you will," Samantha said, and kissed her hair in a way that rewarded the right response.

She passed Sarah a small packet of dry crackers wrapped in parchment. "For your coat pocket," she said. "In case."

Sarah weighed the packet in her palm as if good intentions might prove poisonous. "I'm not a child."

"You're tired," Samantha said. "Different animal."

Sarah slid the packet into her pocket without admitting the victory.

Kevin rose, gathered his tie, reached for the folder, and looked at Samantha like a man about to build a bridge without knowing the river. "I'll be back for lunch," he said.

"There's soup," she told him. "Lentil. I've labelled it. Microwave one minute, stir, one more minute. Don't burn your mouth; you always pretend you haven't."

A crease formed between his brows, deepening the way new lines do when they're told they exist. "Do I?"

"Yes," she said, gentler than she felt. "You do."

He bent to kiss her again—closer to the target this time—and left with the careful tread of someone avoiding a squeaky step. She had oiled that tread last week; it squeaked anyway when it wanted attention.

The front door sighed shut. The house exhaled in a long, satisfied thread through the vent. Samantha listened, set her jaw, and smiled at her sisters with an ease earned by practice.

"Right," she said. "Let's set the day."

***

Sonia gathered the mending as if she could hide inside it. Sarah drained the ginger tea, made a face, and reached automatically for the crackers she had pretended not to want. Samantha rinsed mugs, set them upside down like well-behaved hats, and watched the kitchen become itself—edges aligned, surfaces shining, the whiteboard's lines straight enough to walk along.

She took a cloth and polished the oven door until the glass gave back a clear image. Three women in the reflection, two seated, one standing. For a blink they lined up—same eyes, same mouth, the slight difference in the set of each shoulder. She adjusted her hair, turned her face to the left where the light softened, measured her smile against the mask she had rehearsed.

Samantha believed in walking the perimeter. Not in a military sense—though sometimes the metaphor pleased her—but as a daily covenant with the building. Houses, like marriages, wanted maintenance. If you ignored the creaks and cracks, they widened until nothing held. She would not permit widening.

She began in the hall. The rug had crept half an inch overnight; she nudged it back with her foot so the fringe lay straight against the skirting. The family photographs leaned, as they always did. She straightened the frame that held their wedding portrait—Kevin's arm around her waist, her own smile not the one she wore now but an earlier draft. For a moment she thought the glass quivered, like the face behind it had shivered at the lie. She pressed the frame flat until the nail squeaked in the plaster, then stepped back. Better.

In the sitting room, she pulled the blinds to equal lengths. She fluffed the cushions so their seams pointed upwards, not sideways. She plucked a thread from the carpet, folded it neatly into her pocket. Dust tried to outwit her by settling on the mantelpiece, but she had cloths in every room. Swipe, polish, shine—gone. The house gleamed when she was finished, as though grateful.

Upstairs, she opened wardrobes. Sarah's jumpers were folded in loose, impatient piles. Samantha corrected them, aligning by colour, then by size. Sonia's drawers overflowed with fabric scraps and patterns; Samantha refolded the neatest three and left the chaos beneath. Some people needed the illusion of disorder so they could cling to the person who cleaned it. She had learnt long ago not to rob Sonia of her dependence.

Back in the sewing room, she lingered longest. The sash window slid smooth now—Sonia's work. Samantha ran her palm along the frame, approving. The Singer sat silent, a relic humming faintly with remembered power. On the ledge, the wooden animals had turned outward again. Sarah's rebellion. Samantha pivoted them back to face the room. You belonged to those inside, not to the garden.

The vent above the machine rattled softly. She tilted her head, listening.

"Together," she whispered.

A sigh answered, long and even. Three beats. She smiled. The house listened. The house agreed.

At mid-morning, the doorbell chimed. She opened it before the sound finished, because answering quickly reassured couriers, and reassured couriers didn't linger. A young man held a parcel. She signed her name with the neat, upright S that would survive scrutiny. He handed the box across and hurried off, already dialling his next stop.

She closed the door, carried the box upstairs. Shoes. Identical to the pair Sarah had ruined on the steps last month, mud eating the soles. Samantha slit the tape with a nail, lifted the lid. Leather, grey, uncreased. She inhaled newness. Perfect.

She slid the shoes into her wardrobe, behind the aligned scarves. Rotation demanded precision. One coat fraying? Replace it. One shoe muddied? Produce its twin. Identities relied on seamlessness. Anything less was neglect, and neglect was betrayal.

She checked the bottles of perfume: three lemons, lined like soldiers. Caps polished, levels measured. She checked scarves: grey, grey, grey. She checked notebooks: one in Kevin's study, one in Sonia's bedside drawer, one in her own desk—each with lists, handwriting close enough that even Kevin, with his folder, hadn't seen the seam. He thought he hunted lies. He didn't know he was walking in a pattern she had stitched long before he noticed.

She descended to the kitchen and set out offerings. For Sarah: a glass of water with lemon slices, peel floating for sharpness, blanket arranged on the sofa, remote within reach, paperback novel on the table. For Sonia: a spool of blue thread and a folded note in her careful script—*For always patching the holes.* She knew Sonia would tuck it in her notebook, cheeks pink, conscience steadied. For Kevin: lunch ready in the fridge, clingfilm taut, cutlery in the drawer aligned. He would think himself independent, eating in silence, never realising how many decisions she had already cleared from his path.

The house hummed as she worked, approving. She hummed back, tuneless but steady, like two partners marking time in a dance only they knew.

When the oven door caught her reflection, she stopped to study herself. Hair pinned smooth, eyes calm, smile measured. She practised two versions—one soft, one brisk—choosing which Kevin would need tonight. Rehearsal was survival. Spontaneity was waste.

Her phone buzzed once in her pocket. Not her everyday phone—the other one. The secret. She left it for later, savouring the promise of instruction. Maintenance required order, and order arrived on schedule.

She stood again at the whiteboard, marker ready, and added *Market—apples first, bread last.* The squeak of the nib made her shiver, pleased. Behind her, the radiator clicked twice, pipes giving back their assent. She placed the marker down precisely parallel to the board. Alignment was love. Alignment was law.

***

Then she moved to the table and, for the first time all day, allowed her eyes to rest on Kevin's folder. Still bulging, still hungry. He carried it everywhere now, like armour or a child. She hadn't opened it, but she knew its contents as if she had written them herself. Receipts. Notes. Lists. His trembling photographs. All evidence of the story she was writing faster than he could read.

She touched the cover with two fingers, gentle, like a blessing. *Grow,* she thought. *Grow teeth. You'll never bite the hand that feeds you.*

The house sighed again, low and satisfied.

By late afternoon the house wore its neatness like a pressed shirt. Samantha stood in the arch between kitchen and hall and let her eyes travel the lines she had drawn into the day. The whiteboard's columns were straight and legible. The sink shone. The oven door reflected a world that behaved. Even the lilies had surrendered—spent heads trimmed, stems refreshed, their sweetness dulled to something she could tolerate.

Kevin came home earlier than expected, the folder tight under his arm, the set of his shoulders trying to look casual and failing. His eyes flicked to the whiteboard and away, as if the board might read him back. He made himself busy with the kettle, poured water he did not want, then let the mug sit untouched on the counter while steam climbed and thinned.

"Cold?" Samantha asked, as if temperature were the subject and not the way his gaze snagged on certain corners of the room. She turned the dial on the radiator anyway so he could feel he had been understood.

"I looked at the bell camera," he said, speaking to the steam. "It sometimes doubles recordings. Glitches. That's all."

"Technology loves a ghost," she answered, airy, kind. "It frightens itself and then asks us to soothe it."

He made a non-committal sound. His hands were clean but he rubbed them as if they were dirty. She wanted to take them and press them flat on the counter until they learnt stillness again. She didn't. Correction in public is cruelty; correction beneath the spoke skin is love.

From the hall, Sonia's laughter bubbled—bright, unsteady, quickly apologetic. She entered with her mending tin against her hip, cheeks pink from the heat of the iron. "Blue dress done," she reported. "Tea towel too. It won't fray again; I made it promise."

"Miracle-worker," Samantha said warmly, and meant it. "Take the flowers through, would you? Fresh water."

Sonia obeyed, relief loosening her shoulders simply because a task had chosen her. Sarah followed, saltine wrapper crinkling in her pocket, the same war on her face: fight or accept the blanket she'd already accepted.

"We're going to the market," Samantha said, voice light, unopposed. "Apples first, bread last."

Sarah's mouth twitched. "You're going to the market."

"We," Samantha repeated, gentle only at the surface. "It's good to walk."

***

The four of them crossed the short distance to the high street as if practicing family. The evening had the metallic cool London offers on days it cannot be bothered to rain. In the greengrocer's she redirected Kevin's hand away from bruised apples without appearing to move it; in the bakery she timed their entrance so the rye would still be warm. She greeted the woman at the till by first name—people relax when remembered—and nodded politely at the man who thought he recognised them from somewhere but could not place why they were always the same and always not.

On the way home, Sarah paused outside a charity shop window, caught on a row of baby cardigans knitted by hands that liked to keep other people warm. Samantha stood with her a moment, profile to profile in the glass. She could see the thought form and harden in Sarah, then scuttle off like a crab under a rock. Sarah moved on without comment, so Samantha moved too.

Back in the kitchen, she arranged the market like proof of competence: apples polished, bread wrapped, the receipt flattened under a magnet as if honesty were a document you could display. She watched Kevin glance at it, watched him not quite take a photograph with his eyes. She gave him something else to look at.

"Dinner with the neighbours," she said. "Seven. I'll take a bottle."

"We didn't—" he began, then stopped, because he remembered they had. He nodded.

She set out plates with the quick surety of someone who can lay a table in the dark. It wasn't a performance; it was medicine. She dispensed cutlery and calm. Sonia fetched napkins and folded them like boats, then unfolded and made them squares again because boats felt frivolous when the water was doing what it had been doing lately. Sarah leaned against the counter and let the cool wood take some of her heat. Kevin loosened his tie and pretended not to notice the whiteboard. Samantha's eye caught the marker sitting perfectly parallel to the frame and she felt suddenly, absurdly, safe.

Neighbours did what neighbours do: poured wine, asked after work, made cheerful remarks about the council and its new bins. Samantha let the conversation cross its prescribed bridges and smiled in the right places. When the woman from number twelve said, "I saw you twice on Tuesday—same coat, different scarf—made me think I'd lost it," Samantha laughed and covered the moment with a compliment about the woman's garden. Compliments are lids. The woman beamed and segued to roses. Kevin sat very straight and drank very little. Samantha touched his knee once, under the table; his muscles leapt and then pretended they hadn't.

***

Back home by nine, she reset the kitchen quickly—glasses washed, plates stacked, crumbs chased to the bin with a damp cloth. She let the others drift. Sarah vanished with the swiftness of someone avoiding kindness. Sonia collected the mending tin and hovered like a moth near light; Samantha kissed her hair and sent her up to bed. Kevin lingered, folding and refolding the dish towel until it creased along a line that made sense to no one but him.

"Walk?" he asked finally, as though walking might replace talking.

"Another time," she said, as though refusing something small could hide the fact of refusing something large. "You've had a day."

He watched her for a heartbeat and she felt the examination from the soles of her feet to the crown of her head. It was a weighing, not of weight but of worth. She gave him the soft smile—the one that said *we are not at war, even if your heart thinks we are.* He nodded once, defeated or soothed; she did not care which, only that the evening didn't split.

When he went upstairs, she stayed. Kitchens keep secrets if you thank them. She wiped the whiteboard to a clean sheen, left the faintest ghost of *Market—apples first, bread last* where the pen had pressed too hard earlier, then wrote Tomorrow: call at nine in a non-urgent hand. She turned the marker so the label faced out, parallel to the frame. She aligned the fruit bowl with the edge of the table. She opened the window two fingers and a smidge. Maintenance, not magic. Maintenance is what keeps magic from becoming trouble.

The house made its low music—pipes settling, floorboards answering in polite taps, the fridge breathing. She stepped into the sewing room last, because she always did. The Singer waited with its contained patience. The wooden animals faced the room, not the world. She sat on the stool, folded her hands, and spoke into the vent.

"We're keeping it together," she told the dark metal. "We are. It feels worse than it is because people are looking at the edges instead of the centre."

Air moved, hardly a sound, the faintest exhale in threes. Approval. She closed her eyes and counted it like prayer.

***

Her phone pulsed in her pocket: one discreet buzz. The other phone. The one that never rang unless it meant to. She took it out and shielded the screen with her hand as if light might break something.

Rotation's slipping. Clean the edges.

The words sat black and bare, unmoved by her breath. No greeting. No signature. She stared until they arranged themselves into meaning. Not suggestion. Directive.

Clean the edges.

She thought of edges as she had learnt them: where reflections misaligned, where a scarf knot differed, where a bag zip lay left in one life, right in another. Clean the edges meant remove the snag points. It meant silence the noise.

It meant kindness so exact it looked like kindness even from inside it. It meant, if necessary, choosing the smaller pain now to prevent the catastrophic one later. People used other words for that. She had stopped caring about their vocabulary.

She slipped the phone away, breath steadying, and stood. On the shelf above the Singer, a tin of buttons made a small clack as it settled. It sounded like the beginning of a metronome.

Steps on the landing above. Kevin, moving as if he believed floors were judges. She listened to the weight of him pass the door, pause, move on. Sonia's door clicked shut. Sarah's floorboard gave its familiar answer and then fell quiet.

Samantha turned the sewing-room light off and let the dark declare its boundaries. In the kitchen, she paused by the whiteboard and added one more line, very small, in the lower corner where no one but a vigilant heart would look:

Edges.

She capped the pen. The house answered with three tiny ticks from somewhere she couldn't name. She smiled—no rehearsal this time—and carried the secret phone upstairs, tucking it back under the cool obedience of folded scarves.

In the bedroom, she undressed with the order of someone folding parachutes. Coat, hanger, aligned. Shoes, heel to heel. Lemon bottle rotated so the label faced forward. She lay down and in the mirror of the wardrobe door saw a woman who would be called cold by those who had never had to build warmth from logic. She reached to the lamp, hesitated, and let the house sit with her a moment longer in the half-light.

"Together," she said softly to the room.

The bulb flickered, once, twice, three times—clean, deliberate. Approval. Promise. Or perhaps warning. The meanings lived side by side.

She switched the lamp off and let the dark take the edges. In the next room, a floorboard answered and then remembered how to keep still.

Tomorrow, she would tighten the rotation until it sang. She would sand down the snags. She would be kind enough to look like control and in control enough to look like kindness. If something had to be removed to keep the shape, then removal would be a type of mercy. The pact required maintenance. Maintenance required nerve.

Samantha closed her eyes and kept the count in threes until sleep found her—steady, exact, on time.

# Chapter Seventeen
## Scan Day

S arah hated mornings. She always had, but lately they felt like in-terrogations. The sickness came in waves, sharp and sour, leaving her throat raw. Every dawn was a reminder that her body no longer belonged fully to her, that it had betrayed her, signed some hidden contract she hadn't agreed to.

This morning was worse. Today was the scan.

She dressed slowly, dragging jeans up legs that felt like stone. A jumper too big, sleeves covering her hands. The scarf Sonia had knitted years ago, looped twice around her neck. Samantha had wanted to come, had insisted at first, but Sarah had put her foot down. *It's mine,* she had said. *This appointment is mine.* Samantha had smiled—always that terrible smile—but let her go. Sonia had offered, softly, ready to hover, but Sarah had refused her too. She didn't want comfort; comfort meant giving someone else leverage.

Kevin had asked the question she dreaded. "Do you want me there?" He had stood with his tie half-done, folder clamped under his arm like it might hold the truth if he squeezed it hard enough. His eyes had pleaded, but his mouth had stayed neutral. Sarah had wanted to say yes. She had wanted to hand him the decision, let him carry the weight. Instead, she'd said nothing and walked out.

The clinic loomed grey on the high street, windows reflecting clouds instead of light. She pushed through the glass doors, into the smell of disinfectant and old coffee. A television muttered breakfast news on mute, captions crawling beneath a presenter's face. Sarah took a seat and pulled her coat tight, ignoring the radiator that wheezed out stale heat.

Around her sat lives waiting for definition. A young couple holding hands so tightly their fingers whitened. A woman in her forties leafing through a gossip magazine without turning a page. A teenager chewing gum too fast, eyes glued to her phone as if the next notification might rewrite her life. Sarah folded her arms across her chest, daring anyone to look.

Her name was called.

The sonographer was brisk, kind without fuss, the sort of woman who made her living by repeating the same reassurances ten times a day. "Shoes off, love. Lie back. Jumper up. The gel's cold, sorry."

Sarah obeyed, heart in her throat. The probe pressed into her stomach. The screen flickered, grey static arranging itself into meaning. There it was—her insides betrayed, laid out for strangers to measure. A smudge. A shadow. A rhythm beating steady.

The sonographer clicked keys, measuring crown to rump. "About twelve weeks," she said. "Lines up neatly with mid-March."

Sarah's breath caught. Mid-March.

Her mind reeled. That night. The one she could still taste if she let herself. Kevin had been away on business, his folder of papers travelling with him. Samantha had been on her rotation of rules, Sonia distracted by errands. Sarah had slipped out—her body hers, her face hers, no pact hanging like a chain around her neck. Just one night of rebellion. Of freedom. Of a man whose name she hadn't dared say aloud since.

Mid-March. Twelve weeks. The sonographer wrote it down without ceremony. For Sarah, the world tilted.

"Everything looks normal," the woman said. "Strong heartbeat. Do you want a picture?"

Sarah nodded. Her hand shook as she took the glossy print, still damp from the machine. A grainy outline, a blur that claimed to be hers. A claim she hadn't chosen.

She stuffed the photo into her bag and pulled her jumper down, smearing the gel with a tissue. The sonographer smiled, already calling the next patient's name. Sarah slipped out before she could choke on gratitude she didn't feel.

***

In the corridor, her knees buckled. She gripped the wall until the dizziness passed. Twelve weeks. Mid-March. She knew exactly where she'd been, who she'd been, and who she might have brought home in her body.

The sickness rose again, bitter, unstoppable. She made it to the loo just in time, clutching the sink afterwards, staring at her reflection. Her face looked doubled in the mirror for a moment—two Sarahs overlaying, one calm, one wild. She splashed water on her cheeks until the image blurred.

When she stepped back into the waiting room, the young couple were crying with relief. The teenager laughed at something on her phone. The older woman still hadn't turned her page. Life went on around her, ordinary and intact. Sarah clutched her bag, the scan photo burning inside, and fled to the bus stop before the walls of the clinic could close in.

The bus arrived dull red and wet, its flanks streaked where rain had gathered and run like tired mascara. Sarah climbed to the top deck because upstairs you could rehearse being alone even with strangers breathing near. She slid into the front seat and pressed her forehead to the glass until the cold argued her back into her body. The city moved beneath in slow panes: a man sweeping his shopfront with bored authority; a woman tugging a dog away from a puddle it loved; a teenager vaulting a bollard as if gravity were new.

The scan photo burned in her bag like contraband. Twelve weeks. Mid-March. The date rang in her head with the exactness of a doorbell. She didn't have to do the maths; it had been done for her. She saw the night again whether she wanted to or not: the bar where nobody looked twice at her face, the alley where the wind pinched hard and lively, the room with the window that stuck on one side and the radiator that refused to decide if it was working. The way she had laughed—once, helplessly—at the miracle of not being Samantha, not being Sonia, not being the third in a pact that made every day a costume. She had been only Sarah, a person with edges no one had sanded down. And then a man whose name she kept folded away like a razor in cotton. If she said it, even to herself, the room at home would overhear.

Tell Kevin.
Don't tell him.

The thoughts arrived in two clean columns, as if someone had printed them on the whiteboard and offered her a marker.

Tell him: he deserves truth. He deserves not to be run over by a secret coming at speed. He has already started to look at the world like a detective—what would it do to him to learn that his case file should include her body?

Don't tell him: Samantha will use the information like a tool. Kayfabe kindness, the soft edit of events. "Let's be gentle," she'll say, and the gentleness will take the shape of a cage. Sonia will apologise until she dissolves. Kevin will forgive because forgiveness is his favourite kind of denial. And the house—whatever the house was doing to them—would swallow the story and burp it back as policy.

Sarah toyed with the bell cord. The bus hissed to a stop, took on a flurry of people, shuddered forward. A group of schoolgirls poured into the rear seats with the benevolent self-importance of small gods. One of them wore a cardigan that had been hand-knitted, pale blue, bobbly with use. For an instant Sarah saw a baby sleeve on her lap, the sort of cardigan laid on a charity shop rail by someone with warm hands and time. She blinked hard, and the ghost sleeve dissolved.

Her phone vibrated—Sonia: Do you want me to meet you?
She typed No and deleted it, typed Maybe and deleted that too, then sent I'm fine because it was the lie that kept everybody upright.

Another message, Kevin this time: Everything OK?
She could feel him at his desk, the folder close, his jaw working. She almost told him everything in a single long message that would make their phones heat with trying to carry it. Instead she sent Later. He replied OK and the little dots paused as if more were coming, then vanished. He was learning at least that silence could be a sentence.

The bus lurched. At the front, the driver flicked his indicator, and the convex mirror above his head swung slightly with the motion. Sarah glanced up and froze. The mirror caught her reflection and doubled it, a trick of curve and light. Two Sarahs, side by side: one with colour in her face from the climb up the stairs, mouth set; one paler, a faint smear where the curve distorted her cheek. They looked at each other for a breath. The bright Sarah might tell; the pale one might not. Or the other way round. She couldn't tell which of them was truer.

The driver adjusted the mirror with two quick taps, indifferent, and the second Sarah slid away into metal and sky. Sarah laughed once under her breath, a sound cut short because people looked when laughter arrived uninvited. She put her hand over her mouth and felt the gel she'd missed at the clinic dry into a film on her skin.

She tried to imagine telling Kevin well. There were versions. In one, she sat him down in the kitchen and said the sentence cleanly, as if cleanness were kindness: *Mid-March. I wasn't with you.* In another, she gave him the scan photo first, let him fall in love with a smudge before she made it complicated. In a third, she said nothing at all and chose a different life, one with her name on the door and a kettle that hissed only when she told it to.

All of them required a choice she had put off since the test turned the bathroom into a courtroom: whose life was she living. Hers, or the one Samantha curated.

The bus crawled past Riveredge Road. The chemist's shutters were blue, exactly as "Samantha" had said. Rage pricked her skin; the fact of the shutters felt like an insult, as if the world had chosen sides. She pressed the stop bell and didn't get off. The doors hissed open and closed on no one. The driver glanced in the mirror, shrugged, pulled away. Power lay in small refusals too.

Her stomach heaved, not with sickness but with nervous energy. She took the scan photo out of her bag and held it flat against her thigh so the paper wouldn't tremble in the air. Grey static resolving into a shape that would become a person. The sonographer's scribble in the corner: 12+1. She traced the numbers and felt, absurdly, superstitious—if she touched them too hard the weeks might change.

A man sat down beside her, middle-aged, smelling faintly of cloves and old wool. He kept his elbows tucked in, generous with space. After a minute he said, without looking, "Congratulations," and Sarah hated him, instantly and unfairly, for being kind to a stranger without needing to be asked.

She slid the photo back into her bag. "Thank you," she said, because the version of herself who refused kindness would become the version who refused help, and she was done making new prisons.

The bus turned into a road that narrowed between brick terraces and a small park where two children were kicking a football without regard for physics or traffic. A gust lifted the yellow leaves left over from a season that had not, strictly speaking, finished leaving. Up ahead, a new mother tried to fold a pram with one hand while the other hand kept an infant attached to her. She swore cheerfully when the hinge bit her thumb. The swear word made Sarah want to cry with the sheer good luck of hearing an honest noise.

Tell Kevin, the bright reflection said, the one with colour in her cheeks. You're not guilty; you're alive.
Don't, the pale reflection said. The house turns truth into instruments.

"I'm not a violin," Sarah whispered, and the schoolgirls five rows back laughed at their own joke, assuming she was mad or a poet or both.

She thought of Samantha's morning: mugs aligned, whiteboard measured, her kindness delivered in supermarket portions. *Maintenance*, Samantha called it, as if people were pipes. Sarah's hand clenched. Maintenance also described a kind of abuse: the routine application of "care" to keep another person where you want them. You held them steady until they forgot how to sway.

The bus rattled over a seam in the tarmac and the glass shivered; so did she. She imagined the house hearing the sonographer's number, pronouncing a conclusion. She imagined the vent over the Singer exhaling mine. She imagined the sewing room with its sensible machine and its stupid little animals watching the room like ushers.

She pressed the bell again, abruptly. This time she stood. The driver stopped with a sigh. She clattered down the stairs and out into air that felt newly invented.

***

The bus moved off, carrying away the duplicate Sarah, or bringing her back around the city to meet her again at some other corner.

She walked the last ten minutes home because walking turned panic into heat. Past the charity shop with the pram in the window—crocheted blanket folded over the handle, white worn to kindness. Past the bakery where the boy had said *hoops* and *scar* and named a woman who was her and not her. Past the off-licence where the owner had once let her leave IOU when she'd forgotten her purse and had told her not to tell anyone he did that. People were better than systems; that was the problem and the hope.

Her phone buzzed twice in her pocket. Samantha: How did it go? She didn't answer. Sonia: Are you nearly home? I can make tea. She typed Five minutes and sent a heart, because Sonia counted hearts like fuel.

At the corner before the house, she stopped. The pavement smelled of rain and hot stone. A pigeon dragged one wing in theatrical grief and then forgot to limp when it found bread. Someone had chalked a hopscotch grid on the slabs and left it mid-game at number seven. She stepped through the boxes fast—one, two, three—light on her feet despite herself. When she reached the end she turned and kicked an imaginary stone back through the grid, childish and fierce. She would not ask permission on a pavement. She would not ask permission in a clinic. She would decide when the deciding belonged to her.

As she lifted her eyes, the upstairs curtain twitched and stilled, though no one had reason to be there. The house watched in the way dark glass watches. Sarah adjusted the set of her mouth to neutral and went to her own door with the scan in her bag, mid-March in her bones, and both Sarahs walking in step just long enough to fit through the keyhole.

***

The front gate stuck as it always did, but today Sarah heard the sound differently: like the house clearing its throat. She pushed harder, shoulder to the wood, and stepped into the garden path that had been swept so clean it looked unlived. The upstairs curtains hung square, no drift, no light escaping. She dug her keys from her bag, fingers shaking more from nerves than cold, and opened the door.

Lemon polish hit her like a slap. The scent clung to the air, sharp, rehearsed, a smell she now associated with Samantha's version of love. Rugs aligned, whiteboard gleaming, the day's instructions printed neatly as though the house itself had been briefed.

She paused in the hallway, coat still on, handbag clutched to her chest. The silence was complete, but not passive—it had texture. A listening silence. The kind where you couldn't tell if someone was behind the door, ear pressed close, or if the walls themselves were paying attention.

Sarah hung up her coat slowly, aware that her hands were trembling. She thought she heard the faintest shift upstairs, a weight on a floorboard, then nothing.

She climbed, one step at a time, each creak an echo. Her room lay at the end of the corridor, the door ajar exactly two inches. She knew she had left it shut that morning. Her throat tightened.

***

Pushing the door open with her fingertips, she froze.

On the bed lay a tableau.

A folded blanket, pale cream, edges frayed with age but carefully aligned. Across it, a ribbon tied into a bow, faded pink, ends trimmed sharp. And at the centre, resting with deliberate innocence, an old wooden rattle. The paint had chipped down to the bare grain in places, the handle worn smooth by hands long gone.

Sarah's breath came shallow, a sound almost swallowed before it left her. She staggered back a step, one hand gripping the doorframe as if it might keep her upright.

She hadn't put this here.

She hadn't touched a rattle since childhood.

The blanket was not hers.

The ribbon smelt faintly of smoke, as if it had been pulled from some drawer where moths and secrets had slept too long.

"Who..." Her voice cracked. She swallowed hard, throat raw. "Who did this?"

The house gave no answer.

But the ceiling creaked overhead, slow and deliberate, as if acknowledging her question.

Sarah moved forward, drawn in despite herself. She reached out, touched the rattle. The wood was cool, real, solid. Not imagined. She lifted it, and for a moment the room seemed to lean towards her, waiting to see what she would do.

Her bag slipped from her shoulder and fell open, spilling the folded scan photo onto the floor. She bent, picked it up, and held it against the rattle. The grainy black-and-white outline of the child inside her body; the relic of a child that once belonged to someone else in this house.

Her mind raced. Was this Samantha's doing? A punishment, a warning? A statement that the pregnancy was no longer Sarah's to control, but part of the pact? Or Sonia's guilty conscience laid out in objects, her way of confessing without words?

Or worse—was it the house?

The thought made her stomach lurch. If the house was playing now, choosing props, scripting scenes, then none of them had power left.

She sat heavily on the bed, rattle still in hand. Her pulse pounded so loud she half-expected someone to knock on the door and complain about the noise.

She thought of telling Kevin everything in this moment. She could picture his face, the way his jaw would work, the way he'd try to fold the truth into his folder until it made sense. But she also imagined Samantha stepping in, soothing him, rewriting the scene as she always did.

The floor creaked again. Sarah snapped her head up.

"Hello?" Her voice wavered, too thin.

No reply. Just silence, thick and attentive.

The rattle slipped in her grip and rolled across the blanket, wood clicking softly. The sound was unbearable in its innocence. She snatched it up again, clutching it to her chest like a weapon.

Her eyes fell to the ribbon. She touched it with cautious fingers. The fabric was rough, worn, and carried that strange smoke scent. She lifted it to her nose. Not cigarette smoke. Older. Fire smoke. Burnt paper. Burnt things.

Her mind flashed to Sonia's secret notebook, to the ashes she had once glimpsed behind the panelling. Had Sonia pulled this from hiding? If so, why now? Why place it here, in Sarah's room, on Sarah's bed?

The air grew colder. She felt it along her arms, goosebumps rising beneath her jumper. She looked to the corner where the radiator ticked softly, three beats like a sigh.

The house was answering.

Sarah stood abruptly, scan photo in one hand, rattle in the other. She wanted to fling them both, to scatter them like dice and see what future turned up. Instead she pressed them tight, as if holding both truths might fuse them into one.

Her lips parted, words spilling without permission. "Whose child am I carrying?"

The question echoed in the room.

The rattle shifted in her grip, rolling against her palm as if it wanted to speak. Then, with a soft, deliberate motion, it slipped free and fell onto the blanket, spinning once before stopping.

The click of wood on fabric was louder than thunder.

Sarah's knees gave. She dropped onto the mattress, scan and rattle side by side, staring at them until her eyes blurred. Two futures, two claims. Neither hers alone.

A draught moved through the room, though no window was open. The ribbon lifted slightly, bow twitching as if tugged by unseen fingers. Sarah's breath hitched.

She looked towards the door, half-expecting Samantha's figure to appear, calm and cruel. Or Sonia's, trembling with guilt. But the corridor remained empty.

It was worse that way.

Because it meant someone had set this scene and left. Someone confident enough that the house itself would deliver the message when Sarah returned.

The rattle lay still now. The ribbon fluttered once and settled. The blanket looked ready for a child who hadn't yet drawn breath.

Sarah pressed her hand to her stomach. The beat she felt there was not hers alone anymore. And the question that roared inside her found no answer in the quiet room, only the echo of wood clicking like a clock beginning to tick.

# Chapter Eighteen
## Sonia's Confession Attempt

Sonia waited for the house to yawn itself quiet. It did, eventually: a last cough from the boiler, a settling creak on the landing, the far-off hum of a fridge that believed in duty. She lay on her back counting the beats between each sound, telling herself that courage could be summoned like breath—inhale, decide; exhale, speak. When she had counted to thirty without the floor complaining, she slipped from bed.

She didn't put on the overhead light. Lamps are kinder to the hour, and to the sort of truth you only manage in halves. The kitchen wore its night face: surfaces darkly polished, the whiteboard a pale rectangle with a faint ghost of today's commands, the fruit bowl centred like a pupil in an obedient eye. She filled the kettle and stopped herself at the last second—steam travelled and told on you. Instead she poured water from the jug and waited for her hands to accept the glass.

The table showed a small oval of shine where Kevin's folder had sat at supper. He had carried it upstairs as always, like armour, or a child he didn't trust the house to mind. Sonia stroked the oval once with the heel of her palm, then placed both hands flat as if she could warm the wood into giving her the words. Tonight, she promised herself. Tonight you will say it.

Say what? The sentence broke differently every time she tried it on. *We aren't—* was the honest beginning, and also a precipice. *We aren't what you think. We aren't one woman. We aren't safe.* The words scattered as soon as she chased them. Samantha had taught them all to round their sentences off before the sharp pieces showed.

Someone turned over in a bed overhead. The sound came down the joists with the intimacy of a sigh against a throat. Sonia flinched, felt foolish, then felt angry with herself for feeling foolish. She moved to the sink and ran the tap for a count of five to disguise the tremor in her breath, then turned it off and listened. Silence. Good.

She took the stool nearest the wall—the one that didn't wobble—and placed her notebook on the table with the care of a person setting down a loaded plate. She didn't open it. The false bottom in her wardrobe had taught her the pleasure of secrets that stayed secret. But tonight secrecy was a coward's luxury. Tonight she needed the book not as hiding place but as witness.

The hallway clock ticked two minutes into the new hour. She imagined Kevin behind his door, wearing his tired face and that defensive, patient kindness he deployed when the room frightened him. She imagined him smoothing the edge of a receipt flat with his thumb. She imagined him looking up when she knocked and measuring the shape of her mouth against the catalogue he was compiling. *We aren't*— She practised the word *we* silently, felt its plural weight settle on her tongue like a coin. It felt right. It felt treacherous.

The light over the cooker flickered once, twice. She glanced up. Three sparse blinks had become the house's favourite punctuation lately. Tonight it chose restraint. She found herself grateful and then hated the gratitude.

\*\*\*

Footsteps on the stairs—measured, careful. Kevin. She knew his tread from a childhood spent learning people by sound. Samantha's feet made decisions even when she walked; Sarah's made a promise and then broke it for the pleasure of feeling free for a second. Kevin's asked permission of every step and apologised to the ones that creaked.

He paused in the doorway and saw her. The pause had surprise in it and a little dread, like a man discovering a letter in his post that hadn't been meant for him. He had not shaved. It made him look softer, or perhaps only more eroded.

"Couldn't sleep?" he asked, voice low for the hour.

"Not well," she said. She pushed the glass of water towards him. "You?"

He smiled and didn't attempt a lie. He sat opposite and set his hands on the table palms down, as if showing he wasn't armed. They looked at each other across the polished wood. For a moment she saw the kitchen as a photograph Kevin might one day keep in the folder: two people about to ruin or rescue one another.

"I need to tell you something," she said, then watched the sentence recoil and try to flee. She tightened her fingers round the notebook and made herself continue. "I should have told you months ago."

He nodded slowly. "Go on."

She swallowed. The word stuck. The room thickened. Behind Kevin's shoulder the whiteboard held a faint, stubborn after-image of Market—apples first, bread last, and the ghost of No rules about my body underlined twice. The board made promises it did not keep.

"We," she said, and the chandelier above the table gave a tiny, crystalline ring—one note, bright and cold. She froze, both guilty and absurd. Kevin flinched too, though he pretended he hadn't, and lifted his eyes to the ceiling with an expression that, on another night, might have made her laugh.

She tried again. "We aren't—" The chandelier rang again, a second note answering the first. Her throat closed, and the third note felt inevitable, like a sentence ending where you hadn't planned it to.

Kevin put his palms up now, a slow surrender. "It's all right," he said, though it wasn't. "Take your time."

She could feel the shape of Samantha everywhere: in the aligned mugs, in the edge of the tea towel folded to thirds, in the hole in the rug that had stopped widening the day Samantha measured it. If Sonia spoke, she would be puncturing a system that functioned—cruelly, cleverly, but functioned. People liked functioning. They forgave violence if it arrived with lists.

Her mind leapt sideways to the little brass tag she'd found days ago—S.W.—hidden behind the sash with the burnt flakes of *Rule*. She had written it down like a good archivist. Her private law below it: *Tell the truth when silence harms.* She tapped the notebook now, thumbnail finding the edge of the cardboard like a worry bead. The rule sat under her skin, itchy.

"Kevin," she said carefully, and the act of saying his name steadied her. "I think something is going to happen. Soon. I think..." The words scattered again. She saw Samantha's face tilt into a patient smile and decided to jump before she could be pushed. "We aren't who you think we are."

His flinch was small but real, a muscle near the temple tightening as if a wire had been plucked. He didn't speak. He was good at not speaking when it mattered. She loved him for that, and hated the house for repurposing his gentleness into a tool.

"We," she said again, bracing for the chandelier, and it obliged—this time the faintest tremor of glass, as if the room had learnt discretion. "We've made... arrangements. For a long time. To keep the peace. To keep you. To keep—" She stopped before she said *Samantha happy,* because naming one sister in front of another had always felt like petitioning a god.

He breathed out, long and even. "Arrangements," he repeated, testing whether the word had teeth. "I've... suspected. But I don't know what I've suspected. If that makes sense."

"It does." She smiled without meaning to, wrecked by how decent he was. "You're kinder than this house deserves."

He glanced at the whiteboard as if it might file a complaint and then back to her. "What do you need me to know?"

That I'm afraid, she thought. That there are days I want to take the Singer apart and hide the pieces in the garden so none of us can mend anything ever again. That Sarah is going to be hurt by whatever happens next, and it will be my fault if I keep quiet. That Samantha is not a villain and that is what makes her impossible to stop.

"Just this," Sonia said aloud, because the largest truths would not cross her teeth. "I'm going to tell you something soon. Properly. And when I do, I need you to believe the parts that sound mad. And—" She leaned forward, sudden desperate. "If I don't manage it, if I lose my nerve, ask me the right questions. Don't let me be kind instead of honest."

He opened his mouth and closed it again. "All right," he said finally. "I can do that."

The hallway clock caught the hour and declared it softly. Sonia felt the minute tip over. There was a sound on the stairs then—the light touch of someone barefoot who had practised not being heard. Sonia's stomach lurched. She glanced towards the doorway the way a rabbit glances at hedgerow.

Kevin turned too, slow, as if he'd agreed with himself not to startle. He looked back at her, eyebrows raised: do we stop?

"Not yet," she said, surprising herself with the bravery in it. "Please. Not yet."

She reached for the sentence again, the big one, the one that could tear what needed tearing. "We aren't—" The third note from the chandelier rang clear as a glass tapped with a knife. Sonia sat frozen under it, mouth open, unable to pull the truth through.

A shape moved in the doorway, and the kitchen gathered itself for company.

***

Samantha entered the kitchen like she owned the hour. She didn't hurry, didn't glance between them with suspicion the way an ordinary wife might have. She carried the air of someone who already knew where each piece belonged and had simply come to reset them.

"Still awake?" Her voice was velvet over stone. She glanced at Sonia, then Kevin, then the chandelier, as though the three-note chime had summoned her. "You'll both be exhausted in the morning."

Kevin sat back, hands folding as if instinctively to cover the table's polished surface. He had the expression of a man caught with evidence he hadn't known was evidence. Sonia gripped her notebook so tightly the spiral dug crescents into her palm.

"I couldn't sleep," Sonia said, too fast, too small. "Just water."

Samantha moved behind her and touched her shoulder, not gently but not cruelly either—a grip dressed as comfort. "Of course you couldn't. You think too much at night. That's always been your flaw."

"I was telling Kevin—" Sonia began.

"That apples bruise if you buy them last?" Samantha interrupted smoothly, releasing her shoulder with a squeeze that left heat behind. "He forgets that every time."

Kevin's mouth twitched, half ready to protest, half ready to accept. Samantha smiled at him and crossed to the counter, switching on the kettle with one practised flick. Steam would travel through the house now, carrying the story she wanted it to.

Sonia's chest tightened. The moment had been here—her words on the table like cards—and now they were covered. Samantha spread her kindness like a cloth over everything, smoothing the dangerous edges.

"Tea?" Samantha asked, looking at Kevin. "Chamomile. Helps the mind stop racing."

He hesitated. "I'm fine."

"You're not." Her smile was perfect. "But you will be, if you let me look after you." She placed a mug in front of him anyway, steam rising, scent sweet.

The chandelier gave a faint tremor, one crystal brushing another like teeth. Sonia felt the sound in her ribs. Samantha ignored it, stirring honey into the mug with slow circles, clockwise only.

Sonia looked at Kevin desperately, trying to recapture the moment. "We aren't—" she blurted, forcing the words past the stone in her throat.

The chandelier rang a sharp, clear note, louder this time, and Kevin flinched. Samantha only set down the spoon, each movement measured, as though she had expected the interruption.

"We aren't resting enough," Samantha said over her, calm as prayer. "None of us. That's why we're frayed. That's why words come out jagged at this hour. Tomorrow will sound different. Tomorrow we'll be ourselves again."

Sonia's mouth closed. Her pulse hammered so hard she thought Kevin must hear it. But he only rubbed his temple, confused and tired.

"I think," Samantha continued, "that we've all been carrying too much. Kevin with his folder, Sonia with her mending, Sarah with her... distractions." She let the word linger like smoke. "That's why I've written out a new rotation. To keep us steady."

Rotation. The word landed heavy. Sonia's stomach twisted. Kevin's eyes narrowed just slightly, but he didn't speak.

Samantha slid the mug towards him, closer, closer, until his fingers touched the ceramic as if compelled. "Drink," she said, softer than breath. "You'll sleep."

He lifted it and sipped. Sonia wanted to scream.

She shifted in her chair, forcing out the last shred of courage. "Kevin—"

Samantha turned to her, smile serene, eyes sharp. "Bed, Sonia. You're pale. You'll make yourself ill if you keep worrying. I'll tidy up."

The command slid into her bones the way it always did. She hated how quickly obedience lived in her body. She rose, clutching her notebook to her chest like a shield.

Kevin watched her, confusion softening into apology, as though she'd dragged him into a game whose rules he hadn't learnt. She tried to hold his gaze, to tell him without words that there was more, that she wasn't finished, that Samantha's care was poison dressed as tea.

But Samantha moved between them with practised ease, blocking the line, pouring herself a cup as if nothing urgent had been happening at all.

"Goodnight, Sonia," she said, voice smooth, final.

The chandelier stilled, glass settling back into silence.

Sonia went.

***

Sonia shut her bedroom door and leaned against it, the wood cold against her back. The notebook trembled in her hand, its cover damp from her grip. She pressed her forehead against the panel and listened. The house gave nothing now. The chandelier's three notes had died into silence. Even the pipes seemed to be holding their breath.

She crossed to the bed, dropped onto it, and let the notebook rest on her lap. Her hands shook so badly she could hear the paper rustle. She wanted to open it, to let the rule she'd written days ago stare back at her: *Tell the truth when silence harms.* But looking at it felt dangerous, like inviting Samantha into the room. She placed her phone beside the book instead, black screen watching her.

She switched it on. Kevin's number was already open in her messages, cursor blinking like a heartbeat. She typed:

We aren't what you think. Please listen. Please believe me.

Her thumb hovered over send. She pictured the message arriving on his phone, lighting his room. She pictured him reading it, sitting up straight, folder forgotten, pulse racing. She pictured him storming into the kitchen tomorrow, demanding answers. She pictured Samantha stepping in, calm, capable, untouchable, spinning her honeyed net until Kevin himself doubted he'd seen the words at all.

Her thumb shook. She deleted the sentence.

She typed again:

I tried to tell you. I'm scared. We're not safe.

Delete.

Another attempt:

Sarah's baby—

Her throat closed. She deleted.

She tried again, slower:

If anything happens to me, believe Sarah. Don't believe Samantha. Please.

Her chest ached with the words. She stared at the screen until her eyes blurred. Her thumb touched send. For a second she thought she had pressed it. But the screen remained still, only the blinking cursor mocking her.

Delete.

The phone slipped from her hand onto the duvet. She clutched her notebook instead, flipping it open with a desperation that made the spine crack. She found the page with the brass tag's initials—S.W.—copied in her neat script. Beneath it, her secret rule: *Tell the truth when silence harms.*

Her pen hovered.

She wrote beneath it, hand moving faster than she meant it to:

If I don't speak, someone will die.

The words carved themselves onto the page. She stared at them, horrified at the certainty that had poured out of her. The letters looked alien and inevitable, as if someone else had guided her hand.

A floorboard popped outside her door. Sonia froze, notebook clutched to her chest. The corridor remained silent. No knock, no whisper, no Samantha. Still, she shoved the notebook beneath her pillow, heart hammering.

She picked up the phone again, thumb hovering over Kevin's name. She wanted to send one last message, any message, even a fragment. She imagined Samantha finding it, twisting it, turning Kevin against her. She imagined Kevin folding it into his file and never letting it see daylight.

Her thumb fell. Screen black. No message.

The room darkened as the bulb flickered three times, soft and deliberate. Sonia pulled the blanket over herself and curled around her secret. She whispered into the silence, voice hoarse:

"I will tell him. I will. Before it's too late."

The house said nothing.

# Chapter Nineteen
## The Party

The invitation had arrived as a neighbourly afterthought, scrawled on a postcard with a drawing of a fox that looked more like a cat. *Drop by for a drink, Friday, from seven. Nothing fancy.* Samantha had accepted before Kevin could weigh the cost of people. "It will be good for us," she'd said, smoothing his jacket as if he were the event.

Now the hallway smelt of lemon and wool and whatever courage lived in clean coats. Samantha tied his tie with the easy intimacy of habit. "Relax," she said. "They're nice. They like plants and bins."

"Who doesn't," he said, aiming for lightness and hitting only tired. He picked up his folder without meaning to; it had become a limb. She touched the corner, two fingers gentle, and he set it down. "Half an hour," he bargained.

"An hour," she countered, smiling. "We'll call that compromise."

Sonia appeared on the stairs with a dish of olives she'd marinated to taste like sunnier weather. Sarah came last, hair pinned loose, jumper too big. For a heartbeat they were a painting: three women at the door, the same mouth in three moods, Kevin buttoned into his part. The house gave a soft, approving crack in the radiator. Agreement or warning—he could no longer tell.

They walked the twelve doors to number twelve, carrying politeness like a casserole. Inside, neighbours balanced drinks and small talk with the cheerful competence of people who had rehearsed friendliness. The flat was bright with lamps and the warm pride of recently sanded floors. A record player turned something old and optimistic in the corner, and the air smelled of orange peel and new paint.

"Come in, come in," said Tom, broad, thirtyish, hair making a break for it at the temples. His partner, Maya, elegant and wildly competent, took coats with the grace of a maître d'. "You made it!" She lowered her voice confidentially to Kevin as she hung up Samantha's grey. "We never know who's who. It's thrilling."

"Is it," Kevin said, aiming for droll and landing near exposed. He watched Samantha watch the room, calculating angles like a surveyor. She handed the olives to Maya, praised the fairy lights, asked after the plant on the windowsill by species and temperament. Sarah drifted toward the record player and stood too close, pretending not to be tired. Sonia disappeared into the kitchen with relief and started drying glasses that did not need drying. Everyone took their places in the scene.

\*\*\*

Before the first round of drinks was placed, before jokes about the council had warmed up, the first mistake arrived—light-footed, eager to please, wearing a good jumper.

"I met your sister last week," said a man in a mustard cardigan, smiling at Samantha. "At the greengrocer's. She sold me on a new apple like a proper evangelist."

Samantha's smile didn't dim. "You met *both* my sisters last week," she said, cheerful as weather. "We're a bit of a set."

"Oh!" Mustard blinked, turned to Sarah and performed a little bow. "Sorry—yes—of course. You were wearing—" He stalled, suddenly aware he had been talking to a trick of context. "A different scarf."

"We have a lot of grey," Sarah said, and that was almost a joke. The room rattled with non-committal laughter. Maya topped up wine as if topping up could heal embarrassment.

Another guest arrived late, shaking rain from her coat, and called across the room to Samantha, "You were marvellous about the bins on Tuesday—got them to swap ours back after the mix-up. I owe you biscuits."

"That was... my sister," Samantha said pleasantly, not looking at Kevin. "She likes order."

A man in a denim shirt took Kevin aside to talk football and failed; Kevin stood there nodding at facts about a team he had once loved watching and now couldn't watch himself watch. Over the man's shoulder he saw it: a tiny difference in the set of Samantha's shoulders. An almost-scar—no more than a shade under the right brow—there, and then not, depending on the angle and the lift of the lamp. He blinked, and the skin smoothed. A second later, she turned to laugh with Maya and the faint line returned, pale as a thread. The room had mirrors in it, and none were made of glass.

***

He tried to fix on perfume—Samantha had worn lemon out of the house. Now a warmer scent threaded the air around her, skin and vanilla with a clean metallic tail, the kind of laboratory flower you smell when people who know about "notes" talk about "dry down." He inhaled again. Lemon gone. Vanilla there. Later, lemon would return like a rehearsal remembered. He watched her move and became sick with the knowledge that his wife could be more than one woman inside a minute. He tried to image-capture the moment on the back of his eyelids: *Time stamp: 19:42. Scent change observed.* The folder in his skull turned a page.

Maya shepherded people towards conversation islands: bins, trains, whether the new bakery's loaves justified their price, who had seen the fox in the alley that looked too shiny to be real. Samantha sailed between groups lacing ease into gaps. Sarah stood by the window with a glass she didn't drink and watched the rain pretend to be a curtain. Sonia materialised at Kevin's elbow with a napkin he hadn't needed and didn't know he wanted. Her hand brushed his and he felt gratitude embarrass him.

"Are you all right?" she asked.

He gave the lie. "Fine."

"Good," she said, too quickly, then, lower: "Soon." He didn't know if she meant she would speak or that something would happen without her permission.

Across the room Tom lifted a bottle, caught Samantha's eye and called, "Top up, Sam?"

"Please," she said, and Kevin heard the vowel. The evening version of her voice fell half a tone lower than the afternoon's. It was a tiny thing, but it was a thing. The man in denim continued his monologue about a striker's hamstring as if nothing in the room had shifted. Kevin's glass remained full. He pretended to sip and watched his marriage like a play.

The second mistake came dressed as kindness. A woman from two doors down, pink nails, pinker cheeks, said to Sarah, "I loved meeting you last Sunday in that blue coat—your scarf was different today though, wasn't it?" Sarah smiled and said, "I'm learning," and Kevin almost loved her for how lightly she said it, like a person playing the melody of a song they hated.

Samantha's perfume switched back to lemon near the door, as if passing through that particular square of air reset her. Kevin watched her pass a mirror that was only a framed print and saw, just for a heartbeat, both brows carrying a shine where skin had once been stitched. He blinked and the illusion vanished. Or not illusion—overlap.

When Maya proposed a toast "to neighbours who help with bins and foxes and keeping us sane", Samantha deflected attention to Tom's playlist and Tom deflected it to Maya's ability with basil and Maya deflected it to a guest's new baby, and the baby slept through their selflessness with the confidence of the recently adored. Kevin laughed like a person in on the joke and felt as if he were standing in a lift that had not noticed the floor had stopped.

He found himself at the bookcase because bookcases keep people safe. The spines arranged themselves into declarations: travel, cookery, lives of other people who made mistakes in better rooms. A photograph tucked behind a row of paperbacks showed Maya and Tom in coats that were trying too hard to be ugly. They looked happy, the kind of happiness that stands up to April. He envied them their ignorance of lemon and vanilla, of tiny scars that arrive and exit in the space between a word and its shadow.

Sonia drifted to him again, small gravity. "She won't let me say it here," she said without moving her lips.

"I know," he said. It tasted like failure.

"You'll ask me later?" she said.

"Yes," he said. It tasted like a promise he might not keep.

***

The record jumped a groove and recovered. The room politely ignored it. Kevin thought of the whiteboard at home and the words that lived there even after they were wiped.

At nine, people found their coats while insisting they didn't want to be any trouble. Sarah ghosted through thanks. Sonia returned a borrowed dish the host hadn't known was borrowed. Samantha wrote a note for Maya's fridge because this street ran on notes, and notes ran on Samantha. Kevin watched her hand. The capitals she made for public were neatly upright. The capitals she made for home carried a slight curve. He was learning to see difference like a fluency that made him sick.

On the way out, in the pinch of the hallway where the coats insisted on being bigger than people, the third mistake settled on his shoulder. The woman from number twelve's garden said brightly, "Your sister—sorry, your *other* sister—helped me fix the hinge on the back gate on Tuesday. She said her name was Samantha too. But you're Samantha." She laughed, charming her own confusion. "I've done that wrong, haven't I?"

Samantha smiled, open, indulgent.

"We share well," she said.

***

The woman laughed with relief as if having been offered a moral.

Kevin stood in the rain-soft night holding the bottle they'd brought and failed to finish. Samantha looped her scarf. Sonia linked Sarah's arm. They walked home the long way because short ways make people feel dismissed. The street smelt of wet stone and old leaf. Someone's upstairs lamp lit ivy as if it mattered. Kevin tried to fix his mind on ivy. It had the decency to be itself in all seasons.

When they reached their own gate, the wood stuck and then performed, grudging. Samantha smoothed it with a hand as if smoothing worked on timber. The house exhaled through the vent by the porch and Kevin felt the breath on his cheek though the wind was moving the other way. He thought of himself as a guest in his own hallway and wanted to apologise to the stair.

Inside, coat on peg, bottle on table, neighbours' voices fading to polite ghosts in his ears, he put his foot on the second stair from the bottom. Sonia had fixed it last week—there had been a quiet half hour of whirring and tapping and her pleased noise when the tread accepted its new life. The stair had behaved since.

Tonight it squealed.

***

A sharp, thin sound—metal on wood on message. Kevin stepped back, startled into a laugh, then angry—at wood, at sound, at nervousness. He put his foot down again. The stair squealed again, brighter, as if enjoying him. He looked at Sonia. Her face emptied, then filled with something that looked like guilt. "I—" she started. "It was fine."

"It was," he said, hearing that the stair had lied and that the house had learnt to lie with it. Behind him, the radiator clicked three times like an old song. Sarah flinched as if the clicks had teeth. Samantha reached to steady the banister, not him.

"Upstairs," she said pleasantly. "We've had a night." She was right, and yet the word *we* felt loaded now—plurals as traps. Kevin put his foot on the offending tread a third time, as if to make the point to timber, and it held its breath. He hated that too. The house had learnt performance.

They dispersed like smoke. Sonia to her room because she was practising disappearing. Sarah to hers because the scene in there had been laid by hands she needed to name and couldn't. Samantha to the bathroom, humming in the key of Being Right. Kevin stood in the hallway with his hand on the newel post and felt the wood more alive than he was.

He went to the kitchen to fetch water, as if water could be loyal. On the whiteboard the day had been wiped to a fog, but faint letters clung like bruise-yellow: No rules about my body and beneath in a lighter hand (safely), and beneath both the drag-mark where someone had smudged mercy into coercion. He turned away and stared into the window's dark square. The glass offered him a face with a man behind it carrying a folder he didn't have in his hand. He looked as if he wanted to ask the reflection for identification.

The house made a small sound—barely a tick—and he turned and knew, suddenly and entirely, that he would speak to Samantha without audience. If the truth was an animal that only came into rooms alone, he would wait with meat.

***

He found her at the dressing table, removing mascara with the care of a surgeon. The room smelt of lemon again. Vanilla gone, as if the night had been laundered from her skin. The lamp made a pool of hotel light in which nothing bad ever happens until it does.

"Can we talk," he said, closing the door.

She glanced at him in the mirror, smiled, went on with the cotton pad. "We've been talking all evening."

"Not about anything," he said. He moved into the light so she could see the way his hands had decided not to shake. "I want to ask you something and I want you to answer me without... without helping."

She laughed. "You make my kindness sound like robbery." She turned, facing him, bare-faced now, beautiful and difficult. "Ask."

"At the party," he said. "People said they saw you when you weren't you. The bins. The greengrocer. The hinge on the back gate." He heard himself listing domestic miracles like crimes and hated that there was no other way. "They were sure, Sam. They were sure of *you*."

"People are sure of all sorts of things," she said mildly. "They see what they're told to see. And we," she added, "are very persuasive."

"Are we," he said, and the *we* cut his tongue on the way out. He took a breath. "The perfume. You wore lemon out of the house. At some point it changed. Then it changed back."

She smiled. "Do you want me to put together a schedule for my wrists?"

"The scar," he said, and felt something rise in his chest that might have been grief, might have been relief. "Sometimes it's there. Sometimes it isn't. I'm not mad. I am *not* mad."

She didn't look away. "I've never called you mad."

"You've called my questions untidy," he said.

"Because they are." She stood, stepped close. The lemon came with her. Up close, the right brow was smooth. He could swear he saw, underneath smoothness, a memory of line. He closed his eyes and saw the river again and Samantha's hand pointing and her voice correcting him from Venice to Florence, and the fact of her with him and not with him at once. He opened his eyes.

"I need the truth," he said, steady. "I can carry it. I'm ready."

She cocked her head. The kind smile arrived like weather at a garden party: inconveniently pleasant. "You're not ready for the truth."

"I am." He almost said *please*. He didn't. A scrape sounded somewhere in the house—the stair considering its options. "I am," he said again, and it surprised him that it felt like bravery.

She studied his face with the attention she gave to whiteboards. He couldn't tell if she was categorising or forgiving. At last she nodded once, not kindly. "Then survive it."

It wasn't a threat. It wasn't comfort. It was a condition set down on the table between them, next to the cotton pad and the bottle of lemon. He felt the air move around the syllables as if the house had leaned in.

"Tell me," he said.

She stepped past him to the door, opened it, and listened a second for the house to give them away. It said nothing. She closed the door again, turned the lock slowly, placed the key on the dressing table with a click, and sat. When she looked up, the mask had slipped a fraction, not into cruelty but into clarity.

"All right," she said. "Let's begin."

***

Outside, the stair squealed once and then, as if catching itself in a lie, fell perfectly silent.

# Chapter Twenty
## Fire in the Sewing Room

T he sewing room had learnt to hide its sharpness. By day it looked practical—Singer quiet on the table, tins lined up like obedient soldiers, ribbons coiled into docile spirals. But at night, when the light was wrong and the house listened harder, every object on the workbench seemed to confess its second life: scissors as argument, pins as punctuation, thread as fuse.

Sarah stood in the doorway and let the room take her measure. The blanket from the staged nursery scene had gone—folded away by mysterious hands—but a ribbon end still clung under the table leg, faintly singed. Someone had wiped the surface; the lemon polish only made the memory of smoke cleaner.

She moved inside. The Singer's steel throat gleamed. A chalk wheel lay on its side like a spent coin. The vent above the table gave a soft exhalation she refused to call a sigh. She reached for the little wooden elephant and turned it towards the window out of instinct, an animal wanting weather. The elephant rocked, unsure, then faced the dark glass as if choosing.

\*\*\*

"You moved them again."

Samantha's voice arrived without footfall, the way important weather arrives. She stood in the doorway, grey jumper, bare face, hair perfectly domestic. The scent was lemon at first, then something warmer that Sarah could not name.

"I hate them watching me," Sarah said, not turning.

"They watch over you," Samantha said. "There's a difference."

Sarah laughed and it wasn't nice. "Like a guard. Not like a god."

Samantha stepped in, closing the door with a civil sound. She didn't block the way out; she didn't have to. Doors, with her, learnt to behave. She set her palm on the Singer, an owner checking a loyal dog's temperature. "You shouldn't be down here alone," she said, soft as cotton. "Not now."

"Because you've laid out props upstairs and you don't want me spoiling the arrangement?" Sarah turned. The room caught the new angle of her face and made it bolder than she felt. "Don't dress me for a crib I haven't asked for."

Samantha's smile stayed. "The crib asked for you."

***

"Then the crib can wait."

They held each other's eyes. Thread spools made quiet stacks of colour at their elbows, like arguments too shy to speak. A pair of shears sat open on the table, blades parted as if mid-breath. Sarah slid them shut with one finger. The click sounded like an answer she wanted to keep.

Samantha glanced at the shears and then past them to the wall where Sonia had taped a papery frame of pattern pieces at eye level.

"We can do this gently," Samantha said. "Or we can do it at the speed the house requires. I prefer gentle."

"You prefer control."

"You pretend they're different."

Sarah took a breath she hoped looked like a yawn. "You set the nursery tableau to make me compliant."

"To make you ready."

"You don't get to curate my readiness."

"Someone has to," Samantha said, and there it was—her theology of maintenance. "You won't pick your moments. You choose chaos at every turn. You call it freedom and then complain when it costs."

"What will it cost?" Sarah asked. "Name it. Say out loud what you think I've done."

Samantha's eyes flicked, just once, to Sarah's stomach. The smallest of movements; the largest of accusations. "You know what it will cost," she said. "Don't make me say it."

The Singer's foot pedal sat under the table like a secret. Sarah nudged it with the side of her shoe, feeling rubber give under leather. Her anger felt like a new limb, heavy and dumb until she taught it tricks. "You think you can tidy this the way you tidy everything," she said. "As if my body were the whiteboard and you just needed a stronger cloth."

Samantha tilted her head, patience lacquered on. "Don't do this in metaphors, Sarah. You're not built for metaphor. You're built for ignition."

"Then stop setting things you don't plan to watch burn."

The room tightened. The vent ran a private breath. Somewhere upstairs a floorboard remembered how to creak and then forgot again.

Samantha reached for the shears. She did it slowly, the way you take a knife away from a child. "Let me hem your anger to size before you trip over it," she said, and the charm in the line was the worst of it.

Sarah's hand landed on the shears first. Her fingers closed around the grip, knuckles whitening. Samantha's fingers met hers. For a heartbeat they held the same steel. The Singer reflected a blade-shaped streak of light onto the ceiling like a shouted word.

"Don't," Sarah said.

"Give," Samantha said.

They pulled. Not hard—hard would have been honest. A thin tug, a seam-test. The scissors slid under Sarah's palm. Samantha shifted her stance—not aggression, only engineering—and the shears stayed where they were. Sarah let go first because the fury that wanted to rip the room in half startled her. She stepped back, knocked her hip against the table, and sent the chalk wheel skittering. It hit the floor with a clatter that made the house answer with a deeper one.

"Stop staging me," Sarah said. "Stop laying out bedtime stories on my bed."

"That wasn't a story," Samantha said. "It was a reminder."

"Of what?"

"Of origin. Of duty." Samantha placed the shears flat, blades pointing away, and wiped the table with her palm as if smoothing a wrinkle out of evening. "Of how we got here."

"I know how we got here," Sarah said. "I walked myself. You marched me when I didn't."

Samantha breathed, and the sound made the room smaller. "You want chaos to be a personality trait. It's not. It's a weapon you wave around and pretend isn't loaded."

Sarah reached for the wooden giraffe and turned it again to face the window. "Then step away. I'll wave it at the moon and let everyone sleep."

Samantha moved around the table so they were parallel, twin reflections in the Singer's dull chrome throat. "Tell me whose it is," she said gently, the old question raising its careful head. "There will be a plan if you let there be one."

Sarah held her breath so long her mouth dried. "There is a plan," she said. "It just doesn't belong to you."

Samantha's smile thinned. "So it belongs to a stranger."

"It belongs to me."

"Everything that belongs to you belongs to us."

"Whose rule book says so?" Sarah asked. "The one you hid behind the sash?"

Samantha's eyes blinked, a flash of surprise. The Singer caught it, kept it, gave nothing back. "Sonia told you."

"Sonia told no one," Sarah said, and in saying it she loved Sonia fiercely. "I can smell ash on ribbon, that's all."

They stood so close the lemon on Samantha's skin warred with the metallic tang of the machine. Sarah felt the itch behind her scar-that-wasn't, that phantom mark the city's bakery boy had named and un-named. The room felt like the edge of a map, paper wearing thin over sea monsters.

Samantha picked up the tape measure. "Lift your jumper," she said, voice nurse-clean. "Let me measure how much trouble you intend to cause."

"Put it down." Sarah took one step into Samantha's space and then another. They touched—shoulder, breath, bruise. "Don't touch me like a job."

"Then act like a person," Samantha said.

Something snapped—not audible, not fibre, but a small tendon of restraint. Sarah shoved her.

It was not a dramatic push. Hands to shoulders, a quick, shocked movement. Samantha staggered back into the shelves. A frame tumbled—thin wood, glass brittle with age, some heirloom someone had claimed as neutral décor. It fell face-first and the glass went with a sound that cut through the Singer's dignified quiet. A shard skidded, bit Sarah's ankle through the sock, and the pain arrived as a bright bead. Blood rose neat as punctuation.

The sight of it—her blood, here, now—made the room tilt. Samantha straightened with fury contained into a smile. "Look at you," she said, breath steady. "You can't even bleed without turning it into an argument."

"You staged a nursery," Sarah said, breathless. "You don't get to mock my blood."

Samantha stepped forwards and brushed her thumb under the bead, catching it the way you catch marmalade from a child's lip. The gesture was so intimate and so wrong that Sarah slapped her hand away. Their arms both struck the table; the spool tin rattled like a drum. The shears slid, kissed the Singer's plate, and sang a quick knife-song.

"What will you do?" Sarah whispered. "Label my veins?"

"Only if you keep misplacing them," Samantha said, and for the first time that night her patience had a crack in it.

In the corridor, something—someone—moved. Both women stilled, listening. The house did too. Then it resumed its quiet complicity. Sarah stepped around the broken frame to the window and yanked the sash up with a strength that surprised her. The cold came in like a witness; the curtain stirred; the wooden animals rocked on their hooves.

"You don't get to open and shut my air," she said.

*** 

Samantha followed and set the window down two inches, exact. "You'll make the baby cold."

Sarah swallowed, tongue salt with metal. "Say his name," she said, dangerous. "Say the word baby like you're not eating it to keep yourself fed."

Samantha's eyes flicked, once, to the Singer's treadle. "Step back," she said. "You're bleeding on the rug."

Sarah didn't. The bead swelled, broke, petalled into the fibre like a crimson instruction that declined to be wiped. She looked at the shears, the thread, the fracture in Samantha's voice, and felt the room decide to be a theatre.

She raised her chin. "Try to move me."

Samantha did.

Samantha lunged first. Not wildly—she never wasted movement—but with the precise push of someone who knew where a body bent and where it broke. Her shoulder caught Sarah square, forcing her back against the Singer. The machine shuddered, its iron foot kissing her hip.

"Stop performing," Samantha hissed, her breath lemon and heat.

Sarah shoved back harder, this time with both palms. Samantha's spine struck the shelf; thread spools cascaded, bright confetti bouncing across the floorboards. A tin of pins tipped and split. Silver needles skittered like insects fleeing light.

"You staged my bed!" Sarah's voice cracked. "You think you can choreograph me until I'm nothing but your script!"

Samantha laughed, sharp as snapped chalk. "You were nothing until I gave you lines!"

The Singer's shadow wavered on the wall as if it had grown larger, heavier. Sarah snatched a fallen spool and hurled it. It struck the pattern frame still hanging, and the brittle wood surrendered.

Glass rained down, fracturing into glitter that stuck to their hair and sleeves. A shard traced Samantha's forearm. Blood welled—bright, deliberate, obscene in its neatness.

***

Samantha stared at the bead forming. "Look," she said evenly, raising her arm as if offering evidence. "Even my blood keeps to order. Yours is chaos."

Sarah felt the sting at her ankle where her earlier cut had split wider. She lifted her sock cuff; crimson spread like a slow tide into the weave. "Then let chaos have its turn." She stepped forward, leaving a print on the rug.

Samantha's smile flickered, vanished. She pushed again, fingers gripping Sarah's shoulders. Sarah twisted, shoved back with a cry she hadn't meant to release. They circled the table, tangling, knocking tins and frames, bumping wood. Every contact made the house groan deeper, pipes clicking like an audience.

"Say it!" Sarah shouted. "Say you're afraid it isn't his!"

Samantha's hand flashed, slapping Sarah's face—not cruelly, not kindly, but decisively, like shutting a book. Sarah reeled. Rage blurred the sting into clarity. She caught Samantha by the wrist, twisted, and slammed her hand onto the Singer's steel plate. The machine gave a hollow clang.

Something shifted.

The treadle under the table depressed. Neither foot touched it, but the iron pedal sank, rose, sank again, a rhythm steady and self-propelled. The machine's wheel turned once, clicking its teeth. Thread spools rattled in sympathy.

Both sisters froze.

The Singer's needle arm dipped as though ready to pierce, then lifted. The pedal stopped. Silence thickened, embarrassed, like a room that had spoken out of turn.

Sarah's breath came ragged. "You saw it."

Samantha's jaw clenched. "The house is tired of your theatre."

"No," Sarah whispered. "It's tired of yours."

They stared at each other, chest to chest, ankle bleeding, arm bleeding, air charged. Between them, the Singer sat smug, its brief betrayal pulsing through the silence.

Samantha tore her hand free and backed to the shelf, shoulders rising and falling. She picked a shard of glass from her sleeve, flicked it to the floor. "You think that was proof? It was accident. A weight shift. Nothing more."

"It was a warning," Sarah said, voice hoarse. "And you heard it too."

Samantha wiped her bloody arm on a cloth, movements controlled, exact. "Warnings are for children. We are beyond warnings."

Sarah gripped the edge of the table until her knuckles whitened. "Not beyond consequences."

For a long moment neither moved. The vent above whispered, carrying a cold breath that threaded between them. The Singer gleamed as if pleased with itself. Somewhere upstairs, a stair squealed—a reminder that the house could lie now, too.

The stand-off quivered on the edge of another shove.

And then the door opened.

The door banged open against the wall. Sonia filled the frame, hair loose, cardigan slipping from one shoulder, eyes wide with a panic that came already knowing.

"What are you doing?" Her voice cracked the room like glass.

Samantha and Sarah both froze mid-breath, caught in the thrum that follows violence. The Singer still gleamed with its impossible stillness, as if it had never moved. Blood dotted the rug—two kinds, two shades.

Sarah lifted her chin. "Ask her," she said.

"Ask *her*," Samantha echoed, smoothing her bloody forearm with deliberate calm.

Sonia stepped inside, gaze darting from spool to shard to scarlet. She caught the smell—iron and lemon—and seemed to sag under it. "Enough," she whispered. "You'll kill each other."

Sarah lunged again, but Sonia moved fast, faster than either expected. She wedged herself between them, arms outstretched, back to Samantha, facing Sarah. "Stop!" she shouted, and her voice broke into something fierce, unfamiliar.

Sarah panted, eyes wild. Her ankle bled freely now, crimson petalling into the rug. She gripped the table edge as though it could keep her upright. "She set me up," she hissed.

"She set *all* of us up," Sonia said. Her voice shook but held. "That's the point. Don't give her the theatre."

Samantha let out a short laugh, quiet and cruel. "You finally grew a spine. Shame it arrived late."

Sonia spun on her. "Shut up."

***

The words shocked her own mouth. But once spoken, they stayed. "You don't get to wrap this in kindness anymore. You don't."

For a heartbeat Samantha looked almost impressed. Then the smile returned, tighter, as though she'd measured Sonia's rebellion and marked it down in her ledger.

Sonia turned back to Sarah. "Come away," she pleaded. "Please. You're bleeding."

"I'm fine." Sarah's voice was brittle.

"You're not." Sonia reached for her wrist, but Sarah jerked back. The movement rattled the table, and something skittered from beneath it. A slip of paper, yellowed and curled at the edges.

All three froze.

The paper rocked once on the floor, caught in the draught. Sonia bent first, trembling fingers lifting it. Dust clung to the back. She turned it over.

A photograph.

Three girls, maybe seven or eight, crammed shoulder to shoulder. Identical faces, grinning wide with missing teeth, hair tied with matching ribbons. The image was blurred at the edges, but the girls were clear, vivid with life.

Across the bottom, in thick childish scrawl, one word repeated three times: Sam.

Sonia's throat closed. She handed it to Sarah, who stared, wide-eyed. "This is..."

Samantha snatched it from Sarah's hand, too fast, too sharp. She clutched it to her chest, breathing hard, mask slipping for a fraction of a second. Her eyes blazed with something between pride and terror.

"You shouldn't have seen that," she whispered.

"It's the beginning," Sarah said, voice shaking. "Isn't it? The pact. The lie."

Sonia backed towards the wall, tears burning her eyes. "We were children," she murmured. "We thought we could... we thought if we acted the same, the world would keep us. We thought it was love."

Samantha's jaw clenched. She looked at Sonia with a fury so sharp it felt like grief. "Don't you dare rewrite history," she snapped. "We made a choice. We made it together. We swore."

Sarah shook her head, clutching her stomach. "You swore for me. You dragged me into it and called it family."

The Singer sat silent, pedal still. But the memory of its impossible movement hung over them like smoke. The photograph crinkled in Samantha's grip. Sonia covered her mouth, sobbing once, quiet and hopeless.

The three sisters stood in the ruined room: pins scattered, thread spools rolling, blood drying on rug and sleeve, glass sparkling like accusation. Between them, a picture of three grinning girls, all named Sam.

Kevin's voice called faintly from upstairs. "Are you all right?"

Samantha straightened, face smoothing into her public smile. She tucked the photo into her jumper pocket. "We're fine," she called back, sing-song.

Sarah's breath caught. Sonia's tears spilled.

The house sighed through the vent, long and low, as if pleased with the answer.

# Chapter Twenty-One
## The Lock Rule Breaks

Kevin didn't know when Rule One had become law, only that it had arrived early and never been debated. *No locked doors.* It had been sold as courtesy—airing rooms, airing tempers, never letting the house feel like a set of boxes. "We don't lock," Samantha had said once, in the tone she reserved for gravity and gas hobs. And they hadn't. Bedrooms open unless sleeping. Bathroom latch slid but never turned. Study door on the catch so voices could find you. The house moved through itself like weather.

Tonight he broke it.

He waited until the sisters' voices thinned and the landing went quiet. The hallway clock pushed past eleven. Pipes finished their last conversation and cooled. He took the manila folder from the wardrobe shelf—fat now, edges feathery with photocopies and printouts and the torn backs of envelopes—and held it for a second against his chest. A ridiculous gesture, like checking a pulse through cardboard. It felt heavy with a story he could not yet read.

The spare room had been a neutral place: a single bed with a quilt Sonia had mended into patience, a narrow wardrobe that held out-of-season coats, a low bookcase of paperbacks whose heroes were braver than their readers. He had never loved it, but he trusted it; it had no memories stuck to its skirting boards. He stepped inside and shut the door. The soft click sounded like defection.

The key lived on a ledge above the frame, dusty, unnecessary. He wiped it on his shirt, slid it into the brass, and turned. The lock engaged with a small, decisive clunk—modest, not the thud a film would give you, but the kind of sound a rule makes when it changes its mind. He felt it in his teeth.

He laid the folder in the wardrobe on the top shelf. He had lined the shelf with an old towel because the cardboard corner had started to fray and he could not bear the idea of losing a millimetre of evidence to splintering wood. He set the folder down, adjusted its angle until it sat square. He closed the wardrobe and stepped back. The room looked exactly the same. He stood there for a long moment, breathing, as if he had smuggled a live animal into a library and was waiting to see if it would bark.

The house answered with a small tick from the radiator and then withheld opinion.

On the bed he placed a glass of water no one would drink and a torch he hoped not to need. He sat on the mattress and felt the hollow where a visitor's hip had once pressed a shallow dip into the springs. The room smelt faintly of starch and lemon—the house's default breath these days—and beneath that the dusty vanilla of old paperbacks. He let his hands hang between his knees and looked at the door. Locked. A simple word with too many neighbours: safe, secret, selfish, sane.

Rule One had always done more work than it admitted. *No locked doors* sounded like intimacy until you tried to keep something of your own. Then it became surveillance with manners. He pictured Samantha's face if she found the key turned. The soft frown first, the disappointment. Then the explanation that would make him feel he'd missed an obvious route through the day. "You don't have to hide," she would say, and she would mean *you don't get to.*

He stood, crossed to the door, and turned the key back and forth three times to hear the mechanism learnt his name. Metal on metal, a small lesson. He kept his hand on the knob, felt the shiver through the spindle, and a memory arrived uninvited: the stair that squealed again last night after Sonia had mended it, the way the house had learnt to lie. If wood could pretend, so could locks. He turned the key a fourth time and pulled. The door held.

He clicked off the lamp, waited for his eyes to stop being dazzled by their own courage, and listened. The room settled around the new shape of its evening. A car moved past outside, tyres whispering wet. Somewhere in the walls a slow drip found a new path. On the dressing table—this had once been a real bedroom—stood a comb Sonia had left behind months ago, tortoiseshell cheap and faithful. Three teeth were chipped at the tips, like a smile that had chewed a difficult sentence. He picked it up, turned it over, put it down again with a sense of having touched a boundary and been forgiven.

He didn't intend to sleep in here. He wasn't that brave or that foolish. He intended only to make the new arrangement *true*—to teach the house the change—before he walked back down the hall to the bed where his body could pretend it still knew how to be married. He sat again, counted breaths to twelve the way the sonographer had done for Sarah, and let the anger that had been his engine all week ease into something less hot. He wasn't angry now. He was... aligned. A locked door was alignment. Either that or treason. He was willing to be both if truth required it.

At the threshold he paused and looked back the way people look back into rooms they've just told a story to, as if waiting for applause. The spare room had no opinion. He turned the key, pocketed it—strange weight—and stepped onto the landing.

***

The house flinched. Not loud. A change in pressure that made his eardrums tighten. He closed his eyes and felt along the air for malice. Nothing. Only the new knowledge moving through old lungs: a door, locked. He waited for a reprimand—*We don't*—and none came, which for this house felt like a threat.

He slept badly. Dreams filed past, untidy. In one he was twelve and couldn't remember the combination on a locker that wasn't his. In another he followed Samantha through the house while she wiped each doorknob with lemon oil and said *There,* after each, her voice both prayer and verdict. The worst dream was the simplest: a door handle turning, turning, turning—the quiet insistence of a polite intruder who had all night to be patient.

He woke to the exact sound.

Not the handle itself at first. The scratchy whisper of skin on paint. Then the small metal complaint of a knob tested and held. He sat up. The clock said 3:14 in figures that looked like instructions rather than time. He listened. The sound came again, not dramatic, not forced. A right hand trying, then a left, then the pause of a person tilting their head to hear the lock's opinion. A minute passed. Another. A third. The knob rattled, twice, no more than you might do in a hotel when you're not sure which door you booked. Then silence.

He found himself standing in the hallway in his bare feet before he remembered deciding to move. The carpet felt colder where the landing narrowed by the spare room. He pressed his palm to the wood. The door was cool, indifferent. He leaned his ear to it and waited. The house breathed: in, out, in, out. Far down in the plumbing a pipe gave the sound a throat gives when it refuses speech. Then, through the thin slot under the door, the vent in the skirting—or the mouth of the room—carried a single, clear word that made the hair rise on his arms.

"Mine."

***

He stepped back, heart loud enough to be heard. It hadn't been spoken at the keyhole. It hadn't belonged to a person's mouth. It had travelled the way heat travels, certain of its path. He wanted to say *Who?* and he didn't. He wasn't sure which answer would be worse: the house, Samantha, or the part of himself that had begun to sound like both.

He stood there until his knees hurt. The corridor clock decided it was morning by making four o'clock feel like a promise and five like an accusation. He went back to bed and lay beside a sleeping shape that smelt of lemon and sleep and said nothing in either scent. He kept his eyes open until they closed themselves.

When light came, thin and uncommitted, he rose with it. He didn't stop for tea or for the whiteboard or for the polite conversation mornings are meant to have. He went straight to the spare room and set the key into the brass with fingers that shook less than he expected. He turned it, felt the bolt withdraw, and opened the door to see what the night's visitor—and the house that now had a voice—had left for him.

The door gave easily to the key in the morning, as if it had not resisted all night. Kevin pushed it open slow, careful, prepared to find the folder gone or gutted. His eyes went first to the wardrobe. Closed. The towel he'd lined the top shelf with showed through the gap where wood never quite met wood. He crossed quickly, pulled the door wide, and reached for the folder.

It was there. Heavy. Exact. Every corner intact. He thumbed the edges like a priest handling relics. Nothing had been taken. Nothing added. He almost believed the night had been a dream conjured by his fear.

Then he saw the handle.

The brass knob bore three shallow scratches that had not been there before. Thin arcs, not deep enough to gouge, but enough to speak. Someone—or something—had worked at it in the night. Not violently, not with tools, but with persistence. Skin, nail, perhaps a ring dragged back and forth in patience. He bent close, breath fogging the metal, and traced the marks with his fingertip. They felt deliberate. They felt like the kind of writing a locked door invites.

Kevin straightened slowly. He turned, scanning the room. Bed untouched, water glass half-evaporated, comb still on the table where he'd left it. The ordinary remained, smug in its ordinariness. But in the air hung something else, a residue of listening.

He checked the floor by instinct. The fibres of the rug under the wardrobe bore no new weight, but dust had shifted by the skirting. He knelt, pressed his ear to the vent. A faint warmth still moved through it, the echo of the boiler's sighs. He held his breath and leaned closer.

The word came then, as clear as if whispered into his head, carried on the thin draught:

"Mine."

***

Kevin jerked back, struck his temple against the wardrobe edge. Pain flared white. He clutched the wood and breathed hard. The word had not been a person's—it lacked saliva, lacked human drag. It had the clarity of a bell struck once and left to ring in your bones.

He wanted to ask *Whose?* but his throat closed. His mind supplied the three possible answers anyway: the house, Samantha, or something in himself that had grown greedy. None was better than the others.

He forced himself upright. He needed evidence. He opened the folder, flipped through—receipts, notes, the handwriting test, the duplicated list. All there. Untouched. But on the top sheet—one he knew he had left clean—lay something new.

A comb.

Not the tortoiseshell Sonia had abandoned months ago, but another: identical in shape, teeth whole, as if conjured for comparison. He picked it up. The plastic was slick under his thumb. The teeth bore a faint smear of oil—citrus, sharp, familiar. Lemon.

He sniffed. The scent was unmistakable, the same lemon Samantha rubbed into wood, into whiteboards, into life. It clung to the comb as if brushed on by ritual.

Kevin held it above the folder. His pulse thudded, slow and monstrous. Whoever had entered—or whatever had claimed to—had not taken. It had *marked*. A signature, bold as handwriting, quiet as perfume. The scratches on the handle were footnotes; the comb was the thesis.

The room tilted. He pictured himself carrying the folder to Samantha, slamming it on the table, demanding explanation. But he saw her answer already: the smile, the calm, the kind of denial that felt truer than his proof. He imagined Sonia's tears, Sarah's fury. He imagined the house sighing in satisfaction.

He set the comb back on the papers. Closed the folder. Closed the wardrobe. Closed his mouth.

But the word in the vent did not close. It stayed, vibrating in the air around his ribs.

*Mine.*

He pocketed the key and left the room, locking it behind him, knowing Rule One was not only broken now—it had been rewritten. Not *no locked doors*. Not anymore. Now: *Even locked, they are listening.*

***

Kevin found Samantha in the kitchen, already dressed for the day though the clock said barely eight. She stood by the whiteboard, marker in hand, writing a list so straight it might have been printed. She didn't look up when he entered.

"You're up early," she said, as if it were a kindness.

"I couldn't sleep," he answered. His voice came out hoarse, as though the word from the vent had scratched his throat.

She capped the marker and turned. Fresh jumper, hair plaited tight, lemon scent hovering like armour. She smiled. "Another late night with your notes?"

He stepped closer, the key still warm in his pocket. "I locked the spare room."

Her smile faltered, then returned, tighter. "You know the rule."

"I broke it." He watched her eyes. "And someone tried the handle. Scratched it."

"Old metal scratches," she said lightly. "That's age, not trespass."

"The vent spoke."

She laughed once, soft, patronising. "Vents whistle. Houses creak. You've been listening too hard."

"It said mine." His voice cracked on the word.

That stopped her. For a moment her eyes flicked to the ceiling, then back to him. She set the marker down with deliberate care, aligning it to the board's edge. "And whose voice was it?"

"That's what I want to know," he said. "Yours? The house? Me losing my mind?" He swallowed. "Or all three."

Samantha crossed the room slowly, her expression a study in patience. She laid her hand on his arm. "You're not ready for the truth."

"I am," he said quickly, too quickly, because if he paused she'd steal the moment. "I am ready. I've been building it. Notes, receipts, handwriting tests, every inconsistency. I know I'm close."

Her smile thinned, almost sad. "Close to what, Kevin? Madness? You've always liked puzzles, but not every knot was meant for you."

He pulled his arm free. "Don't talk to me like I'm a child. I've seen enough to know you're hiding something."

"Of course I'm hiding something," she said, and for the first time her tone sharpened. "I've been hiding *us*. For years. Keeping us safe, keeping you safe, keeping everything balanced. You think you can survive the truth?"

"Yes." He forced the word out steady, though his heart thumped like a fist.

Samantha's eyes searched his face, weighing him as if he were fabric she might cut. She nodded once. "Then survive it."

It wasn't a threat. It wasn't reassurance. It was a condition.

The house gave a single, sharp click from the radiator, as if marking the end of a sentence.

Kevin stood in the lemon-scented air, folder locked behind him, comb burning in his memory, the word *mine* echoing through the vents. He didn't know if he was about to learn the truth—or be devoured by it.

# Chapter Twenty-Two
## The Father Question

S arah chose the café because it was ordinary. Ordinary was what she needed: a small room with steamed windows, a bell that rang on the door without menace, a counter that smelt of burnt milk and cinnamon. She arrived early and chose a table by the window, where the glass misted faster than the barista could wipe it clear. Outside, the high street made its winter noises: tyres hissing on damp tarmac, a woman laughing into her phone, a delivery driver swearing at a pallet that hadn't been told what to do. Ordinary. She could be anyone here. She could be just a woman waiting to see a man about nothing in particular.

He messaged running late at twelve past the hour. At twenty past: two mins. At twenty-two past the bell rang and the air stirred and he walked in—taller than memory, or perhaps carrying height more carefully. He looked the way men look when they've slept badly but refuse to admit it, clean-shaven to make up for the eyes. He saw her and the waiting left his shoulders.

\*\*\*

"Sarah."

"Hi, Reuben." She tried the name on her tongue and decided it fit the day. Not the night she was thinking of—no name had been allowed there—but the day. "Want a drink?"

He glanced at the blackboard, economic with attention. "Tea. Strong." He managed a half-smile. "I know. Not very London."

"I'm not either," she said, and felt the lie and the truth sit down together in her chair.

They drank the first five minutes. He had always been good at silence that didn't accuse. They watched a man outside drop a bag of bread and pretend he hadn't. They watched a mother unfold her pushchair with a curse that made the barista grin into his sleeve. They watched the rain decide between needle and mist. Finally, Reuben rubbed his palms together like a man making fire of nerves.

"You said it was important."

"It is." She looked at his hands instead of his face. Long-fingered, clever. He'd held her differently to Kevin—less certainty, more discovery. She took a breath and set the words out like cutlery. "I need to ask you about a night."

He didn't look away. "All right."

"Mid-March," she said. "Second week."

His eyebrows twitched towards each other. "That's... specific."

"I've had a lot of practice at being vague." The smile didn't go anywhere near her eyes. "Not today."

He nodded slowly. "The bar on Hammersmith Road."

"Yes."

"The radiator that whined." He smiled with the relief of memory aligning. "The window that wouldn't open."

"Yes." Her mouth went dry. The radiator's whine unfurled in her head like a wire. "You were there."

"I was there in February," he said, gently, as if correcting a child's pronunciation. "End of. Twenty-fourth. I remember because the home side lost and the bartender turned the volume up to hurt everyone equally. I was back up north most of March. My dad had a... well." He shrugged the way men shrug when the facts are heavy and private. "I can show you the train tickets if you like."

Sarah's hand found the edge of the table. The wood was sticky. She didn't look down. "It wasn't February."

"It felt cold enough for February," he offered, still kind.

"It was March," she said, and the glass turned the word back into her face. She kept her voice level. "There was a mural outside the Italian place. A fox drawn like a cat."

"That mural's been there ages."

"Maybe," she said, softer now. "But you weren't."

He reached for his phone. "I wasn't trying to... I'm not—" He stopped, closed his palm over the battered case. "You're asking if—"

"Yes."

"And you want me to say—"

"I don't know what I want you to say." She thought of the scan photo burning in her bag like contraband, the sonographer's neat 12+1 in the corner, the bus mirror splitting her face in two. "I just want the arithmetic to behave."

He watched her, measuring kindness against truth. "We were February," he said at last. "We were very much February." He let humour in as a bandage: "And you were... you were extraordinary." He paused, choosing from the things men shouldn't say and saying the best anyway. "But I wasn't here in March. I'd swear on... I don't know. I'd swear on the trains. If I could swear on the cold seats, I would."

She smelt lemon for a second and shut her eyes. Memory was a vandal. "All right."

"I'm sorry."

"Don't be." She swallowed. "I wanted you to be a solution. That's unfair."

He sat back and played honestly with the coaster. "Do you want me to lie?"

She opened her eyes. "No."

"Do you want me to come with you anyway and stand up in someone's kitchen and make a shape of a lie so big it casts a believable shadow?"

She almost laughed. "I don't want you anywhere near my kitchen."

"That bad?"

"It's a place where truth becomes policy." She rubbed her thumb against the table's ridge, wanting the pain of a splinter. "It was good, though. February."

"It was very good," he said, and they both allowed themselves two seconds of softness to honour that. Then he straightened, practical again. "Do you have someone you can...?"

She thought of Sonia biting her lip until it bled rather than speak out of turn. She thought of Samantha polishing reality like cutlery. She thought of Kevin in a hallway holding a door handle as if apology were a tool. "Yes," she said, because she wasn't going to scare a former good thing with the science of her current bad one. "I have many someone's."

Reuben grimaced sympathetically. "Too many someone's, from the sound of it."

She decided to be kind to him. He had given her February, and February had been a door that opened in a locked house. "You were a good someone," she said. "Thank you for telling me a truth I didn't want."

He nodded. "Are you safe?"

"No."

"Are you going to be?"

"Eventually." She held his gaze until she believed her own answer. "I'm going to make it so."

He finished his tea. "If you need me to say we were March, I won't. If you need me to say we were *we*, I will."

"Fair bargain," she said, surprised by gratitude. "Keep it."

He stood and she did too and for a second it seemed they might hug, but they didn't. The bell rang for someone else and the sky outside brightened by a shade that meant nothing really. He left her with his hands deep in his coat pockets, shoulders braced for weather.

***

She sat until the cup was cold enough to accuse. February had turned to evidence and then politely stepped aside. She took out the scan photo and laid it flat on the table, running her finger over the grey shape as if it had edges she could learn. The sonographer's numbers had not shifted while she talked. Twelve weeks. Mid-March. She had wanted an alibi and had collected one that collapsed on examination. That, at least, felt true to form.

On the way home the city displayed itself with hand-waving honesty: a bus making the wrong kind of hiss, a cyclist swearing at a sleek car that had confused hazard lights with permission, a fox trotting past a pile of black bags as if late for a meeting. She walked through it all with her scarf tight and her hands in her pockets like someone carrying smuggled hope. Outside the charity shop where the pram still stood with its crocheted blanket folded like church, she paused to look at the window. Glass made the world manageable. It turned air into frame.

Her reflection offered itself up as usual: pale face, hair pulled back, jumper trying and failing to look like a decision. Then, with the slow, merciless adjustment of a lens choosing a subject, the reflection changed. She wasn't empty-handed any more. She was cradling a baby. Not a trick of angle—an addition. A weight she could see in the way her arms bent. She could make out the curve of a cheek, the suggestion of a hat. The reflection Sarah held the reflection child with a competence she did not currently own.

She did not move. She waited for the world to correct. A bus passed and smudged the glass with red; the baby remained. Wind pushed a smear of rain across the pane; the baby remained. Her breath fogged the view and she wiped it away with the edge of her sleeve; the baby remained. She lowered her eyes and saw that her real arms were empty and shaking.

"Fine," she said out loud, to the shopfront or the house or the part of her that refused to keep secrets. "Fine. I see you."

The baby remained half a heartbeat longer, then the reflection returned her hands to her pockets as if embarrassed to have told the truth. She stood very still until the pavement remembered how to be pavement and the window remembered its job.

She walked home the long way, because short streets made her feel observed. The house showed its face from halfway down the road—curtains straight, bricks pretending modesty, the front step recently scoured. Sarah climbed the gate, because the gate liked to stick, and walked up the path with the slow tread of someone arriving at a verdict.

Inside, lemon smelt like a choreography. The whiteboard gleamed, new writing crisp in a blue she associated with Samantha's best manners. The message was neat enough to be a rule, polite enough to be a threat.

KEEP THE PACT OR LOSE THE HOUSE.

She stared. The handwriting carried that slight lean towards virtue that had always made her skin itch. Beneath it, smaller, in brackets: (no exceptions).

Sarah put her bag on the table with a thud. She didn't take off her coat. She didn't go upstairs to discover what else had been staged. She walked to the drawer, took out a black marker, uncapped it with her teeth, and wrote in a line so straight it surprised her:

THEN I'LL LOSE THE HOUSE.

The marker squeaked. The sound made her feel twelve years old and taller than she'd ever been. She capped it and set it down with a click that belonged to a stranger who refused to remain strange.

The house breathed. Not a sigh this time. A long intake, as if preparing to hold its breath. The kitchen bulb flickered once, twice, three times, then steadied. The vent above the oven exhaled a note that was not quite a word and not quite not.

Behind her, a floorboard in the hall remembered how to complain. She turned, half expecting Samantha with a cloth and a smile to wipe her defiance into something more presentable. No one stood there. Sonia's door remained shut. Kevin's footsteps did not arrive. It was just her and the board and the message on the wall that had already begun to ghost under the gloss.

She took a step back and looked at the pair of sentences: the house's and her own. She imagined one devouring the other overnight and leaving only a faint underline, a suggestion that someone had tried to speak and then agreed not to. She uncapped the pen again and drew a box around her words. Not tidy—this was not a tidy day—but definite. She shaded the corners until they almost whistled.

The vent above the cooker breathed again, a light thread that traced her neck and made her hair move. She thought she heard a word buried in the breath—mine—and for once didn't care who had said it.

"Not any more," she told the metal, the walls, the pact that had taken to signing its emails in her kitchen.

She went to the sink, filled a glass, and drank water that smelt faintly of the pipes' old sadness. She felt the baby's presence stiffen under her ribs as if the child had tensed for a fall; she touched her stomach through the coat and said, "We'll be fine," not caring whether the house took it as promise or provocation.

On the way out of the kitchen she paused and added one more line to the whiteboard, smaller, a private note to the future version of herself who might wake to find her certainty smudged:

I MEANT IT.

***

Then she put the cap on firmly, placed the pen parallel to the frame because petty rebellions worked best when the rest of the lines held, and walked upstairs to collect the things you carry when you're prepared to leave a house you once mistook for a home: a coat with deep pockets, a bag that didn't squeak when it protested weight, a memory of a reflection that had told her the truth on a wet pane of glass.

At the landing she stopped, because the second stair from the bottom squealed again—a bright sound, delighted with its own treachery. She looked down and smiled in a way that showed all her teeth and none of her forgiveness.

"I'm not negotiating with wood," she said, and the house, in its baffled good manners, let her pass.

Outside, the light had decided to be afternoon. The pavement offered itself like a destination. Behind her, in a kitchen that had become a court, two sentences faced one another in blue and black: KEEP THE

PACT OR LOSE THE HOUSE and THEN I'LL LOSE THE HOUSE. The first had history. The second had heat.

Up the street, the charity shop rearranged its window: pram moved, blanket refolded, a space where a reflection had stood. Sarah walked towards it with an acceleration she trusted. The question of fatherhood had not answered itself. The arithmetic could continue to fight all it liked. The decision, at last, was not a sum. It was a sentence, written in a hand she recognised as her own.

The house let out a long, thin exhale behind her, like someone watching you leave and promising to change. She didn't look back.

# Chapter Twenty-Three
## Sonia Breaks

Sonia waited until the house sighed itself into silence. The sewing room slept, the radiators whispered their small metal lullabies, the landing clock gave its steady tick. She carried a torch the size of a finger, nothing that would rouse suspicion if the wrong eyes caught a glimmer. Her hands were clammy; she wiped them on her skirt twice before she knelt by the wardrobe in her room.

The false back was hers. She had cut and hinged it years ago with a precision she thought of as loyalty. A space for things no one must see, for words that might dissolve the pact if they were read at the wrong time. She pressed her palm against the panel. It gave slightly under pressure, wood against wood, as if the house itself debated whether to grant permission. Then, with a faint scrape, the latch clicked, and the back swung in.

Inside lay the book.

It wasn't much to look at: a battered hardback ledger, its cloth frayed to threads, corners scuffed down to board. She had started it when they were fifteen, copying rules in neat script, numbering them, refining them. As the years passed, the book absorbed more: drawings, notes, torn bits of receipts, even a feather she'd once thought meant something. Samantha had always scoffed at keepsakes. Sarah had mocked it as Sonia's "ghost diary." But Sonia had kept it because keeping was her job.

She lifted the book out with reverence, settling it on the bedspread. The ledger felt heavier than its pages. She opened to the middle, where new entries had begun to crowd the margins. Taped there were photos—quick snaps with her phone—capturing the whiteboard on mornings before Samantha wiped it into her version of the day. Words ghosted through ink: NO RULES ABOUT MY BODY, later overwritten, later softened into (safely). The message Sarah had left in black marker still glowed through faint smudges. Sonia had photographed them all.

She pressed a fresh print into the book now, gluing it with the edge of a Pritt Stick kept for this ritual. The ink was sharp, the letters clean:

KEEP THE PACT OR LOSE THE HOUSE.

and beneath in stubborn black,

THEN I'LL LOSE THE HOUSE.

She whispered as she smoothed it flat: "So it will be remembered."

Her throat tightened. The ledger was no longer history; it was indictment. And she was its custodian.

For years, her role had been quiet maintenance, smoothing quarrels, tidying the pact until it looked almost kind. But something had shifted. The Singer had breathed. The stair had lied. The vents had spoken. And Sarah had written back. Sonia's hands shook as she closed the book and pressed it to her chest. *If I don't speak, someone will die.* The rule she had written only days ago gnawed at her.

She slid the book back into the closet, tucked behind the panel, but this time she left the panel ajar. A symbolic act: she would not hide from herself. She closed the wardrobe doors, sat on the bed, and felt the tremor in her fingers settle into resolve.

Tonight she would speak.

***

The kitchen clock said 2:17 when Sonia padded down in socks, the floor cool beneath her. The house at night smelt of lemon over dust, a marriage of pretence and neglect. She took paper from the drawer—the kind Samantha used for shopping lists—and a biro that stuttered before it gave in.

She wrote slowly, her hand careful, the letters slanting forward like they wanted to run ahead:

Kevin—
Meet me at the river. I'll tell you everything.
S.

Her heart hammered. She read it three times, folded it once, twice, slipped it into an envelope. On the front she wrote his name in block capitals so he couldn't mistake it.

For a long moment she stood by the whiteboard, staring at the faint shadows of words that refused to vanish completely. Rules bled through even when scrubbed. She thought of Samantha standing here with her marker, rewriting, correcting, instructing. She thought of Sarah's furious black scrawl refusing to fade. She thought of Kevin's folder—his secret mirror of her ledger. They were all writing the same story in different alphabets.

She laid the envelope on the kitchen table where Kevin would see it at breakfast, weighed down with a salt cellar so it couldn't drift or be lost. She touched it once with her fingertips, as if blessing it.

The floorboard by the door knocked once. She froze.

Then again.

Then a third time.

A pattern, deliberate. Three knocks, slow, steady, patient.

Her mouth dried. She whispered, "Who?" but the house gave no answer.

***

Only the hush of the vent above the cooker, carrying a breath that smelt faintly metallic.

She turned out the light and left the kitchen, pulse loud, praying she had been braver than foolish.

Morning arrived too bright, slicing through curtains she hadn't drawn tight. Sonia dressed quickly, fingers clumsy on buttons. She went down early, hoping to catch Kevin before Samantha's morning choreography began.

The table was clear.

Her heart stuttered. The salt cellar sat where she had left it, but the envelope was gone.

She checked the floor, the counter, under the fruit bowl. Nowhere. She straightened, breath ragged.

Kevin walked in a moment later, folder under his arm, tie already knotted. He gave her a tired smile. "Morning."

"Morning," she said, throat raw. She waited. Waited for him to mention the note. To ask. To look at her with new eyes.

He poured tea, buttered toast, sat down, folder beside him. No envelope. No question. No sign.

"Sleep?" he asked, as though life were still small talk.

"A little," she whispered.

Then Samantha entered, lemon trailing her like perfume, hair smoothed, jumper folded at the cuffs. She smiled at them both. "What a calm morning," she said, and reached for the salt cellar to sprinkle her egg.

The envelope peeked from under her sleeve as she lifted the shaker. Just a corner, just enough. Sonia's breath caught.

Samantha's smile didn't falter. She set the cellar down, sat opposite Kevin, and poured herself tea as if her hands were spotless. The envelope was gone again.

Sonia's chest hollowed. She looked at Kevin, willing him to notice something—anything. He unfolded his folder instead, pulling out a receipt, lips moving as he scanned numbers. Samantha buttered her toast with precise strokes.

Sonia's pulse roared. She had left a message that might have changed everything. Now it belonged to Samantha.

Too late—for the note, not for her.

She pressed her nails into her palms until pain steadied her. She wanted to scream, to knock over the tea, to force the truth out of the air itself. Instead, she sat, folded her hands, and watched Samantha sip lemon tea with perfect composure.

The note was gone. The pact remained. And Sonia realised she had broken—not Samantha, not Sarah, not Kevin. Herself.

Sonia left the table on legs that didn't entirely belong to her. She rinsed her mug under the tap, wiped the rim as if a clean circle could be a spell, and set it upside down on the rack. Samantha and Kevin were talking about bins—bins, of all things—Samantha's voice a soft metronome, Kevin nodding with the politeness of a man learning a foreign alphabet. The corner of the envelope flashed again under Samantha's cuff when she reached for the tea towel. Then it vanished.

"I'm popping out," Sonia said, too brightly.

"Bread?" Samantha asked, as if Sonia were announcing a mission.

"Air," Sonia said.

The hall smelt of wool and old weather. Sonia took her coat, her scarf, no bag. Outside, the day had chosen a grey that wasn't sulking, just diligent. She walked fast past the pram in the charity shop window (blanket refolded, as if truth practised tidiness), past the bakery where the boy had once named scars, past the chemist with its shutters remembering blue. The river met her with that cynical kindness water has in cities—it would hold your secrets and kill you with equal competence, depending on the angle you asked.

She stood at the rail where the paint had rubbed off to iron. Barges shouldered along, heavy-hipped, pretending not to notice the under bridge wind. A gull hung motionless for three seconds and then remembered physics. Sonia folded her hands and waited.

Kevin would come, she told herself. Even without the note, he would come because the day had learnt a shape and the shape included courage. Ten minutes. Fifteen. Twenty. The bridge clock's minute hand jumped with shocking authority and then apologised by pretending not to have moved.

She took out her phone and typed Where are you? and deleted it. If Samantha had the note, Samantha had the day. Sonia turned her face into the river gust until her eyes watered, and when she blinked the water away she saw a child on a scooter skimming the promenade, one foot wild with confidence. A woman jogging behind him smiled like she'd just remembered her body was built for moving forward.

Sonia stayed another ten minutes. The cold got inside her gloves and set up housekeeping in the bones of her fingers. Finally she put both hands on the rail and said, quietly, "I tried." The river answered the way rivers do: by continuing.

She walked back the long way, because short ways are for people who aren't thinking. A fox trotted along a wall as if it owned the brick. She felt a pang of envy at how thoroughly it belonged to itself.

At the gate the wood performed, sticking then obeying. In the hall she paused, listening. The house made its careful noises, none of them confessional. From the kitchen came the occasional punctuation of a teaspoon chiming against porcelain. Sonia wiped her palms on her pockets and stepped in.

Samantha looked up with summer in her smile. "Good air?"

"Bracing," Sonia said. Her gaze dropped, as if of its own accord, to the bin. The swing lid was down. She pressed the pedal and the lid rose with the prim sigh of a well-brought-up secret. Inside: onion skins, a crumpled kitchen towel, the plastic band from a broccoli stem, and—tucked down the side as if hiding from daylight—the torn corner of an envelope. White, good paper. The rip was clean. A scent rose from the bin that had nothing to do with broccoli: lemon. Her note had been opened with a cloth that had been kindly, violently polished.

She let the lid close. When she looked up, Samantha was watching her with that exact patience she used on blind hems and difficult people.

"Everything all right?" Samantha asked gently.

"Yes," Sonia said, voice reasonable, because rage would be a confession. "Everything is exactly all right."

Kevin came in then with his folder under his arm like a child he had promised not to drop. "Need anything from town?" he asked, generous, doomed.

Sonia shook her head. If she spoke, she would say *Meet me at the river* and watch the words fall dead at Samantha's feet.

She went upstairs before her face could betray her, closed her bedroom door softly—still not locking; even now the rule reached up and cupped her hand as it fell. She leaned against the wood until the grain printed her shoulder blades and waited for the first of the three knocks that had answered her note in the night. They came on cue: one, two, three, patient, proprietorial.

"Please," she whispered to the floor. "Not now."

Silence, obedient and superior. The house, she thought, had decided to be a person.

She crossed to the wardrobe, pressed the panel, and took out the ledger. It had weight like grief pretending to be paper. She laid it open and slotted a new item into the chronology: a small square cut from fresh notepaper, her own hand copying the lines she had written on the kitchen board last night before courage sank: Tell the truth when silence harms. If I don't speak, someone will die. Beneath it she added the morning's arithmetic: I spoke. She intercepted.

Her hands moved without her. She took another photo of the whiteboard—Samantha had already neatened Sarah's black box around THEN I'LL LOSE THE HOUSE into a shape that looked like "consideration." Sonia printed and glued it in, noting the time. She wrote a caption in her neat schoolgirl script: House: edits dissent into good manners. It felt like blasphemy to write, which only made it truer.

Her phone buzzed. A message from an unknown number: Rotation's slipping. Clean the edges. She stared until the words blurred, then turned the phone face-down as if that could unwrite a command.

Her thumb hovered over Kevin's name again. She typed Samantha took my note and watched the letters gather. She imagined the app obligingly turning her courage into a little blue speech bubble that would float across the room to a man who wanted to be brave but had to look at his own fear every time he shaved. She deleted the message, then typed River at six. Please and deleted that too. She settled for a coward's compromise: Are you in later? Send. Three dots. Nothing.

She shut the ledger and slid it into the closet, left the panel open a finger's width—another tiny treason. She went to the landing and listened. The house breathed like an animal considering a bite.

Downstairs, she heard a soft clatter: post through the slot. She went to collect it and found, on the mat, a single flyer for a river clean-up day—JOIN US in cheerful blue, a cartoon gull smiling at a bag of rubbish. The coincidence made her bark a laugh that sounded like crying. She took it to the kitchen, dropped it on the table.

Samantha glanced at it. "Community spirit," she said. "We should volunteer."

"We already do," Sonia said, unable to help herself. "We clean up what you make."

Samantha's eyes flicked up, sharp, and then gentled. "Careful," she said softly. "You're tired."

"Furious," Sonia corrected, and the honesty shocked them both.

Kevin came in again, searching for his keys with the panicked dignity men give to losing small things. Sonia watched his hand hover above the fruit bowl, the drawer, the folded tea towel. She willed him to notice the bin, the lemon, the torn corner.

He didn't.

"Found them," he said, relief a little boyish, holding the keys up like a medal. He kissed Samantha's cheek, missed Sonia's shoulder by an inch and apologised to the air. "Back by five."

"Good," Samantha said, and the word closed the room like a lid.

When the door shut, Sonia felt the day tilt. The house took the weight without complaint. She walked to the whiteboard and stood in front of the twin sentences—KEEP THE PACT OR LOSE THE HOUSE and THEN I'LL LOSE THE HOUSE—and tried to imagine the version of herself that would rub her own message away because neatness felt like love. She didn't move. She didn't blink. Three slow knocks sounded from the floorboard by the door, precise as a metronome. She lifted her chin and stared at the ceiling as if the knocks had a face.

"I hear you," she said. "I'm not obeying."

She went back upstairs, sat on the bed, and opened the notebook to a fresh page. The words arrived without hand-wringing, clean and legible:

New rule: If the truth cannot travel by paper, it will travel by breath. Meet him in person. No notes. No phones.

She underlined breath twice. She closed the book and tucked it under the pillow, the old place for old promises. As her head lowered, something crinkled—the tiniest sound. She reached beneath the case and drew out a scrap. Paper. A ghost of an envelope corner, lemon faint on the fibres.

Samantha had been here too.

Sonia's throat tightened, but the fear had a new edge now; it could cut the other way. She stood, smoothed the coverlet, and laid her palm flat on the wardrobe door. "I'm going now," she told the room, the house, the air. "You can knock. You can lie. You can breathe words into vents. I'm going."

Three knocks answered, patient as ever.

"Good," Sonia said. "Practice listening." "She'd learnt to. "

She put on her coat, took the stairs lightly—avoiding the one that squealed like a snitch—and let herself out into a daylight that had decided to be almost kind. At the gate she glanced back just once, not for nostalgia but to memorise the sight of a house that believed itself to be a person.

The letterbox lifted a fraction and settled, as if the door had tried to speak with its mouth full.

***

"Later," Sonia told it, and turned towards the river without leaving anything behind that mattered except fear.

# Chapter Twenty-Four
## Kevin at the River

Kevin didn't know why he went to the river that evening. He hadn't been asked. Not aloud, not on paper, not even in a message he could hold up to the light. But something tugged him—stronger than curiosity, quieter than reason. He told himself it was exercise, that a walk by the water cleared a mind clogged with lists and whispers. He told himself he was stretching his legs after a day sat at his desk turning numbers into patterns and then doubting them. But he knew better: it was hunger.

He carried the folder under his coat like contraband. He hated himself for it—what sort of man took evidence to a stroll? But leaving it behind felt worse. He had begun to imagine it whispering in his absence, aligning itself with the house, offering up its receipts like prayers.

The air down by the water smelt of rain and riverweed. Dusk settled in strips—gold at the horizon, grey climbing fast from the ground. He walked the path past the old crane and the new graffiti, past benches that had forgotten the weight of ordinary couples. A gull screeched once overhead, derisive, then wheeled away.

He reached the railing where paint had peeled to bare iron. His hand touched it automatically, like a pilgrim's touchstone. Cold. Honest. The river below moved like a muscle flexing.

A woman with a pram passed, humming to her child. The tune snagged in Kevin's ear. A lullaby, though he couldn't name it. He watched them vanish under the bridge, shadows elongating.

He set the folder on the railing for a moment, fingers still clamped to the edge. The papers inside seemed to vibrate with the breeze, eager to take flight. He pressed them down and exhaled. "What am I supposed to do with you?" he muttered.

The river gave no answer. But in the metal under his hand, three faint vibrations pulsed—knock, knock, knock. As if the floorboards had followed him.

Kevin looked up sharply. No one was near enough to have tapped. The knocks had come from inside the iron itself, or through his bones. He shoved the folder back under his coat, sudden sweat slicking his palms.

He had the sharp sensation of being late. Not late for a meeting—late for his own understanding, as though an appointment had been booked without his knowledge and now he was failing to attend.

He waited until the lamps along the path flickered to life, orange halos smeared by drizzle. Still no one came. But he stayed, because something in him whispered that absence was also a message.

Kevin stayed where the railing turned slick with condensation. A barge pushed upriver, engines working like tired lungs, and the wake licked at the embankment with the persistence of something trying to erode stone. He adjusted his grip on the folder beneath his coat, aware of how absurd he must look—a man hugging paperwork while the city went about its Friday dusk.

A movement caught his eye.

Downstream, near the bench with peeling green paint, a figure stood watching the water. Small, hair loose, coat hanging open in a way that suggested hurry. His chest clenched. Sonia. It had to be. The shape of her shoulders—sloped with worry, rounded by kindness—was unmistakable.

He started towards her, steps quick, shoes clicking against the damp pavement. But when he reached the bench, the figure turned and it wasn't Sonia at all.

The woman was younger, her face sharp with unfamiliarity, scarf patterned in bold red and black. She glanced at him without recognition, annoyed to be mistaken for someone else, then walked off briskly, boots hard against the stone. Kevin stood watching her vanish into a side street, the phantom of Sonia still clinging to his sight.

"Bloody hell," he muttered, dragging a hand across his face. The adrenaline left him shaky. For a second he had believed the pact was breaking, that Sonia was stepping out of shadows to hand him the truth. Instead he was left clutching air.

He turned back to the river. A man had taken her place on the bench—appeared almost out of nowhere. Stocky build, dark coat, cap pulled low. Kevin hadn't seen him arrive. He sat slouched, hands in pockets, but his head was tilted in Kevin's direction. Watching.

Kevin forced himself to stay still. The folder weighed heavy under his arm. His breath clouded.

The man raised a hand in greeting. Casual, as if they were acquaintances.

Kevin hesitated, then lifted his own hand half an inch. The man's smile was small, knowing, a smile that said *I know where you've been, I know where you're going*. Then he stood, sauntered off, leaving only the smell of tobacco and the scrape of boots on damp stone.

Kevin's stomach twisted. The greeting had been too familiar. The smile too confident. Yet he could swear he had never seen the man before.

He looked again at the bench. On the seat, where the man had been, lay a folded newspaper. He approached, cautious, and picked it up. The paper was damp, but legible. The front-page date was a week old.

Tucked inside was nothing—no note, no clue. Just newsprint smudged with rain.

Still, the act of leaving it felt deliberate. A placeholder. An almost-message.

Kevin dropped it back on the bench, suddenly unwilling to take home anything the river had chosen to give him.

The lamps brightened overhead. The path filled with couples, joggers, teenagers with skateboards. The ordinariness of them made him dizzy. They had no idea a house could breathe, that rules could be commandments, that three women could share one name and one man until the seams of reality gave way. They were safe in their own stories. He was a ghost in theirs.

Sonia hadn't come. Or maybe she had tried, and someone had stopped her. He felt it like a bruise beneath his ribs: the sense of a conversation that should have happened and hadn't, a truth aborted.

The folder pressed against him like an impatient child. He thought of the scratches on the spare room handle, the comb slick with lemon, the vent's whispered *mine*. He thought of the photo Sarah had shown him—her defiance in black marker on the board. He thought of Sonia's glance the other night in the neighbour's kitchen, the plea she had hidden inside the word *soon*.

None of it added up. Or maybe it added up too cleanly, and the sum was something he couldn't name without shattering.

Kevin turned from the water. He felt watched as he walked back along the embankment, but when he glanced over his shoulder the benches were empty, the lamps steady, the river content to keep moving without him.

By the time he reached the corner where the estate agents always left their lights on, his decision was set. He would ask Sonia outright. Not tomorrow, not "soon." Tonight. Even if Samantha was in the room.

Even if the house answered. He would drag the truth into daylight by force.

He tightened his grip on the folder, nearly dropped it when the wind shoved hard at his back. The gust carried a sound that made him stumble.

Three knocks. Clear, deliberate, metallic. Not from the houses, not from the bridge. From the iron railings themselves, travelling the length of the path like a message tapping its way home.

Kevin broke into a run.

*** 

Kevin ran until shame made him stop. Men his age weren't supposed to sprint along the embankment clutching folders like stolen children. He walked the rest, breath a rough file in his chest, and told himself he was only hurrying because of rain. The river fell behind him with a last, indifferent slap against stone.

By the time he reached their street the lamps had chosen a deeper orange, the kind that forgives bricks for being old. Number Twelve's fairy lights twitched in the window; someone laughed on a landing; a fox arranged itself at the edge of a hedge like a footnote with teeth. Kevin opened the gate. It stuck, performed, then yielded—the little theatre it loved.

The front door unlocked as if pleased to see him. Inside, the hallway had been reset to calm: shoes paired heel-to-heel, coats breathing their faint wool into the air, a lemon brightness that had gone past pleasant into ritual. He stood a second, letting his eyes adjust to domestic light. The house seemed to angle itself toward him, the way a cat pretends it isn't watching you from a chair.

"Hello?" he called, because etiquette mattered even when fear was in the room. His voice sounded like it had put on a tie.

From the kitchen: "In here," Samantha's voice, even, afternoon-clean. No echo of river in it.

He stepped in. The table was set for not-quite-dinner: three plates stacked, cutlery aligned, a loaf in paper. Sonia stood by the sink with her hands under the tap as if washing something off that water couldn't help with. Sarah sat at the table, chin propped on palm, eyes half-lidded in a way that made her look furious with gravity. The whiteboard had been cleaned, then written on again in a blue so crisp it made his teeth ache.

6PM—SUPPER.

7PM—ROTATION DISCUSSION.

8PM—REST.

Beneath, a thinner line, almost apologetic:

No more notes.

His gaze snagged on that. Samantha followed it and smiled, soft as mercy. "The board was getting... noisy," she said. "We need quiet to think."

Sarah's mouth twisted. "Quiet to obey."

Sonia flinched. Kevin caught it: the fast, involuntary jerk of a body that's realised it has betrayed itself. He looked at her hands. The water ran and ran, uselessly persistent.

"Good walk?" Samantha asked, as if the room hadn't noticed the folder at his ribs.

"Fine," he said, and hated the word for being both true and not. He slid the folder onto the end of the dresser, out of reach of bread and sentiment. He couldn't stop himself glancing at it again as if it might have grown teeth.

Samantha moved to the oven, checked the dial, checked it again, a woman rehearsing normal. "Sit," she told him. "You're clammy."

He sat because sitting seemed like a way to survive the next ten minutes. Sarah's gaze flicked to him and away. Sonia dried her hands as if preparing to touch something delicate.

Three knocks came then—faint, from the floorboard by the door. Knock. Knock. Knock. A rhythm that had become a signature.

Kevin stared at the wood. Samantha didn't turn. She reached for a tea towel and smoothed it in thirds. "Pipes," she said. "Always the pipes."

He stood, unexpected, his body surprising itself. He went to the board and, without asking—and what a revolution that was—picked up the marker from its parallel rest. He wrote, under No more notes:

Then speak out loud.

The squeak of the nib made the air seem thin. He capped it and put it back exactly where Samantha would have put it, a small act of treason dressed as good manners.

Sarah barked a laugh that had gratitude tucked in it. Sonia made a tiny sound that might have been a sob, or a laugh, or both. Samantha stepped closer, read the words, and didn't erase them. Her restraint felt like a loaded gun placed gently on a table.

"After supper," she said evenly. "We'll speak after supper."

\*\*\*

They ate badly. Bread that pretended to be crustier than it was, soup that had decided to go on being tin even after heating. Kevin swallowed shapes instead of flavours and tried not to look like he was keeping time with the radiator's clicks. Three. Pause. Three. Pause. An orchestra's warm-up for a performance he hadn't paid to see.

At seven, obedient to the board, they set their plates in the sink and stayed in the kitchen, because where else do families stage their collapses. Samantha stood with her back to the counter, palms flat, as if she might push the whole house away if it lurched.

"Rotation," she said calmly. "It's kept us safe. It needs to tighten to hold."

Sarah grinned without humour. "We're not tyres."

Sonia's fingers worried the hem of her cardigan. "We can't... keep pretending," she said, and the sentence shook like new glass. "Kevin knows."

"I know enough to know I don't know enough," he said, and the admission felt like strafing his own pride.

Samantha nodded, as if marking a pupil's essay. "Then here is what you will know. We share. We have always shared. The pact is older than your folder. It is older than Sarah's anger. It predates lemon." A flicker of smile. "It began when we were small and the world liked us better when we were one."

"And now?" Kevin asked.

"Now the world is not to be trusted," she said. "Nor is your curiosity."

He heard the word *your* like a slap. "My curiosity is the only reason I'm still standing."

"Your curiosity is dynamite with polite handwriting," she said, and the worst part was the part of him that admired the sentence. "You want a confession so you can keep loving us. I can give you truths only if you agree to live in them."

"Meaning?"

"Meaning you stop locking doors at random," she said, eyes flicking like knives to his pocket where the key still weighed. "Meaning you stop teaching the house bad habits. Meaning you handle knowledge with gloves."

"Whose gloves?" Sarah murmured. "Yours?"

Sonia reached across the table and touched Sarah's sleeve, a gesture of ceasefire. "Please," she said, to both of them, to all of them.

The lights flickered then: once, twice, three times. The house doing its party trick. On the third flicker the bulb didn't steady immediately; it hovered in a thin, indecisive hum. Kevin felt the hair on his arms stand and thought, wildly, of static building for a bolt. The hum softened, the light held.

Samantha exhaled as if she had been waiting for permission. "One rule," she said. "Tonight. No more notes. If you need to say something, say it. No cameras. No phones. No whiteboard as diary. Mouths, not pens."

Sarah stood. Her chair complained just enough to register its vote. "Fine. Mouths." She jabbed a finger at the board. "I'm keeping mine." She left the room before anyone could edit the moment into kindness.

Sonia followed more slowly, the way a tide withdraws after an argument with a wall. At the door she turned back to Kevin. "I tried," she said. He didn't yet know what she meant, but the words laid a weight on his chest. He nodded, which wasn't enough, and she went.

Kevin and Samantha remained. The clock declaimed seven-fifteen in a language only punctual people love. He looked down at his hands so he wouldn't have to look at hers. Flour dusted one knuckle from bread with too much brand; the other hand bore a faint line where the folder had bitten. Marked. Property of—he didn't finish the thought.

"Walk?" he said, because moving felt safer than staying still.

"Here is fine," Samantha said, and there was a finality to it that made the kitchen seem enormous.

A draft slid through the vent above the cooker. When it reached them it shaped itself around a syllable.

"Mine."

Kevin swallowed. He chose to pretend he hadn't heard it. To say otherwise would be to argue theology with an air duct. He stepped to the board instead and read the lines again, needing the comfort of legible threats.

6PM—SUPPER.

7PM—ROTATION DISCUSSION.

8PM—REST.

No more notes.

Then speak out loud.

He turned to Samantha. "All right. Speak."

She regarded him for a long beat, and in that beat he saw the gears behind her calm. Then she shook her head. "Not here," she said. "Not while the house is taking dictation." She picked up the marker and, for the first time since he'd met her, her hand trembled. She wrote a new line under his:

Tonight, after midnight. Sewing room.

The pen squeaked; the letters came out smaller than her usual certainty.

He stared at the words until they ghosted under the gloss. "All right."

Samantha placed the marker down parallel to the frame, old habit refusing to yield. "Eat something at ten," she said, absurdly practical. "You're worse when you're hungry."

He almost laughed. Instead he nodded, because the only thing worse than being managed was being unmanageable.

At midnight, he told himself, the truth would walk into a room and sit down and agree to be named. He didn't notice, not at first, the tiny smear the marker left on the board where she lifted it too soon. A lemon thumbprint in blue.

When he finally looked back to the dresser for his folder, his breath hitched. He had left it closed. It lay closed still. But on top of it, aligned with the edge, lay a single item that had not been there before.

A ticket stub. Paper curled from damp, printed in the inky purple of the local bus company. The date: Mid-March. The time: 23:17. The stop name was their street. In the corner, someone had drawn a small, neat lemon with three tiny lines radiating: scent made into a stamp.

Kevin didn't touch it. He leaned close enough to smell citrus, and the folder below gave a small creak like a chest trying to breathe.

He straightened, heart pounding, and felt rather than heard the floorboard by the door offer its opinion.

Knock.

Knock.

Knock.

The house had added itself to the evidence.

He looked at Samantha. She looked at him. Midnight was suddenly a cliff he had agreed to jump from.

# Chapter Twenty-Five
## The Death

The storm came in sideways, not in stately curtains but in knots and fists. Rain rattled the windows as if the weather had arrived with an opinion. Wind took the gutters in its teeth. Somewhere up the road a bin lid launched, clanged, spun, and settled like a cymbal dropped by an exhausted drummer. By nine the sky had mislaid the idea of colour; by ten it had forgotten the idea of time.

Kevin stood at the back door and watched the garden try to leave. The rosemary thrashed, the washing line erected itself at impossible angles, and the ivy on the brick wall behaved like an animal the house kept as a joke. Every few seconds lightning pressed a pale hand against the clouds, and the garden revealed its bones: slabs, path, the rusted handle of a spade he'd never thrown out because throwing things out felt like treachery. Thunder followed late, as if embarrassed to be obvious.

Inside, the house had gone bright in the way fearful people go bright. All the lamps they owned were on. The kitchen threw light at its own corners and still didn't look reassured. The whiteboard gleamed, more mirror than instruction. The words Tonight, after midnight. Sewing room. hung there in small, uncertain blue, Samantha's letters tided into something timid by the storm's indifference.

Sonia made tea. She always made tea when the world frayed. She moved with the careful violence of a person trying not to knock anything over, which never fooled objects as much as she hoped. She placed mugs on the table and failed to drink. Sarah sat hunched, jumper sleeves over her hands, eyes narrowed as if scanning the wind for a sentence. Samantha checked sockets, then rechecked them, unplugging and plugging in with a competence that wanted applause.

"Don't," Kevin said, and wasn't sure which of them he was addressing.

Samantha looked up. "Power cuts like this," she said, "set people on fire." She was matter-of-fact about catastrophe, as if calamity were only a poorly organised afternoon. "We'll keep it tidy."

The lights dimmed once, twice, and then agreed to continue. The fridge hummed like a monk. The vent over the cooker breathed its thin metallic prayer. Down the hall the chandelier in the sitting room tinkled—no draft that he could feel, but a draft the house could.

He put his palms flat on the table to anchor the room. The folder sat on the dresser, closed, wearing its new ticket stub like a crown. He had not touched it since finding the lemon-drawn stamp. Evidence that scented itself. He felt both foolish and devout.

"Do we still...?" Sonia nodded at the whiteboard.

"Midnight is midnight," Samantha said. She had rolled her sleeves to the same exact height on both arms. Her plait showed no interest in damp. "We won't let the weather rewrite us."

"Maybe the weather knows more than we do," Sarah muttered.

Lightning flattened the kitchen into a photograph. In the picture, they looked like people imitating themselves: the organised one, the appeaser, the rebel, the man who loved them because love had seemed like the safest story. Thunder followed, a little closer, a little louder, as if it had eavesdropped and decided to comment.

At half past eleven the lights finally failed. It wasn't a drama. They thinned, trembled, made one last brave glow, and went. Darkness fell smart, decisive, like a lid.

Sonia's breath hitched. "Candles," she said, already at the drawer. Matches rasped. One flame bloomed, then another. The kitchen became smaller, more honest. Faces within a few feet; everything else suggestion. Lemon hid beneath wax. Shadows climbed the walls and held on.

"Upstairs," Samantha said. Calm. Command. "We sit together. Sewing room. One room is safer than four."

"Since when," Sarah said, "is that room safe?"

"Since always," Samantha said. "Since it's ours." She took a candle in a jam jar and moved for the door, the glow throwing her profile into confident lines. Even in the dark she walked as if the floor had been ironed.

Kevin took a second jar, Sonia a third. Sarah didn't move. Lightning found them again. The room flashed bones and vanished them. "We could wait here," Sarah said, as if refusing geography might win.

"Together," Samantha replied. It wasn't up for debate. The house seemed to lean with her. The jam jars made little planetariums on their hands.

The sitting room chandelier sang as they passed—a well-bred ring, then another, then a third, notes glass-true, spaced like breath. Samantha did not look up. "Loose fittings," she said, which was the sort of explanation that people who loved order preferred to the sensation of being addressed by metal. Kevin could not help it: he looked, and in the candlelight the pendants seemed to tremble in recognition.

On the stairs the second tread squealed. Sonia had mended it twice. It squealed anyway, delighted with its treachery. Kevin felt a childish urge to stamp until it understood seriousness. He didn't. He put his foot carefully, and it squealed again, quieter, as if whispering its joke to itself.

"Hold the banister," Samantha said over her shoulder, which would have irritated him in any other weather and tonight soothed him. He held it. It was warm, as if the house had already put its hand there.

The landing was black. Sarah's candle wobbled like a thought. The air carried that wet, expectant smell old houses borrow from churches during storms. Somewhere a gutter overflowed and poured its boredom down brick. The sewing room door stood ajar, a thin coin of light inside where someone had left a lamp on earlier and the bulb still held a grudged, cooling memory.

They filed in. The Singer's silhouette rose from the table, chrome and iron translated into shadow. The wooden animals on the shelf made watchful humps. The sash rattled, uncertain which allegiance to choose: weather or house. Samantha set her candle down and the room formed itself around that small sun.

"Sit," she said.

Sarah didn't. She stood by the window, stubborn in profile, like a saint refusing canonisation. "Say it," she told Samantha. "You dragged us up here; say it."

Sonia put her candle on the Singer's table and winced at her own presumption, then knelt and set it on a tin instead. "Careful of the varnish," she whispered, then hated herself for minding. Kevin took the spare stool and found it puzzled by his weight. The Singer's treadle sat under the table like an idea.

Outside, rain took a deep breath and redoubled itself. Wind rummaged the gutter for stories. Lightning unzipped the sky again, white and indecent. For the beat that light allowed, Kevin saw the room like an x-ray: the line of the Singer's wheel, Samantha's gaze rotated toward them all at once, Sarah's jaw arranged to fight, Sonia's hand flexed into a prayer she had not been given permission to finish.

Thunder spoke in a voice old houses recognise. The vent above the table swallowed the last of the kitchen's warm air and exhaled cold. The exhale lasted too long to be only weather. It seemed to shape itself around the briefest syllable—mine—and then dissolved into draft.

"Right," Samantha said. She rested her palm on the Singer's top as if calming a well-bred dog. "It's midnight."

The house, which had no business with clocks, rang the chandelier once in the sitting room to agree.

***

For a second—one exact second—the room held. Four people occupying four corners of a square you could draw only because the storm had erased everything else. Samantha drew breath to begin.

The Singer woke.

Not promiscuously. Not in a horror-film thrash. The treadle depressed with the slow courtesy of an elderly person lowering themselves into a chair. The wheel turned once. The needle arm dipped, rose, dipped again. No feet moved on it. No hands touched it. The motion sounded like an oath being repeated to itself. In the jar lights the chrome caught and returned small, guilty stars.

Sonia made a sound like a prayer ending. Sarah flinched and stepped back, her heel crunching a stray shard of old glass from the night the frame had shattered. The crunch rang too loudly. The house listened harder.

"Draft," Samantha said, breath measured, as if the word could be a cloth over the machine. She pressed her palm to the Singer's throat and the metal answered with a hum, a purr so fine Kevin felt it in bone rather than ear. "Sit," she added, but it was unclear if she spoke to machine or family.

From somewhere along the landing a door banged. Cold ran down the corridor. The chandelier in the sitting room rang a bright, brittle chord—one, two, three notes, each a fraction sharper than the last. The vent above the Singer breathed in, out, in, then roared; not loud, but full, as if the house had decided lungs.

Sonia's candle guttered. She cupped it, protecting flame with fingers that shook. "Please," she said, though it wasn't clear to whom. "Please don't."

"Enough," Samantha snapped, the word a whip-crack not at Sonia but at the storm, at the machine, at the idea of chaos itself. "This is *our* house."

As if offended by grammar, the bulb in the hall, already dead, flared once—a corpse remembering a joke—and went black again. From upstairs came a sound that took a second to identify: someone running.

A scream followed, raw, human, not Sarah's, not Sonia's, not Samantha's, not any single sister's; it had the shape of their shared throat. Kevin was on his feet before his fear had time to stand. The scream cut, then rose again, wordless. A heavy thud answered—furniture struck or flung—and then the unmistakable patter of something small and hard skittering along floorboards: pins, a tin spilled by air or hand.

"Stay," Samantha ordered, already moving to the door with her candle held high like a punishment. "No one—"

A second scream tore the command in half. It came from the bedroom at the far end—Sarah's, or the room they used to call Sarah's until rooms had to earn their names. Kevin ran. He did not register his choice to disobey; his legs chose. Behind him, glass chimed, the Singer hummed, the vent gave the lowing sigh of metal reconsidering its loyalties.

The landing had become a tunnel. The rain's percussion took over every surface. Candle flame tore itself small on the run. On the second tread the stair squealed as if excited to participate. Kevin cursed it and leapt three at a time, useless hands stretched out for a rail that wasn't where rails belong in nightmares.

At the doorway he stopped dead. Candlelight spat shadows against the walls. The room was unmade in a way that had nothing to do with bedding. Drawers stood aghast. A wardrobe gaped like a gossip. The curtains fought the window for jurisdiction.

Two figures struggled near the bed, tangled—hair, sleeves, breath, a flash of shears, a hand batting them aside, a knee—then separated and collided again. He saw only outlines, the storm's light cutting their edges. One gasped, "Stop," not as plea but as command. The other made a sound he had never heard a human make and feared he would never stop hearing.

"Samantha!" he shouted, but which of them was she?

He lunged in. Someone's shoulder met his chest hard enough to take his wind. His candle swung, flung a comet of wax, and went out. Dark took the room in its mouth. Lightning bit the window. In the white-blue instant he saw: a hand flat against a sternum, pushing; an ankle twisted under a bed leg; eyes wild and wet; hair in ropes; the shears on the rug like a decision.

Then dark swallowed them again.

He grabbed the nearest wrist and was punished for his faith. Teeth flashed, bit his palm quick and sure. He yelped, reflex loosened his grip, and the body he'd held tore free with a hiss. Another body hit him from the side—Sonia, small and determined, or Sarah, furious and living—and they all staggered into the corridor like furniture being moved in a hurry.

"Stop—stop—" Sonia's voice now, definitely Sonia, right in his ear, breath hot with human fear. "You'll—"

The chandelier in the sitting room shrieked. Not a note now, but a scraped scream as if glass had found ways to hurt itself. The vent roared open. The Singer, three rooms away, found a new gear and whirred, brisk, industry resurrected; its wheel turned like a metronome disappointed in its orchestra.

Rain bullied the sash. Wind shouldered the landing. The stair waited.

A body slammed into the banister. Wood complained. Another hand flailed for purchase and found only air. Kevin saw, because lightning insisted, a face twist—not terrified, enraged—and then a foot missed the tread that squealed when it liked attention.

Someone fell.

It wasn't a graceful fall. It wasn't theatrical. It was the ugly, efficient collapse of physics doing its unsentimental work: hip to wood, shoulder to post, head to tread, tumble, thud, bounce, slide. Skin and hair and cloth and sound. An end made in a series of insistences.

The scream at the beginning did not return to finish itself.

Silence tried to form around the stairwell and failed. The house still made its noises—singer humming, chandelier complaining, vent bellowing—but they felt decorative now, like a band playing a cheerful tune after a grenade. Somewhere a jam jar shattered and the smell of cheap wax pitched itself into lemon as if perfumes mourn.

"Sarah?" Kevin bellowed. "Sonia?" His voice came out broken. His candle was gone. He ran blind, following the cold that falls down stairs faster than anything else alive.

He found the floor with his hands and then his knees. The hall felt like a throat. He reached forward and met hair. Warm, heavy hair, tangled, wet—not with rain. He slid his hand higher, met skin slippery with something that made the floor tack. His breath left him. "No," he said, because the word exists. "No, no—"

"Don't move her," Samantha's voice said from above him, very calm in the way people are calm when the world has ended twice and they have chosen the smallest task. "Don't touch her neck."

He did as he was told without agreeing. His fingers shook. His knees slid. The body lay at a wrong angle a human body doesn't choose. The storm, rudely disinterested, insisted on weather. The Singer whirred down the hall, making its little professional sounds. The chandelier produced one pure, perfect note as if it had been asked to bless proceedings.

"Sonia?" Kevin tried again, and then, because the word was cheap, "Sarah?" His voice begged for an answer he could hate.

No answer arrived from the floor. A ragged sound came from the landing—someone crying without air. After a second he knew it for Sonia's. He tried to be grateful, then tried to be not a monster for the relief.

"Light," Samantha said. "We need light."

Flame nicked the darkness. A match. Another. The hall filled with little oranges that made the black worse. Samantha descended, sure-footed, candle in one hand, the other out for balance. She arrived like an officiant, knelt, put the jar down. The flame played on hair that hid a face. Blood made its self-possession down the stair's angle and into the hall rug where it found old patterns and improved them.

Samantha didn't touch the neck. She touched the wrist instead and held it for the smallest scientific count. Storm, Singer, chandelier, vent; they all kept talking. She closed her eyes for one precise beat and opened them again in a face that looked like itself and also didn't.

She looked at Kevin. "Don't let Sonia come down," she said, and because he had no more arguments left, he obeyed and put his hand up toward the landing like someone warding away a shadow. "Stay," he said to the sobbing shape above them. "Please. Stay."

"Sarah?" Sonia got out. And then, smaller, terrified of bargaining with the dark, "Sonia?"

"Stay," Samantha repeated, the word hardening. "Do not come down."

Kevin took the jar in his free hand and tilted it. The light moved over the body: hair, throat, collarbone, the place where a jumper had given and skin had torn, a hand folded under itself like a forgotten tool. He was afraid to move a strand of hair. He was more afraid not to. He put the candle on the stair, used the back of his knuckles to nudge, gentler than he had ever been with anything.

A face revealed itself in unflattering pieces: cheek, mouth, a scrape, the half-moon of an eyelid. Not enough. The jaw carried a necklace of red that had nothing to do with jewellery. He swallowed bile. He nudged again, gathering hair with fingertips, dragging it away from the mouth that would not be asked anything again.

The house chose that second to suck its breath in. The flame licked long and almost went. The jar glass clouded with his sweat. Samantha steadied it. Her other hand hovered above the brow—not touching, never touching—and then withdrew.

"Is it—" Sonia started from the landing, then couldn't finish.

Kevin leaned so close his own face touched cold hair. He found the brow with the careful tenderness of a man trying not to hurt a statue. He wiped the tack away with his shirt cuff once, twice, revealing skin pale where the blood had refused to bead. He peered, hunting a seam he had become a student of. Lightning obliged, whitened the hall, gave him the clean, sharp relief of detail.

There. Or not. A faint shine where a line sometimes lived, or only the trick of candle and storm. The right brow, too smooth—no, the suggestion of something mended long ago—no, he couldn't tell, he couldn't—

He made a noise. He had meant to say a name. It came out like a person failing to lift a heavy thing.

Samantha looked at him steadily. She did not look at the face. She looked at him, and when she was sure he was looking back, she said, very softly, in a voice with no more lemon left in it:

"This is what truth costs."

***

Time didn't stop. That would have been a kindness. Time stuttered; then it behaved. Rain still hammered the sash. Wind still talked with its mouth full. The Singer ticked itself to silence because even machines understand when to be polite. The chandelier sang a last small note—almost apologetic—and made itself dull.

Sonia crept to the top step despite orders not to, knees under her, hands white on the banister. In the feeble light she looked like a child who had reached the top of a slide and changed her mind. "Who is it?" she whispered, and the whisper landed like a stone. "Please. Who is it?"

Kevin opened his mouth. A name hovered on his tongue, uncommitted. He did not trust his eyes; they had lied before. He did not trust the house; it had learnt to imitate. He did not trust the storm; storms prefer theatre to accuracy.

He tried logic. Sonia's voice was here, unbroken, alive. The figure on the floor was one of two. It should have been simple arithmetic. He thought of the photo Sonia had found—three girls labelled Sam. He thought of the whiteboard—No more notes—and his own defiance—Then speak out loud. His mouth made the shape of Sarah's name and then of Sonia's and then chose neither because choosing would turn the night into a fact.

Samantha put her palm flat on the stair, next to the candle, as if calming wood. "We don't speak that word yet," she said. "We speak no names."

"You can't—" Kevin began, and then he stopped because he could. She could. She could make rules out of breath. She always had.

"We call an ambulance," Sonia said, hope a small flame absurd against physics.

"We do," Samantha agreed. Her calm had returned, a cloak shrugged back on. "We ring. We do what decent people do. Kevin—" She handed him her phone; his hands had forgotten how to find the right buttons.

He dialled. The voice on the other end was bright with professionalism. He gave the address; he gave the words he could: "fall," "stairs," "unconscious," "bleeding." He did not give a name. He did not answer the question "Are they breathing?" because he could not force his mouth to feel for breath and say the truth. Samantha leaned very slightly closer to the unmoving chest and shook her head minutely. Kevin said, "I don't know," which was accurate enough to pass for useful.

"They're on their way," the voice said, sympathy institutional and therefore bearable. "Stay on the line."

He stayed. The phone became a warm rectangle he could hold to stop his hands looking stupid. The operator's reassurances travelled into his skull and arranged themselves like furniture for a party that wouldn't happen. Samantha adjusted the candle by a centimetre; light threw the face into relief and then softened it again.

On the landing Sonia rocked, keening under her breath—the sound new to him, terrifying because it was small. Sarah did not speak. The absence of her voice—if absence it was—made the storm louder. Or perhaps that was what grief is: everything is louder and less clear.

The house exhaled long through the vent. It did not say mine. If it had, Kevin would have stood and broken the grille off with his bare hands and thrown it through the window. It breathed like any house, which is to say like a thing that refuses to confirm what it has witnessed.

Far off, a siren began to grow. It was the least gothic sound the night had to offer and therefore the most beautiful. Kevin swallowed and spoke into the phone. "We can hear you," he said, as if the ambulance were a person and not a promise of people.

Samantha stood. "Sonia," she said, not unkindly, "go down to the door. Let them in. Don't come further than the hall."

Sonia obeyed. Her knees stuttered on the second step. She stopped, hand to mouth, then continued. When she reached the bottom, she didn't look at the body; she held the wall like a handrail and slid past with the tact of someone ignoring a sleeping animal.

"Kevin," Samantha said, and he braced for an order that would offend him and found himself grateful when it arrived. "Get towels. The old ones. And the blue sheet from the airing cupboard. We don't move her. We don't... disturb. But we don't let the neighbours see more than they must."

He moved because moving is easier than naming. He went to the cupboard where sheets become acceptable to strangers, took the blue one, took two towels that had once been white and had become honest. He brought them back and handed them over like offerings. Samantha unfolded the sheet with the steady competence of someone laying a table for a guest she both loved and feared. She draped it in a way that covered and did not pretend to erase.

"Who?" he asked through his teeth.

Samantha didn't answer. The ambulance wail rounded the corner into their street. Lights pulsed through the fanlight, blue washing the hallway in the colours of a bad dream. The fox in the hedge bolted. Neighbours stirred behind curtains, or pretended not to. The storm went on, uninterested in human arrivals.

Boots. Voices. The door opened to cold. Sonia's silhouette in the hallway, small, brave. "In here," she said, and the *here* hung between the life they had been living and the life that was arriving.

Paramedics filled the space with the righteous bustle of people who can still be useful. "Evening," one said, absurd and therefore perfect. "Let's see." Gloves. Torches. A case opened to reveal other cases. The blue sheet lifted. The torch made a small moon across a throat, a cheek, a brow. Kevin watched their faces because watching theirs was easier than watching the one he might have to love or grieve.

They did the steps: pulse, pupil, breath. Their language narrowed to numbers he could not hear. The older one met Samantha's eyes and shook his head once in a language people who have done this long enough speak to people who are forced to learn it quickly.

"I'm sorry," he said, then because protocol requires more, "We'll confirm, but—"

Sonia made the sound of a rope fraying. Sarah said nothing. Kevin put his hand on the stair to keep from floating into the space between the blue light and the candle flame and the smell of lemon pretending to be order.

"Do you know the name of the patient?" the younger paramedic asked, pen poised.

Samantha's mouth opened and closed. She looked at Kevin and then at the whiteboard in the kitchen as if it might have written this down. She said, "Yes," without supplying it. Her voice didn't crack.

The pen hovered. Rain attempted a new angle at the window. The chandelier upstairs behaved.

"Any allergies?" the paramedic tried, because the form does not leave room for silence.

"No," Samantha said, still administrative. "None."

They worked because working is what their bodies understood: lines, tubes, a question to the ceiling that had no ceiling-appropriate answer. At last, after all the small, brave acts had been attempted, they stilled.

"I'm sorry," the older one said again, and this time he placed his hand on Samantha's forearm, a piece of human contact he would get told off for if he believed in rules more than people. "We can— we'll need..." He faltered, looked past her to the stairs and the landing and the house, which had opinions about procedure.

"We'll call family," Samantha said, businesslike, and the cruelty of plural barely registered. "We'll do what is done."

The men nodded and made a phone call that asked another van to arrive at a different pace. The radio in the van outside chuckled with unrelated tragedies. Sonia pressed her forehead against the cool paint of the hall, then turned and inched back up two steps and sat and stared at her own knees like a person who needed instructions on how to kneel.

Kevin sat too, three steps above the body, as if height might protect him from the specific gravity of the dead. He touched his bitten palm and watched blood bead and thought of how blood does exactly the thing it is made to do until people get in the way. He rubbed his face with that hand and left a red smear on himself he would not notice until morning.

Samantha stood. She looked at Kevin, not for strength—she did not borrow—but for witness. She looked past him to the landing where the dark held Sarah or held her absence like breath. She looked down at the sheet that covered the face he could not name, then up at the ceiling where the house listened without blinking.

"This," she said, almost kindly, almost to herself, almost to the house, "is what truth costs."

The storm answered with a crack over the chimney, a last grandstanding before the weather exhausted itself. Somewhere down the street a car alarm woke and complained.

The Singer in the sewing room, good machine that it was, finally forgot its old lesson and gave up humming.

The paramedics worked around the body with the choreography of restraint.

*** 

The blue light washed the hall again, then faded; the second van arrived without drama, men with quiet hands and a folded stretcher, politeness weaponised against catastrophe.

Sonia stood when they asked her to. She stood as if borrowing legs from the air. Sarah did not come down. The house did not speak. Kevin put his hand on the banister because wood was older than rules and less inclined to lie.

They lifted. The sheet shifted. Hair slid. Candle gave one last brave flare and guttered, then caught again because Sonia cupped it with both hands as if saving a life mattered whenever you could manage it.

"Name?" the younger man tried again, gentle but required.

Samantha breathed once through her nose, a tiny act of rebellion against oxygen, and spoke a single name into the hall.

Kevin flinched. The sound of it rearranged the furniture of his chest. Sonia's hands shook and the candlelight danced as if pleased to be included in grief. The house took the name into itself without comment.

The stretcher moved. The front door opened to a night newly tired of itself. The sheet, the hair, the silence, the last of the paramedics' compassion went out into rain that had begun to lose interest. Sonia followed as far as the hall and stopped. Kevin did not move. Samantha stood on the stair like a person who has finished a speech to a room that isn't going to clap and is deciding whether to bow.

At last the door clicked shut. The clock in the kitchen made a single, brave tick and then remembered itself: time was not, tonight, a service the house would offer.

Samantha looked at Kevin. If there were lemon on her skin, the storm had washed it away. She laid her palm flat again on the stair, next to the candle, and said it once more, quietly, as if to confirm the receipt.

"This is what truth costs."

The house—good host, terrible witness—kept the secret of which sister lay at the foot of its stairs.

# Act III — Truth and Ruin

# Chapter Twenty-Six
## After the Fall

They carried the body out as if it were a secret already told. Blue light rinsed the hallway, then retreated with the stretcher into rain that had calmed to a fretful drizzle. The fox from the hedge watched the little procession with the calm of a creature that never expects things to improve. Neighbours arranged themselves at windows: faces halved by curtains, eyes the size of coins. Someone lifted a phone and then thought better of it. The ambulance door closed with the soft, adult click of equipment that has learnt not to startle.

Kevin stood three steps up from the hall, one hand on the banister, because he could not discover what else hands were for. The sheet's edge brushed the rug, nudging a thread that would fray later, long after the night had cleaned itself away. He could smell lemon under the damp outside—the house's default story continuing as if nothing had happened. Sonia leaned against the wall by the door, head bowed, palms pressed to distemper as if hoping the paint might cool something under her skin. Sarah remained on the landing, unmoving, a cut-out in shadow, as if the dark had been shaped with scissors to hold her.

Samantha had no place in the procession and yet she organised it. She moved before and after the paramedics with a kind, tidy competence, clearing the way, holding the door, offering to fetch a towel for the stretcher rails, then not fetching it when told no. When the men checked they had their equipment she counted the items with her eyes,

reassuring herself the house would not be left with stranger's para-
phernalia. She spoke softly to Sonia as the gurney rolled past—"Don't
look"—and to Kevin when the back doors closed—"Sit down"—and to
the air as if the house were capable of taking instruction—"Still."

"Do you need anything?" the older paramedic asked, voice pitched to
the steadying register they teach you between the CPR dummies and
the tea urn.

Samantha shook her head once, decisive, as if she knew what everyone needed better than they did. "We'll make tea. Thank you for coming so quickly." She meant it, and also she meant: we will choose the
next movements of this house.

When the ambulance pulled away the street exhaled. The neighbours' curtains deflated back into their day shapes. The fox flicked a
paw as if erasing a line from a sentence. The rain recommenced its
ordinary work of turning things into themselves. Silence wrapped the
house like a sheet that didn't fit.

Kevin descended two steps and stopped. He looked at the place on
the tread where the candle had sat a long hour ago and found a ring of
wax like a target, white against wood, already hardening into a fact that
would outlast breath. He wanted to scrape it up with his thumbnail and
couldn't make his body move.

Sonia lifted her head. Her eyes were swollen into small storms. She
tried to speak. What came out was a sound he had never heard from
her, a little dry creak like a hinge that has forgotten which way doors
open. "Kevin," she said, and then covered her mouth, because names
were now dangerous—every name committed you to an answer you
couldn't bear to give.

"Upstairs," Samantha said gently but in the voice that knows its
orders will be obeyed. "Both of you. I'll... I'll sort the hall."

"You don't need to sort anything," Sarah said from the landing, voice flat with a courage she held between her teeth. "There's nothing left to sort."

Samantha looked up. For a heartbeat the mask slid and something in her eyes showed through—grief or fury or the terror of a person who has been proved mortal in her own home. Then it closed, not unkindly. "We have to live here in the morning," she said. "We keep it decent."

She found a cloth—of course she did—and knelt to blot the stair where blood had turned to a dark, tacky sheen. She didn't scrub; she pressed, lifted, turned the cloth to a clean square, pressed again. The movement had the rhythm of prayer. Kevin wanted to snatch the cloth and fling it at the wall, to refuse neatness. He gripped the banister harder instead.

"Stop," Sonia whispered. "Please."

Samantha paused, cloth held in her fist like surrender. "I can't," she said, and for the first time it sounded like confession rather than defiance. She stood, folded the cloth into itself so the red was inside, and carried it towards the kitchen like a midwife clearing linen.

Kevin followed because following was easier than thinking. In the kitchen the whiteboard wore the bright emptiness of a hotel room: wiped to shine, every ghost-letter chased to the corners. Only when he stood close did he see the faint greenish bruise of old ink that refused to die: THEN SPEAK OUT LOUD paled to a whisper under the gloss. Someone—Samantha—had tried twice. The words clung. Letters don't leave a house that has learnt to keep them.

Samantha set the folded cloth in a bowl and filled it with cold water. The red bled out in threads that faded fast, as if memory were efficient tonight. She turned the tap off cleanly. "Kevin," she said without looking at him, "wash your hands."

He looked down at his bitten palm. The half-moon marks stood out, dark now, drying. The blood on his other hand had printed his jaw a dull brown he hadn't felt. He obeyed the instruction because she was right: there would be officers in the house in minutes, and officers dislike the untidy. Lemon soap jumped into the water when he squeezed the bottle. The scent climbed his throat like a rule he had tried to swallow. He scrubbed until the skin itched and turned his face to the towel and came away with a brown smear he didn't understand until he pictured himself kneeling at the stair. His stomach lurched. He breathed through it.

Sonia reached for a mug and missed it by an inch. The mug fell into the sink and survived, which somehow seemed cruel. She put both hands flat on the worktop like a diver considering the water. "We should call..." she began, and trailed off because there were too many numbers and too few names she could imagine saying to them.

Samantha set three mugs on the table and made tea with the practised economy of a woman who can keep a room from drowning by changing its temperature. Steam moved through the kitchen with a prim sense of purpose, as if it had been told to put itself to work. "We'll do calls after," she said. "We give a statement first. We give the same statement."

Sarah came in, slow, as if the doorway were a border with expensive guards. She didn't sit. Her eyes fell on the whiteboard and held there, reading the nothing as if it were the most threatening paragraph she'd ever seen. "Leave the ghosts," she said, too softly for Samantha to pretend not to hear. "They're the only honest thing."

Boots sounded in the hall. A knock, polite. Samantha moved to answer. She pressed her palm to the whiteboard frame in passing, a touch she might not have realised she'd made, and the plastic rasped a little under her skin as if it remembered being dragged at speed. She smoothed her hair with the other hand, found no rebellion there, and opened the door.

Two officers entered with their hats in their hands, rain combed into neat beads on their sleeves. The older—sergeant, probably—had a voice that made even the phrase "I'm so sorry" sound procedural, which Kevin found oddly merciful. The younger carried a notebook he seemed embarrassed to own. They were careful with their eyes. They saw the stair and didn't stare. They saw the kitchen's brightness and didn't flinch. They took in the three women and the one man and the table set for four, then three, then two, depending on where you stood.

"We'll be as quick as we can," the sergeant said. "Just the basics tonight. We'll arrange to follow up in the morning."

"Of course," Samantha said. "Tea?"

He hesitated, then said, "No, thank you," and looked both grateful and sorry, which is the face authority wears when it recognises hospitality as defence.

Kevin sat because everyone else did. The chairs made their small, domestic complaints. Sonia wrapped her hands round her mug and didn't drink. Sarah stood, still, at the whiteboard, as if guarding its transparency. Samantha arranged herself with poise that walked on the edge of catastrophe.

"Tell me what happened," the younger officer said gently, pen poised.

It surprised Kevin that Samantha did not speak first. She looked at Sonia and said, "Please." Sonia blinked, startled into seniority, opened her mouth, and the night tried to come out in a rush. Samantha put her hand on Sonia's wrist—barely a touch—and the flood slowed to a stream. Between them they told a story of storm night, of a power cut, of moving upstairs together because candles in one room are safer than candles in four. They did not say *the house spoke* or *the Singer woke* or *the chandelier sang*. They said *noise*, they said *confusion*. They said *a fall*. The words slotted themselves into the shape of a narrative that would fit in a form.

Kevin listened to his own life simplified and felt both rescued and erased. When the officers turned to him he repeated the same architecture in his own mouth, holding back the parts that would make the younger man's pen stop moving. He said what could be true. He did not say *I could not tell whose skin I touched* or *I wiped blood from a brow to name the woman it covered* or *the house has learnt how to lie*.

They asked for times. He made some. They asked for who was where. He arranged his three sisters along the corridor in a way that looked sensible. The sergeant made a small hum that might have been approval.

The officers rose, promised a follow-up, promised contact details, promised the dignity of a process. The sergeant's gaze skimmed the whiteboard on his way out and hesitated, so slightly Kevin might have imagined it. He saw nothing written there and frowned at the sight of faint ink where there should have been none, and then the politeness of the job moved him on.

When they were back in the hall, Samantha went after them with the cloth to wipe the banister where gloves had touched. She didn't see Kevin watching her, or she did and decided he didn't count as witness. She put the cloth back in the bowl, pressed it down, watched the red find water again and lose itself.

Kevin stood at the whiteboard. The words THEN SPEAK OUT LOUD hovered like bruises under skin. He touched the gloss. It was cold and patient.

Three slow knocks travelled through the floorboards from the front room—soft, almost thoughtful. Sonia flinched. Sarah closed her eyes.

Samantha returned to the doorway without looking at the boards at all, as if refusing to acknowledge a language keeps it from being spoken.

The sergeant lingered just inside the door, hat under his arm. "Mr Hayes?" he said, tone changed now that the paperwork part of the night had been fed. "A moment, if that's all right."

Kevin turned, heart tightening as if the house had pulled a cord. "Yes," he said.

"In private," the officer added gently, glancing past him at the three women.

Samantha opened her mouth, then closed it, nodded, stepped back. For once she let a door close without arranging what would be said behind it.

Kevin followed the officer into the sitting room, where the chandelier still pretended innocence. Rain bowed at the windows and let them go. The room smelt of cold fabric and lemon oil that had been asked to do too much. The officer didn't sit. Neither did Kevin. The house leaned, listening.

And the night, obedient to cliffhangers, held its breath.

***

The officer's voice was pitched low, as if conscious of the house's inclination to echo.

"We'll just confirm some details, Mr Hayes," he said. "And then I'll leave you to your evening."

Evening. The word felt obscene, as if the hours after a body left could be folded back into ordinary time. Kevin nodded, because nodding costs less than honesty.

***

The younger constable remained in the kitchen with the sisters, his pen scratching while the kettle reheated needlessly. Samantha had insisted they all stay in one room, calling it *efficient*. She stood a little behind Sonia's chair, one hand resting lightly on the back, almost maternal. Sarah stayed standing by the whiteboard, arms folded, gaze fixed on the faint ghost of ink. The constable followed her line of sight once, frowned at the empty gloss, then looked away quickly.

Guided statements

"Start from when the lights went," the constable prompted. His voice was careful, the kind that wants to hold pieces without cutting itself.

Sonia tried first. Her throat caught and the words fell out too soft. "The storm... we were worried about candles... we decided—"

Samantha stepped in smoothly. "To go upstairs together. Fewer risks if we shared one light. I thought the sewing room would do." She looked at the constable as if daring him to disagree.

He nodded. "And then?"

"There was shouting," Sonia whispered. "The machine—"

Samantha's hand squeezed her shoulder, a soft correction. "The wind rattled the window. It startled us. One of us tripped. The stair is tricky when it's wet."

The constable scribbled. "And which one of you fell?"

Silence pinched the air. Sonia's lips trembled open, but Samantha was faster. "We're not sure. It was dark, loud. By the time we reached the hall..." She let the sentence trail, shaping it into grief rather than fact.

Sarah laughed once, dry, bitter. "Not sure. That's convenient."

The constable glanced up. His eyes were young; he didn't yet know how to stop a room curdling. He scribbled again, pen scarring paper harder than necessary.

Kevin shifted in the sitting room doorway, half in shadow. He felt the weight of his own throat pressing back words. He could correct, could say he knew exactly who had screamed, could admit he had touched the wrong brow searching for a scar. But he didn't. He watched Samantha's hand remain on Sonia's chair until the girl stilled, obedient to touch.

Tidying grief

When the officers excused themselves to radio updates, Samantha moved fast. She gathered stray mugs, stacked them in the sink, straightened the tea towels, turned the whiteboard marker parallel to its frame. She wiped the edge of the table with her sleeve where Sonia had left a wet ring from her cup.

Kevin recognised the choreography. This was what she did in every crisis: tidy. Not comfort, not cry. Neaten. Put the world back into lines and squares until the mess blurred into habit. He wanted to scream at her, to knock every mug to the floor, to show her that order did not resurrect. But Sonia sat with her shoulders hunched and her hands tight round her knees, and Sarah pressed her forehead against the window's condensation, and Kevin lacked the cruelty to make the room worse.

Instead he leaned against the wall and closed his eyes. He let the noises of the house filter through: radiator ticking its three-count, the chandelier sighing overhead, the faint hiss from the vent that might have been weather. It sounded like the house laughing into its own sleeve.

***

The faint ink

When Kevin opened his eyes, he found himself staring again at the whiteboard. Samantha had wiped it twice. He'd watched her lean into the plastic with deliberate force, cloth biting at gloss. Still the words bled through. Faint, greenish, like veins under skin.

THEN SPEAK OUT LOUD.

The constable returned and caught Kevin's gaze. "Something written there earlier?"

Samantha answered before Kevin could breathe. "Just shopping lists. I cleared them. Nothing useful."

The man nodded, half-accepting, but Kevin saw his eyes linger on the ghost-letters. He wanted to step forward, to say *yes, there was something, and it was mine, and it matters*, but his tongue felt sewn to the roof of his mouth. The Singer's phantom hum seemed to run through his jaw, reminding him of the cost of words.

Sarah turned from the window. Her reflection still clung to the glass, delayed, as if the storm outside needed a moment to digest her face. She pointed at the board. "Ghosts," she said. "This house never forgets."

The constable shifted, uncomfortable. He jotted nothing down.

Pre-wiping

Later, while Sonia fetched blankets for the spare beds the police insisted they rest in, Kevin caught Samantha in the hall with a fresh cloth. She moved along the banister, wiping each spindle, each rail. Her motions were practised, efficient. She stopped only when she noticed him watching.

"We don't want stains," she said softly.

"You mean fingerprints," he replied.

She didn't flinch. She folded the cloth once, twice, three times until the damp red patch was hidden inside. "It's the same thing."

He stepped closer. "Why are you so sure what story they'll believe?"

"Because I know what stories people need," she said. "And because you'll repeat it too, when they ask."

Her certainty made his chest ache. He wanted to deny it, but already he felt the narrative lodging in his throat: storm, confusion, candlelight, a fall. A story neat enough for forms.

***

The silence stretches

The officers reconvened. They offered a time for tomorrow, they left a card on the table, they said words that filled space without filling sense. When the front door shut behind them, silence expanded like breath held too long. Sonia sank onto the sofa and pressed her face into a cushion. Sarah stood in the hallway, arms crossed, staring at the stairs where wax and blood still left faint shadows despite cloth and water.

Kevin sat at the kitchen table, eyes fixed on the whiteboard. He could see the words now even without looking: THEN SPEAK OUT LOUD. They pulsed behind his eyelids. He thought of speaking, of breaking Samantha's script, of telling Sonia and Sarah what he had seen at the river, what the man with the cap had smiled, what the comb with lemon meant. He thought of opening his mouth and becoming honest.

But he stayed still, because stillness was safer.

And then came the three knocks, faint but undeniable, from the floorboards beneath the table. Sonia sat up, wide-eyed. Sarah closed her fists. Samantha, returning with a fresh tea towel, didn't even look at the boards.

She wiped the corner of the table, neat, decisive, as if nothing had spoken at all.

The sitting room felt staged for someone else's evening: cushions equal, rug squared to the hearth, the little bowl of matchbooks that had never seen a flame. The chandelier wore its silence politely. Through the window, streetlight softened the rain into strands of wool. The officer remained by the door, hat tucked under his arm, posture respectful in the way of men who enter other people's nights and try not to bruise them.

"Mr Hayes," he began, voice low enough that the room had to lean in, "I want to thank you for your patience. It's... never easy." The slight pause before *never* told Kevin the man meant *always*.

Kevin nodded. He was tired of nodding. He hooked a thumb into the pocket where the key to the spare room still lived, then took it out again as if he'd been caught fiddling a coin. "What do you need?"

"Just a little clarity," the officer said. "About the household. About tonight." He cleared his throat, glanced up at the chandelier as if the pendants might ratify honesty. "You described a power cut, candles, a move upstairs for safety. Then an altercation—" His eyes flickered; the word sat there awkwardly, a bureaucrat at a wake. "—then a fall. Your wife—" He paused. "Mrs Hayes—who is Mrs Hayes?"

Kevin felt the floor dip under the question. "Samantha," he said too quickly, like a boy answering roll call.

"And the other two ladies?" The officer's tone remained neutral. His pen stayed pocketed. This wasn't for forms.

Kevin swallowed. "Sonia and Sarah. Samantha's sisters. They've... been staying."

"For some time?"

"A while."

The officer let that float, then nodded, as if time were an elastic he wouldn't test tonight. "And you've lived here...?"

"Eight months," Kevin said. "Give or take." Eight months of lemon and lists and a house that learnt his name and made up better uses for it.

"I see." The officer's gaze skimmed the mantelpiece: a framed postcard of Florence (or Venice), a jar of dried rosemary, an old Singer manual propped like a relic. He did not touch anything. "No children in the home?"

"Not yet," Kevin said, and then bit the inside of his cheek until heat rose. The word had been an instinct, a habit. *Not yet* was a phrase for couples who kept soft hope in drawers. Not for this house. The officer's eyes registered the slip and moved on with mercy.

"You said upstairs there was... noise." He didn't say *machine*. He didn't say *singing glass*. "Who was with you at the landing when the fall occurred?"

Kevin's mouth went dry. Memory returned in strobe: shoulders slamming; the hiss of breath; the squeal of the second tread like a delighted child; lightning's white cruelty; hair, blood, the fussing of a candle. "Two of them," he said carefully. "In the corridor. The third—" He stopped. The silence shaped itself into an answer and refused to be said aloud.

"The third?" the officer prompted gently.

"In the room," Kevin said, and the vagueness curdled his tongue. "Then... it was dark."

"I understand." The officer didn't write it down and Kevin was grateful not to see the sentence in ink: *It was dark.* "There's something else," the man added, softer still. "May I ask—has there been any... confusion around identities in the home?" He lifted a palm. "I'm not trying to be intrusive. It's just—we have statements from neighbours. More than one mentioned seeing 'Samantha' on two separate errands at the same time. A mix-up with the bins. A gate hinge at number twelve."

Kevin let out something like a laugh and failed to land it anywhere. "They're triplets," he said, which was both explanation and the beginning of any interesting disaster. "People... mistake them. Even we do, sometimes." *We.* The word came out easily now, harmlessly. It had teeth in it.

"I see." The officer nodded again, thoughtful. "I ask because when I spoke to your neighbour just now, she said—and I quote—'You never can tell which one is Mrs Hayes.' I told her that's not our business tonight. Still—" He spread his hands. "It's a small street."

Kevin stared at the rug. The fibres offered no counsel. Lemon hovered under the colder smells of wet cloth and extinguished candles. Somewhere underfloor a pipe ticked three times, waited, ticked again. He thought of the spare room's scratched handle; the comb on the folder; the word in the vent. *Mine.*

"Mr Hayes," the officer said, and the room narrowed. "How many women live here?"

It was not asked to trick. It was asked to anchor. A simple datum, clean for a form: one line, a number.

Kevin opened his mouth and nothing came out. He had the answers he'd always given to council tax, to deliveries, to well-meaning colleagues who thought moving house meant a baby next.

*Three sisters, one wife.* But saying *one wife* felt like lying in front of a mirror. Saying *three wives* turned him into a man he wasn't ready to despise. The house, sensitive to theatre, exhaled faintly through the vent, the faintest of breaths, and he swore it shaped itself—just for a heartbeat—around the syllable he had heard in dreams. *Mine.*

He tried again. "Three," he said, then immediately, helplessly, "One." The officer's eyebrows drew together in patient confusion. "Three women," Kevin clarified, choking on grammar, "live here. One is my wife." The sentence sounded like a problem set in a school where the answers always disappointed the teacher.

"Which?" the officer asked. Not a trap. A bridge.

Kevin saw Samantha's hands, steady on the banister cloth. He saw Sonia's notebook hidden behind a false back. He saw Sarah's handwriting in black defiance on a whiteboard that refused to forget. He saw the photo of three girls labelled Sam. In his mind he stood by the river, watching a stranger raise a hand in greeting. In his body he stood in a lemon-scrubbed room where a chandelier trembled with the memory of song.

"Mr Hayes?" the officer prompted.

Kevin licked his lips. The key in his palm pressed a small moon into his skin. He could speak the tidy answer and deliver them all into a bearable morning. He could speak the untidy truth and invite the house to finish the night for them.

A floorboard, somewhere under the middle of the sitting room, knocked—once, twice, three times—polite as a summons. The officer's eyes flicked down; he composed his features into what people wear when they decide to believe in plumbing.

Kevin stared at his reflection in the dark window: a man in a house that changed its mind about numbers, a face already learning how to forget in the shape of remembering. The rain's woolly threads blurred his outline. Behind him, faint and insistent, the glass seemed to gather three figures into one and split them again, as if the weather were practising their magic.

He opened his mouth to answer.

Lemon rose in his throat like a vow.

# Chapter Twenty-Seven
## The Ledger Opens

S onia did not sleep. She lay on her side with her palms pressed together the way children pray when they're trying to remember the words. The house breathed its thin, practical draught past the gap under her door; somewhere a pipe ticked like a metronome learning to count to three; on the landing the second stair rehearsed a squeak in dreams. When she closed her eyes she saw the blue sheet and the candle ring on the wood, and when she opened them she saw the wardrobe. Behind its false back waited the thing she had promised herself to show him. If she hesitated any longer, the house would make a rule out of it.

At half five she gave up the pretence. She dressed in yesterday's cardigan and moved lightly across the floor, toes instinctively missing the nail heads that lived under the rug. The wardrobe door breathed open. She pressed the little hidden catch; wood thinned to a secret; the panel swung inward. The book lay where it had lain for years, battered cloth and blunt corners, the ledgers of her cowardice and her care stitched together. She lifted it out and held it to her chest for a heartbeat, as if it could heat her. It didn't. Paper holds cold better than people.

\*\*\*

The hall was grey with the sort of morning that demands explanation and receives none. She knocked softly at Kevin's door and then opened it before he could pretend to be asleep. He was sitting with his back against the headboard, a man taught upright by a night. His eyes went first to the book. She hated that; she wanted them to go to her face.

"I know what that is," he said, voice speaking inwards.

"You don't," Sonia answered, and sat at the foot of the bed, ledger held like a pet that might bite. "But you will."

He rubbed his jaw; his fingers came away clean. The brown smear he'd left on himself in the night had disappeared under a flannel and the lemon soap that made grief smell respectable. "Samantha—"

"Samantha isn't up yet," Sonia said. It was true and it was also a prayer. "Please, before she is."

He nodded—quick, guilty—and moved to the chair by the window where the light came without judgement. She opened the ledger on the bedspread between them and breathed in the old scent of glue and paper and the slight mineral note of whatever the house leaked into everything. The first page was the first sin: *Rule One: One face. One voice. One wife.* Her handwriting at fifteen: neat, obedient, eager to be accepted into law.

Kevin reached out and stopped himself an inch above the paper. "May I?"

She nodded and felt shame flood her cheeks like warmth. "I wrote them down because I thought keeping them neat would make them kinder."

He turned the pages carefully, as if pages could shatter. There were rules she remembered as if she still had to recite them at the door—*No locked doors; no private friends; we speak with one mouth; money is for the house*—and others she had written for herself in the margins like defensive spells—*Don't make her angry in the morning; don't speak if the whiteboard is wet; tell the truth when silence harms.* Kevin skimmed, stopped. He touched a taped-in photograph. The whiteboard in one of its angrier days: NO RULES ABOUT MY BODY, Sarah's black jab, and beneath it someone's smaller mercy (safely), a word that had never felt less honest.

"You took these?" he asked.

"Every time I could," Sonia said. "Before they were wiped. I thought... if I kept them, then what we did wouldn't rot into nothing." She pointed. "Here. The day Samantha wrote KEEP THE PACT OR LOSE THE HOUSE. And Sarah answered. You can see the felt tip bleeding through even after it was scrubbed. The board remembers. So did I."

He turned another page. There, feathered with soot, was the brass tag she had found behind the panelling, glued beside a rubbing of its letters. S.W. He frowned. "S.W."

"We don't know whose," Sonia said. "It could be anything. Somebody Ward. Somebody Wright. Somebody... Sam something. It was behind burnt paper. As if someone else made their own rules and then tried to cook them into ash."

Kevin's thumb stroked the rubbing unconsciously. "How far back does it go?"

"The tag?" Sonia shrugged. "Someone's past. The ledger?" She tapped the spine. "Fifteen years. I added receipts, the whiteboard. And this." She turned to the middle where, glued across two pages, sat the photograph they had pulled from under the sewing table: three girls with the same grin, ribbons, missing teeth. Across the bottom, in a child's determined scrawl, Sam Sam Sam.

Kevin flinched as if he'd been struck by paper. "You were... what? Practising?"

"We were told we were better when we were the same," Sonia said. "By teachers. By aunties. By neighbours who liked neatness. Samantha heard it as a calling. Sarah heard it as a plague. I heard it as a duty. We held hands and said we'd make the world easier by being one good girl. And then we grew up and found out *one good girl* lands better than *three complicated women*. We mistook the applause for love."

Kevin kept turning. Here were the days when Samantha's lists overlapped entirely with their lives: rota diagrams, tidy grids—*S = Monday shop; S = Tuesday, Lido; S = Thursday, Kevin's work do*. The little S's all the same, rounded, perfect; the lie built into graph paper. Here were the weeks of Sarah's rebellion in thick black blocks that smudged the lamination. Here, now, the fresh prints of the kitchen last night, the ultimatum and the answer: KEEP THE PACT OR LOSE THE HOUSE / THEN I'LL LOSE THE HOUSE boxed in anger that the whiteboard refused to forget.

He stopped at a page she had glued only a day ago: the comb resting on Kevin's folder, photographed in nauseous clarity, its teeth glistening. Beside it, a bus ticket stub. In the margin Sonia had written, The house leaves notes. Lemon is a signature.

He gave a small, miserable laugh. "I thought I was the archivist," he said. "My folder. My tests."

"You are," Sonia said softly. "Yours has numbers. Mine has weather."

He turned more pages. Photographs of the Singer's treadle; of the sash catch that cut the light into thin permissions; of the stair with its candle ring; of the little brass screws in a jar that had lived in the sewing room long before them. The ledger had become a museum of unnerving, and the curator was ashamed.

Kevin closed his eyes for a second. When he opened them he was careful again. "Sonia, why show me now?"

"Because last night happened." The sentence lay between them like a cold thing that would never warm. "Because once something is dead in your hall you either lie forever or you start telling the truth before it

kills someone else. Because I wrote a rule and I'm trying to keep it." She
pointed: *Tell the truth when silence harms.*

He nodded. "We leave, then."

Her heart lurched as if it had been tugged by thread. "We leave,"
she said. Saying it didn't make it safer. "Today. Before she wakes. We
can get the train north. I have an aunt who still thinks I'm sweet. We
can come back with... with help." The last word felt treacherous in the
mouth, like grass in church.

"We can't just—" he said, and stopped because yes, they could. They
could. People leave houses. It is allowed. They teach you how at school
(Fire Drill), and again as an adult (Escape Room), and again in books
(Pilgrims). Even if the house made it feel like treason.

"We can," Sonia said, fierce for once. "We take bags and the ledger.
You take your folder. We tell the truth to someone whose job is to hold
it even when it breaks people."

His gaze flicked instinctively to the door, to the landing, to the hall
where the house liked to listen. "She'll stop us."

"Not if we go now," Sonia whispered, as if speed could trick law.
"Kevin, please."

He stood and the bed complained at being relieved of him. "Ten
minutes," he said. "I'll pack. You—" He looked at the ledger and back
at her. "Guard that."

She hugged the book as if it were a baby. "I will."

***

They moved with a furtive, unnecessary quiet, the ridiculous hush of
people creeping away from their own life. Sonia put on shoes that
didn't squeak and folded two jumpers into a bag with the efficiency of

someone betrayed by weather. She wrapped the ledger in an old cardigan because cardigans believe in decency. In the corridor, Kevin's door opened and shut without fanfare. Sarah's door remained dark-still. The landing air smelt faintly of damp and candle. Somewhere downstairs, a clock remembered how to be precise and made half-six sound like an insult.

They met in the kitchen. It had been tidied in the night—of course it had. Mugs rinsed and upturned, tea towel smoothed, chairs square. The whiteboard shone; if you looked straight on it was blank with zeal. If you slid your gaze, the ghost letters showed: THEN SPEAK OUT LOUD the faintest of bruises.

"Keys?" Sonia asked.

Kevin patted his pocket. The spare room key printed its crescent in his skin. "Yes."

"Phones?"

He held up his. "Yes."

Sonia reached for her coat and found it was not where she had left it. She frowned at the peg as if it might be playing a small joke. The coat hung on the peg to the left, neat, out of the way where the house likes to keep things that intend to disobey. She took it down with more force than needed. "We're going now," she told the room.

The room shook a picture on the far wall—barely—a cheap print of a fox that had always looked a little too shiny to be real. It straightened itself a second later. Sonia felt the hair on her arms lift. "We're going," she said again, but softer, as if the house liked manners.

They made it as far as the hall. Kevin lifted the latch. The door stuck—not on swollen wood; on will. He leaned his shoulder. The wood yielded with a sly little sigh, the way pets forgive you. Rain had eased to that light, defeated spin that cities do when they've finished threatening and gone back to work.

"Bags," Kevin said. "Folder—"

"My bag," Sonia said, and turned back to pick up the cardigan-wrapped ledger from the kitchen chair where she'd set it a moment ago.

It wasn't there.

She stared at the empty seat, at the indent her book had left, at the neatness of absence. She turned slowly, as if she could rotate herself to exactly the angle where the past continued. The book lay on the table, atop the tea towel, centred as if set down by a person who liked fruit bowls. She had not set it there.

"Kevin," she whispered.

He came back, door still ajar, a pane of damp air leaning in. He saw her face, then the book. He did that thing men do when they have to decide whether to believe the story objects tell. "You...?"

"I didn't move it."

He approached as if the ledger might startle. He placed his palm atop it, as if to hold it still. The room exhaled through the vent with an air of patience. Sonia lifted the book, wrapped it again, placed it into her bag, zipped. The bag felt heavier than it should. Weight of paper. Weight of rules.

They turned toward the door again. Sonia slotted her arms into her coat sleeves. Kevin picked up his folder from the dresser. When Sonia reached for her bag strap, the bag wasn't on her shoulder. It stood two feet away, propped against the chair leg, mild as a pet that will not be coaxed into the carrier.

She laughed—a thin, high mistake. "No."

Kevin's mouth set. He stepped to the bag, placed his hand on the strap, lifted. The strap slid through his fingers. He gripped harder and felt the absurd pull of a thing that did not want to be lifted. "Stop it," he said to no one, and to the house, and to the fear that makes people stupid. He picked up the entire bag in both hands and brought it to the door.

The hall mirror caught them at an angle: a man holding a bag like a child, a woman with her mouth too thin, a house practising being a person. They crossed the threshold. The bag strap wrenched once—petulant, or his imagination—and then behaved. The step swallowed them. The door remembered to click. On the pavement a woman with a pushchair went past with breakfast-in-hand and the dignity of people who do not have operas in their kitchens.

"Go," Sonia said. "Before it decides we need to stay."

They made it five paces. A thought that wasn't a thought arrived in Sonia's mouth out of nowhere and she stopped. "Keys," she said. "Did we... did we lock the—"

Kevin blinked rain off his lashes. "Leave it," he said. "We're not coming back this morning."

"We should lock," she said, because being tidy is a narcotic. "It's responsible."

He turned back with the defeated grace of a man who knows how to lose to habit. Sonia stood with her bag clutched and watched him check the latch, watched him half-close the door to test it, watched him put his palm on the wood the way Samantha had done last night as if doors answered to touch. The act took three seconds. Three seconds in which a house exercises all the rights you concede to it.

When they stepped into the kitchen once more to collect the train tickets Sonia had left on the table (she had not; the table insisted), the ledger lay open.

She had zipped the bag. Wrapped the book. Carried it out. The bag still hung from her shoulder. It was lighter than it had been; she had known it in her heart and chosen to lie.

The ledger was open to a page she did not recognise. The paper was hers, but the ink wasn't. In the exact middle, in letters that looked printed but had the small human wavering of hand, one word had been written:

MINE.

The dot of the I was a lemon smear. Not drawn. Dabbed. The faint oily sheen caught the wet morning light.

Sonia reached without meaning to and touched the dot. Lemon rose, polite and triumphant. She put her finger to her nose and smelt Samantha and whiteboards and the good, clean destruction of polish. Her stomach went cold.

Kevin stood very still. "You didn't write that."

"No." She swallowed. "Did you?"

"Of course not."

They both looked at the door. The hall stood unconvincing in its innocence. The vent breathed a thread of air that skirted her knuckles. Somewhere above, the chandelier gave one modest note as if to underline.

"Take it," Kevin said, jaw set. "Take it anyway."

Sonia closed the ledger carefully. The word MINE shone through the paper as if ink could be a light source. She could feel the lemon tack on her fingertip drying to nothing, leaving only story. She slipped the book back into the bag and zipped and triple-checked the zip, as if metal teeth could keep a house out of paper. She slung the strap across her body like armour. "Now," she said, and did not care whether she sounded brave. "Now we go."

***

They reached the door again. The latch was obedient. The wood pretended to like them. They stepped out into a morning that had decided on drizzle. Sonia put one foot onto the pavement and felt it give her weight, which was, briefly, a miracle.

Behind them, very gently, very decently, the door closed. It did not slam. It clicked, a courteous mouth shutting on a sentence. The second stair inside squealed quietly to itself.

Sonia didn't look back. She gripped the strap where the ledger rode her hip and walked down the path with a pace that surprised her.

Three houses along, at the corner where the fox poster in the estate agent's window pretended to be a map, the bag tugged again. She tightened her grip and refused the tug. Kevin matched her stride. The train, she told herself, lived at the end of a series of pavements and she knew how to win pavements. She had walked them every day of her life and stayed in the house anyway. Today she would continue.

They turned the corner. Rain wrote its tiny script on her cheeks. She looked up and watched the sky hold its water the way people hold their breath when someone difficult is talking.

"Don't stop," Kevin said.

"I won't," Sonia said.

She didn't.

Behind them, the house exhaled once through vents and chimneys and keyholes. It sounded like laughter in a throat that knows it's not polite.

Sonia did not quicken. She did not slow. She thought of the word on the page she had not written, the lemon dot above the I, and felt something in her spine harden that had been chalk for years.

The ledger knocked once against her hip, twice, three times, polite as a metronome.

"Not yours," she told it softly.

But when they reached the end of the street and she checked—because you check, even when checking breaks you—the bag had zipped itself a fraction open.

And inside, the ledger had opened again to the page with MINE. The lemon dot had smeared to make a tiny, radiant halo.

Sonia zipped it shut with shaking hands and didn't look at Kevin because if she did she would ask him to carry it and that would be a theft she could not forgive in herself.

They walked on.

The house behind them let the chandelier sing one last, silvery note into the empty hall and then went about putting their shoes back into pairs.

# Chapter Twenty-Eight
## The Swap

Kevin hadn't meant to find her there. He'd left the bedroom because the walls were too close, the bed too neatly made by hands that weren't his, and the silence pressed like an unwanted second skin. He padded barefoot to the living room and discovered Sarah already claimed it.

She sat at the far end of the sofa, knees tucked to her chest, cardigan sleeves bunched in her fists. The only light was the orange spill of the streetlamp through lace curtains. It dappled her face into patterns, hiding more than it showed.

"You're awake," Kevin said, trying for neutral.

"You too," she murmured.

He lowered himself onto the opposite cushion. The sofa sagged, and he felt the dip drag them a fraction closer. Between them lay the cushion with a threadbare patch Sonia had promised to mend. The Singer in the sewing room hadn't stopped humming in his head since the night of the fall; he could almost believe the stitches were still being laid somewhere in the dark.

For a long moment, they let the house do the talking: radiator clicks, the faint hiss of pipes, the polite groan of the second stair even though no one stood on it. Then Sarah whispered, "Do you remember?"

Kevin frowned. "Remember what?"

She uncurled slightly, her voice a whip crack and a plea all at once. "Nights. In bed. The way she smelt sometimes—not lemon, but smoke.

The way she moved slower, or not at all. The words she used, different ones. You noticed. Don't tell me you didn't."

His breath snagged. He had noticed. Once, Samantha had whispered "darling" instead of "Kev." Another time, her hair smelt faintly of the cheap roll-ups the neighbours smoked out back. He had filed those moments away under marriage: moods, quirks, tiredness. Now they returned sharpened, accusing.

"I thought—" He stopped, tried again. "I thought it was her. Just her being... different."

Sarah's laugh was bitter. "It wasn't. It was me."

***

The words knocked the air from him. "What?"

"Sometimes," she said, looking at him now, eyes black with truth. "Some nights, we swapped. She asked, or I offered. To keep the peace. To keep the lie neat. One face, one wife—that wasn't just for the neighbours, Kevin. It was for you. So you wouldn't see the cracks."

Kevin's throat closed. The room tilted. "No. I'd have known. I would have known."

"Would you?" she pressed. "You didn't. That's the point. You never saw. You never asked. You thought you were tired. You thought she was moody. But that was me you touched, Kevin. Me."

He put his head in his hands. The memories swarmed, corrupted. Every night blurred into another. Which voice had said "I love you"? Which body had turned towards him in the dark? Which face had he kissed half-asleep, trusting it belonged to his wife?

"Oh God," he whispered, "I don't even know who I touched."

Her expression softened for a heartbeat. "Now you understand. Why she wanted it. Why I hated it. Because if you couldn't tell, the pact held. You were hers. We were hers. And I was just... a substitute."

Kevin dragged his hands down his face. He wanted to scream, to wake the whole street, to drag the neighbours from behind their curtains and shout the truth. But the truth was contaminated. Every memory he owned was suspect.

Sarah leaned forward, elbows on her knees, hair falling in a dark curtain. "I'm done being her shadow," she said. "The baby changes everything. She'll want to claim it, fold it into her rules. But it's mine, Kevin. Mine. And I'll prove it."

The chandelier above them trembled once, releasing a faint, silvery note into the room. The sound settled into Kevin's chest like a bruise.

He stared at her, hollow. "Prove it how?"

"Science," she spat, as though the word were a weapon. "Not her lists, not her board. A test. Numbers. Results. Something she can't wipe away with a cloth."

Kevin closed his eyes. For a moment he wished he could return to ignorance, to the days when odd scents and strange words were nothing but quirks of marriage. But that door had slammed shut. He could still hear the echo.

Sarah stood and moved towards the curtained window. Her outline blurred against the streetlamp glow, the lace pattern cutting her into fragments. Kevin stayed seated, palms pressed into his thighs as if anchoring himself to the sofa.

"It started when we were girls," Sarah said without turning. "Games. Harmless, we thought. Swapping places to confuse teachers, friends, strangers. Samantha kept the score. Sonia always laughed. I..." She hesitated, fingers brushing the curtain edge. "I hated it. But I played along, because saying no made her look at me like I'd ruined the show. And ruining the show was a sin in our house."

Kevin's voice cracked. "You carried it into marriage?"

"She did," Sarah corrected, glancing over her shoulder. "Samantha said it was necessary. That one wife with three faces was safer, easier, more perfect. That you didn't need to know. That if we took turns, the burden would be shared." She gave a small, jagged smile. "Shared, like chores. One night I'm the dusting, the next I'm the bedding."

He recoiled. The metaphor lodged like glass. "And Sonia?"

"She stayed out as much as she could," Sarah said. "She's too soft. She patched the holes, smoothed the edges, made excuses. Sometimes she covered for us in daylight. But she didn't... she didn't go into your bed. Not like we did."

Kevin clutched at his head. "Christ."

Sarah's tone hardened. "Don't you dare play the victim. You never looked close enough to notice. You let yourself be fooled because it was easier. You smelled smoke and thought nothing. You heard different words and told yourself it was mood. You wanted one neat wife, Kevin, and you let us provide her."

The accusation landed heavy. Kevin opened his mouth, closed it again. His mind raced back over years of marriage: the dinner parties where Samantha's laugh rang unfamiliar; the mornings when the kiss was gentler, hesitant; the nights when the sheets smelt of someone else's shampoo. He had known something, deep down. He had chosen not to dig.

Sarah crossed the room and crouched before him. Her eyes blazed with tired fire. "You think I liked it? Being her stand-in? Being your wife when I never chose you? I did it because she demanded it. Because saying no meant war. And because... sometimes, just sometimes, I wanted to be seen. Even if it was through her mask."

Her confession shook with rage and something like grief. Kevin wanted to reach for her hand but stopped, unsure which part of her he would be touching—the rebel, the victim, or the liar.

"You said you'll prove the baby's yours," he said at last, voice unsteady.

Sarah's hand went instinctively to her stomach. "Yes. Because if I don't, she'll take it. She'll fold it into the pact, raise it as another shadow, another mask. I won't let that happen."

Kevin whispered, "And if it's not mine?"

She flinched. "Then at least it's not hers. At least it's mine to keep."

Silence swelled. The house pressed its weight around them, listening. A faint draught rolled down the chimney, lemon-scented and smug. The chandelier gave another tiny tinkle, like polite applause.

Kevin stood abruptly, pacing. His mind whirled with images: Samantha writing rules on the board, Sonia smoothing them into lies, Sarah clawing her way out with rebellion. And himself, centre of the storm, blind.

He turned back to Sarah. "You should have told me. Years ago. Before—"

Her laugh was harsh. "Told you? And what? You'd have stayed anyway. You'd have chosen her version of the story. You always do. You like your truth tidy."

The words cut, because they were true. Kevin thought of his folder, his tests, his attempts at investigation—all neat, all boxed, all desperate for order. He was no better than Samantha, just clumsier.

Sarah rose, defiant. "No more tidiness. No more masks. I'll get the test, Kevin. And whatever it says, I'll be free. For once in my life, I'll be myself."

Her hand pressed harder against her stomach. The gesture was fierce, protective, almost sacred.

Kevin watched her, heart pounding. For the first time, he saw her not as "the third wife" but as a woman trying to claw her way out of a labyrinth built by her sister.

The radiator ticked its three-count. The chandelier stilled. The house seemed to lean closer, listening, as Sarah vowed to break the pact.

***

Sarah fetched her phone from the mantel where it sulked between a jar of rosemary and a postcard of a city Kevin refused to name aloud. She unlocked the screen with a thumb that shook only a little. The blue light painted the bones of her face. Kevin stayed where he was, arms folded as if his ribs needed guarding.

"Private clinic," she said, more to herself than him. "No GP. No paperwork that can be tidied by someone else."

She typed deliberately, each tap a blow: paternity test London clinic same day. Links bloomed. She chose one with a reception that answered in her head before she dialled—brisk, kind, mercenary. The website was too white, too clean; photographs of handsome people telling the truth with digits. She filled a form: name (she used one), contact (hers), gestation (she winced and wrote it), preferred appointment (Thursday, 10 a.m.). She pressed Confirm. The screen thought, then softened into a calm sea of tick marks.

Kevin exhaled. "Done?"

"Done," she said, and for a second she was a person turning a corner into a new street.

The confirmation email arrived with a delicate chirrup. She opened it to admire her victory:

Subject: Appointment Confirmation — Paternity Consultation

When: Thursday 10:00
Where: *Clinic address*

The words steadied her. "I'll go alone," she added quickly, before Kevin could volunteer himself like penance. "You'll only make it look like permission."

He didn't argue. He rubbed his thumb against his bitten palm instead, as if reading his own skin.

The email shimmered. That's the only way to describe it. Not a glitch, not really; a blink. The timestamp in the corner hiccupped and the body of the message refreshed as if embarrassed.

When: Wednesday 15:00

Sarah froze. "No." She stabbed the back arrow, reopened. Wednesday 15:00 blinked back, serene. She swore under her breath—Sonia's word, learnt years ago, small and precise. "I didn't pick Wednesday."

"Refresh it," Kevin said, already crossing to her.

She did. The wrongness persisted, polite as a new plaque over an old name.

"You put Thursday," he insisted, voice thin. "I saw."

"Then look." She thrust the phone into his hands. He read, lips tightening, as if he could bite the text into obedience. The chandelier above them gave a shy tinkle, three notes spaced like coins placed carefully on a counter.

Sarah snatched the phone back and opened her calendar app. The clinic's invitation had already installed itself. It sat there in Wednesday, not Thursday, a neat blue block between Midwife Qs (a note she'd made and never kept) and Supper (Samantha's recurring fiction). She pressed and held to drag it. The square moved obediently under her finger into Thursday, slotted into 10:00, glowed as if relieved, and then—just as her breath began to lower—slid back on its own into Wednesday at 15:00, smug as a child returning to a favourite seat.

Kevin let out a sound like a swallowed shout. "It's synced to something."

"To her," Sarah said.

She opened Settings with ruthless taps. Notifications, calendars, accounts. Samantha's email wasn't on her phone; it never had been. But the house loved a network the way ivy loves brick. In Calendars a new colour had appeared: a cool, lemon-tinted green labelled Home. Sarah's thumb hovered over the toggle. "I didn't—"

She switched it off. The calendar went briefly blank as if sulking, then repopulated itself without the offending colour. The clinic appointment remained. Wednesday. 15:00. She switched Home back on; switched it off again; swore; switched it on. No difference. The event might as well have been carved into the screen.

"Phone them," Kevin said. "If it's a clerical thing—"

She hit Call before he finished. The ring purred. A woman answered, brisk kindness turned into vowels. "Good evening, Westgate Diagnostics."

"Hi," Sarah said, fighting for civility. "I just booked a consultation for Thursday at ten. Your email says Wednesday at three. I need it to be Thursday."

"Let me check," said the woman, and her keyboard made little obedient sounds. "Hmm. I have you down as Wednesday at fifteen hundred."

"That's not what I selected."

The keyboard clattered more thoughtfully. "It may have auto-allocated based on availability."

"I didn't consent to auto-anything," Sarah snapped, and immediately smoothed her tone. "Please. It has to be Thursday."

"We don't have Thursday morning. I can offer Friday at nine."

"Thursday," Sarah said again, like a spell. "Or I don't come."

A pause. The receptionist sighed in professional regret. "We can't hold Thursday morning. I can place you on a cancellation list."

Sarah closed her eyes. The chandelier chimed once, bright and unhelpful. Somewhere in the walls a vent gave a slow, satisfied exhale. "Fine," she said. "Put me on the list."

"Done. You'll receive an updated email if a slot opens." The woman brightened, reading from script. "Just to confirm—Wednesday at three remains your current appointment."

Sarah ended the call without thank you. Kevin didn't chastise her. The house could be polite for them both.

"Different clinic," he suggested.

"Five clinics," she replied, already typing. She booked a second, a third. Each confirmation arrived with the same neat betrayal: Wednesday 15:00. On the fourth, the website crashed while loading the payment page and returned her to an unrelated advert for lemon oil. She pressed the X so hard she thought she'd bruise the glass.

"Landline," Kevin said. "Let's try something analogue."

They used the old phone Sonia insisted on keeping for power cuts. Sarah watched the handset like it might grow a rule. She dialled, booked, insisted on Thursday 10:00, spelt her chosen alias twice. The clerk repeated Thursday back, cheerful. "You'll receive an email in just a moment."

The landline clicked and replaced itself with the faint noise of weather. Sarah stared at the receiver like it might explain loyalty. Her mobile chimed. She looked. Wednesday 15:00. The subject line had grown a little at the end, as if someone had learnt emoji to mock her.

Kevin swore into his fist. "This is impossible."

"It's her," Sarah said, notable for not shaking. "She's already in my future. She's moving the hours like furniture."

She walked to the printer by the Singer—a concession to modernity the Singer tolerated with poor grace. "Fine," she said. "Paper. Paper is harder to edit." She hit Print from the email. The machine woke, grumbled, dragged the sheet through its throat, and spat a page that smelt faintly—impossibly—of lemon. The ink was damp. Wednesday 15:00 dried in glossy certainty. She printed again, changed nothing. Wednesday 15:00 slid out, patient. On the third try the printer paused, as if thinking, and delivered a blank page. When she held it to the light, watermark faint, she saw a word soaked invisibly into the fibre: OURS.

She dropped the sheet like it had bitten her. The chandelier shivered, very pleased with itself.

Kevin moved to her shoulder. He read the word and went grey. "We leave the house to book. We go to a café."

She nodded, already shrugging into a coat. "Now. Before she decides we need sleep." The Singer gave a soft tut. The vent breathed lemon. "Now," Sarah repeated, and the room obeyed by letting them pass.

They walked two streets in drizzle, to a café that didn't belong in their lives—chrome chairs, stale pastry smell, a barista with a tattoo of a fox reading a book. The phone struggled with the café Wi-Fi like a person learning manners. Sarah booked again, slow, deliberate. The barista's radio hissed into a song about honesty and then lost signal. The confirmation arrived. Kevin leaned over the screen. He read it like a man checking a pulse.

Thursday 10:00.

They both exhaled. Sarah forwarded it to Sonia, to herself, to a redundant email she kept for beginnings. She screenshot the message, printed it to PDF, saved it to Files. The café's printer? The barista shook his head. "Sorry, love. Out of ink." He smiled with teeth he'd paid to straighten. "Screenshots last forever," he lied.

They stayed long enough to drink two cups of something that claimed to be tea. The confirmation stayed Thursday. The radio found its station again as if ashamed.

***

"Home?" Kevin said.

"For now," Sarah answered, hating the words. On the walk back, the rain arranged itself into needles. The house at their street's turn looked like a woman waiting in a doorway, arms folded, patient.

Inside, the kitchen had been tidied again—someone had straightened the tea towels into faith. Sarah placed her phone face-down on the table, as if that could hold time still. She didn't pick it up again until the house's evening made a shape around them. When she did, it vibrated like a guilty heart.

The clinic had sent an "update"—just in case she hadn't seen. Appointment Reminder: Wednesday 15:00.
Underneath, a calendar invite accepted "on your behalf".

Sarah stared until the battery icon looked like a mouth.

She opened the Thursday email from the café. It still read Thursday—for half a second. Then the text swam, neatened itself, and settled into Wednesday 15:00, with a new, chirpy See you soon! added to the signature. She scrolled to the header. The time-stamp belonged to twenty minutes ago, while they'd been walking home past a fox that wouldn't meet their eyes.

Kevin put both hands on the table to stop the room tipping. "We'll go anyway. We'll turn up on Thursday and demand it."

"We'll turn up on Wednesday at three," Sarah said flatly. "Because that's when the door will open. She's already written it."

She lifted the phone and held his gaze over the slim, traitorous rectangle. "She won't steal the result," Sarah said. "I will know. Even if I have to take the test in the street."

Behind them, the chandelier allowed itself three delicate notes, evenly spaced, the sound of someone amused into patience.

On Sarah's screen, another email arrived.

Subject: Courtesy Call — We tried to reach you

Body: *Just confirming your attendance tomorrow at 15:00.*

Tomorrow. The house had changed the tense.

Sarah smiled without humour and pressed Reply. Her fingers didn't shake this time.

Attending.

She hit Send. The whoosh noise sounded too cheerful. She turned the phone face-down again, as if playing dead could fool a predator.

The vent breathed once more, lemon-bright, and then the house went still, satisfied with its scheduling.

Wednesday, 3 p.m. was now stitched into their calendar like a seam the Singer approved of.

# Chapter Twenty-Nine
## The House's Story

Kevin waited until the house chose its afternoon hush, the hour after lunch when pipes settled and the stair forgot to squeal for the pleasure of it. Sonia had gone out for paracetamol and air; Sarah was upstairs with her phone face down as if that could pin a day to the table. Samantha—wherever Samantha was—had left a trace of lemon that clung to the skirting like policy. The quiet felt staged, but it was enough.

He took a flathead screwdriver, a torch, and his folder, because superstition is only ever carefulness with different clothes on, and went to the sewing room.

The Singer sat with its throat bared to light, polished out of habit. The treadle waited like an invitation to repent. The sash window admitted a grey that made everything honest and unappealing. On the wall, the strip of panelling Sonia had prised away weeks ago sulked against the skirting, a secret that had been interrupted and put back on hold.

He knelt and pressed his palm to the panel as if asking permission from a piece of timber. The house offered him a thread of draught in return, not quite an answer, not quite not. He set the screwdriver's tip to the first paint-scarred nail and worried it loose with the care of a man retrieving a splinter from his own hand. When the nail squeaked free, the room seemed to draw breath. He told himself not to be ridiculous and worked the others out in turn.

The panel came away with a faint stick of dried paint against paint. Behind it, the cavity waited: an oblong dark enough to think things in, with lath and brick advancing at the edges like audiences in old theatres. The smell rose—dust, mouse, cold, and that faint, clean bite of something once burnt and long apologised for.

He angled the torch into the gap. Light slid over nothing and made it important. On the bottom ledge lay a scatter of blackened paper flakes, curled to themselves like dead moths. To the right, half-lodged behind a splinter of lath, glinted the brass tag Sonia had already found. He left the tag; he wanted to earn it differently. He reached in and pinched a flake between finger and thumb. It dissolved to whisper. He tried another, larger, and it held just enough to reveal the ghost of a printed letter: a serifed R becoming ...ard... or ...wright, or nothing at all. He let it go before it could demand a name.

There were more serious fragments further back, caught where the brick bit shallow into the cavity. He slid his hand deeper, skin rasping on old dare. Something scraped his knuckle—wood, nail, the memory of nails—and he gritted his teeth and kept going until he felt the corner of a page. He eased it out the way you ease a sleeping child's arm from under your ribs. It came in one piece, brittle, edges singed to scallops as if a fire had been hungry and then distracted.

It wasn't a page as such. It had the look of a pasted thing torn from its host: browned paper, lines faint, the ghost of glue. Across it, in a hand stiffer than Sonia's but no less careful, were three short rules:

One face in public.
One voice in rooms.
One name to call and answer.

Underneath, a date, half-eaten by scorch, offering only 19— and then ash. Beneath that, in smaller writing, an initial and a second letter that might have been a surname starting: S. W— The rest was gone. Smoke had kept those letters and refused to return them.

Kevin sat back on his heels. The floor under him pushed a complaint into his knees and he ignored it. He read the rules again and felt the cold knowledge slide into place: none of this had started with them. The pact might have been their invention, but the house had taught it the steps.

S. W. He ran the alphabet and its appetites. Sophia Ward. Sarah Wright. Susan Wheeler. Sabine West. Samuel something—no, that pulled the brain in an easier direction he didn't trust. The letters were both promise and misdirection, too generous and not enough. He rubbed the edge of the paper and came away with a smear of old soot.

***

He leaned back into the cavity, hunting more. The torch slid over a bundle of something wedged into the far corner—cloth or paper stiffened to cloth. He reached again and met the cold slick of an old spider's bequest. He shook it away with disgust more social than real and gripped the bundle. It resisted like a person pretending not to have heard you. He tugged harder. The bundle came, trailing dust. When he opened it on the floorboards, the smell found him first: the baked, clean stink of a fire that had done its work years ago and left the linen to rot with dignity.

It was muslin. Or had been. A scrap only, ragged at two sides and scorched at the others, with a pattern of hand-stitches so small and regular he had to squint to see them. It might have been part of a curtain, a baby's swaddle, a dress lining, a rag caught up to save something else's life. Near one edge a line of red thread darted back and

forth across a few centimetres and stopped abruptly, as if the needle
had been interrupted between vow and proof. The stitches formed no
letter in particular, but the rhythm was familiar: the rhythm of someone keeping their hands busy because the mind might misbehave if
allowed to idle.

He set the muslin aside and took the brass tag from its berth. He held
it up to the window to read the stamp proper: S.W. The initials wore
dented pride; the surface carried the scratched shine of something that
had known fingers. There was a tiny hole at one end where a thread
or chain might have gone. A luggage tag, a work token, a name from
a collar. He wanted a full name so badly he felt ridiculous, like a man
trying to bribe a coin to grow a face.

He put tag, muslin, and rule-page together on the Singer's table and
looked at them. The machine, offended by new company, refused to
purr. Its wheel contented itself with a small reprimand. The vent above
offered a draft that smelt faintly, obliquely, of polish: lemon watered
into manners.

For years he had approached the pact as a modern catastrophe: three
women, one man, a stupid romance turned monstrous by cleverness.
Now the room flexed and revealed a second frame. The pact had a
genealogy. Someone had lived here before—S. W.—and written rules
on paper rather than on the whiteboard, the same rules the house now
remembered for them even when wiped. Someone had tried to burn
those rules. Someone had failed, or the house had failed to let them.
That wasn't supernatural, strictly. Houses absorb what you say often
enough. He'd read it in a piece about old pubs and their smoke-yel-
lowed ceilings: how shouting becomes part of the paint.

Still.

He took his folder out of habit and set it beside the Singer's manual
Sonia kept propped like a prayer-book. His notes were almost embar-

rassed by the company: receipts, lists, handwriting tests, the ticket stub with the lemon-sketched sun. Sonia's ledger had contained weather; this corner of the sewing room contained archaeology.

He photographed the rule-page on his phone, though it felt wrong to bring that cold blue light into a room that preferred glow and guess-work. The camera, unbothered by desire, recorded the scants of letters. He tried a filter; the char went darker, the ink lightened. The partial date remained coy. The initial and its partner letter were no more forthcoming. He gave up before he began to invent.

He put the panel back neither fully on nor fully off and sat at the Singer with the muslin under his palm. He ran his thumb along the line of red stitches and felt the bump of each small decision. He thought of Sarah's phone tugged to the wrong hour; of Sonia's ledger being carried to the door and carrying itself back, bookish and stubborn; of the whiteboard that refused to forget; of three little notes from a chandelier accepting its role in the day. He pictured S. W.—whoever she was—writing rules in a hand that had never been taught how to forgive. He pictured her setting flame to the paper and then, perhaps, hearing the Singer start to hum without a foot on its pedal, and in her terror letting the half-burnt page drop behind the panel as if walls could be a confessional.

He should have been afraid; he was, a little. Mostly he felt the pre-posterous, practical urge to set things in an order that might survive daylight. He folded the muslin once, twice, the way shop assistants taught you to make cloth obey. Then he unfolded it again and laid it beneath the Singer's foot for no reason he could explain.

***

The foot came down of its own accord.

He flinched hard enough to knock his knee against the table and send a judder through the wood. The foot was down, and on the table the wheel ticked a fraction forward, then held. No badge of lemon here, no stagey note from the chandelier, just the heavy, intimate whisper of metal answering some pressure he had not supplied. He waited for the fantasy to pass.

A thread he did not remember leaving in the needle glimmered in the odd light, thin and ordinary, the colour of unbleached string. It ran back through the machine's path as if hands had just threaded it. He put a finger to it and felt the slight, living tension of a line under instruction.

He spoke aloud because nobody was there and someone had to be. "Don't."

The machine, which had spent a whole previous night proving it did not care for advice, made a small, obstinate sound. The wheel turned, slow, private. The needle dropped and rose, took a bite of the muslin, dropped and rose again. He snatched his hand up and then, finding himself ridiculous, made himself lower it to the table near the cloth, ready to pull it away if the machine made a bid to feed his skin. It did not. It took the muslin by a fraction of an inch at a time, a bored tailor making a demonstration stitch.

He looked toward the door despite himself. No one stood there. On the landing, perhaps, someone held their breath professionally. In the hall, the house tried out a pipe tick that might have been a knock. He waited for the predictable three, and the waiting was its own kind of apology.

The needle worked. The first centimetre of stitching came straight, then broke its patience and walked up and left, up and left, as though the machine had changed its mind mid-seam. He bent close. The thread formed an angle, then another. His scalp prickled. He told himself it was personality looking for pattern and then watched the pattern present itself anyway.

The Singer wrote with thread. A letter formed, plain as a child's block print: S.

He stood without meaning to, chair legs shrieking against the boards, and his shins hit the table so that the machine gave a sulky hiccup. It didn't stop. The thread made its juddering course, needle dipping and rising with method. The second letter arrived with even less ambiguity. Two strokes down, two across, two gentle diagonals. A.

It struck him with a force more numbing than fear that his own hands had been producing letters for weeks—shopping lists, annotations, his childish block-cap test—and the house had decided, with exquisite mockery, to show him how handwriting worked when you taught a machine to pretend at it.

"Don't," he said again, and meant *not this; not on cloth; not in this room; not with some other woman's initials on a tag turning into a word that belonged to the person who governed his day*. He reached to snatch the muslin and then didn't, because his brain flashed him an image of the needle spitting through his skin and fastening him to the cotton like an unruly patch in someone's quilt.

Another letter, quick now: M. The Singer paused in the middle of the last stroke and then, as if satisfied, lifted its foot a fraction and spat a tail of thread as tidy as the end of a sentence.

SAM.

He swallowed hard enough to taste iron. The room altered its weight about him. He lay his palm flat on the table and was absurdly grateful to find old wood there rather than the hungry mouth of a myth.

He had expected, perhaps, an after-show: a polite tinkle from the chandelier, a theatrical sigh from the vent. The house, having delivered, chose to be dignified. It gave him no applause, no overt gloat. It took back its afternoon hush and waited to see what he would make of the word laid in plain stitches on the cloth.

He looked at the brass tag—S.W.—and at the rule-page that had smuggled a half-name through fire, and at the muslin with its new alphabet. He let his eyes move from one to the other and felt the tilt of inevitability that makes people mistake ritual for destiny.

S. W. might have been *someone* Ward, *someone* Wright, a woman who had once written One face. One voice. One name and tried, belatedly, to burn the lesson out of the house. Or S. W. might have been only what you saw when you looked for what you already believed. Sam was both a person and a project now, a word men used to shorten a woman's ambition into something worn on a key ring.

He lifted the muslin and was surprised by how light it was now that it had agreed to speak. He folded it once, careful not to crease the new-made name, and slid it under his folder, as if paper could weigh cloth down. The Singer, pleased to be relieved of its duty, let the thread go slack.

Three knocks came from somewhere down in the bones of the house. Not the hurried rapping of accident, not the impatient tap of pipes, but the measured knock-knock-knock the house had adopted for statement. He closed his eyes as if he could hide from sound.

When he opened them, nothing had moved except him. The panel leaned where he'd left it. The tag shone where he'd set it down. The scorch on the paper went on making its case.

He slid the panel back into place and left the nails crooked, a promise to pretend to finish the job. He carried the tag and the rule-page and the muslin to the dresser and laid them with the caution you give sleeping creatures. He placed his folder on top as if it were a lid that could keep meanings from evaporating.

He stood a long moment, the way you stand at a grave when you're not sure whether to speak, and then turned to the door.

Behind him, the Singer's wheel twitched once—no more than a shrug—and the slack thread lifted of its own accord and lay neatly along the seam where the muslin had taken its new name. The foot patted the cloth, twice, like a teacher approving a pupil who had finally written their letters right.

He walked out into a house that had learnt how to tell its story.

# Chapter Thirty
## The Ultimatum

**M**orning performed itself to Samantha's standards: kettle at the first click, cups set lip-to-lip, knives aligned with their shadows, lemon sliced thin enough to pass for virtue. The house had been left unruly by grief; she would not let it bask in that. Order was oxygen. Maintenance, she told herself. Not denial. Maintenance.

She took from the printer a warm sheaf of paper and squared it on the kitchen table. The title sat in a font so clean it looked disinfected:

ROTATION — INFANT CARE (ONE FACE)

Below, a grid: blocks of time, initials, duties. Under NIGHT FEEDS a slender column of Ss; under CLINIC APPTS the same; under VISITORS a blank space containing instruction: S PRESENTS. O SUPPORTS. A RESTS. The baby's name line was unfilled, a dignified underscore waiting for reality to behave.

Kevin came in with the careful gait of a man who has taught himself where to tread. He paused at the table and saw the grid before he saw her. His jaw tightened. "What's that."

"Maintenance," Samantha said brightly, setting down the lemon. "We've had chaos. This puts us back in a shape we can live with."

He looked as if she'd slapped him with paper. "A rota. For a baby that hasn't—"

"For a baby whose needs won't wait while we argue," she said. "You like schedules, Kevin. They calm you. This one calms the house."

Sonia hovered in the doorway as if deciding whether she was allowed to cross. She wore a cardigan that had lost a button; she had mended one cuff with small, ashamed stitches. Her eyes went straight to the grid, then to Samantha's face. "You printed it," she said softly, as though the printer were the indecency.

"It's better than the whiteboard," Samantha said. "Paper doesn't bleed. It goes in a folder. It stands." She held out a copy to each of them, polite as a host with menus. "I've left room for flexibility."

Kevin didn't take his. "There will be no rota," he said. "No *one face*."

Samantha kept her smile, the one that never cracked. "It's a phrase, not a sentence."

"It's a prison," he said.

***

Sarah arrived behind Sonia, hair damp from a shower taken like an act of resistance. She clocked the grid, snorted. "Look at that. She's printed the cage."

Samantha laid her palm on the paper, not rough, firm. "It is my job to keep us safe."

"You failed," Sarah said, and the room reverberated, not with thunder, but with the memory of it.

Samantha went still. For a moment her expression thinned to nothing. Then it smoothed. "We manage what remains," she said. "We will not let this house become a public spectacle. We will not permit strangers to decide the words that describe us." Her hand tapped ONE FACE with a gentle, bureaucratic finger. "This keeps us from tearing."

Kevin laughed without humour. "One face tore us."

"Your folder tore you," she returned, mild. "Your appetite for proof. Your refusal to let love be enough."

He stepped closer to the table. "Say the word 'love' again in that voice and I'll put a match to every list you've ever written."

Sonia winced. "Please."

Samantha drew a breath. "The rota is sensible. Nights are heavy; days have errands. We'll present stability to the world and stability to the baby. We'll decide what she's told. We will—"

"—lie to her," Sarah cut in.

"—protect her," Samantha said, and the sparkle in her eyes hardened. "She will not grow up split into pieces for other people's entertainment."

"She will not grow up in a cult," Kevin said.

"We are a family," Samantha said. "This is maintenance."

"Grief isn't a boiler," he said. "You don't book it in for service."

Sonia had taken her copy without meaning to. Her eyes travelled the columns with the hunger of a person desperate to be told how to live well. Under SLEEP TRAINING: S. Under NAMES: One agreed diminutive only. Under PHOTOS: S approves. Sonia's mouth moved before her courage could stop it. "Why am I *support*," she asked. "Why am I never *present*."

Samantha turned to her with patient kindness. "You hate being looked at," she said. "Presenting is hard for you. It exhausts you. I'm sparing you."

"I don't want to be spared," Sonia whispered.

Something shifted at the edge of the room—air, or allegiance. The house let a draught come low through the vent, lemon diluted to politeness. The chandelier, which had chosen to be grave since the night of the fall, chimed once, cautious, like a child testing a parent's mood.

Samantha ignored the house the way she ignored anything that didn't knock on the front door and give its name. "We'll trial this for a month," she went on, reasonable, managerial. "After the paternity appointment, we'll reassess."

Sarah laughed. "*After* the appointment you moved. You've already written time, Samantha. I can't move it back."

Samantha's gaze didn't flicker. "Wednesday suits everyone. We'll go together."

"No," Sarah said. "I go alone."

"Not alone," Samantha said. "We are not leaving our story unattended in a clinic corridor."

Kevin spread his hands. "You hear yourself. *Our story.* She's a person. Not a press release."

"She is our face," Samantha replied. "Our continuation. She must be kept in one piece."

"By being three pieces," Sarah said. "You never tire of the joke."

Silence. Not because there was nothing to say, but because the words in the room had all learnt they would be cross-examined and opted to lie down.

***

Kevin picked up one of the printed pages with two fingers as if it might soil him. He read down the schedule until his eyes caught on a line halfway down:

BIRTH CERTIFICATE — FATHER: K H.

His chest tightened. "You've filled this in."

"It's a draft," Samantha said. "We'll confirm."

"You filled it in."

"I have a pen," she said. "That's its job."

He met her gaze and thought—not for the first time—that he had married a woman whose tools had become her creed. She wiped boards and believed in erasure; she wrote grids and believed in fate.

Sonia's hand trembled. "Samantha," she said, "the ledger—"

Samantha's eyes cut to her at the word. "What ledger."

"The one I kept," Sonia said, and felt her body prepare to be told she had no right to time. "The rules. The photos. The *S.W.* tag. We're leaving. We—"

"You are not leaving this house with our history," Samantha said calmly. "It doesn't belong in a stranger's boot."

"It belongs to us," Sonia said, and the line of her jaw found a strength it had not practised for years. "Not to you."

Samantha's smile was one she saved for birthdays, now misplaced. "You're frightened," she said. "Maintenance makes fear worse before it makes it better. Read the rota. You will feel steadier."

Sonia's eyes filled so fast she had to look down. The letters swam. She tapped the page with a finger that wouldn't play along. "Why is *I can rest* not on here," she asked. "Why is there no column for that."

Samantha's head tilted. "You rest when the system runs. I can't write it down for you."

Kevin slid the rota back across the table. "Listen to yourself."

"I am listening," Samantha said, and her voice shimmered between sincerity and something like threat. "I hear chaos wanting to claim us. I hear strangers at the door. I hear our name on other people's tongues. I won't allow it."

"You can't stop it by printing it," Sarah said. "You can't stop it by making the baby a mask."

Samantha's gaze moved to Sarah's hand resting on her stomach. Whatever softness she had trained into her features fell away. "You will not take her away to perform truth at men in rooms," she said. "You will not make her a weapon to hurt me."

"She isn't a weapon," Sarah said. "She's a person. She's *mine*."

The word struck like crockery on tile. Samantha did not flinch. "She is *ours*," she said, and the pronoun crept down Kevin's spine like a cold thumb. "You may carry her. I will carry the world around her so it doesn't crack her open."

"By telling her there is one of us," Sarah said. "When there are two. When there were three."

Samantha's stare hardened to glass. "There is one. There must be one."

"Why," Sonia asked, the small word enormous in her mouth. "Who told you there must be one."

Samantha did not answer immediately. She reached for the lemon and the knife and made two, three perfect rounds as if precision could repair what the question had broken. "Everyone," she said at last. "Teachers. Aunties. Neighbours. Men who look longer when there's one face to look at and look away when they realise they've miscounted. The lady at the registry. The bank. The landlord who preferred *Mrs Hayes* to *the sisters at number twelve*. The early days when we learnt how the world softens if you present the simplest version of yourself."

Kevin remembered the photograph Sonia had shown him: three girls with the same grin, Sam Sam Sam stamped across the bottom in childish certainty. He remembered the scorched rule-page in the wall: *One face in public. One voice in rooms. One name to call and answer.* He thought of the Singer writing S A M as if obeying an old spell. His anger didn't vanish. It became older.

"We won't do to the baby what was done to you," he said quietly. "No rota. No one face. She will have a name and it will be hers."

Samantha met his calm with her own. "You may believe that until the first time someone asks a question you don't know how to answer. Then you will call for me, and I will arrive with a folder that fits into their forms."

He shook his head. "No."

Sonia folded her rota till it made a small, neat square in her lap. Tears sat on her cheekbones and didn't fall, as if unwilling to trust gravity. "Sam," she tried, using the old comfort to see if it still worked, "please."

"I am Samantha," Samantha said without turning. "Now more than ever."

Sarah pushed her chair back so hard it bit the floor. "You can print as many cages as you like. I'm going to the clinic. I'm going to speak to a person who doesn't know our faces and won't pretend to. He'll take blood and spit and maths will tell us something you can't edit."

Samantha's mouth softened into pity. "You think maths is stronger than love."

"I think it's stronger than your pen," Sarah said.

Samantha picked up the rota and held it so the light glossed the title. "This is not love," she said. "It is maintenance. So that we can love."

Kevin stepped between them, not as a shield, but as a wall that declared the room divided. "There will be no *one face*," he repeated. "If you hang it on the fridge, I'll tear it down. If you put it on the whiteboard, I'll write over it. If you try to put it inside her name, I'll teach her to answer only to herself."

Samantha looked at him for a long time in which she aged ten minutes and ten years. Then she set the rota back on the table and smoothed the margin with two fingers. "You'll tire," she said. "You always do. And when you do, I'll be here, and my grid will have held the shape of your days for you."

Sonia stood suddenly, knocking her chair over with a clatter she would ordinarily apologise to. "Stop," she said, hoarse. "Please. You're doing it again. You're making words into handcuffs. I can't breathe."

For a second—not longer—Samantha's face showed true distress. It made her younger and more dangerous. "I'm trying to keep you," she said. "All of you. I am doing the job no one else will do."

"You're doing the job you gave yourself," Sonia said, and the courage it cost her trembled in her hands.

Samantha turned away. Her attention slid towards the cooker, the dials aligned, the metal vent above it that had learnt more vocabulary than metal needs. She walked to it with no more theatre than crossing a room and stood under its grille as if stepping onto a small stage she had used before anyone knew it was there.

"Enough," Kevin said, sudden anger lifting his voice. "Don't."

She rested her fingers against the tile and leaned in, her mouth close to the vent's black slots. When she spoke, it was hardly speech, more a breath pressed into consonants. "We're not finished," she whispered. "We will hold."

The vent answered.

Not loudly, not with words a stranger could transcribe, but with a soft return of breath shaped around the memory of a sentence. A thin, obedient murmur ran along the metal and came back as if the house had practised listening and found that it liked being useful.

Sonia made a sound that might have been her name broken in half. Sarah's chair scraped backwards as if repelled. Kevin felt the hair lift on his arms.

Samantha drew back from the vent, her expression smoothed into the calm she wore like a uniform. "There," she said, and the satisfaction in the single word was almost tender.

The house exhaled once, twice, three times—measured, domestic—then went still.

# Chapter Thirty-One
## The Nursery Witness

T he house hated her being here. That was enough reason to do it.

Sarah carried a book she didn't want to read and a mug of tea she didn't want to drink. The stair whined under her foot as if asking her to reconsider; she didn't. The nursery door was half-open, shy of its own purpose. Someone—Samantha—had left the cot dressed, the blanket folded with a show-home's precision, corners aligned like soldiers, ribbon tied in a little bow that pretended not to be a noose.

The room had that lemon-brightness she had come to associate with being managed. Even the light through the sash arrived in tidy rectangles. She set the mug on the sill, wiped her palms on her leggings, and tested the rocking chair. It answered with a single breath and then held, as if not wishing to over-familiarise itself with her weight.

She told herself she'd come up to plan. The appointment lay on her phone like a loaded word—Wednesday 15:00—and she needed to list the things she would say if someone tried to come with her. But the lists would not start. Her head was noise and cotton. The house's silence instead began to speak.

Under the ordinary hush—pipes thinking, radiators tick-tick-ticking in their new habit of threes, a faint draught making a ribbon lift and lie again—there was something else. A hum. It came so low she noticed it with her ribs before her ears understood. She stilled. The hum gathered, found a thread of tune, and climbed.

Above the cot hung a mobile she had not consented to, all smooth beech animals—fox, hare, bird—kept in tasteful colours that would look good in other people's photos. It moved. There was no breeze; the window was shut. Still, the wooden fox drifted, tapped noses with the hare, tipped its head politely to the bird. The hum shaped itself into a lullaby without words. Not the one their mother used to sing (that had teeth); not the one Samantha favoured (that had instructions). This was... practice. A song trying on a name.

She waited for it to stop. It didn't. Instead a second line slipped under the first, cunning in its timing, and a third answered a beat later. Three voices weaving one cradle tune, each almost the same and not. Her skin went tight.

***

"Stop," she said, absurdly formal, as if speaking to a child in a supermarket aisle.

The tune softened but did not die. The fox and hare clicked each other again like teeth being counted. Something cold laid itself on the back of her neck and remained: the knowledge that if she called downstairs and told them the nursery was singing, Samantha would come with a cloth and a rule and wipe the sound off the air.

Sarah put the book in her lap. The words on the page lost their nerve and scrambled. She stared at the paper until her eyes watered and still the music threaded through. She tried humming back, a childish counter-spell. Her voice sounded like a person pretending not to be frightened.

She stood. The chair released her with a sound like an elderly person approving of her manners. She crossed to the cot and put two fingers on the mobile's arm. It stilled at once, obedient as a child caught mid-trick. The room's quiet widened in satisfaction. Then, without any movement she could detect, the mobile began again—one slow turn, the fox rotating with the same patience she remembered in Samantha's face when people tried to change her mind.

"You've made your point," she said to the room. "I'm here."

The sash was cold under her fingers. She pressed her palm flat to the glass and felt the nursery's breath come back at her, warm, damp, human. On the outside the world made drizzle out of its earlier tantrums. On the inside a shape bloomed where her hand had been. She wiped it away with her sleeve, annoyed with herself for having left a trace, then watched as, quite neatly, the condensation wrote a single curve where her palm had cleared.

O.

Her stomach dropped. She told herself it was childish to read meaning into weather. The window continued, calm as handwriting practice. U. R. S. Four broad, fat letters, each stroke rounded and confident, as if a careful infant had been given a fingerful of water and a lesson to please someone important.

OURS.

Sarah put her fist to her mouth. The taste of tea—cool, tannic, embarrassed—sat under her tongue. "No," she said. "No, she isn't." Her breath fogged the glass and muddled the letters, but the shapes returned a second later, patient, crisp. O U R S, running down like small rivers. The word watched her with a politeness she hated.

She refused to be chased out of the room by damp and melody. She lifted the sash a fraction and let the outside in. Cold threaded itself through lemon; rain's smell shouldered the polish aside for once. The mobile faltered, uncertain which air to obey, and paused. The lullaby split into silence.

A car passed on the street below, tyres sighing through shallow puddles. Somewhere a neighbour's radio made a cheerful lie of morning. She tried to find those sounds and make them more important than the room she stood in. When she shut the window the letters had run. A trick, she told herself, in a house where tricks were simply craft performed well.

***

Her phone on the sill lit up with a new message. She reached for it—then stopped. She had learnt something in this house. There were acts that made you visible to the wrong eyes. She left the phone facedown, a little slab of refusal, and sat again. The chair gave its consenting sigh and held. She folded her arms on the book and let her head sink onto them. She would rest her back, not sleep; she would assert the right to exist in this room quietly without fleeing; she would breathe until she believed she could do it at will.

She woke to lemon.

The scent was bright enough to make her eyes sting. For a second she didn't recognise the room. The lullaby had bled into her dreams and constructed a corridor she had tried and failed to run down; the corridor had rearranged itself into childhood; childhood had spat her out at the Singer with her foot pressed where it shouldn't be. Now she was in the chair, neck stiff, the kind of small sweat that comes from shame cooling on her skin. The light had advanced to the particular grey that made everyone look as if they belonged to the house.

On the cot sheet lay a comb.

It was one of the combs Kevin had found in the other rooms and pretended not to have found before he started writing things down.

Plain plastic, neat little teeth, the length of a lie in a pocket. It had been placed just off-centre, a fraction to the left, the way Samantha always shifted a vase to make it belong to a table. The comb smelt like a citrus that had learnt to pass as cleanliness. Lemon rose from it like a signature.

Sarah put a finger to the comb's spine. It was warm. That was the worst of it. Not stage-prop cold from a cupboard, not a found thing pretending to be old. Warm from a palm.

Her jaw tightened. "No," she said again, and this time the no had marrow in it. She took the comb and set it on the window ledge as if returning a borrowed thing. Her finger smelled of lemon. She scrubbed it on her leggings and the scent brightened, triumphant.

She picked up the phone at last. The screen greeted her with good news she had not asked for: Appointment Reminder — tomorrow 15:00. She deleted it; the reminder popped back a second later, cheerful, determined. Beneath it a message from Sonia:

*Are you all right? Heard something. Like a song.*

*Nursery fine,* she typed. *Window being clever. Lemon on everything.*

Sonia replied with a heart she probably hadn't meant to choose. Then: *Come down? Tea?*

Sarah stared at the comb on the sill, its teeth catching the light like a sentence. *Five minutes,* she wrote.

She didn't move. The nursery did its patient theatre. The mobile swung one degree and then thought better of making itself too obvious. The cot held its breath like a person pretending to be asleep. The letters on the window melted into rivulets, making the glass look like a face that had cried and gotten away with it.

"If you think I won't go," she told the room, "you're wrong." Her voice came out steady. It surprised her and made something in her stand taller. "If you think you can schedule me into being yours, you're wrong.

And if you think you can make her a mask—" She stopped because the rest of the sentence was too big. "She's mine."

The vent above the door breathed and was silent, a prim little intake of the house's opinion of her speech. She snorted and stood. The chair objected, then forgave her. She picked up the comb between finger and thumb as if it might try to prickle her, and carried it to the door the way you remove a spider you do not wish to encourage.

***

On the landing she paused. Downstairs, plates made the tiny music of being placed into a rack. Sonia, probably, clinging to decency. The second stair squeaked as if excited that something was happening. Sarah put the comb on the top of the banister. "There," she told it. "Stay. Be useful."

She went down. Sonia met her with a mug and a face full of sentences she wasn't yet brave enough to say. "You look pale," she managed.

"I'm fine," Sarah lied. "The room's a child. It wanted attention."

Sonia's gaze flicked to the ceiling. "It wanted a mother," she said. "Or three."

"Not three," Sarah said, more sharply than she intended. "Never three again."

Sonia flinched, not at the word but at its certainty. "Tea," she said, defaulting to the only liturgy they still shared.

They drank at the kitchen table. The whiteboard across from them had been wiped and wiped again, the gloss showing the faint bruises of THEN SPEAK OUT LOUD when you caught it wryly. The rota sat under a magnet shaped like a lemon. ONE FACE looked impossibly neat next to the ghost of defiance under the board.

"Did you sleep at all?" Sonia asked.

"In a chair. It dreams for you." Sarah took a mouthful of tea and swallowed resentment. "The window wrote OURS."

Sonia's eyes shone with concentration, the way they did when she was holding panic still to see its shape. "Of course it did."

"Of course?"

"I mean—of course it would choose that word." Sonia folded her hands in her lap so she would not have to watch them shake. "It always chooses the word that sounds like kindness and behaves like a command."

Sarah raised her mug in a bitter toast. "You've become very wise."

"I've become tired," Sonia said. "Tired of pretending not to see what shapes the house likes."

They sat a while in the quiet. The clock remembered its job and ticked. The vent kept its opinion. Somewhere, very lightly, the chandelier tapped its pendants together to reassure itself they hadn't gone anywhere.

"Will you still go?" Sonia asked at last, voice so small a person might have missed it.

"Yes." Sarah did not say *unless I'm dead*. The house had taken a taste for stairs.

"And if she follows you?"

"Then the clinic will learn it's possible for a corridor to hold two versions of the same person." Sarah smiled without humour. "London will cope."

Sonia looked at her with love that had spent too many years apologising. "Let me come."

"No."

"Please."

"No," Sarah said, gentler. "If she's going to punish someone for it, let it be me. Not you."

Sonia stared down at her tea and saw nothing in it. "I made a rule," she said. "Tell the truth when silence harms."

"You're doing it," Sarah said. "You told me you're scared. I told you I'm going anyway. That's enough truth for a breakfast."

A shift of air made them both look at the doorway. Samantha stood there, not intruding, simply existing in the space with the certainty of a piece of furniture that refuses to be moved because a catalogue says it belongs there. Her face was calm. Calm had become her most frightening expression.

"Morning," she said. "You're up early."

"Nursery," Sarah said, as if that were an explanation rather than a provocation.

Samantha's gaze flicked to the ceiling as if she could see the room through the floorboards and approve of its alignment. "Good," she said. "She should hear voices. She'll arrive into a house that has learnt to speak properly."

"She'll arrive into a house that knows how to shut up," Sarah said. "If I have anything to do with it."

Samantha let that pass. She went to the whiteboard, wrote MILK in neat blue, and underlined it once. Then, without looking round, she said, "The comb belongs upstairs."

"I know," Sarah said. "It's waiting on the banister."

Samantha wrote BINS on the board as if the information were domestic rather than insurgent. "Put it where it lives," she said. "It's part of a set."

Sarah didn't salute. She took her mug to the sink, rinsed it slowly, made the water take its time. She imagined lifting the comb and throwing it at Samantha's face. She imagined the perfect way Samantha would catch it by the spine, turn it into an object lesson on manners, and place it, smiling, back in the dish with the other combs that had learnt to be friends.

"Going out later?" Samantha asked, a phrase so ordinary it might have belonged to a different kitchen.

"Yes," Sarah said.

"For an appointment?"

Sarah dried the mug. She put it upside down. "For air."

Samantha capped the marker and aligned it with the frame. "Don't be late for lunch."

Sarah left before she could say a thing she would then have to stand still and repeat. In the hall the comb had migrated. It sat no longer on the banister, polite and visible, but back on the cot sheet upstairs where it first had been, a line of white teeth waiting to be named useful.

She found it there when she returned to fetch her phone. The lemon was louder than before, as if proximity had made it brave. On the window the condensation—cleared by her earlier hand—showed a faint bruise where the word had been. She ran her fingertips over the glass and felt nothing. That was, somehow, worse.

She picked up the comb and dropped it into the drawer of the changing table without looking; the drawer clicked like a mouth that had been fed. She shut it with more force than necessary and the mobile stirred in its frame. The wooden fox spun once, approving something.

As she turned to go the lullaby started again—soft, cunning, plausible. She paused on the threshold and listened. One line, then a second, then the third, familiar now, all braided so the ear might call it one voice if it wanted to be lazy.

"Sing to yourself," she told it. She shut the door. The song softened as if sulking.

On the landing the stair squeaked exactly three times, like a person with nothing left but habits. Sarah took each step as if it were an argument she had already won. When she reached the bottom she felt the house press its palm against the back of her head the way a parent steadies a child for a photograph.

She ignored it and went out.

In the nursery, the comb lay where a more obedient version of her had left it a minute ago: centred, lemon-bright, its teeth glinting like a promise the house intended to keep.

# Chapter Thirty-Two
## The River Again

He told himself he was going for milk. It was the kind of sentence you could show to yourself later like a receipt. He put on his coat, took no bag, and left by the back door because the front had started to feel like a mouth. It was late afternoon, the city rinsed clean by a shower that had already forgotten itself. Clouds ran fast and pale, their undersides smudged with the sort of light that made you think of old photographs.

He walked without choosing. Past the bakery that no longer sold anything he wanted to eat. Past the launderette whose warm, damp breath used to comfort him and now smelled like a lie about cleanliness. Past the bus stop where a timetable made grand promises to people who believed in numbers. At the corner, a fox trotted ahead with the confidence of someone who knew what bins would be out on which day. It did not look back.

*** 

His feet selected turns as if a hand inside his bones were guiding. The houses shifted from neat terraces to the sulky Victorian stock that preferred to lean. The road dipped. The air freshened in the way air does when it has somewhere to go. When he looked up, railings were already at his hands—flaking black paint, iron scalloped with old weather—and beyond them the river stretched long and colourless, quilting itself with wind.

He put both palms on the rail because that was what you did at a river: you held yourself to it so it didn't take you. The water moved with the relieved determination of a thing that has remembered its job. To the right, a bridge steepled its back, iron triangles building belief out of repetition. To the left, a bend hid what came next in a way that comforted him more than he would have admitted.

"Afternoon," said a voice at his shoulder, as if they had agreed to meet and Kevin was late.

He didn't start. He looked, and there the man was—the same thin coat, the collar turned too high, the face made of ordinary features that refused to add up. The stranger's hair had that river damp you can't buy. His hands were bare and held nothing. He wasn't old—forty, fifty?—or he was very old and the river had ironed him flat. It was impossible to tell.

Kevin found himself smiling the way people smile at old enemies in supermarkets. "You again."

"You keep saying that," the man replied, a little amused. He leaned on the rail as if it was his, forearms set just where the paint had worn to smooth iron. The coat smelt of wool and rain and something faintly metallic. He didn't look at Kevin yet. "How's the house?"

Kevin made a noise that wasn't a laugh. "Hungry."

"They get like that," the man said, as if houses were a breed you could read about in a book. "Yours has a good ear."

"For what?"

"For what you refuse to say out loud." He cocked his head, listening past Kevin in the direction of the street he had come from, as though the house had chosen to send its voice down on the river wind. "Busy place. All those notes, all that wiping. I thought you'd be deaf by now."

Kevin stared at the water. He thought of the Singer writing S A M as if practising a signature. "You know the house."

"I know houses," the man said. "Yours is only the most recent to fall in love with a story."

"Whose?"

"All of yours." He smiled now, not unkind. "And that's the problem, isn't it. You want one story. Houses hate one story."

He said it as if it were not a line but a law. Kevin felt the sentence slot into place the way a true thing does—too heavy to be tidy. "Who are you?"

"A river man," he said cheerfully, which meant nothing and might have meant everything. He pinched the railing between finger and thumb, as if testing an old tooth. "The kind you meet when you're too proud to ask your neighbours for advice."

"You've been to the house." Kevin didn't frame it as a question because the man's coat smelled faintly of their lemon, impossible and distinct, like a gloved hand already in the conversation.

"Long time ago," the man said. His attention wandered to a reed bent double by its own ambition. "Or not long. Rivers reconsider the calendar."

Kevin pictured S. W., the scorched rules, the brass tag that felt too heavy for its size. "Did you know her?" he asked, surprising himself with the pronoun.

"Which her." The man's mouth twisted sympathetically. "You're learning you'll have to be better with names."

"The one who wrote the rules."

"She wasn't the first to write them," the man said mildly, "but she had the cleanest handwriting." He tapped the rail twice, light, like the beginning of the house's three-knock habit. The tap travelled along metal as if someone had laid a string. "One face, one voice, one name. Sounds like protection until you live inside it."

Kevin thought of Samantha's rota with its disinfected font: ROTA-TION – INFANT CARE (ONE FACE). "It sounds like a threat when it's printed."

"They always print it," the man said. "Paper looks like mercy until you see who's allowed to write on it." He turned his head suddenly and looked Kevin full in the face. His eyes were unremarkable and therefore disarming. "How many women live in your house, Kevin?"

The use of his name landed like a cold coin dropped onto tongue. "Three," he said, and then, because the word had become complicated, "One."

The man's smile deepened, not mocking. "You see."

"Do you—" Kevin swallowed. "Do you know which of them—" He couldn't finish. The river could. It performed a small, indifferent clap beneath the bridge.

"Death's a poor archivist," the stranger said. "You're imagining sub-traction. Try rearrangement." He peered along the water as if reading a line there. "You'll know when you need to know. Or when the house gets bored of watching you guess."

Kevin's fingers tightened on the rail. "I need to know now."

"Do you?" The man's voice softened. "Or do you need to live five more days believing you can choose what sort of man you've been."

"That's not fair."

"Rivers aren't." He lifted one shoulder, a shrug edited for politeness. "Houses either."

***

Wind came low across the water, bringing with it the scent of mud and old metal. Under it there was the faintest joy of something sweet—florist's bin bags torn, blossom beginning somewhere else. Kevin found himself naming smells the way other men name birds.

"You're not a neighbour," he said, more to give himself a sentence than to prompt an answer.

"No." The man rocked back slightly on his heels, considering the opposite bank. "Neighbours come calling with sympathy. I don't sympathise. It doesn't help."

"What does?"

"Leaving," he said promptly. "Or speaking. In that order." He moved his hand like a conductor coaxing a gentler tempo out of a stubborn orchestra. "But you'll do neither."

"You don't know me."

"I know your kind." The river ran a rippled bar across his words like a joker in a pack. "Men who think the right evidence will tame a story. Men who hold their breath until a house stops singing."

"It's not singing," Kevin said. The bridge clanked in a way that suggested disagreement. "It's... rehearsal."

"Ah," the man said with real pleasure. "Now you're getting somewhere."

They stood together a while in a grief that had decided to be sociable. A runner passed behind, worn shoes slapping compromise out of damp path. A cyclist coasted, looking past them for a fairer future. The river carried a supermarket trolley, anonymous as regret, until the weight of its own absurdity toppled it and it sank with a sound like a short laugh.

"You're going to the clinic," the man said, as casually as you would say *you're buying bread.*

"She is," Kevin said.

"Same thing," the man replied; and whether he meant the women or the days or the lies, Kevin couldn't tell. "You'll think math will save you."

"Will it?"

"For a minute," the man said. "Then the house will change the clocks again."

Kevin pressed his lips together until they whitened. "You talk as if it's a person."

"It talks as if it loves you. I'm only translating."

"Translate this," Kevin said. "S. W."

The man's head tilted. The corners of his mouth lifted as if he'd been offered a riddle at a party. "A name," he suggested, gentle. "Or a warning. Or a trick you play on yourself so you don't have to say Samantha out loud."

"You know her," Kevin said, absurdly.

"I know her type," the man said. "People who can't bear a room unless it answers to them. People who tidy grief so it won't make a mess on the good rug." He glanced back towards the street. "People who call maintenance love."

The word landed and shattered where it fell. Kevin saw the rota in his mind, the line where Samantha had filled in FATHER: K H. as if pens could declare paternity. He wanted to crush something small and safe in his fist. The only small thing near was a receipt in his pocket, and he didn't want to grant it the privilege of being destroyed.

*** 

"Why the river," he asked, because he needed to pull the conversation out of his kitchen. "Why meet me here."

"Because houses tell the truth better when they can see their reflections," the man said. "And because currents know something about not being the same water twice. Stand still long enough and you'll learn to let it pass without naming every eddy. Or you'll fall in. Either path is a kind of education."

"I can't just watch," Kevin said. "I have to keep them—" He saved himself from completing *safe* at the last second. The river would have thrown the word back.

The man's attention returned to him, fully, and it was like standing in clean light. "You can't keep anyone," he said, with no malice in it. "You can choose whether you become the fourth."

Kevin's mouth went dry. "The fourth what."

The man didn't blink. "The fourth face." He smiled again, gentler this time. "You've been auditioning for months."

"I'm not—" Kevin began, and realised he was about to say *that man.* He swallowed it and tried again. "I won't."

The man nodded as if Kevin had passed a test or failed it. "We'll see."

A gull invented a crisis above them, all noise and white. Somewhere upriver a siren tried to compete and gave up. Light thinned by increments; the water learnt pewter.

"Do you want me to go," the man asked, friendly as a shopkeeper turning the sign.

"No," Kevin said, before he could tidy the answer. "Yes. I don't know."

"Good," the man said. "Questions are honest. Answers breed rot in houses like yours."

"You haven't told me your name."

"You haven't asked me the right thing."

"What's the right thing."

The man tilted his head as if listening to instructions from further down the bank. "Ask what you came to ask."

Kevin felt a small click in his chest, like the second hand of a clock coming level. He didn't think. "Is the baby mine."

The man sighed, and it wasn't unkind. "That's not a river question," he said. "That's a kitchen question. Rivers don't do kingship. They do flood. They do drift. They do silt. Take your kitchen question to a person who likes forms."

"We're booked," Kevin said, and hated the pride that had snuck into the sentence.

"Of course you are," the man said, and the line was so like Samantha's he almost laughed. "Go at three."

"It's on Thursday," Kevin said, hearing himself offer the lie to see if anyone would take it from him.

The man's face went listening-blank. "It's on Wednesday," he said, as if correcting a child's spelling. "Houses do prefer the middle of things."

"You talk like you've been inside mine."

The man smiled. "I've been inside worse."

"What happened to them."

"They learnt not to hum," he said. "Or they burned."

The word dropped between them like a stone and kept falling. Kevin found himself thinking of the scorched scraps, the rule-page half eaten by heat. He felt the new scar in the house—the place on the stair where wax had made a white ring of refusal. He smelled, absurdly, lemon.

"What are you," he said, the pronoun slipping into something larger than a person.

"A reminder," the man said, almost kindly. "That you can't have one story in a house built for three."

"Four," Kevin said, before he could stop himself.

The man's eyes creased. "There we are."

***

Wind came up again, this time from behind, lifting the hair on Kevin's neck. The river tilted. The man's coat shifted as if it had a body of its own. Kevin half turned to look behind him—nobody, nothing—and when he looked back, the stranger wasn't there.

No fading footsteps. No polite cough and farewell. Only the lean of railings, the wet air, a smudge where an elbow had polished iron to honesty over a long, habitual time. The place where the man had stood held his absence like a shrine.

"Right," Kevin said, out loud, to prove he had a voice, and it blew thin downriver.

He took his hands off the rail, intent on punishing himself with the long walk back, and felt something in his coat pocket like a polite animal. He slid his fingers in and closed on card.

A bus ticket rested on his palm. Single fare. The paper's blue had the washed-out innocence of children's exercise books. The date was mid-March—this year—and the time printed in unapologetic digits: 15:00.

He stared until the figures doubled, then steadied. The corner of the ticket had softened as if warmed by skin. There was a darker smudge where a thumb might have pressed. The route number was one he knew by muscle memory: the bus he took when he went to the river without meaning to.

When he turned the ticket over, a thin lemon stain marked the back in the crescent of a thumbnail.

He closed his fist around it and stood very still. The river lay ahead, innocent as only long guilt can make a thing. Behind him, the way back to the house rearranged itself helpfully, street by street.

He walked. Halfway home, a bus passed. He looked up in time to see its digital display glitch, just for the length of a breath: WED 15:00 slid across the number before sense returned and the route reclaimed its face.

At the top of their street the fox watched him from the hedge, eyes the colour of old coins. It didn't move when he passed. He had the quiet, irrational certainty that if he put out his hand the fox would place the good paw on it and press, once, twice, three times, a benediction or a warning.

He let himself in by the back door. The lemon from the hall greeted him like a signature on a cheque. In the kitchen, the whiteboard shone too clean. Stand in the right place and the faintest bruise of THEN SPEAK OUT LOUD showed itself, like blood under newsprint.

He placed the bus ticket on the dresser under his folder as if weighing a small animal so it wouldn't run. The house settled round the gesture with the politeness of a hotel he couldn't afford. Upstairs, the chandelier gave a shy, exploratory note, then a second, then a third, trying out the room.

Kevin stood a long time with his palm flat over paper that shouldn't have been his. When he lifted his hand, the ticket had left a pale impression on his skin, a rectangle you could almost believe was printed.

He went to the sink, turned on the tap, and held his wrist under cold water. The mark did not hurry to leave.

On the dresser the ticket lay where he'd put it, mid-March ink patient and perfect. The time refused to blink. 15:00 held its breath.

He exhaled, and the house listened.

# Chapter Thirty-Three
## Sonia Collapses

It was the towels that did it. Not the blood on the stair or the rota on the fridge or the lemon that had learnt to behave like law—towels, white and already folded, made and remade beneath her hands until the hems knew her fingers better than her own face did. Sonia stood at the end of the landing with a neat stack balanced at her hip, and she understood, with a tired clarity that made her want to cry, that if she folded one more rectangle into obedience she would disappear inside its corners.

She took the towels to the cupboard, placed them on the shelf—edges aligned, labels facing, an arrangement she'd copied from a magazine once when she was trying to convince herself you could keep a life in order if you just taught your linen how to behave. The shelf accepted them without gratitude. The house breathed its small approval through the keyhole and went on waiting for her to be useful.

*** 

Samantha's voice—calm, managerial—stayed tucked under Sonia's skull, the way a pin will hide in a hem no matter how carefully you swipe your palm. *Maintenance, not denial. One face keeps us safe. We present stability.* Each sentence had been ironed before it touched air.

Sonia had repeated them so often to other people she had forgotten how to hear them as threats.

She shut the cupboard. The stair gave its small squeal of excitement at being noticed. Sonia placed her hand on the banister and let the weight of her sink down her arm into the wood. Her head throbbed, not with the sharpness of pain but the heaviness of a thought finally deciding to stand up.

If I don't speak, someone will die.

She had written it in her secret notebook with a blunt pencil, the sentence crouching between shopping lists and whiteboard photos like a creature afraid of being thrown out. She had written it because writing was what women in this house did to make reality behave. It hadn't been enough. The sentence needed air.

She went downstairs, careful of the second step (stupid to be careful of wood when blood made a better case), and found the kitchen the way Samantha liked it: counters cleared, tea towels smoothed, the whiteboard shining too hard. If she stood at a particular angle she could see the greenish bruise of THEN SPEAK OUT LOUD under the gloss. The first time she'd noticed it she had laughed. The second time she had cried. Now she just nodded at it like a person passing a neighbour at the bus stop.

She took the mug with the fox on it—Sarah's, strictly—and boiled the kettle because that's what the living do, they boil water and apply it to leaves so the hands have something to do while the rest of you tries not to be frightened. Steam climbed into the vent with the same politeness it had shown since the night the vent learnt English. Sonia watched it go and didn't speak. She had learnt not to say things when metal was listening.

On the table, Samantha's printed rota lay under a lemon-shaped magnet, ONE FACE in a font that pretended not to be a threat. Sonia had read it ten times. Under VISITORS she was SUPPORT. Under NAMES the baby was a line waiting for a pen that never ran out. Under PHOTOS: S approves. There was no column for *I can't breathe* or *I have loved you and I don't know how* or *I am sorry*. There had never been a box for apology on any of Samantha's forms.

She drank half the tea and didn't taste any of it. Across the room, the sewing room door was ajar by a width a sensible person would not remark on. The Singer sat beyond, polished. Someone had dusted its throat in the night; she recognised the clean shine Samantha gave to anything that might speak out of turn. A scrap of muslin lay on the table near the foot, folded to conceal something and failing. Thread teased out of one corner like a fuse.

***

Sonia put the mug down very carefully and pressed her palms together the way children pray when they're trying to remember the words. The headache eased. Resolve replaced it, heavy and welcome. She could not put the confession on paper; paper belonged to Samantha and Samantha's pens. She could not text it; Samantha would find a way to correct the autocorrect. She could not speak it to Kevin; she had tried at the sink and learnt how fast a woman can be interrupted by the person who taught her not to finish thoughts.

Voice, then. A voice that lived outside the whiteboard and the rota and the polite vent. A voice you had to hear even if you wanted to wipe it off a surface.

In the sewing room, under the bottom shelf where she kept wool she liked to think she might turn into comfort, was the tin her grandmother had given her when she was thirteen and still believed she would make beautiful things. Enamel roses, chips at the edges, a lid that clicked like a gossip closing her mouth. Sonia had hidden the dictaphone in it weeks ago, in the small hour after she'd seen S.W. on a brass tag and realised the house had kept earlier women's rules for dessert.

She knelt. The floor was cold through her tights. The tin's lid stuck and then yielded, and the smell of old metal rose—pennies and time. Knitwear she had pretended not to have abandoned lay soft and accusing: two blue skeins, one lemon (she flinched, petty, at the colour), a half-knitted square with a mistake she hadn't had the heart to unpick. Beneath, the black plastic rectangle slept—cheap, practical, nobody's idea of art.

Sonia held it like a small animal. Her thumbs found *REC* before her courage could find an excuse not to press it. A red dot lit, steady. She sat cross-legged on the floor because it felt important to be a child if she was going to tell a secret.

"My name is Sonia," she said, and stopped because the house shivered in a way only she would have noticed. She started again. "My name is Sonia Hayes. I'm married to Kevin. I live with my sisters, Samantha and Sarah. That's not the truth. The truth is we live in Samantha. The truth is I've been quiet because it made her love me." She took a breath, and the tin made a tiny amplification of the air. "If anyone hears this: I'm sorry. I'm sorry for all the parts I kept neat so nobody would see the mess."

The red dot watched her with a patience she envied. She pressed STOP, then REC again, because breaks made bravery possible.

"Rules," she said. "We have rules. We wrote them when we were girls and we wrote them again when we were women and then the house learnt to write them for us. One face. One voice. One name. No locks. No private friends. Money is for the house. Kevin doesn't need to know. That last one wasn't on paper; that one lived in our throats." She could feel the whiteboard behind her through the wall, listening. She leaned closer to the microphone. "I kept a ledger. I know I wasn't supposed to. It has photos of the board before she wiped it. It has the S.W. tag. There was someone else before us who tried to burn the rules. I don't know her name. I think about her a lot. I want to say sorry to her too."

Her mouth was dry. She licked her lips and tasted lemon, which seemed unfairly poetic when you were just a woman kneeling by a tin. "I have a rule I wrote for myself," she whispered. "*Tell the truth when silence harms.* I wrote it small. I didn't keep it. I'm trying now."

A sound in the hall made her pause—the particular hush that follows a person changing their mind. Sonia waited. The hush decided to be the house after all, not a person. She pressed on.

"Kevin," she said, to the dictaphone, to the future, to herself. "I didn't stand between you and her the way I should have. I kept you comfortable. I told you were right when you were just... normal. You never looked too hard and I loved you for it because looking hard made Samantha angry and everything was easier when she wasn't angry. I am telling you now because Sarah is going to tear the house open and if you aren't ready you'll cut your hands on it."

The red dot held steady. The headache did not return. Sonia felt, absurdly, almost peaceful. She clicked STOP. She didn't play it back. Not yet. The thing existed outside her now; that was enough. She slid the recorder under the fat blue skeins and closed the tin. The lid made its gossip click and she understood, with the tired relief of someone finishing a chore, that she had crossed a line she would not be able to uncross.

When she stood, her knees ached. She took the tin with her. The Singer watched as she left, the treadle lifting and settling once like a curtsey that could be read two ways.

On the landing she paused. Samantha's door stood closed, the kind of closed that is also a statement. Sarah's door was ajar, a habit that said *come in if you dare* and *don't you dare* in the same breath. Kevin's door was open on an empty room; he had gone out to the river to ask questions only water would answer badly. Sonia carried her confession into her own room, set the tin on the dressing table, and looked at herself in the mirror.

She did not look brave. She looked like a woman who had been careful for so long she had forgotten how to wear any other expression. She pressed her fingertips to the glass. It felt cool, innocent. In its surface, her face doubled and doubled again for a second, as if even reflections in this house had learnt the trick.

She sat on the bed. The mattress dipped, the way it dips after someone leaves. She placed the tin in her lap and folded her hands over it. Her head throbbed once more—not pain, not exactly. The body objecting to being honest. She waited it out with the patience that had kept three women alive in one lie longer than anyone had a right to expect.

Downstairs, the vent breathed, once, twice, three times, polite as always. Sonia didn't move. She had begun.

***

Sonia waited until the house had settled into its evening posture before she dared return to the tin. The others were scattered: Kevin out on one of his walks, Sarah shut upstairs, Samantha busying herself with a rota she'd already lost to Kevin's refusal. That left her a pocket of time—a dangerous, fragile silence that felt like a gift she wasn't supposed to unwrap.

She lifted the tin from the dressing table and placed it on her lap. The roses on the enamel lid had lost their blush long ago, rubbed pale by decades of hands, but she ran her fingers over them anyway. Grandmother's tin, grandmother's gift, grandmother's steady voice telling her: *Needles never lie if you watch their tips.* She wondered what her grandmother would have thought if she knew the tin held not knitting but proof.

The dictaphone was still there, pressed between skeins of wool as if wrapped for safekeeping. She pulled it free and set it on the quilt. Its surface was dull, a student's tool, unremarkable. And yet it felt heavier than it should, as though it had already learnt the weight of what she'd spoken.

She hadn't played it back. That was deliberate. Words on paper Samantha could erase. Spoken words could be dismissed, interrupted, woven into another script. But this—the dictaphone was her anchor. The red dot meant truth, and truth deserved to be frightening.

Her pulse thudded as she pressed REC again. The light glowed steady.

"My name is Sonia Hayes," she said, firmer this time. "And this is the first time I've said it out loud without apologising for existing."

Her throat closed; she forced it open.

"I've been part of a lie my whole life. We were taught to be one person, to fold ourselves into each other until the world couldn't tell us apart. Samantha told us it was safety. Sarah said it was a prison. I chose to pretend it was love. I smiled for Kevin when it wasn't me, I smoothed the rules when they hurt, I patched lies the way you darn socks. I thought if I kept the seams neat enough, no one would bleed through."

She glanced at the door, half-expecting it to open. Nothing. Only the faint hum of pipes.

"I'm guilty," she whispered to the machine. "Guilty of silence. Guilty of smoothing over. Guilty of letting Kevin think one woman could keep him, when it was three of us, taking turns like shift workers in a factory. He never saw it because he never wanted to. But I knew. I *helped*. I told myself I was protecting him, protecting Sarah, even protecting Samantha from herself. But really, I was protecting the pact. Because I was too afraid of being left behind."

Her voice cracked. She stopped, breathed, pressed her palms flat to the quilt until the tremor steadied. Then she leaned back in, almost urgent.

"If anyone finds this: Samantha writes rules on a whiteboard. They're wiped, but the house remembers. I've taken photos, kept them hidden in my ledger. The ledger has more—fragments, names, the tag stamped S.W. We weren't the first. Somebody else lived this life before us, and she tried to burn it away. She failed. The house doesn't forget."

The red dot blinked in steady rhythm. Sonia swallowed.

"My own rule was supposed to be different. *Tell the truth when silence harms.* That's what I wrote. But I kept silent anyway. Even when Sarah begged me to back her. Even when Kevin looked at me with that half-realisation in his eyes. Even when Samantha turned our grief into timetables and rotas. I was the glue. Glue holds even when the cracks are poison. And glue dies first, because it's never meant to be seen."

Tears stung her eyes, but she refused to stop. "The baby... The baby changes everything. Sarah wants freedom, Samantha wants ownership, Kevin wants clarity. And me? I want her to grow up not knowing what it feels like to vanish into someone else's face. I want her to be herself, even if that self breaks the house in half. Even if it kills me. That's what this is: my truth. My permission to be blamed."

The words filled the room in a way she hadn't expected. The house listened—she could feel it in the boards, in the faint tingle of air moving through the vent. She half-expected Samantha to burst in, neat as ever, to confiscate the tape like a contraband book.

But nothing came. Only the sound of her own breathing, captured, stored, made undeniable.

She pressed STOP.

For a moment she just sat, clutching the dictaphone to her chest as if it could pass for prayer. Then, with shaking fingers, she tucked it back into the tin. She layered the wool over it—the lemon skein, the blue, the half-finished square—and shut the lid with a click that sounded final.

Her chest felt lighter, though her hands trembled. She had spoken. Not to Samantha, not to Sarah, not even to Kevin. But to the world beyond the house, to ears that might never hear. She had created a version of herself that could not be silenced by a cloth or a marker.

Still, guilt nagged. Would it be enough? Would the truth survive if Samantha found the tin?

She slid it beneath the bed, out of sight, and sat back, spine against the wall. The room felt different now—more aware, like a stranger you've just confessed to who hasn't yet told you whether they forgive you.

Sonia whispered into the quiet: "It's done."

But the house only breathed in reply. Once. Twice. Three times.

***

Night gathered with that particular unkindness the house favoured—no drama, only a steady thickening, as if someone were turning a dimmer down on her life one notch at a time. Sonia tried to make herself busy: rinsed two mugs that weren't dirty, set out plates no one had asked for, folded a dishcloth into a perfect square. Each small decency felt like an apology she hadn't earned the right to offer.

She lasted an hour.

The tin under the bed tugged at her mind like a loose tooth. She could taste metal. At last she knelt, lifted the bedspread, and drew the enamel roses back into the light. The lid stuck again—as if it had opinions—and then yielded with a click. Wool breathed that faint sheepish scent of old shops. The dictaphone lay where she'd left it, weightier now that it contained her.

"Just to check," she told herself, out loud, as if narration could make caution look like courage. She sat on the edge of the mattress, feet flat on the rug like a child waiting to be told off, and pressed PLAY.

Her voice filled the room at once: thin, higher than she imagined herself, the vowels of a girl who learnt not to take up space stretched over a woman's truth. *My name is Sonia Hayes... We share one life...* She winced as if a hand had closed round her throat again, then forced herself to sit through it. The rhythm steadied. *One face. One voice. One name.* The words wore their years.

Nothing else bled in—no hiss, no trick, only her. She felt a bubble of absurd hope rise: perhaps the house had decided not to interrupt. Perhaps it was enough to have said it and stored it.

Then the tape reached the second recording and the hope burst like soap.

At first the interference was only a thin hush, the sort tapes make when they remember they are made of plastic and magnets. It eased under her words as weather does under a door. Sonia leaned forward, straining to understand. The hush thickened. It found a pulse.

A syllable formed—less sound than shape. Not.

Her own voice kept speaking, unaware, like someone being followed who refuses to run. The hush shaped itself again, clearer. Not yours.

Sonia flinched, thumb hovering over STOP, then held. The words repeated. Not yours. Not yours. Not yours. Three perfect measures, as if someone had scored them for a metronome.

Her confession wavered but did not vanish beneath the overlay; instead the two threads twined horribly, like two songs a child insists fit together because they like them both. Sonia's voice: *I'm guilty of silence... I kept the seams neat...* The other: Not yours. The timing was almost tender, slipping into spaces, refusing to touch. It sounded like consideration. It sounded like ownership.

"Who are you," Sonia whispered to the room, and the room behaved itself, which was somehow worse.

She stabbed STOP. The red light died with a little dignity, as if it had never been on. For a long moment she sat very still, shaking, listening to the blood in her ears. Then she pressed PLAY again, because disbelief is a muscle and she had always kept hers strong for Samantha's benefit.

The same. Her voice, then the other. The whisper so clear now she could hear the shape of a mouth around it. Not breathy—decisive. A spoken stamp. Not yours. Not yours. Not yours. Between each triplet the faintest rustle, as if cloth were being folded the proper way by hands that had never failed at folding.

She pressed STOP and REW together—an old trick learnt off a Walkman. The machine complied, tape whining as it spooled backward. She lifted her finger. Silence. She pressed PLAY and advanced in jerks: her throat, her shame, her rule. Then the intrusion. The words fitted themselves into the same slots as before, as if recorded along a second track she had never consented to.

She turned the dictaphone over as if a name might be stamped on the back of it. Only brand, model, battery cover that didn't quite sit right. The screw head bore a scratch. She imagined Samantha's screwdriver, Samantha's patience. But Samantha hadn't been in this room—she

would have noticed, surely. Unless noticing had gone the way of speech
in their house: something you did only when Samantha had written it
on the board.

"Try again," Sonia said, and her voice steadied of its own accord, as
if tired of shaking.

She rewound to the very beginning. PLAY. *My name is Sonia Hayes.*
Nothing; nothing; then Not yours—soft as a hand patting a child's hair.
The phrase followed her into the ledger, into S.W., into *I'm trying now.*
It even found its way under *the baby changes everything*, and Sonia's
stomach clenched because the whisper changed, a nuance, a tilt: Ours.
Once. As if it were practising.

"No," she said so quickly she surprised herself. "No, she isn't."

Her vision blurred. She pressed her thumbs into the corners of her
eyes until false stars burst and cleared. When she looked again, the LED
was still. The machine lay there, blunt and honest, as if innocence were
a shape.

She pulled the batteries out. Set them on the quilt. Counted to ten,
because numbers still behaved when nothing else would. She put them
back with a click. The little screen blinked, blank, then found itself. She
pressed PLAY.

Her own voice ran. The other voice ran with it. Batteries did not stop
belief. *Not yours. Not yours. Not yours.*

She stood, too fast, the tin sliding off her lap onto the rug with a metal
sigh. Wool uncoiled like secrets. The dictaphone landed face-down and
continued politely, unmoved by its new angle: Not yours. Not—

Sonia snatched it up and hit STOP so hard she thought the button
would refuse to forgive her. Silence arrived too obediently. Her breath
made the only noise.

A thought came, unwanted as a salesman: *Show Kevin.* She pictured
him listening, his face closing in the way it did when kindness ran

out and judgement began. She pictured him saying, *It's interference.* She pictured him being gentler and saying, *You're tired.* She pictured Samantha appearing in the doorway to call them both dramatic and to ask for the machine because she kept *records* and this should be with the *records.* She pictured herself handing it over because habit was a religion and she was an altar boy who couldn't remember the prayer but could mimic the genuflection.

"No," Sonia told the carpet. She walked to the wardrobe, slid the recorder into the knitting tin again, dug it down under the lemon skein like burying a sin in fresh snow. She shut the lid and felt the click in her teeth.

From the landing came the softest sound: toe on stair, weight checked, retreat. Someone had half-decided to come and then thought better. Sonia kept still until the air resumed neutrality. Only then did she put the tin back under the bed.

She sat again, hands open on her knees, and listened to the room make its small noises: the heating flexing a pipe, the fox poster in the street stirring to no wind, the whiteboard downstairs being blank as an argument. Her heart slowed from its panicked gallop to a pace a person might maintain while walking beside someone they loved.

It was almost over when the dictaphone spoke again.

She hadn't touched it. The tin hadn't moved. But from under the bed—a muffled mouth, a little distance—came the click of REC engaging, unmistakable as a throat clearing before a speech.

Sonia froze. A second's stillness. Then her own voice, faint through metal and wool, emerged—not the confession she had made, but a fresh breath, present tense, as if it had begun to describe her. "My name is—"

Her name cut. A different voice overrode it—hers, and not hers; a closeness she recognised with the accuracy of a lifetime. The syllables of her name came again, tidied. Then the whisper returned, patient, explicitly arranged into three beats as if instructing: Not yours. Not yours. Not yours.

She dropped to the floor and dragged the tin out so fast it scraped a line into the rug. The roses flashed accusation. She flipped the lid. Wool slithered aside, half-strangling the machine. The dictaphone's red light was on, steady, though she had not pressed anything. REC.

"Stop," she said, and her voice sounded like someone else's decision.

She thumbed STOP. The light extinguished. The room opened its palms, empty.

Sonia stared at the recorder, waiting for an honest machine to remember what honesty feels like. It lay inert, a student's tool, a shop's guarantee.

Then, very gently, PLAY clicked of its own accord. The red eye didn't return—the screen did, marker inching forward—yet the sound came anyway, low and unmistakable, ribboning out under the bed as if the carpet itself had chosen to speak:

Not yours. Not yours. Not yours.

# Chapter Thirty-Four
## The Night of Truth

The storm found its old path back to the house. It arrived without hurry, as if returning a library book—first a restless wind, then the first shy taps on glass, then rain committed to its task. Somewhere a streetlamp flickered and remembered itself. The house lifted its chin to meet it, pleased to have weather that matched its temperament.

Downstairs, the whiteboard had been wiped again—polished until it reflected the room like a cheap mirror. Yet when Sonia came into the kitchen for water, two lines stood there, bold as if written with a new hand:

NO MORE NOTES
MIDNIGHT. NURSERY.

The letters were not Samantha's tidy, confident script. They looked like the house had learnt, at last, to prefer print.

Sonia set the glass down with both hands. Her throat tightened. She wanted to fetch a cloth. She wanted to run to the nursery and sit in the rocking chair and hold the room at the level of breath until midnight found some other house to haunt. She did neither. She stood in the doorway and watched the board as if it might write something else—an apology, a reprieve. It didn't. It gleamed with certainty.

Behind her, steps in the hall paused. "You saw?" Sarah asked.

"Yes," Sonia said, and would have said more if Samantha's reflection hadn't joined theirs in the whiteboard's shine—three faces stacked into one, the trick they had practised since childhood now suddenly intolerable to all of them.

"Whose writing?" Sarah asked, without turning.

"The house's," Samantha said, so simply that for a moment neither of the others remembered to be angry.

"Midnight," Sarah echoed. "What is this, theatre?"

"It's maintenance," Samantha said, which would have been funny any other night. She moved closer to the board, almost tender. "No more notes," she repeated, softly. "Good."

"Good?" Sonia turned, helpless. "It's not a suggestion, Sam. It's a summons."

Samantha capped the marker and aligned it with the frame without looking. "Then we present ourselves on time."

The chandelier chose that moment to sing—a clean, bright chime rolling through its glass like a throat warmed for performance. The vent above the cooker sighed in reply, a sound that made words without needing to borrow any. From the sewing room, the Singer gave a single, genteel hum, as if checking the pitch. The house had set its orchestra.

Kevin came in on the last note. Rain freckled his coat; his hair contained the river's memory. He read the whiteboard once and did not ask who had written it. He looked from one woman to the next and said, "Then none of us go alone."

Samantha's glance cut to him, evaluating, not hostile. "We go together," she agreed. "Three faces. One truth."

Sarah snorted. "You've mislaid the definition of that word." She had slept, briefly, and looked as if sleep had taken offence at being misused. She leaned on the edge of the table, palms flat. "If this is your little pageant, Sam, remember: I don't dance."

"Then stand," Samantha said, calm as surgery. "Just arrive."

\*\*\*

The clock on the mantel, which had been sulking since the last power cut, decided to be useful. It ticked with renewed authority towards midnight.

They did not speak much while they waited. Words felt like crockery—too easy to break, too hard to clean. Sonia made tea because hands require employment in the hour before a reckoning. Kevin stood by the window and watched the storm rehearse the street. Samantha gathered stray paper, smoothed a tea towel, lined a knife with its shadow. Sarah sat, then stood, then sat again, energy choosing the least safe route through her body. The house, delighted by its own restraint, breathed in threes at the edges of the room.

Five minutes to midnight. The whiteboard did not amend itself—no second line, no revised venue. Samantha lifted her chin. "Time," she said.

"Together," Kevin said, because superstition is only a synonym for attention when you're protecting people you have already failed.

They climbed the stairs. The second tread squealed and then, very distinctly, squealed again, as if practising nerves. Sonia said "Hush" to the wood and hated herself for it. The landing waited—long, lamplit, a corridor that had been kind to secrets. At the far end the nursery door stood open to its own shadow.

They stepped inside and the room received them like a chapel behaving badly. The cot sat dressed, the blanket folded just off-centre as if by a person who believed imperfection made a thing more believable. The mobile hung still; the wooden fox was poised mid-nod, courteous, false. The rocking chair in the corner faced the window, the way people prefer to confess to glass.

At first nothing moved. Then the chandelier's voice reached them even here—one, two, three clear notes as if counting them in. The vent in the nursery's ceiling returned the count, breathing the number back. The Singer in the next room offered a bass hum thin as a threat.

Samantha took three steps forward and stopped beside the cot. She did not touch it. "We are here," she said, not to anyone in the room.

"Speak for yourself," Sarah answered, but quietly.

Sonia found the wall and leaned against it because her knees had begun to consider a future in which they didn't hold her. Kevin placed himself between his wife and his not-wife and the not-not-wife they had all taught themselves to rely on. He hated the geometry of it—women arranged like furniture so a man could feel useful.

\*\*\*

The window fogged at the edges. Sonia told herself it was weather. Words began to form in the condensation with an indecent eagerness. Not big, nothing theatrical—small letters, careful, a child learning to please:

OURS.

"We know," Samantha said softly, as if soothing a child who has just announced it can count to three.

Sarah's jaw clenched. "You don't get to answer on behalf of the air."

The mobile moved the smallest amount. The fox tapped the hare's nose twice, their beech muzzles clicking with a sound too neatly like teeth. Sarah reached up and pinched the mobile's arm to still it. It obeyed like a child caught stealing a biscuit.

She faced Samantha. "One last time," she said. "You don't get to keep her. You don't get to keep me. I don't belong to your rota. I don't belong to your whiteboard. I am not a name you can print in a neat box and underline."

Samantha's expression did not alter. Only her hands betrayed her—fingers opening, closing, as if counting on an abacus only she believed in. "You think I want a rota because I like control," she said. "I want it because it keeps you alive."

"You mean obedient," Sarah said.

"I mean alive." Samantha's voice thinned. The storm lifted its voice as if offended for her. "You don't understand the cost of being more than one person in a world that likes its women single-use. I learnt it for you. I paid it. I'll pay it again if I have to."

"On my body," Sarah said. "With my child."

"With our name," Samantha said.

Kevin stepped between them then, not to be a hero, only to put his skin between two engines. "Enough," he said, which was a naive word in this house. "No more rules. No more rotas. No more *ours* stamped on things that breathe."

Samantha's gaze slid to him. "If you had paid proper attention years ago, none of this would be necessary."

The blow landed. Kevin took it and said nothing because the rebuttal would be a list and lists were her country. He lifted a hand. "No one moves near the stair." It sounded foolish; it sounded like hope. "Whatever happens, you do not step back."

"Then don't push me," Sarah said, but she had softened by a hair; care had got in through a crack.

Sonia found her voice's thread. "Please," she said, and the word surprised them all with how much authority it held. "We can argue without making the house clap."

*** 

The house had been waiting for its cue. The chandelier downstairs sang again, louder. The vent in the nursery returned it like a learnt line. The Singer's hum lifted into a note that wanted to be music. The window's letters brightened and began to run, thinning into watery bars that moved as if breath had turned to script.

"Stop performing for it," Sarah told Samantha. "Face me."

"I'm facing you," Samantha said, and she was. For the first time since they were girls, she let the mask sit on a chair and kept only her face. It looked tired. It looked old. It looked like love delivered in the wrong wrapping. "Sarah, please," she said, echoing Sonia's word but bending it into a rope.

"Please what."

"Please don't make me break you to keep you."

Sarah moved so fast it surprised even herself. She was on Samantha in two strides, the air between them cracking with a sound that was not thunder and might have been history snapping. Hands at wrists, wrists at hair, a twist, a shoulder bucking free—the ugly, ordinary choreography of sisters who had practised not hurting and now couldn't remember how.

"Stop," Sonia said, and reached for them, but the cot was between. Kevin rounded the cot and caught at Samantha's elbow. She wrenched. Sarah stumbled. The rocking chair skidded, heel catching its rocker; one leg lifted, struck the skirting, thumped back.

They spilled towards the doorway like water taking a corner too quickly. Kevin got an arm around Sarah's waist and took her backwards step with her, matching the movement to bleed off its violence. Samantha bared her teeth in a laugh that had no joy in it. The vent gave a long exhale that could have been language in a worse house.

"Let go," Sarah said through her teeth.

"I will," Kevin said, and did, and immediately regretted it as Samantha surged, and in surging clipped Sarah's shoulder. It was a minor contact, the sort that makes a person swear and rub a bruise in the morning. Tonight it altered geography. Sarah reeled, pivoted on her heel, and the landing welcomed her like a mouth.

"Sod this," Kevin said, out-loud prayer, and grabbed for her.

The second stair squealed.

***

It was the sound that had been a joke on easy mornings and a balm on hard ones, a line in the house's lullabies. Tonight it was a blade. Sarah's foot found the edge of it wrong. She went backwards, arms flung wide not for drama but for balance. The storm outside chose that second to drum both palms on the roof.

Kevin's hand closed on her forearm.

Everything else paused.

The house held its breath the way crowds do in bad theatres. Samantha's face emptied, then filled with something that might have been horror if it had survived longer in her mouth. Sonia made a small, childish noise and surprised herself by not being ashamed of it.

"Got you," Kevin said, not as triumph, as fact. He pulled. Sarah's body righted, just enough; her heel came back to the landing. Her knees buckled and she sat down with an inelegance that preserved her spine. She laughed once, helpless and fierce, and then pressed both hands to her face, elbows on knees, as if to hold herself in.

Samantha had reached out too late; her hand hung in the air with a single answer in it and no one to give it to. She lowered it slowly. Her lip trembled—the tiniest betrayal. She bit it. "You can't keep doing this," she whispered, and it wasn't clear who she meant.

"Doing what," Sarah said, voice hoarse. "Refusing to fall for you?"

"Falling at all," Samantha said. "Insisting on gravity when I have built you a level."

Sonia slid along the wall until she could take Sarah's hand. She squeezed. Sarah squeezed back. The two of them held that small, ordinary pressure as if it could outvote the house.

Downstairs, the chandelier gave three soft notes, almost apologetic now—as if even it understood spectacle had been denied. The Singer in the next room dropped to a murmur and then stopped, needle stilled, foot patted twice like a teacher praising handwriting. The vent took a breath and let it out without shaping it. The storm changed key.

Kevin did not let go of Sarah's forearm until he felt her put weight back into her feet. When he did, he found his own hand shaking. He curled it into a fist so he wouldn't have to watch.

The window in the nursery cleared itself with a shudder. New letters didn't write. The old ones returned, faint, stubborn as bruises.

OURS.

"No," Sarah said, steady, almost calm now. "Not tonight."

They stood in the doorway and did nothing dramatic. It felt like the bravest act the house had asked of them yet. The second stair complained again as if embarrassed by its role. Samantha stepped back from the edge, one careful pace, a concession she made no comment on.

"Midnight's done," Kevin said, and the sentence rang plain as a bell. "Go to bed. All of you."

Samantha looked as if she would argue with the clock. Then she nodded once, a tiny bow to a fact she hadn't written. Sonia exhaled a long-held breath. Sarah rose, slow but willing, and let herself be steadied by hands that had hurt her and would again, because that is how families behave in houses that make habits.

***

They left the nursery as they had entered it: together. On the landing, the storm rolled its shoulders and decided not to perform for them any more. At the stair, Kevin went first. When his foot met the squealing tread it made its small, familiar noise, and no one fell.

Behind them, in the quiet of the nursery, the mobile made a single, private turn. The fox nodded to the hare as if acknowledging that a scene had nearly found its old ending and then failed to. The cot lay dressed for a child who had not yet arrived and had already been claimed and unclaimed, and the window held no word at all—only the mist of four people choosing, for the moment, not to be written for.

# Chapter Thirty-Five
## One Face

The storm had gone, but the air still crackled like a wire sparking unseen in the walls. Rainwater dripped from the eaves in slow intervals, a metronome for nerves. The house had learnt silence for the moment, though it was the kind of silence that smirked—it knew it could break it whenever it chose.

Sarah stood in the nursery, one hand braced on the cot, the other pressed against her stomach. She had come here at first to breathe, but breathing had grown difficult inside these walls; every inhalation seemed shared with someone else. The crib was made up neatly, though not by her hand. The blanket lay folded in the same off-centre precision Samantha preferred, a silent flag of occupation.

She leaned into the cot, whispering words she hadn't intended to say aloud. "You'll be mine. Not ours. Just mine." Her palm smoothed the edge of the blanket, and the words felt foreign in her throat. Her child had been claimed so many times already—by Samantha, by Sonia, by the house itself—that Sarah feared she would never get to hear the word *mine* without contest.

The mobile swayed faintly above the cot, though the air was still. She caught it with her hand to stop the movement, but the carved fox rattled as if laughing.

"You won't grow up this way," she said. "You won't grow up splitting yourself into parts. You'll have one face, your own. Not three. Not borrowed."

\*\*\*

Behind her, the door clicked open.

Samantha entered without ceremony. Her hair hung loose, damp at the ends, as though she had prepared herself in haste. No rota papers, no board marker, not even the lemon scent that usually preceded her. She looked raw, stripped of her armour, but her eyes carried their usual determination—the kind Sarah had always mistaken for confidence until she learnt it was control.

"You shouldn't be in here," Samantha said. Her voice had no rise, no fall. Just a line, straight and severe.

Sarah didn't turn. "Neither should you. It isn't yours."

"It's not yours either."

Sarah gripped the cot until her knuckles blanched. "Don't start with that. I'm finished with the pact. I'm finished with pretending one person can own three lives."

"That's not what it was," Samantha said quickly, stepping further into the room. The floorboards didn't complain; the house, unusually, gave her its grace. "The pact kept us together. It protected us."

"Protected us?" Sarah spun to face her now, fire sharp in her eyes. "You call this protection? Hiding behind names? Making Kevin believe a lie? Turning us into one woman because you were too afraid of being just yourself?"

The chandelier in the hall rang three clear notes. Both sisters stiffened. The vent above the cot sighed like a warning. From below, the Singer hummed once, needle striking air.

Sarah laughed bitterly. "Even the house knows what we're doing. It's joining in."

Samantha's jaw tightened. "Because it understands."

"No," Sarah snapped. "Because it's feeding on us. You've trained it to sing our rules back until they're written in the walls." She jabbed a finger towards the cot. "But she won't be fed to it."

***

Samantha's eyes flickered to Sarah's stomach. "You don't even know if she's yours."

The air dropped half a degree. The words hung there, the kind of statement that could split a room forever. Sarah's breath caught, but she forced her expression not to crack. "That doesn't matter," she said. "She's mine because I'll love her as myself, not as your idea of us."

"You don't get it," Samantha said, her voice breaking for the first time. She stepped close to the cot, fingers brushing its rail. "One face is how we survive. Alone, we're weak. Together, we're invincible. The baby doesn't change that—it makes it more important."

Sarah slapped her hand away. The sound cracked sharp in the small room. The mobile began to turn again, slow and deliberate, though neither had touched it.

"You've always needed me to keep your world neat," Sarah hissed. "But I'm not your mirror anymore. I won't let you script her life like you scripted mine."

The vent gave a deep, rumbling exhale. Letters bloomed across the window in condensation, bold and wet:

OURS.

Samantha's lips curved, almost tender. "You see? Even the house agrees."

Sarah turned, teeth clenched. "Then the house is wrong."

For a heartbeat they stood across the cot, twin silhouettes in the moonlight, each woman claiming the same air, the same life, the same shadow. Their faces mirrored but their stances worlds apart: Samantha stiff, precise, her body a wall; Sarah raw, trembling, fierce enough to burn herself down if it meant light for the child.

The chandelier sang again. The mobile spun harder. The Singer hummed, pedal twitching. The house rehearsed its finale.

Neither sister moved. Not yet. But the storm inside the walls had found its stage.

The landing boards groaned, a warning before the man himself arrived. Kevin appeared in the nursery doorway, shoulders squared as if bracing against weather that was no longer falling. His coat clung damply to him, hair plastered to his forehead. In his hand he clutched the battered folder that had grown into his second heart—stained receipts, photos, test lists, the mess of evidence he'd built like a barricade.

He froze when he saw them: Sarah at the cot, hair loose, chest rising too fast; Samantha opposite, composed yet trembling at the corners. For the first time in their lives, the illusion broke cleanly. He saw them both. Same face. Same mouth. Same eyes. But separate, undeniable.

"God help me," Kevin whispered. His voice was paper-thin. "There are two."

The sisters stilled, as if his words had sliced something open they had been nursing in secret. Sarah's hands tightened on the cot rail until wood creaked. Samantha only blinked once, slow, as if absorbing a blow she had rehearsed for.

Kevin's throat bobbed. "All this time..." His eyes roamed from one to the other, then down to Sarah's stomach. "What did you do to me?"

Samantha answered first, voice soft, coaxing. "We gave you love, Kevin. Whole. Complete. More than any one woman could give. We kept you safe in one face."

"Safe?" His laugh broke ragged. "Safe from what—truth? From recognising the woman I was supposed to know better than anyone? From myself?"

Sarah's voice cut in, sharp as glass. "Safe from her," she spat. "From Samantha's rules. From the house she made into a shrine for lies."

The chandelier chimed three crisp notes above their heads, as if applauding. The mobile began to twirl again without breeze, wooden animals clacking teeth together. The house was enjoying itself.

***

Kevin took one halting step inside. The folder trembled in his fist. "Tell me," he said, louder now, desperate. "Whose baby is it?"

The silence swelled, thick and wet. Sarah and Samantha both stiffened, but it was Sarah who broke first.

"It's yours," she said, steady but hoarse. "Or hers. Or both. Does it matter?"

Kevin's eyes burned. "Of course it matters. I need to know who I—" He cut himself off, choking on the memory that surfaced. Nights when "Samantha" had smelt different—woodsmoke instead of lemon, hair falling the wrong way. Nights when her cadence had shifted, whispers changed. Times he had thought, fleetingly, *this isn't her*, before dismissing it as fatigue or fancy.

He dropped the folder to the cot. Papers spilled like entrails—receipts, handwriting samples, two lists that should have matched but didn't. "I don't even know who I touched," he whispered, horrified. "I don't know who I loved."

Samantha's eyes softened, and in that softness was triumph. "You loved us all," she said. "That was the gift. That was the pact. You don't need to know whose. You only need to know you belong."

"No," Sarah snapped. She shoved the folder aside, scattering papers to the floor. "He deserves the truth. Even if it breaks him. Especially then."

Kevin looked at her, his face caught between longing and betrayal. "Then tell me," he begged. "Tell me the night. Tell me if it was you."

Sarah's lips trembled. She glanced at Samantha. The pause was answer enough.

Kevin staggered back a step. "Oh God," he muttered. "You swapped. You swapped places in my bed."

Sarah shut her eyes. "It was the only way to survive her rules. To keep the peace. To keep the lie running smooth."

Samantha's voice sharpened, cutting through. "He doesn't need details. He needs to choose. Either he stays, or he goes. Either he is part of us, or he is no one."

"Stop it," Kevin said, voice cracking. He shook his head violently. "No more rules. No more pacts. No more one face."

The chandelier answered with a dissonant chime. The vent whispered, a hiss forming into syllables that sounded horribly like laughter. The Singer thrummed a bass note through the floorboards. The house was swelling towards climax.

Sarah reached out, hand trembling, as if to steady Kevin. "Listen to me," she pleaded. "You don't have to be part of her game. You can choose me. Choose the baby. Choose reality."

"Reality?" Samantha scoffed. "He doesn't want reality. He never has. He chose blindness. He chose comfort. He chose one face because it's easier to love a mask than a mess."

Kevin's hands went to his hair, clutching at his scalp. "Stop," he said again. "Stop talking like I'm not here." His chest heaved; his heart felt like a clock wound too tight. "It's mine, isn't it? Tell me it's mine."

Sarah's eyes filled. "It might be. It might not. That's the truth."

Samantha smiled faintly, pityingly. "You'll never know. That's the truth."

The mobile spun harder, animals whipping into a blur. One snapped loose from its string and dropped into the cot with a hollow clatter. Kevin flinched at the sound like a gunshot.

He looked between them—two faces, same eyes, one child. His knees buckled, and he clutched the cot to keep from falling.

"I can't do this," he whispered. "I can't live in a house that lies every time it breathes."

Sarah moved towards him, arms half-lifted. "Then help me end it. Help me break her grip."

Samantha stepped in front of the cot, her shadow stretching tall in the moonlight. "Or accept it. Accept us. It's the only way you survive."

The chandelier rang again, three perfect notes. The vent breathed back. The Singer shuddered.

The house wanted blood.

And Kevin, caught between two faces of the same mask, realised he had already lost.

***

The room broke.

It happened fast, though Kevin would later recall it as slow, agonising frames, like a film reel losing speed. Sarah lunged, hands out, not towards him but towards Samantha. Samantha braced, expecting it, her body already half-turned to make the push seem like balance. The cot rattled as Sarah's hip caught it, the mobile spinning wild, animals colliding until splinters cracked in the air.

"Stop!" Kevin shouted, reaching for both, but neither heard. They were locked in a fight older than the walls—two halves refusing the pact that had glued them together too long.

Samantha shoved Sarah back against the window. Glass trembled but held. Sarah clawed her way free, striking with the desperation of someone protecting more than herself. A nail tore a line down Samantha's cheek. She gasped, not from pain but from shock, as if she'd never believed her mirror could leave a mark.

"You'll kill her!" Sarah spat, hand on her stomach. "You'll kill us all!"

"She was mine before she was yours," Samantha hissed back. "Everything was."

The chandelier exploded into song—seven mad, discordant chimes. The vent roared a wordless chorus. The Singer hammered like a drum, pedal pumping though no one touched it.

Kevin shoved between them, arms out, folder crumpled underfoot. "Enough!" he bellowed. "You'll tear the house down!"

"Let it fall!" Sarah cried.

"Let it stand," Samantha countered.

They grappled again, bodies colliding into him. Kevin dragged them apart, holding one in each hand, but the strain ripped through him. Sarah jerked free, lunging again. Samantha twisted, spinning from his grasp.

Momentum betrayed her. She staggered backwards out the nursery, heels striking the landing's edge. The banister loomed, the stair yawning beneath.

Kevin shouted her name.

Time slowed. The second stair squealed, gleeful. The chandelier gave three soft notes, like a countdown.

Samantha's arms flung wide, not from panic but from poise. For one terrible instant she looked crucified against the moonlight, hair a dark halo, eyes locked on his.

Kevin reached for her. His fingers brushed hers, but too late.

She tipped.

***

Her body curved over the banister, falling into the stairwell. The sound when she struck—first wood, then floor—split the house in two. The chandelier trembled. The Singer shrieked and stopped. Even the vent seemed to choke.

Kevin stumbled forward, half-dragging Sarah with him. They peered down into the darkness below.

She lay crumpled on the hall floor, hair veiling her face. Blood spread slow from her temple, black in the moonlight. But her eyes found him. Clear. Calm.

Her lips moved once, a faint gurgle shaping the words with dreadful clarity:

"One... face..."

Then her eyes shut.

The house exhaled, long and satisfied, as though it had been waiting for this exact moment.

Kevin dropped to his knees at the top of the stair, heart hammering. Papers from his folder drifted past him, floating down like snow into the dark where she lay. Receipts, notes, rules, all useless.

Beside him, Sarah pressed both hands to her mouth. Tears streaked her cheeks, but her body shook with something more complicated than grief. Relief. Terror. Freedom. Guilt. A whole storm in flesh.

"She's gone," Sarah whispered. "She's gone, Kevin."

But even as she said it, Kevin wasn't sure. The calm in Samantha's eyes lingered in him, terrible and steady. He thought of her last words, that final insistence, and shuddered.

One face.

The house, too, seemed to believe it. The chandelier gave a single lingering chime. The vent exhaled like a satisfied sigh. From the nursery behind them, the mobile gave one last turn, though no hand touched it, no wind stirred.

Kevin took Sarah's arm and pulled her back from the edge. "We don't know what's gone," he said, voice raw. "Not yet."

They stood together on the landing, staring down into the dark where the body lay, waiting for the house to declare whether death had been subtraction—or merely rearrangement.

# Chapter Thirty-Six
# Epilogue: The Fourth

The house learnt to be quiet after the fall. It wasn't repentance—houses don't repent—but a newly careful hush, like a child who has broken a vase and now moves as if porcelain grows out of air. Rain still visited when it pleased. The second stair still squealed, though less brazenly. The chandelier sang only when the wind got it drunk. And yet, for weeks, every sound seemed padded, deliberate, as if someone had laid felt beneath the days.

***

A baby arrived into this carefulness—small, red, affronted by light, fists curled as if already holding court. There were photographs taken that would later look staged: Kevin in a hospital chair he didn't remember finding, a blanket folded and refolded by hands he could not name, a midwife with the mercy not to stare at how many shadows a man can cast when he doesn't know who he is. He learnt to hold the child with the unteachable competence of terror. The little body burned hot against him, a star introduced to a pocket. He watched her mouth find the world and claim it and felt something in him move its furniture.

Neighbours were kind in the way neighbours are when they are sure they have a story. Cards arrived with rabbits and moons on them and sentences about blessings. Someone left a casserole on the step with a ribbon that suggested apology. At the door, faces gentled themselves. "How are you getting on?" they asked, like people trying not to look into a window after dark. Kevin said "Fine" and meant "We're breathing" and the house let the lie pass without tidying it.

*** 

He told no one how the lullaby came into the nursery uninvited, how the mobile turned under a sealed window, how the chandelier downstairs tuned itself to the baby's cries. He told no one that even in silence he could hear a song made of three threads, braided so deftly that the ear—if it were lazy—might call it one.

They did not talk, either, about the fall. An accident, the GP had said, voice respectful to the point of suspicion. An accident, said the officer with notes in her hand and the good manners to keep her doubt in her eyes rather than her mouth. An accident, said the neighbours when the foxes shrieked at four in the morning and the street needed a reason to be awake. An accident, said Kevin, to the mirror in the bathroom, because it's easier to wash your face if you are cast as victim by the glass.

The house did not say accident. Houses don't use that word. It let dust settle into places no one touched. It let lemon fade to something more like memory. It kept the whiteboard clean as a plate at the back of a cupboard, though, if you stood just so, you could still see the bruise of THEN SPEAK OUT LOUD under the gloss.

***

The ledger stayed in the wardrobe behind sweaters he no longer wore. The brass tag—S.W.—lived in his top drawer, face up, as if waiting for its surname to grow. The scrap of muslin with S A M stitched by the Singer's sudden literacy lay under the baby's basket like a talisman he refused to admit was a talisman. On nights when he slept, he dreamed himself sewing letters into cloth and waking with the taste of string in his mouth.

He learnt the baby's weather. The hours she preferred for hunger; the noises she made when gas wanted to be a person; the small, satisfied sigh she produced after an exact amount of milk—as if she had signed something. He grew precise about temperatures and the tilt of bottles, expert in matters that had never concerned him when he thought marriage was a room that arranged itself.

Outside, leaves set themselves properly on trees and then took themselves off again. Weeks moved in squares across a wall calendar that kept trying to insist on appointments he would not make. Time, which had been theatrical, returned to the workaday job of being endured. The house learnt to knock softly: once to remind them it was there, twice to collect interest, three times when it wanted to be obeyed. He called the three a draught, then a settling, then nothing at all. Words do light work when you ask them to.

***

He took the pram out in a way that felt like apprenticeship. Mothers recognised him and nodded, charitable, as if men who walk infants had done something extraordinary rather than ordinary well. In the park, the river performed its endless rehearsal. He stood at the rail and did not lean. The wind rifled the baby's blanket and she frowned, and he earned her forgiveness with a soft shushing that was not the house's song. He tried to find the stranger in the river's face and found only his own, distorted enough by current to look like a warning.

At home, he learnt which creaks underfoot woke her and which cocooned her, and he told no one that the cot sometimes shifted itself a quarter-inch to the left as if preferring a different geometry for sleep. On good days he laughed and called it settling. On bad days he stood in the doorway and told the room, just above a whisper, "No."

***

He did not speak the surviving sister's name aloud when he could avoid it. He discovered you can live for weeks on pronouns if you hold your breath and move carefully. In front of strangers he used singulars like prayer beads. *My wife. She's resting. She's coping as well as can be expected.* Singulars soothed people. Singulars raised fewer questions. The house approved. It liked a man who had learnt his lines.

At night he lay beside a warm back and listened to a breathing that sometimes smelt of lemon and sometimes of smoke and sometimes of nothing at all, and if he dared to wonder which woman's history had written the shape of that breath he told himself it was unkind to ask questions once you had committed to an answer. He had chosen complicity, he thought; he had chosen to be the fourth face the house had been auditioning him for since the first comb turned up with citrus between its teeth. He would keep the baby safe by making the world simple at the front door and untidy in the kitchen. He would be polite to whispers. He would tidy what could be tidied and forgive what could not.

\*\*\*

He kept expecting the lullaby to stop. It didn't. It refined itself instead, learning his footsteps, pausing when he entered so he could pretend it hadn't been happening, picking up again when he left. Sometimes he caught it halfway—a single line, then its shadow, then the third, the mischief, the split. He never asked the room to prove itself. He knew better. The house loved a man who kept faith with what he couldn't name.

When the baby was six weeks old—a number the health visitor loved because it looked like a solution—he found himself awake at an hour with no clock, the light a weak blue that either promised morning or lied. The baby fussed, not angry, just exploratory. He lifted her and walked the long oval parents perform in the dark, shoulder to hip, hip to door, door to chair, chair to window, window to cot. Outside the glass the street performed a slower version of the same loop. In the kitchen, a bottle remembered its job.

He paused at the whiteboard and wrote MILK in blue on a corner, only to wipe it off a second later, unnerved by how quickly his hand had found the old rhythm. The gloss showed the faint ghost of what he had written for a breath too long. He turned the baby so she faced away from it. "Don't learn that," he murmured, and she obligingly stared at the light fitting, an early expert in pretending not to understand what the room demands of you.

\*\*\*

He took her back to the nursery and sat. The rocking chair remembered him in its wood and moved without squeaking. He counted the breaths between her sighs. On the wall beside the cot, the nightlight threw shadows that startled him—one large, one smaller, a third that shouldn't have been there and yet was, all of them wavering inside the mobile's slow circulation. The fox nodded to the hare in time with the baby's swallow. The third shadow turned its head and looked at him. He did not look back, because that's how such things become facts.

From the landing came the three knocks. Not loud. Not theatrical. The kind a person makes before entering a room they already live in. He didn't answer. He kept rocking. The knocks came again, patient. He stood, put the baby down, covered her with the blanket that always lay just off-centre no matter how he folded it, and crossed to the doorway.

"Not tonight," he said softly, and the sentence surprised him with its authority. The house obeyed. Or the person in the hall did. He could not decide which answer he preferred.

***

He went back to the chair and watched his daughter—or the baby, or the child; he was still negotiating pronouns with himself—sleep. Her hand opened and closed in a tiny rehearsal of ownership. In sleep, her face made expressions it hadn't learnt yet. At one moment she looked like a man he had been, at the next like a woman he had loved, at the next like a stranger who had introduced herself to the family and refused to leave. He could have watched for hours. He had. He would again.

Later that morning—a map of minutes he would not be able to re-draw—there was a knock at the actual door. Not the house's knock: real wood on wood, neighbourly, apologetic. He opened it to find Mrs Henderson from two doors down cradling a foil-wrapped loaf like a child. She peered past him, not rudely. People who have lived on the same street for thirty years think their gaze is part of the rent.

"Just checking in," she said. "Thought you might like something warm. Smells like a Sunday."

He thanked her. She sniffed—not at him, at the air. "Lemon," she said, approving. "Clean."

He smiled. "We do our best."

"Who doesn't," she replied, and handed him the bread. "Is your—" She bit the pronoun before it could commit. "Is she sleeping?"

"Just now," he said. "Finally."

"You're doing well," Mrs Henderson said, as if she had the authority to confer competence. "And if you ever need me to sit with her, you knock. I'm old but I can hum."

***

He pictured her in the rocking chair, humming against the house's three-part, and had to steady the bread to stop it sliding. "Thank you," he said, and meant it. When he shut the door, the hallway seemed to have been spruced by kindness. The vent breathed once in approval, and he decided to let it.

By the time he returned to the nursery the baby had shifted herself slightly and put her hand out on the sheet as if testing the feel of the world. The comb dish on the changer—he had left it empty on purpose—now held a single white comb laid teeth-down in a way that suggested someone kind had made sure it wouldn't scratch. He did not pick it up. He did not say a name. Names made things happen.

He took the comb to the bathroom instead and dropped it into the cupboard under the sink, where dust and toothpaste caps could educate it about irrelevance. When he came back the dish was empty again. He laughed, quietly, helplessly, at his own optimism, and the house—pleased—tapped the second stair with what might have been affection.

***

Afternoons made peace easier. He learnt to sleep when the baby slept, to apologise less to visitors for the mess, to accept tea in mugs that didn't match. He and the surviving sister got good at nodding across rooms, an economy of speech that sounded, to strangers, like marital ease. Sometimes he saw her watching the baby with a hunger he could not assuage and a possessiveness he could not condone. Sometimes he saw a softness so wide it frightened him. On those days he remembered the river man telling him you can't have one story in a house built for three. He would make two stories, then. Two would be enough. Two would be survivable.

At dusk, when streetlamps mislaid their certainties, the lullaby put its shoes back on. It climbed the stairs politely. It made itself known with one line, then two, then three, and when he stood in the doorway the music behaved, as if embarrassed, and turned into the ordinary sounds of a small life: breathing, shifting, a sigh that conjured a woman he could love without having to label her.

***

One night, exhausted into honesty, he broke his rule and asked the air a question. "Is she mine?" he said to the dark. "Tell me at last. Please."

The house said nothing. The quiet went on and on until it became an answer of its own. He felt ridiculous, kneeling to a room. He felt relieved. He felt punished. He stood, put his hand on the cot rail, and repeated the sentence he'd found that worked on wolves and neighbours and lies: "Not tonight."

The lullaby obeyed the shape of the words, if not their meaning. It softened, spread itself, split again, and when he met its divisions with a steady gaze it turned into weather and left him alone.

Spring took itself seriously; the baby learned to smile at nothing and then at everything; he began to recognise the expression she wore when she was about to learn something that would change the shape of the day. He tried not to count. He tried not to arrange. He let the whiteboard remain blank, a sentinel of refusal. He put the rota in the bin and then took it out again and burned it in the sink because some gestures deserve to be theatrical. The smoke alarm performed morality and he removed the battery and told it to mind its business.

On a warm afternoon that tilted towards evening, he took the baby back to the river. He did not look for the man, though he felt watched by water anyway. The baby slept. He leaned on the railing—carefully, not as a supplicant—and looked down at the surface, which pretended to be a story because it moved. He said nothing to it. He had learnt that rivers enjoy the sound of their own advice. Instead he told the baby, in a voice that belonged to no pact, a list of things that would be hers and only hers: the name of a fox that owned their street; the taste of strawberries with too much sun in them; the scratching sound pencils make when they tell the truth; the joke you can make out of your own name when you are bored of being certain.

On the way home, he bought milk and forgot the bread he hadn't needed. He reached into his pocket and found a bus ticket that hadn't been there, mid-March, 15:00, and folded it into a small square and dropped it into a bin because sometimes superstition wants a ceremony and sometimes the ceremony is letting go of paper.

That night the three knocks came again. He let them. He did not answer. The house clicked its tongue against the second stair, disappointed but willing to wait.

He would have liked to end in certainty. He told himself he had chosen complicity—outward singularity, inward management—and that the choice made him strong. He would be the fourth if it kept the baby safe; he would wear the mask until masks were out of fashion. He would, in a pinch, hum the house's lullaby back to it until it fell asleep.

\*\*\*

At two a.m., he went into the nursery to check her because fathers in houses like his do that. Moonlight had learnt the lesson of summer and came thin, delayed, like a visitor who will stay too long if you let them. The mobile was still. The cot made the shape of a small body breathing. He stood, hand on rail, and listened.

The quiet gathered its courage and became a song. Not loud. Not cruel. Three lines, braided. He stared at the wall and saw his shadow; then another, a woman's; then a third, smaller, next to the cot. He didn't turn his head to count in case numbers made it permanent.

He leaned over the cot, kissed the air just above his daughter's forehead, and spoke softly, almost amused at himself for needing to say it, almost frightened of what would happen if he didn't.

"Tell me," he whispered. "Tell me she's yours... not *ours*."

\*\*\*

The baby sighed the sigh of someone who has already learnt how to be kind to a man. The mobile turned once, with no wind. From the landing, very gently, the house knocked three times.

# Acknowledgements

Writing *The Third Wife* has been a journey of late nights, early mornings, and more tea than I care to admit. It would not have been possible without the support and encouragement of those around me.

To my family — thank you for your patience, your belief, and for giving me the space to disappear into a world of words when I needed it most. You kept me grounded while I explored the darkest corners of imagination.

To the writers who inspire me and the readers who love psychological thrillers as much as I do — your passion fuels mine.

And finally, to you, the reader: thank you for stepping into this story. Without you, the pages would remain silent. I hope *The Third Wife* lingers with you long after the last word, whispering questions and shadows you carry with you.

# Author Bio

**A**.M. Jones is a UK-based author of dark psychological thrillers. After turning forty, she began writing seriously, inspired by a lifelong intrigue with thrillers and the human mind's capacity for deception.

When not writing, she spends time with her family, exploring the bush on off-road motorbikes, and filling notebooks with latest ideas for her next novel.

Her debut, *The Third Wife*, explores identity, obsession, and the terrifying cost of love — hallmarks of the dark, psychological stories she loves to tell.

# Also by A.M. Jones

*T*he Third Wife

*The Silent Twin (Forthcoming)*

# Readers Note

F inal Note to Readers

Thank you for reading *The Third Wife*.

If you enjoyed the story, please consider leaving a review. Your reflections help keep the story alive and guide new readers into these shadows.

I am so grateful for your time, your trust, and your imagination. Until we meet again in the next book — don't look too long into the glass.

— A. M. Jones